THE EXECUTIONER'S BLADE

THE EXECUTIONER'S SONG BOOK 3

D.K. HOLMBERG

CHAPTER ONE

F inn lingered at the edge of the street that led to
Declan Prison, working through the series of questions he'd ask to find the missing girl. The prisoner had
posed a unique challenge. The prison towered in front of
him, a simple stone building that took up most of one block
in this section of Verendal. He stared at it for a moment
before moving along the street toward the entrance to the
prison. Iron doors blocked access to most, though there
usually weren't many people interested in heading into the
prison. Today was different.

A woman and a small child stood off to one side of the
street, watching the foreboding doorway. The woman wore
a tattered dress, one that had been patched many times,
while the boy had cutoff pants and a scrap of cloth that
served as a shirt. Neither wore shoes. Were it late spring or
summer, such dress wouldn't be out of place, but as the
weather had started shifting colder and the occasional

snowflakes fell some evenings, their threadbare clothing left much to be desired.

The child struck a chord within him. Finn hated seeing children in the streets like that. Hungry. Poorly dressed. Ignored by the city around him.

The woman noticed him and they scurried away, disappearing into the shadows of a neighboring alley. Finn still remembered the alleys of the city from his time as a thief, so he knew where those particular alleys would lead. Not anywhere suitable for a child. All he could hope was that they managed to find the warmth of a fire, a compassionate person who might offer them some clothing and food, perhaps even shelter for the night.

Finn jogged to that side of the street and reached into his pocket for a stack of coins. All he had on him today were silvers, so much more than he once would have carried.

He looked into the depths of the alley. They were still there. They had to be.

He stacked the coins on the ground. "For you and the boy," he said, calling along the alley. There seemed to be a faint shuffling sound. "There's a place nearby, the Carina Inn, that doesn't overcharge for meals. They've got clean beds. Ask for Berthel."

Finn waited. It was more coin than he should leave, but seeing the boy…

He turned away and headed back across the street and to the prison. Pulling the ring of keys from his pocket, he sorted through them until he came to the key for Declan, stuffed it into the lock and twisted.

Finn took a deep breath before heading into the prison. The air inside had a different feel to it from outside. The prison itself wasn't heated. That by itself added a torment. A soft stirring of air fluttered past him as he stepped across the threshold and pulled the door closed, locking himself inside once again.

"You still not used to it?" Gord, one of the iron masters standing near the door, asked Finn. He wore the black leathers of the guards, with a smear of what Finn hoped was dirt on his face.

Finn grimaced and let go of the breath he'd been holding, inhaling the smell of feces, rot, and hopelessness that permeated every corner of the prison.

"I don't want to get used to it," he said, heading past the guard.

Getting used to it meant that he would be spending more time there than he wanted. It was bad enough that he had to come for questioning.

The prison was poorly lit. Mostly, that was by design. The effect was intended to be disorienting to all who came to the prison. An occasional lantern illuminated the hall, giving off a pale light that barely revealed the dark stone. Shadows slithered between the lanterns like something alive. There was a time when that would have disturbed him more than it did now. Truth be told, it *still* troubled him a bit.

Finn contemplated heading straight toward the man he had come to question, but decided Meyer would be irritated if he didn't at least ask a few questions of the warden.

Stopping at the warden's office, Finn knocked and waited.

"Come in," a gruff voice said from the other side of the door.

Finn shifted the keys in his pocket. He suspected he had a key that would let him into the warden's office. That wasn't something he had ever tested, nor something that he thought he should test unless there was a real need, but it was a strange feeling to know that he could go anywhere within any of the city's prisons.

When he entered, he closed the door behind him. "Warden James."

The warden looked up from a stack of papers. The topmost page appeared to be from the magister detailing the sentence of one of the prisoners.

"Finn," he said, smiling warmly, and setting down his quill. "Don't tell me Meyer has sent you to question the new prisoner already."

"New?"

There hadn't been any word of a new prisoner. Typically, Meyer would get an accounting of all the new prisoners. As the lead executioner and inquisitor for the city, he was ultimately responsible for all the prisons within the city.

"Ah. Not him." Was that relief that swept across James's face? Finn watched him for a moment, trying to gauge just what emotion James might be hiding from him. Perhaps none. He and James had become friendly over the years, even sharing a pint of ale on occasion. There weren't too

many people who *wanted* to spend time with an executioner's apprentice, so finding those who did, and who were the
kind of company that he wanted to be around, was rare.
"You're here for Holden again."

Finn drew a heavy chair away from the wall and perched
uncomfortably, his feet tucked behind one of the many
sculptures of the gods that littered James's office. The office
was not large. There was space for the desk cluttered with
papers James had stacked on the surface, the only free area
around the lantern that gave light to the room. A chair situated on the other side looked to be too big—and ornate—
for the room, as if it were crafted by a master carpenter for
someone in one of the nice sections of the city and confis-
cated to be brought here. A bookshelf next to the desk
looked to be crammed in and almost unnecessary, considering that James didn't have any books on it. What he did
have were what looked to be small sculptures. Finn had
asked him about it once and learned they were items made
by the prisoners that he'd pilfered from them over the years.
Most of the small sculptures were carved from the stone of
the prison itself, somehow pried free by the prisoners to
work on during their confinement. In that way, James
figured he had a right to those items. All of them were
markers of power, and of the power James had over the
prisoners he kept there.

"Have your men been questioning him?"

"You know that we wouldn't do anything to disrupt an
ongoing investigation."

Finn smiled at him. "I know you wouldn't. Come on,

James. I'm not Meyer. You can tell me what you've uncovered."

James watched him a moment. "You're not Meyer, but you're starting to act like him these days. Damn, Finn. When you first started coming around, you still looked like you'd rather be out in the streets. Now..."

"Now what?" Finn asked carefully.

"Now... now you belong. The Hunter." He chuckled softly as he said it.

It was a nickname he'd heard about in whispers. The iron masters didn't talk too openly about it, but they *did* talk.

It was a nickname that stemmed from the first case Meyer had assigned to him. It had been Finn's opportunity to prove himself. He'd tried to take everything that he'd learned from Meyer in the time that he'd been working with him and use it to understand the reasons behind the crime. Understanding was key to ensuring the proper punishment was carried out.

"*Hunter* is better than what I used to be called."

"What was that?"

"Shuffles."

James tilted his head off to the side, grinning. "Shuffles? Why is that?"

Finn held his gaze, saying nothing.

"Come on. You can't share a detail like that and not tell me *why*. There's got to be a story behind it."

"Not so much of one that it matters. When I was working in the streets"—Finn didn't bother to keep that a

secret, since most knew of his time in the prison anyway—
"there was a man I worked with who thought I made too
much noise when I walked. Complained that I shuffled.
Nothing more than that."

"Gods. That's a terrible nickname. If it were me, I'd have
wanted something more intimidating."

"That's the thing about names in the street. You don't get
to choose them." Not that Finn hadn't tried to turn things so
that he could be called something else. He didn't want to be
Shuffles any more than he wanted this new nickname. He
wanted something that conjured an image that others might
respect or even fear. At the time, that had been something
like the Hand. Wolf. The King. All of them had *names*.

"Well, now you're the Hunter. Guess it could be worse."

"I could be called the Lion."

James sniffed. "That poor bastard," he said, shaking his
head. James shuffled a few pages and pulled another one to
the top of the stack. "I know you probably don't want to
hear it, but you and he would have gotten along. The man
could be a real bastard like you say, but he got answers."

"Meyer never cared for him."

"Meyer never had an apprentice until he got you. Had
the Lion for a while, but that wasn't a real apprentice. He
was a journeyman before he ever came to the city."

Finn only nodded. There wasn't any point in rehashing
all that. The Lion was gone, killed because of the information that someone *thought* that he'd acquired, and left to rot
in the river.

"Your men haven't gotten anything from Holden?"

"Not much," James admitted. "We've tried. Knowing the time is short, we've been pushing him, but he's not the kind to break. As you've seen."

Finn sighed. "Then it's back to work for me." He got to his feet, and started for the door. "Who's the new prisoner?"

"Nothing all that interesting, I'm afraid. Archers brought him in earlier today, which was why I would have been surprised that you had heard something about him already. We've still been trying to process him before sending word to the magister."

And by *processing*, that meant James and his iron masters were trying to question the new prisoner. There were times when that helped and Finn could overlook it, such as when they were dealing with someone like Holden, who supposedly had captured a woman and had her hidden somewhere, but there were other times when James and the iron masters went beyond what they needed to do.

"What's he accused of doing?"

"Cutpurse. Caught on the road outside of Verendal."

Finn paused and turned back to James. That was a strange crime for someone to come to Declan Prison for, which suggested there was more to it. "What else?"

"There were bodies, Finn."

"Bodies?"

James nodded, glancing to the page in front of him. "Three. A family. All left somehow dried out. They'd been dead for a while, from what the Archers said. This man carried them with him. Kept them in a cart."

Finn inhaled deeply and wished that he wouldn't have.

The smell within the prison got to him again. "I can question him when I'm done with Holden."

"You don't have to do that yet. Like I said, we've still got to get him processed. I'll send word like I always do when he's ready."

Finn considered pushing but decided against it. Doing that would not only disrupt his friendship with James but it would put him in a strange situation of having to override the warden. As he remained only an apprentice and not the lead executioner, his responsibility was to report to Meyer and let him handle anything more that would need to be done.

"That sounds fine."

"Do you want me to walk you down to Holden?"

Finn chuckled. "I think I know the way."

He stepped out of the warden's office, closing the door behind him. When he was out, he looked along the hall before heading toward the stairs at the end of the hall. From there, he went down into the depths of the prison.

He stopped at one of the landings where Mather, a lanky iron master, stood guard. "Bring Holden to the chapel," he said.

The iron master nodded and hurried off.

Finn turned and made his way toward the chapel. The room was a strange construct in the prison. The curved ceiling had been long before painted and worked with art of the gods. A small window high overhead let some light in, though this was filtered by the filth covering the window. A pair of small lanterns rested on a table at the far side, where the tools of his trade rested, the metal gleaming from the reflected lantern light.

He'd spent quite a bit of time in this room over the years. Time had made this room familiar to him, but Finn had never gotten over what had once been done to him there and that he had to do something similar to those who were brought here.

At least the chapel didn't smell quite as bad as so many of the other places in the prison. There was only a hint of sweat mixed with what Finn had come to think of as fear. Mostly, that was tied to the men—and it was only men in Declan—who were brought into this room for their questioning. Almost all were afraid. How could they not be? Even the strongest eventually cracked there.

The door opened, and Mather and another iron master guided Holden inside.

He was a thin man with hollowed, almost haunted eyes. His pale brown hair hung limp in front of his face. The iron masters had to drag him into the room, though Finn wondered how much of that was because of what Finn had done the day before and how much of it was because of what the guards themselves had done during their questioning. He hoped they hadn't been too aggressive. There was an art to interrogating men like Holden, and he didn't want the iron masters to have interrupted that art.

The guards settled him into the chair in the center of the room and strapped his arms and legs into it. Meyer rarely needed men to be strapped in, but Finn still preferred the comfort of having them confined like that. It made him feel more in control of the situation.

"Thank you," Finn said to the iron masters.

They stepped out of the room, closing the door behind them.

When he was alone with Holden, Finn stopped in front of him and crouched down to look directly into his eyes. His shoulder twinged a bit with the movement, the result of the door-hanging exercises he'd been doing the evening before.

"How are you doing today, Holden?"

It wasn't how he wanted to start the questioning. He needed answers—and quickly. A woman's life depended upon it, but Holden needed the right approach. The problem Finn had was that he wasn't sure he knew the right approach.

Holden looked up and glared at him, though he didn't say anything.

"I'm going to need you to talk to me. If you want to get this over with, you're going to need to answer questions."

"You don't care what I have to tell you."

"You know that's not true."

Holden lowered his head again.

Finn got to his feet and headed to the far side of the room, suppressing the frustration within him. "When you were here yesterday, we used the boots. I'd rather not have to do that again. To be honest, I'd rather not have to do any of this, but you haven't given me much of a choice."

He made a point of moving several of the implements

around the table. It was a rare thing these days for him to need to use any of them. For the most part, he could start with the less-aggressive approaches and talk his way through what he might do so that they wouldn't need him to step up to the next technique.

Holden had proven difficult.

Finn had expected that of him, given what Holden stood accused of doing.

There was a time when Finn had first been learning his trade where he'd begun to question whether someone who held out like this could actually be guilty of what they were accused of doing. That was before he'd come to learn how *hard* people could be.

He had known that men could hold out. Gods, *he* had held out when it had been him sitting in that chair. But he had underestimated the limits of what a man could endure.

Meyer had taught him to find those limits and exploit them.

"Let me tell you a little more about what we might do together today, Holden," Finn said. "We've used the boots. Most people find them unpleasant enough that they will do anything to have them removed. It can be a terrible sensation to have that boot strapped to your leg, the screws continuing to burrow deeper and deeper, the pressure building around your shins…"

Finn paused, letting the words settle for a moment.

Holden didn't flinch.

He hadn't flinched when he'd been questioned the day before. Or the one before that.

They had only so much time. Finn didn't like being on a timeline like this and didn't love the fact that even were he to get Holden to answer his questions, he still wouldn't know what he needed. It wasn't about the man's guilt. Holden had admitted that the day before. This was about something more.

"There are other ways of augmenting the boots," Finn went on. He tapped a metal spike on the table, the sound a soft ringing. "I could add a little sharper feeling to the ongoing pressure."

He lifted the boots and brought them over to Holden, setting them on the ground. He left them there for a moment. Part of the torment was letting Holden's mind do some of the work. Seeing the boots, remembering how they felt when they'd been applied, would be difficult for most. Holden didn't even give it a second look.

Finn returned to the table, lifted the spike, and carried it over to Holden, setting it on the ground near the boots. "This will focus the pain. I don't have to use it, though. All you need to do is answer what I've asked."

Holden still didn't react.

Finn would have to be more aggressive. He could see that.

It was a fine line he had to walk. Partly, he needed to try to convince Holden that it was in his best interest to answer, and partly he needed to make him answer. Either way would provide Finn with what he wanted.

"All of this will be over the moment you tell me where to

find Rachel Herns," Finn said. "I know you haven't been in the city for long, but I will learn what happened to her."

The one piece of information he'd been able to learn was that Holden wasn't a local.

Which made it worse.

Holden looked up then. A dark smile crossed his face. "You won't find her. Not before it's done. Maybe the dogs will lead you to her." He laughed, and the hollows of his eyes seemed even darker than before.

Finn suppressed the flash of anger.

One of the lessons Meyer had worked to instill within him was that he needed to control his emotions. The one doing the questioning could not lose control of himself. That was the way to failure. Not only was that a way to getting the wrong kind of information, but it led to vengeance rather than justice. And that was not serving the king, along with the people of the city.

That was why he did the job. Not so much serving the king, though there was a part of him that felt that he needed to do it. Growing up, King Porman had never been anything other than a distant threat, one that became more acute as he'd become a thief. Finn had never thought that he would have a chance to see the king, let alone speak to him.

"I think we will begin. You know the question. When you share with me where to find Rachel Herns, your suffering will be over."

That was what Finn wanted. To find her—hopefully alive.

There had been other missing women over the last

month, though Finn hadn't managed to pin them on Holden and doubted the man would acknowledge his role now.

Finn applied the boots. They were fitted on either side of the prisoner's leg and then screwed tightly so they sealed around them. With a turn of the screw, he could apply increasing pressure. Finn quickly tightened them and then began to apply even more pressure. He had made a mental note about how much Holden had been able to withstand the day before, so that when he began to add more now, it *should* be enough that he wouldn't tolerate it well.

Holden barely made any sound.

When it had been like that the day before, Finn had known there was a danger in continuing with this line of torment. The boots worked most of the time, but they weren't infallible. There were people they wouldn't work with.

With the first boot in place, Finn moved on to the next.

He watched Holden the entire time.

There was still no reaction.

Using the spike now would only injure him; it wouldn't draw the answers that Finn needed out of him. For that, he would need a different approach.

Finn took the spike, noting the way Holden looked at him, and carried it over to the table. There were a few other options there that he hadn't attempted.

He took a spool of thick wire, which he carried over to Holden.

This wasn't what he wanted to do, but he kept thinking about what he'd heard about Rachel Herns. A young woman about his sister's age, trapped somewhere in the city, possibly injured.

Finn didn't want to fail her.

There were times when this job was more than what he thought he could do. There were times when he hated it and hated what it made him do. There were other times when he knew it was necessary.

This was one of those times when it was all of them.

He crouched in front of Holden. "Seeing as how the boots haven't bothered you, I'm going to try something different. The wire will penetrate your skin and go deep into the muscle. If I push hard enough, I can even strike bone. That's when it really hurts. With this spool, I have plenty of wire. What's better, the gauge of the wire is such that it won't leave much in the way of a marking, so when it's time to face your sentencing, there won't be a delay."

Finn watched Holden, hoping that he'd say something.

He didn't.

"When you tell me how to find Rachel Herns, this will be over." Finn took a deep breath. "Let's begin."

CHAPTER TWO

The sun had set, leaving the city in darkness. Finn hurried along the streets, heading back toward home, before pausing and taking a different direction. What did it matter if he returned early tonight?

Besides, he thought that he might visit with Oscar. It had been long enough, and he knew what Oscar would say to him, but more than that, he wondered if Oscar might be able to help him with this case. He made his way to the Olin section and to the Wenderwolf tavern. There were times when he wished he could visit more often, because it was familiar and the ale was good, but the memory of what he'd done in the tavern and who he'd once been made that difficult for him.

The tavern was situated near the nicer part of Olin, if any part could really be considered nice. When he was younger, Finn had viewed the sections of the city differently than he did now. Olin was perfectly fine, though it paled compared to the central sections of the city in terms of the wealth found within it.

A sign hanging out front had been recently painted, depicting the massive head of a wenderwolf etched into the wood. It wobbled in the faint breeze gusting through the streets that carried some of the scent of the nearby forest, that of pine and damp earth and cold. Music drifted into the street from inside, a jaunty sound meant to get people dancing.

Finn sighed before entering.

The tavern hadn't changed much over the years. Several booths took up space near the front of the tavern, with tables near the back that could be pushed out of the way for those dancing. The troupe performing at the back included a lutist, a singer, and a drummer, the steady rhythm of their music even louder inside the tavern.

Finn made his way toward the back corner and an empty booth there, taking a seat. It wasn't long before a young blonde waitress in a snug-fitting dress that revealed ample cleavage came by, nodding to him.

"Hey there, Gina," he said.

"Finn. It's been a right while since you've been in." She shifted the tray she held and smiled, a hint of a dimple forming in the corner of her mouth.

"I know. You see him recently?"

Gina looked around the tavern briefly, lingering on the door a moment, before settling her blue-eyed gaze on him. "You asking for work or for your friend?"

"My friend. Only my friend."

She regarded him a long moment. "He's been here. Should be back soon. Can I bring you a mug of ale while you wait?"

"That would be great."

She sauntered off, flashing wide smiles at others around the tavern as she went.

Finn leaned back, tapping his foot in time to the music. The troupe was skilled, though that wasn't surprising. Annie only hired the best she could get.

When Gina brought a mug of ale over and set it in front of him, she leaned forward. "What's got your goat tonight?"

"Nothing I can talk about."

"That right?"

Finn took a sip of the ale. The ale at the Wenderwolf really was some of the best in the city. "It's more that it's not anything I want to talk about."

"Something like that?"

"It's bad, Gina. Real bad."

"You want to share anything, you know I'll listen."

Finn nodded and Gina disappeared. He took a few more sips of his ale and had nearly finished the mug when a shadowy form took a seat across from him.

"Shuffles," Oscar said, sliding into the booth across from him. He was dressed in an inky black jacket and pants— clothing thieves referred to as darks. He had a lean, angular face, and his graying hair was cut short. He leaned forward, resting his elbows on the table, leaving the light to reflect upon the pale scar on his cheek. "I wasn't expecting to see you tonight."

Finn frowned. Oscar was connected throughout the city. "Why not tonight?"

Oscar regarded him, leaning back. The scar twitched just a little. "Looks like I know something you don't. Might be there's a price involved in such knowledge."

"The price being me having saved your life?"

Oscar grunted. "How long do you figure you get to use that?"

Finn grinned at him. "I was hoping for a few more years out of it."

Gina slithered over to the table, carrying another mug of ale, and set it in front of Oscar. He offered a hint of a smile to her, nothing more, before she went scurrying away from him.

"What's this about?" Oscar said, leaning back and taking a long drink.

"Can't it be about me wanting to see an old friend?"

Oscar grunted. "Getting older every day, too." He was quiet for a few moments as he sipped his ale. The music behind him came in a rhythm that Finn struggled to ignore. Oscar didn't seem to have the same difficulties. "You don't come here often enough for there not to be a reason, Finn."

Finn this time, *not* Shuffles.

"I can come for the ale."

"Nobody going to stop you coming in here like you used to. Annie don't much care for what happened to the King, but I've made sure she understood what he was doing to us."

Finn looked around the tavern until he saw the owner. She was about Oscar's age and had always had an easygoing smile when it came to Finn. At least, before Finn had not only turned on the King but been the one to carry out his execution.

"I wish she'd let me apologize," he said softly.

"For what?" Oscar leaned forward. "That's something you've got to come to terms with, Finn. You didn't do anything other than what you were supposed to do. The King got what was coming to him, the same as so many people in this section. The only thing that troubles her is…"

"Is what?"

"Don't matter." Oscar took another drink and set the mug down.

It had seemed to Finn that he'd been drinking quite a bit of the ale, but now that he looked at Oscar's mug, he realized he'd barely had more than a few swallows. That was a measure of how much Oscar felt uncomfortable with Finn's presence.

"I'm looking for a girl," Finn finally said.

"So, you *are* here officially."

Finn shook his head, letting out a long sigh. "Not really. A man named Holden is held in Declan—"

"Holden? As in Holden Grimes? The Pale Bastard?"

Finn snorted. "I didn't know he'd been named."

"That one is dangerous," Oscar said. When he tipped back his ale this time, he took a long swallow. "Came to the city only a few weeks back. Got settled in quickly. Turning down easy jobs that a new crew shouldn't ignore. Damn bastard already had a crew and thinks he can swing his dick around here and push us out?"

It was more irritation than he'd expected from Oscar, but then, a competing crew would do that. At least now he knew that Holden had a crew.

Which made abducting a girl all the stranger.

Crews were for thieving and protection. Not crimes like kidnapping and rape.

Unless they intended to ransom her.

So far, that hadn't appeared to be Holden's intention.

"What did he do?" Oscar asked.

"Probably many things, but we've got him held because of a girl. A woman by the name of Rachel Herns. She's not the only one he's taken lately and probably not the last. I... I want to find her, but I need to know if there are others we can save."

"So, you were hoping that I might be able to help you figure out where he's got her stashed before he ransoms her."

That was *if* he wanted to ransom her. Or any of the others he might have. "That, and I came to see an old friend."

Oscar rested his hands on the table. "The Pale Bastard isn't someone to mess with, Finn."

"He's in Declan."

"As were you. And Rock, if I remember. There are ways of getting in and out of there, even if you don't want to see them. The Pale Bastard has already proven to be dangerous. If he's started in with abductions already, that means he's got a bigger crew than I thought. You'd better be careful, Finn."

"He's in Declan," Finn said again. The warden and the iron masters weren't about to let someone like that out. "And I need to find this girl before whatever he intended for her happens."

"She's already dead," Oscar said, squeezing his hands around the mug of ale, knuckles going white. "You'd be better off focusing on carrying out his sentence—and preparing for the possibility that his crew is going to try to spring him."

"He hasn't been sentenced yet."

"What?"

Finn shrugged. "We wanted to find this girl. He's made it clear that he has her and that something awful will happen to her if we don't find her, so we've been focused on that. And learning how many others he's taken."

"When is he getting sentenced?"

"I don't know. Meyer probably does."

Most of the time, Meyer included Finn in the sentencing. Finn had gone to City Hall often enough that he knew the Archers working by name, along with the names of all of the jurors, though that still didn't mean it was a place that he enjoyed visiting. He still had his own memories of the place.

"If you want my help, it's this. Make sure he gets sentenced quickly. Take care of that man before he does the same to you."

Oscar lifted the mug of ale and started to drink.

Finn sighed. He'd thought there might be some help coming there. "If you hear of anything, let me know."

"I'll see what I can do. Can't make any promises about this one, Finn." Oscar flicked his gaze up at him before looking back at his ale.

Finn nodded. There weren't too many times where his job and his responsibilities put him at odds with Oscar. Finn had made a point of avoiding hearing anything that might pose difficulty for him with Oscar, not wanting to be placed into a position where he'd be the one to need to do something about Oscar. Not that Meyer would even try to put Finn into that position. He understood the connection Finn had to the man known as the Hand, even if he never questioned Finn.

Finishing his drink, Finn got to his feet and tapped the table. "Anything you might be able to tell me, Oscar."

"I heard you," Oscar said, this time his voice more strained.

Finn nodded to Gina before making his way out.

Once outside, he stood looking over at the tavern. The music sounded muted outside, the jaunty songs now shifted, something less than what they had been before. Finn backed along the street, shaking his head, disappointed in Oscar for the first time that he could remember.

There wasn't honor among thieves, but there was respect. Even fear.

It might be fear that drove Oscar now.

Finn needed to better understand the reason why.

Here he had thought that he understood Holden, but apparently, he needed to find out more about him. He had a crew. Getting a handle on Holden would require him to try to do something that he hadn't in a while. Could he even look the part any longer?

Finn had only a few items of clothing from that time. Most were buried in his wardrobe, forgotten over the years. There hadn't been much of a reason for him to hold on to them. Not when most of his days were spent with Meyer, visiting prisons, investigating what they uncovered, and collecting various healing balms from the apothecaries that Meyer liked to frequent.

He made his way through the streets, his mind racing as he struggled to come up with what he would need to do. Find answers. That was the key.

Oscar had given him some information about where to start.

As he headed back to Meyer's home, he had a vague feeling that someone followed him. Finn paused. He didn't worry about being out in the streets the way he once would have, even if he was out beyond the curfew, but someone trailing after him left him a little troubled.

Maybe it's the Hand.

Oscar might not have wanted to be seen offering him help in the Wenderwolf. That wouldn't be altogether surprising. Oscar had built up his own crew over the last few years. They didn't handle any jobs that were particularly dangerous, though Finn had heard some rumors about the kinds of things they did. It would fit that Oscar wouldn't want to be seen sharing too much with the executioner's apprentice.

Finn stood fixed in the middle of the street, staring into

the shadows as he tried to make out what had moved, but couldn't. Finn thought there *was* something there. Even if he couldn't see it, whatever was out there was real. There was an absence of sound that left a burst of adrenaline in his belly.

Which meant that someone *was* following him.

He moved along, but now some of the old training that he'd received all those years before from Oscar came back to him. He snuck carefully so that he wouldn't be seen paying attention to anyone behind him, even though he used every opportunity to look over his shoulder, or to try to catch reflections in glass, or even to turn as if he were looking for someone behind him.

Finn never caught a glimpse of who was back there.

He quickened his pace.

As he neared the end of the street, a demarcation between Olin section and the next, he felt as if there was more movement nearby. The buildings lining the streets there were mostly shops. At this time of night, they were all closed, sealed off until the next morning. None even had any lights in the windows.

Finn glanced along the intersecting street.

It had been a while since he'd been uncomfortable navigating the streets. He probably wouldn't be, if not for what Oscar had said to him about Holden and his crew.

Could that be one of Holden's crew? If it *was* one of his crew, then Finn would have to be prepared for whatever Holden might have his men try.

The sound of footsteps started to loom louder behind him.

There weren't any Archers out.

That surprised him.

There were plenty of crews who had ways of influencing the Archers. A few coins flashed in the right way would change a man's mind. When Finn had been in his crew, the King had used the Archers in that way.

He turned, ducking into a nearby alley.

The alleys in Verendal could be twisty and confusing. Most avoided using them unless they'd spent considerable time navigating the alleys, knowing that otherwise they could end up getting lost—or trapped.

In this case, Finn *thought* he knew where this one would lead, but there was a possibility it would veer off from where he expected it to go. He jogged through it, trying to step over anything unpleasant that might be there.

A shadow at the end of the alley cut off the little bit of light that had been here.

There *was* someone following him.

His heart hammered. A cold sweat worked along his back, up his neck.

Finn sprinted.

If he remembered it the right way, he would reach the street not far from Meyer's home. As he ran, he glanced behind him every so often, looking to see who trailed him, but he couldn't make anything out in the darkness.

Still, it *felt* like they were getting closer.

Finn raced ahead. He scraped along the walls of the alley,

bouncing from them, and then noticed light in the end of the alley.

He was close.

Darkness filled the alley.

Someone was there. They would try to trap him.

He couldn't turn. There wasn't any other way out.

The only choice he had was to keep going.

Lowering his shoulder, he slammed into the person at the end of the alley and barreled through them.

Pain bloomed in his stomach, but he ignored it.

Then he was out. Back on the street.

He stumbled.

Something hurt more than it should.

Finn looked down.

Blood?

It poured from a wound on his stomach. He'd been stabbed. He turned but didn't see the attackers. The alley was a dark smear behind him.

Finn staggered forward.

The river running through the city was near him. He could hear it burbling, though now it sounded almost as if it were rushing past him, a loud *whooshing* in his ears.

Meyer's training started to kick in.

That sound in his ears wasn't a good thing for him to notice. It meant that he was more injured than he'd realized. That the stab to his belly might be more than he would be able to survive.

Meyer's home was near. Help would be there.

Reach Meyer.

That was all he had to do.

Finn staggered.

When he reached the gate leading to the home, he could feel movement behind him.

A shadow appeared out of the darkness.

For a moment, he thought he saw Holden, but that had to be his imagination.

He shoved on the gate.

Something struck him from behind. Heat worked up his back.

Finn grunted, then fell through the gate.

He sprawled out, lying in place. Not moving.

He lost track of how long he'd been lying there. Moments or hours. It all felt the same. Another attack didn't come.

He crawled toward the home.

That was the only thing that he could think of doing.

Move one leg.

Then another. Force himself to keep moving.

His back and his belly hurt. The injuries he'd sustained were likely fatal. He'd seen enough in his time with Meyer to know that he wouldn't be able to survive what he'd gone through. Gods, Finn had questioned enough men to know that what he'd gone through wouldn't be survivable.

Reach the door.

That was the only thought in his head.

He dragged himself farther.

Just a little bit more.

Finn sagged.

No.

He forced himself to go on.

With everything that he'd been through, he wasn't about to let some street attack be the reason that he died. Meyer would be able to save him. He was as skilled as any physician in the city.

Finn reached for the door.

It seemed so impossibly far away from him.

All he needed was to reach it.

Stretching his hand out toward the door, Finn struggled. He wanted to get to the door. To pound on it. Get Meyer's attention.

He couldn't even get his arm out that far.

Finn tried dragging himself farther. Trying to get just a little bit closer to the door, but he couldn't.

Everything hurt.

The *whooshing* in his ears increased.

Weakness washed over him. There was a dizziness with it. Colors flashed around the corners of his eyes.

I'm dying.

He'd been responsible for death. Ever since Meyer had claimed him, Finn had come to know death in a way that he hadn't before, but he'd never felt it so acutely as he did now.

Would the gods welcome me back?

He strained again but still couldn't reach for the door.

When he'd been sentenced to die, the priests had claimed that all he had to do would be to embrace Heleth and he would be claimed by the gods in the afterlife. Finn had never been faithful. Even after coming to work with

Meyer, his faith had been one of requirement, not one of true belief. It was better for him to use the gods during his questioning, so he never made it seem to the condemned that he didn't believe.

Now... now he wondered if this was retribution. That was the thought that stayed with him as he collapsed, his face sinking to the ground.

Somewhere behind him he swore he heard laughter.

CHAPTER THREE

Finn came awake to pain.

There was darkness all around him, and at first, he thought this was the afterlife. Most of those stories about it spoke of lights. Colors. Many who nearly died had images that were impossible to believe, as if those people had gone to sit near the gods themselves.

This was nothing like it. It had darkness and pain.

Pain didn't mean the afterlife. Not unless he were punished.

Which meant he'd lived.

"Easy," a distant voice said.

Finn recognized the voice.

There was pressure on his face. Cool, almost cold. Then the darkness eased.

Finn could see.

Everything was a bit of a blur, though he was able to make out just enough that he could see a pale orange light nearby coming from a lantern. Lena stood off to the side, her mouth pressed in a tight frown.

Were he not dying, Finn might have laughed at that.

There was a time when he wouldn't have expected Lena to worry about him. They had never been close. When their father had been pinched, she had taken the responsibility of caring for their sickly mother. There had never been any concern for him other than disgust at what he'd done to try to provide for their family. That had changed when she'd come to stay with Meyer.

"Lena?" His voice came out in a whisper.

Lena stepped forward. "What happened?"

Finn tried to move but still couldn't. There was too much pain.

Even thinking about moving caused pain to shoot through him.

"I don't know. Attacked."

Speaking was difficult.

Finn focused on his injuries, thinking about what he *could* feel. That was the key to knowing just how injured he actually was. He remembered parts of the attack. The heat in his belly when he'd stepped out of the alley. The sharp pain in his back when he'd been stabbed from behind. Then falling.

In addition to the stab wounds, he would have lost a lot of blood. There were limits to what men could withstand.

"Should be dead," he said.

Lena squeezed his hand. Somehow, even that hurt. Finn didn't remember getting injured there, but he must have.

He looked around. Lena was the only one in the room with him.

"How. Long?"

"Only a day," she said.

A day lost looking for Rachel Herns might mean the difference between life and death. He needed to get Holden to talk, but he wouldn't be in any shape for questioning for a while.

"Meyer?"

She leaned forward. "Henry was summoned away to the palace earlier. He hasn't returned."

"You?"

He tried to reach for his belly, but his hands didn't feel like they worked.

"There wasn't anything that I could do for you. When you were brought here, you were pretty far gone. You'd lost a lot of blood. You... you weren't going to make it."

Finn struggled to keep up with what she was telling him.

Brought here?

He looked around the room, this time *really* trying to look around it.

"Where am I?" he asked.

There wasn't anything about the room that gave him any clue as to where he was. Just the lantern and Lena.

He took a deep breath. A faint hint of a strange spice came to him. That was different. Unique. Familiar.

If Meyer hadn't helped him, then had Lena brought him to an apothecary? With wounds like he would have sustained, an apothecary wouldn't have been enough to help heal him. He'd need a surgeon at worst, or a physician at best.

This didn't look like a physician's home. They had seemed better lit. Given what they charged, they could afford to burn oil night and day.

He took another deep breath.

There was something recognizable in the spice.

One truth that he'd learned in his time working with Meyer was that there really wasn't much difference between what Meyer knew and what most of the physicians in Verendal knew. He had the knowledge of the apothecaries, the skill of the surgeons, and the wisdom of time.

Finn had trained with Meyer, trying to gain an understanding of the types of medicines he used, studying anatomy and concoctions with as much fervor as he studied the other aspects of his profession. Meyer had demonstrated that most of his considerable income would come from healing, not from serving the city.

He took another breath and realized why the spice smelled familiar.

"Hegen," he whispered.

Lena squeezed his hand again. "We didn't have any choice."

Finn tried to lick his lips. "What. Price?"

She leaned close. "I don't know. Whatever it is, I'll pay it. If it means that you survive, it will be worth it."

Finn rested his head back. "Won't. Be you."

"What? It will. I was the one who brought you here." She ran the cold cloth across his forehead again.

That was where the strange scent of spice came from. The odor invigorated Finn. He tried not to think of *why* or what might be in it.

Lena might have to pay some price, but he doubted she would be asked much.

It was me.

They had already used him before. Finn had been caught up in their strange machinations, not really knowing how, but coming to understand that they planned far more than what he had ever believed when he was younger.

Lena wasn't the one of value to the hegen.

That was Finn.

He tried thinking about what they would ask of him, but his mind didn't work the way it should. He was tired. Some distant part of his mind knew that tiredness was dangerous and that he should fight to stay awake, but he couldn't. His eyes fell shut and he drifted.

Finn had strange dreams.

This time, there were colors. Flashes of bright lights. A tingling that seemed as if it were real. Distantly, he felt as if there was some sort of darkness coming for him.

Could that be one of the gods coming to collect me?

When he came awake, the lantern light remained the same. Pale light that glowed in the room. Nothing else.

Finn tried to move and found that he could this time. The pain in his body had eased.

Hegen magic.

That had probably been the reason for the dreams. They'd been using their magic on him. If he didn't hurt, then could he sit? Finn shifted on the bed and lifted his head.

He was alone. Lena had left him.

Either that or the hegen had demanded something of her.

Finn tried to get up and out of the bed, but his legs didn't work quite the way that he wanted them to. He focused on moving, on trying to get his legs shifted and out of the bed, and found that he could.

There had been a moment during the attack, nothing more than that, where he'd begun to wonder if he might have been paralyzed in the attack. A knife to the back could do that. Even a sharp blow to the back could do that.

Finn wiggled his toes. Tested his legs. They worked.

Then he sat upright.

He wobbled for a moment. A wave of dizziness washed through him. *That would be the blood loss.* The hegen might be able to heal with their particular magic, but could they replenish his blood?

Finn remained seated on the edge of the bed for a long moment.

He was still dressed in the same pants he'd worn during the attack. His shirt and jacket were missing.

Looking down, he found the wound on his belly.

Or what remained of the wound on his belly.

Little more than a pink line remained. It looked as if it had been stitched by the finest surgeon and completely healed.

Tracing his finger over the scar, he shook his head. He knew that hegen magic was powerful. He'd never *felt* it.

"That was a particularly difficult wound to close."

Finn looked over to the door. Esmerelda stood in the other room in a pale yellow gown that accented her figure, dark wavy hair falling to her shoulders. A trace of a smile curved her full lips as she carved through a long length of bone with an enormous knife. It cut through it as well as Justice cut through everything.

"Did she find you or did you ask her to bring me to you?" Finn asked, shifting himself to test his feet. The ground was rough against his bare skin, and he looked for his boots, finding them near the door. He would need a shirt, though Esmerelda would likely have some task he would have to complete in order for him to be clothed properly.

She turned to him, looking up from her work. "You fault them for bringing you to me?"

"Them?"

Esmerelda stepped into the room. "You don't know."

Finn stood. He wobbled for a moment but then managed to stand. There wasn't any pain in his stomach or his back. The hegen healing had saved him.

He should be pleased. At least, he should be thankful. Finn couldn't help but worry about the cost. What would Esmerelda ask of him this time?

"Such wounds," she said, sliding over to him and touching his belly.

Finn tensed. Her touch was cool, reminding him of the

way the cloth had felt on his forehead, and his skin tingled where she touched.

That wasn't all that tingled.

Esmerelda was beautiful in a strange and exotic way, but he'd spent time with the hegen before. His relationship with Jasmine had been brief and the differences between them too difficult to overcome, mostly because of his commitment as an executioner, not because she was hegen. Few people wanted to spend time with an executioner, and he'd hoped things would be different with Jasmine, though it had been his duties that had kept him away rather than any feeling of avoiding the executioner like he found with so many he'd pursued. Anything with Esmerelda would have the same difficulties, and that assumed she would even be interested.

He pushed those thoughts away.

"I suppose I should thank you."

"That is customary when one friend helps another."

Finn stepped back. "Is that what we are now?"

"Are we not?"

"What's the price?"

She frowned at him. "Must you immediately turn to such questions?"

"There is a price, isn't there?"

She smiled, somehow making it look sad. "All magic comes with a price, Finn Jagger."

The times that he'd been around the hegen before, there had been no admission of magic. There had been an acknowledgement of what they did, but nothing more than that.

"What will you ask of me?"

She held her hands out and then twisted them slightly. Finn wasn't surprised when a card suddenly appeared in her hands. Esmerelda offered it to him.

The card was blank.

"What's this?"

"The price."

"There's nothing on it."

"Not currently," she said.

"You haven't decided your price. I see."

She smiled at him. "There are some wounds that are easy to heal. Others require a different touch." She reached over and Finn refused to jerk away. When she touched him, he closed his eyes, sighing as the tingling washed through him. "Were it only the one, you would have been easy. The second was the one that posed more of a challenge."

"My back."

She nodded.

"Would Meyer have been able to save me?"

She touched her hands to her upper chest as she looked up at him. "You regret what they did?"

"I don't even know who they are."

"You saw your sister, I believe."

"I did."

"But not the other."

Who else?

"Oscar," he breathed out.

Esmerelda flipped her hands and another card appeared. An outline of a hand covered the face of the card, but then she flipped them and it disappeared. "He cares for you."

Finn grunted. "I suppose now he's going to think we're even."

"Why is that?"

"I saved him from the Archers before. Now he's saved me."

Esmerelda smiled. "All debts must be paid."

Finn looked around the room and finally found his shirt hanging from a hook on one wall near the bed. He lifted it and held it out. The blood that must have stained it was gone. The holes where he'd been stabbed were mended, leaving only a fine stitching, reminding him of how finely *he* would have been stitched.

As he pulled on the shirt, he looked over to Esmerelda. "What's the cost for this?"

Esmerelda laughed. It was a soft and airy sound. "There is no payment needed for your clothing, Finn Jagger."

That was a surprise, but he would take it.

"Did Oscar say what happened to me?"

He must have followed him. Could Oscar have been the one in the alley?

Finn didn't think so. If anything, Oscar had followed to ensure his safety.

He took a step toward the door, wobbling slightly.

Esmerelda watched him, though he couldn't tell what she was thinking. It seemed to him there was some calculation behind her eyes, as if she watched him and debated whether she would be able to use his weakness in another way.

"Thank you for healing me," he said.

He made his way from the back room and into the main entrance to Esmerelda's home. Finn had been there before and recognized it. It was cozy, with magical decorations around the room. Some of the items looked familiar, though that might be because he'd been here a few times.

Hesitating near the door, he leaned on it a moment. Now that he'd recovered—at least mostly—he would have to return to his duties. He would go to Holden. If his crew was somehow responsible, let him see that Finn hadn't died.

There was still the issue of finding Rachel Herns.

Finn didn't think he would have the time to do so.

He looked back at Esmerelda, finding her watching him. Did she know the question in his mind?

"What did you ask of Oscar for payment?" he asked.

"That is between him and me."

"And my sister?"

"The same."

"I can just ask them."

"If you think they will share it with you."

Finn didn't know. There was something to be said about keeping the details of what was owed to the hegen to oneself. In the case of the others, he didn't know if they would even share anything—or if they could.

He reached into his pocket, fingering the card that was there. It was even possible that they wouldn't know what had been asked of them. Much like Finn.

"Will you require an escort back to the city?" Esmerelda asked.

"How much extra will that be?"

She smiled, gliding toward him, and rested a hand on his arm. "Do you always think in terms of what you must pay?" She smiled, reaching past him and pulling open the door. "Not everything requires a transaction, Finn Jagger."

He watched her for a moment before heading out into the street.

The hegen section was outside of the city, situated to the north of the road and near the edge of the forest. Most of the buildings looked to be little more than shacks, though considering what he knew of Esmerelda's home and how it appeared from the outside, he suspected much of that was for show. The streets were narrow though straight, unlike the twisting roads leading through the city proper. None were very long, forcing Finn to make several small turns as he wound his way through the section, trying to get free.

He passed a few others out but not many. Those who were visible turned away from him. Finn had some experience with the hegen to know not to take offense at it, though he didn't know why they thought they needed to avoid him. Unless they didn't care for his responsibility either. Many within the rest of Verendal felt that way. Executioners were valued, but no one wanted to spend time with them.

Reaching the edge of the hegen section, Finn looked back. It was a colorful section, vibrant red and green and orange splashed over the buildings. In the rising sunlight, those colors all drew his eye, almost as if they created a pattern. He breathed in, noticing a hint of the spice that he'd smelled when at Esmerelda's home. It lingered in his nostrils.

Finn turned away. The path back to the city from the hegen section led past the gallows. Finn paused at the Raven Stone, a massive stack of stone where the condemned were brought to carry out their sentencing. He didn't feel about the Stone the way most in the city did. The Stone had a purpose. A meaning. It was there to carry out the king's justice, but it was more than that. Were it only about the king's justice, they wouldn't sentence those like Holden who had committed no crime upon the king himself. It was more about how Finn served the people of Verendal. It had surprised him that it mattered.

The gallows rose from atop the Raven Stone. The solid wood had been rebuilt several times during Finn's tenure as apprentice because they needed to ensure that the gallows wouldn't crack during a sentencing. Meyer made certain that Finn appreciated the gravity of their duty, something that Meyer didn't take lightly. Part of that was ensuring each sentencing was carried out efficiently.

It had been a few weeks since they'd been to the gallows. That was unusual.

Holden would be next.

There was more to question him about, especially now that Finn had suffered an attack.

When he reached the gate, the Archers waved him in. They were city Archers, not palace Archers, and Finn knew them both, having gotten to know many of the Archers over the years. They weren't necessarily friends, though they were friendly. It made his job easier.

The farther he went, the easier it was for him. He began to feel refreshed in a way that he hadn't before, the weakness that he'd awoken to beginning to fade. He tugged on his shirt, twisting it, and noticed a twinge of pain in his stomach and his back, though not like what he had felt before.

The hegen magic.

Were it not for the cost, more people should be offered that kind of magic. It was because of that magic that his mother had been returned to him, though she hadn't been able to recover for long. It was because of that magic that his sister had gotten caught up with the hegen, forcing her to serve. Finn had suspected her service had been a part of getting him bound to the hegen, though he didn't know for certain.

When he reached Meyer's home, he looked at the ground around the small iron gate leading into the yard. The low stone wall surrounding the yard was more decorative than a real barrier. This was where he'd been attacked. There should be blood but he saw none.

Finn pressed the door open and headed inside. He looked there for signs of what had happened to him, but there was nothing there, either.

Hadn't I fallen there?

Finn thought that he remembered the attack.

He remembered coming out of the alley. Looking up, he

turned toward the alley on the far side of the street. It wasn't directly across from Meyer's yard, but near enough that Finn thought that was where he had to have come out of. The presence around him had unsettled him, but it hadn't clouded his thinking. It was only when he'd been stabbed that his mind had stopped working the way that it should.

Either the blood had been washed away—and considering that Finn didn't know quite how long he'd been out, that was a possibility—or he hadn't fallen there.

Stepping back out of the gate, he made his way along the street.

He looked for blood.

Then he found it.

A lot of it.

A pool of blood covered the street outside of a house three down from Meyer's. Much like Meyer's home, a low wall surrounded it, along with a gate. The gate was different from Meyer's, without the same ornamentation.

Finn looked through the gate.

On the other side of the gate was another pool of blood. This was even more than the last. Finn had seen bleeding like that—and knew that he shouldn't have survived.

Not only had he been stabbed and bleeding heavily, but he'd crawled to the wrong house. Had he made it to the house, he wouldn't have gotten the help he needed.

Oscar had saved him.

Finn looked toward the alley again.

He would need to find out who was responsible for what

had happened to him. If it was because of Holden, then Finn would ensure that he paid the price. If it was someone else...

He couldn't think like that. There wasn't anything more that he could do.

Tugging down on his shirt, he headed toward Meyer's home.

CHAPTER FOUR

The inside of Meyer's home had a welcoming feel to it. It was comfortable. Filled with the fragrance of flowers collected in the garden and that of baking bread, Finn breathed it in, finally able to move past the strange hegen smells that had lingered in his nostrils even after leaving their section of the city.

He found Lena and Meyer there. Lena stood over the stove, cooking eggs and bacon, the sizzling leaving a pleasing odor in the air. She looked over when he appeared.

Meyer sat in a chair near the corner of the kitchen, his hands resting on the table. The gray-haired executioner was already dressed for the day, wearing a neatly tailored jacket and pants of a deep blue wool. His mouth pressed into a tight frown when Finn came in.

"Finn? You shouldn't have come back here on your own!"

There was an unreadable expression in Meyer's blue eyes.

"It seems that I wasn't as injured as it seemed."

"The blood on the street and near Merand's home would say otherwise."

Finn shrugged. "I saw that."

"Care to tell me what happened?" Meyer asked.

Finn took a seat across from him, leaning back in the wooden chair and resting his hands on the table. So many mornings started like this, with Lena cooking for them and Meyer and Finn having a conversation about the upcoming day. It had been a while since he had felt guilty with what he needed to share with Meyer.

"I'm not entirely certain."

"What do you remember?"

Finn flicked his gaze over to Lena. She had her back to him. Over the years, she had begun to follow Meyer in the evenings and often listened, paying attention to him as he healed, offering her own insights, and gradually improving her skill. While Finn would one day be an executioner, and through that have the opportunity to heal in his off time, Lena was also serving something of an apprenticeship with Meyer.

"I'd finished questioning Holden for the day and had gone looking for help to find the missing girl."

Lena stiffened.

"Why would you need help?"

Finn leaned forward. "Because he's not going to tell us anything. The girl doesn't have much time, if she still lives. I figured that if anyone would be able to find anything about what had happened to her, it would be—"

"Someone who has access to that kind of information," Meyer finished. His brow furrowed, and the wrinkles in the corners of his eyes seemed to deepen. "You went to the Hand?"

"Oscar," Finn said.

Meyer nodded. "Did he help?"

"I needed to know about Holden's crew. They did this to me."

"Thieves don't like to reveal secrets of their kind."

"I was one of their kind. At least to Oscar."

Lena turned and set plates of scrambled eggs and bacon in front of each of them. She looked over to Finn, as if she wanted to say something, before spinning away. "I will clean up later."

With that, she left the kitchen.

"She worried about you," Meyer said between bites.

"I wouldn't be here were it not for her."

Meyer grunted. "Probably not."

"You don't think you could have saved me?"

"I could have stitched the wounds, but with as much blood as you'd lost, there wouldn't have been much more that I could have done." He took another bite, focusing on his food.

Finn looked down at his plate. His stomach rumbled and he knew he should eat. Food would help him recover. Even a magical recovery would need him to eat in order to ensure that he gained his strength. Hegen magic had helped, but now was a time for him to let his body finish the recovery.

"I don't know what happened. I was followed. Went into the alley. Got caught between a pair of attackers." Finn patted his stomach. "Stabbed here. My back."

"Thought you were making it here?" Meyer asked.

Finn nodded. "Where were you?"

"Summoned to the palace."

That was what Lena had said. Finn should have remembered. Maybe his mind wasn't as clear as he thought. "King Porman?"

Meyer set his fork down and looked up. He'd already finished eating. Finn still hadn't started. "The king arrived two days ago."

Finn blinked. "There was no sign of it."

Usually when the king came to Verendal, which wasn't that often, there was plenty of notice and a procession leading into the city and to the palace. It wasn't much of a secret.

"Not this time. He didn't want his coming to be known."

"What did he call you for?"

Meyer shook his head. "A warning."

"That's all you're going to tell me?"

"It probably means nothing, though he wanted me to be alert."

"Why you?"

Meyer grunted. "I serve the king."

"I know that. Why would the king need to alert you of a threat?"

That was what it had to be. Though what kind of a threat?

"Because there's concern about the prisons. As I serve as master of prisons, he wanted me to have the warning."

"If there's something we need to be concerned about with the prisons, then don't you think that I should be alerted as well?"

"What do you think I'm doing?" Meyer motioned to the plate. "Eat."

Finn turned his attention to his food and began scooping the eggs into his mouth, chewing quickly and swallowing. He didn't taste much this way, but he needed it to recover.

When he was done, Meyer motioned for Finn to join him. Finn set their plates into the washbasin before trailing Meyer out of the house.

The executioner had grabbed a hat on the way out, using it to cover his balding head and to shield against the bright sunlight. He headed toward the center of the city, with Finn following.

"What do you need me to do today?" Finn asked.

"We'll be together today."

"Are you sure? I have supplies I need to gather, a few men to question, and preparations for—"

"We'll be together today," Meyer said again.

That was strange enough. Most of the time these days, Finn worked on his own. That was the advantage of having progressed in his training. He would gather the necessary supplies for questioning, healing, and for other purposes.

He would be responsible for questioning lower-level prisoners. He would even be responsible for presenting some of the prisoners to the jury on his own. Occasionally, he would make preparations to carry out a sentencing, though so far had not done so alone. There was an expectation that he would still do that with Meyer.

"Another girl was taken," Meyer said.

"Another?" Holden was captured, but his crew was still free. "If it's tied to Holden—"

"We don't know that. This one is different, though."

"Why?"

Meyer paused, taking a deep breath. "The king's chancellor had come to Verendal to work through the final pieces of the Alainsith treaty. His daughter came with him."

He handed Finn a folded paper.

When he unfolded it, a small portrait of a lovely golden-haired young woman looked up at him, as if coming alive in the portrait.

"Her name is Elizabeth Jarvis. Her parents are in the palace, miserable at the thought that they've come out to Verendal only to lose their daughter. The king has taken a personal interest in our case."

"We can have the Archers round up the full crew—"

"We are trying. It is not so easy. As this is a relatively new crew in the city, learning their whereabouts has proven problematic."

He heard the frustration in Meyer's tone.

"What can I do?"

"Get him to break," Meyer said.

They continued through the streets before Meyer paused.

Finn frowned. "This is the alley I went down last night." He looked over to Meyer. "You're trying to see what you can find of my attack?"

"I doubt we'll be able to uncover much about it. When you mentioned coming through the alley across from my home, I suspected this was where you had entered it."

Finn hadn't known that Meyer knew the alleys that well. They were confusing for most and created something of a maze that would be hard to follow. Mastering the alleys was not something most ever bothered with, especially since finding a way through the streets could be difficult enough.

"This was. I had been followed ever since leaving the Wenderwolf."

Meyer glanced over at him. "How long were you there?"

Finn shrugged. "Long enough for a mug of ale."

"Were you affected by it?"

Finn frowned at him. "I can handle a mug of ale."

Meyer reached the alley and leaned forward, breathing in.

Finn resisted copying him. There was no point in smelling the stench from the alley; he had done it the night before and found the smell not particularly pleasant.

"Are you sure that you were followed from the Wenderwolf?"

"Not completely," Finn said. "It might have been once I headed toward your home."

Finn tried to think back to it, but it was difficult for him to remember what he had experienced.

He understood what Meyer was getting at. If he were followed from the Wenderwolf, then he had to be concerned about who might have known that he was there. Finn hadn't hidden his presence, but it would be unexpected for someone like himself to have spent much time in that tavern. Now that he served as Meyer's apprentice, he filled a role of serving the king more directly.

"You're concerned someone at the Wenderwolf tipped off Holden's men."

"I'm concerned you aren't necessarily welcome there. I know your friend remains welcome, but he didn't betray Leon Konig."

"I didn't betray him either."

Meyer looked over. "I suppose you didn't." He motioned for Finn to follow and they continued along the street, heading toward the Olin section.

In the daytime, everything looked different. It was easier to see that this section was a bit more run-down than some of the more central parts of the city. Buildings weren't as well maintained here as they were in other places. Signs had faded. The cobbles weren't set quite as neatly. Refuse didn't get cleaned up the way it would in other places.

Still, this was a part of the city where Finn had always felt welcome. When he'd lived in a poorer section of the city, he'd longed to progress to live in Olin. It was a far cry from Brinder, where he'd grown up. In Brinder, the streets were narrow. The people were dangerous, and most were tied to the city's underground in some way. Not like Olin, where there actually were some reputable people.

When they neared the Wenderwolf, Finn felt a flutter of anxiety. That surprised him. There was no reason for him to be uncomfortable coming to the tavern, especially in the daylight and with Meyer; still, he couldn't shake the feeling he had.

"Are you going to go and question Annie?" Finn asked.

Meyer looked over. "I'm not. You are."

"Master Meyer—"

"You were attacked while in service to the king."

"I was in a section of the city that I had no business being in after dark."

"Do you really believe that?"

Finn looked toward the tavern before shaking his head. "No."

"Then go along. I will be here with you."

Finn grunted. "You just want to make sure I'm going to do what you want."

"Yes."

Finn shook his head and headed toward the tavern. Though each step was difficult, he forced himself to make them. When he reached it, resting his hand on the door leading inside, he hesitated. Everything was silent, as if the tavern itself waited on him to pull the door open and enter.

When he did, the tavern was darkened and empty. Even in the evenings, there wasn't much light in the tavern, but there was usually a fire in the hearth, the sound of voices all around, the music from the musicians Annie would hire.

At this hour it was quiet. Somber.

It reminded him of when he'd come when planning jobs with the King and the crew. They had used the Wenderwolf as a base before, coming at all hours. Annie had permitted them to do so. Finn didn't really know what relationship she and the King had, but they'd been close.

Meyer joined him inside. "To hear you speak of this place, I would think it nicer."

"She has the best ale. And music."

A door to the kitchen opened and Viera, a younger waitress Finn had started to know when he'd been working with the crew, emerged. She carried a bucket, and stopped as soon as she saw Finn and Meyer.

"I see," Meyer said.

"She's not the reason I came."

"I'm sure she's not."

"Anymore," Finn said. He stepped forward, smiling at Viera. "Is Annie here?" he asked.

Viera backed toward the kitchen. She looked past Finn, toward Meyer, her eyes wide.

"We're only here to ask her a question," Finn said.

Viera licked her lips, her attention coming back around to Finn. "She didn't do anything," Viera said.

"I'm sure she didn't. We just needed to ask her a few questions. Can you have her come out?"

Viera dropped the bucket and scurried back into the kitchen, letting the door swing closed behind her.

Finn could only sigh. There had been a time when a quick smile would charm Viera. Not that she needed much charming, but he thought that he could pull it off. Now that he was known to be the executioner's apprentice, there wasn't the same opportunity, even were he to want it.

"It is difficult, returning to place you once knew," Meyer said softly.

"The alternative would have been worse," Finn said.

Meyer grunted. "When I first met Maria, she didn't know anything about my profession. I tried to keep it from her as long as possible. I was an apprentice at the time, so there was still the possibility that I might change careers. It wasn't until we had known each other for a few months that I revealed that truth."

Meyer never spoke about his family. Finn knew that whatever had happened to them would have to have been tragic. There was a child. The room Lena used at the house had once suggested that, though Finn didn't see anything else in the house that would be a reminder of that child.

"How did she react?" Finn asked.

"Anger."

Finn grunted, shaking his head.

"Because I had kept it from her. She didn't care. Not the way her father had. It took some convincing and a visit from my master to explain the income of someone in my profession and how I would be able to provide for her. Maria only cared that I had kept something from her."

Finn looked over. Meyer wore a tight expression, his eyes narrowed, almost sad. "That's where you get it from?"

Meyer looked to Finn. "I learn from everyone in my life.

That happens to be a lesson she taught me. The truth is better than a lie, even when difficult."

The door leading to the back of the tavern opened and Annie came out. She was dressed differently than she did in the evenings. There was no low-cut dress. No heavy makeup. Only a high-collared blue dress. Her hair twisted into a bun. It was almost as if she had gotten dressed for this visit.

Finn found himself smiling slightly. Did she really think this would make a difference for him?

"Finn," she said, tipping her head politely. "Master Meyer, I presume. What may I do for you?"

Meyer only waited. This was to be Finn's questioning.

"Can we sit and visit for a moment?" he asked.

Annie looked to him. "What is this about?"

"Me."

Annie's gaze narrowed slightly and then she nodded.

She waved them over to one of the tables. Not a booth. Those were for the crews. Not that Meyer would know that, though maybe he did. Finn waited until Annie had taken a seat and then followed, sitting across from her. Meyer remained standing a few paces away, watching.

Annie looked over to Meyer before turning her attention back to Finn. "I presume this is an official visit?"

"Official enough," Finn said.

"Very well. Am I charged with anything?"

Finn shook his head.

"But you think I might be."

"I don't think that," Finn said.

"Then he does." She flicked her gaze to Meyer, watching him a moment before settling it once more on Finn.

Finn waited for Meyer to answer, but he didn't intervene.

"I don't think so."

"Then why are you here, Finn?"

He watched her. He had gained experience reading people, and when it came to questioning her, he would need to make sure that he could read her reaction. That was what Meyer wanted from him. Meyer probably watched so that he could read her reaction as well.

"I was attacked a few nights ago."

She frowned. "After you were in here?"

He nodded.

"That's why you came to me. You think that I'm responsible."

"I don't know who's responsible, to be honest. All I know is that after I left here, someone followed me into the alleys. They stabbed me."

She leaned forward, looking at him. "You don't look like you'd been stabbed."

He hesitated. Revealing that was probably too much.

Annie was smart. She would have to be in order for her to run the Wenderwolf the way that she did. She'd run it as long as Finn had known about the tavern, despite the dangers that tavern owners often faced.

"How badly were you attacked?" she asked.

"Does it matter?"

"You came to me, which suggests that whatever

happened was significant. Otherwise, you would either have come alone or not at all." She turned toward Finn. "It seems to me that you must have been significantly injured." She frowned. "Seeing as how I watched you coming along the street and there wasn't a sign of injury..."

"I was stabbed in the stomach and the back."

She watched him and then started to smile. "What do you owe them?"

She didn't even need him to tell her what had happened.

"Nothing."

"Nothing? Finn, I've lived in this city a long time. I've known more people than I can count who've gone to the hegen for help. You don't do that without paying a price. If you want my answers, then I'm going to need yours. Consider that *my* price."

Finn sighed and reached into his pocket, pulling the card out and sliding it across the table. There was a part of him that worried the card would suddenly have an image on it, but it remained blank.

"No price," he said.

"A marker. That's worse."

"I know."

"With the hegen, they can turn that marker into... you know." She frowned at him, looking up from the card and meeting his eyes. "You've owed the hegen before."

He nodded.

"Interesting. How long have you been tied to them?"

"I'm not tied to them."

"If you have their marker, you are. How long?"

Finn shook his head. "I paid my debt."

"That's the thing with the hegen. There's no paying off the debt. They find ways to tie you to them until you can't do anything but what they want. Those who know better make a point of not getting tangled up with them." She looked over to Meyer. "Isn't that right?"

Meyer didn't say anything.

"I've answered your questions," Finn said. "Now you need to answer mine. Did you have anything to do with what happened to me last night?"

"Why would I want to attack you?"

Finn hesitated before answering. "Because of what happened to Leon." And maybe because she was helping Holden, but Finn didn't know that for certain.

Her brow darkened. "Leon Konig was a stupid man. He kept taking on more than what he should until it got him caught. That wasn't on you, or on you." She nodded to Meyer. "That was on that foolish man. Had he only listened when I told him to quit while he was ahead…"

Finn couldn't tell if she told him the truth or not. There was something about the way she said it that left him wondering if she were trying to mislead him, but he couldn't tell with any certainty. Annie would be skilled. Having spent most of her days around men like Leon and Oscar, she would have to have a gift for misleading him.

"What about Holden?"

"Who?"

The confusion on her face was genuine.

Annie wasn't tied to it, then.

"Do you know who was responsible?" Finn asked.

She looked up at him. "I don't. And you could have just come here and asked me that rather than coming in like this."

"He was on official business last evening," Meyer said. "An attack upon a servant of the king during official business is a different magnitude of crime."

"Official business? Meeting with the Hand?" she asked, turning to Finn.

Finn smiled. If she had thought to disarm him by revealing what he'd been doing, she was mistaken.

"Meeting with the Hand was official business," Finn said.

Annie leaned back, crossing her arms over her chest as she considered Finn. "You're starting to act like him."

"Like Oscar?"

She shook her head. "Like *him.*" She flicked her gaze to Meyer.

Finn grunted softly. There were worse things in the world to be accused of. Time with Meyer had proven how the old executioner was diligent and respected, and served the way that he believed he should. Finn didn't necessarily try to act the same as Meyer, but he didn't try not to, either.

"Do you know anything about what happened?" he asked.

"No. Now, that's not to say I won't be able to come up with answers. If you want, I could check around with some of the regulars who were at the tavern last night. I'm sure with the right kind of questioning, we can find out what happened."

Finn could tell she knew more than she let on. There was a twitch to the corners of her eyes.

It hurt him.

Not that he had ever expected Annie to protect him, but there had been a time when he had come to the tavern and had been treated well. Even a few nights ago, when he'd come to the Wenderwolf, he felt as if he was treated well, even if he was an executioner who served the king. It seemed to him that had now changed.

Finn got to his feet. "Why don't you look into it? I can stop by later this week and see what you've uncovered. It's important, Annie. Women are missing and we're trying to find them before something worse happens to them."

He would play on her sympathy. Finn didn't know if it would work.

Annie looked up at him. "That's it?"

"You expected more?"

"You come here like this... I thought this was official business."

"It was," Finn said.

"Didn't seem official to me. Seems personal."

Finn glanced to Meyer, who nodded.

They reached the door when Finn paused. "If you hear of anything about what happened to these women, I would appreciate you sharing that as well."

"Especially Elizabeth Jarvis," Meyer said.

That would be the chancellor's daughter.

Annie's eye twitched slightly. "She someone special to you?"

"Someone who matters to the king," Meyer said.

They stepped back out into the street and put some distance between them and the Wenderwolf.

"She's an interesting one," Meyer said.

It was a significant compliment, coming from him.

"She's had to run the tavern for years. Considering the kind of people who frequent the tavern, she's had to be strong."

"The kind who frequent it because she's set it up that way."

"Probably," Finn said. "She knows more than she's letting on."

"I would agree," Meyer said.

"Not just about me." That was what had surprised him. The comment on the missing women had been a bit of a throwaway, just because he wanted to cast as wide of a net for her as he could. When he'd said the name, Annie had twitched. "She recognized that there were missing women."

"I would agree. What do you intend to do about it?"

It was a measure of how far that he'd come in his training that Meyer didn't force himself into it. Finn appreciated it.

"I think I need to find out what Annie knows."

"How will you go about that?"

There were various different ways that he could do it, though none of them were the ways that Meyer had taught. The ways that came to mind were how he had once operated in the city, slinking around and following a person. That might not even work when it came to Annie.

Finn didn't *need* to use those tactics, anyway. He had different strategies available to him now. They were devious in their own way, especially with someone like Annie who depended upon a specific livelihood.

"I might ask the Archers to patrol here a bit more than usual. We can put a little pressure on the Wenderwolf."

"You understand the consequences."

Finn looked back at the tavern. Pressure like that would cause the tavern to suffer.

He kept coming back to something that he'd felt while talking to Annie. She knew something. And if she knew something about what had happened to him, he needed to hear it. More than that, if she knew something about what had happened to Rachel Herns, he needed that as well.

"I understand the consequences."

Meyer nodded. "Do what you think is necessary."

"There's something else I think I need to do."

"You intend to return to Declan today?"

"You knew?"

"It is what I would do. If Holden is responsible for the attack on you, at least if his men were responsible, it would be interesting to see what sort of reaction your arrival will cause."

"We'll need to watch the prison afterward."

"I agree."

"You'll help?"

Meyer looked over, regarding Finn for a few moments before laughing softly. "I suppose so, though shouldn't it be the other way around?" His face turned serious. "We must work quickly, Finn. The king himself will want us to find the chancellor's daughter."

"Then let's start now. Will he meet with us?"

Meyer frowned at Finn. "The chancellor will be difficult for the two of us to reach."

"We have to investigate every aspect of what happened, Master Meyer."

Meyer turned and looked off toward the center of the city. Finn could practically follow the direction of his gaze as it drifted to the palace. It would be more than just difficult getting to the chancellor. Getting into the palace required an invitation, but given what they needed to find, Finn thought it prudent to try.

"We should start with her mother, then. I suspect we'll find her more accommodating." He sighed. "Let's get on with this."

"You want me to come?"

"You are still *my* apprentice."

Finn flushed briefly. He knew better than to question Meyer like that, but there were so many different things that he needed to be doing, not the least looking into Holden and his crew. These days, Finn was more accustomed to working alone, so having Meyer pull him away from what he considered his responsibilities felt like a waste of time.

"Of course."

Meyer chuckled. "Don't worry. This won't take all day."

They started through the city, crossing the river and passing through a merchant section but veering away from the palace. When he mentioned something about that to Meyer, he only nodded.

"The chancellor's wife has family in the city. She's been staying with them while he's busy. Elizabeth was to have been with her. That's where she disappeared."

They stopped in front of a massive home with ivy growing along the exterior. A small wall surrounded the home. The home's size spoke of wealth, but the symbol on the door told Finn what kind of place this was.

"A physician," he breathed out.

Meyer looked at him. "Is that a problem for you?"

Finn shook his head. "Not at all."

Meyer nodded, as if were settled.

There was a part of Finn that still struggled with what the physicians in the city charged for their services. He remembered all too well how he'd been turned away when he'd gone looking for help for his mother, only because he didn't have the money to pay for their services. Now he no longer needed a physician's help. Meyer knew as much as any physician, and now Lena did as well.

They knocked and waited.

When the door came open, an older woman with bright blue eyes and graying golden hair looked out at them. She would have been lovely in her youth. "I'm sorry, but he's not taking any patients today."

Finn frowned. A physician would turn someone away? Meyer never did.

At least they weren't dismissed out of hand the way Finn had been when he'd last come to a physician. That probably had as much to do with the way Finn was dressed as anything else. That, and Meyer's demeanor. He could fit in anywhere in the city.

"Mistress Jarvis?" Meyer asked.

She frowned, tugging on her navy dress. "Yes. Who are you?"

Meyer tipped his head politely. "I'm Henry Meyer. I'm investigating your daughter's disappearance. I had hoped to ask a few questions about her."

She stood in the doorway, making it clear that she wasn't going to invite them in. "About her? Is that necessary? She's missing, Mr. Meyer. I would expect a crown servant such as yourself to do whatever is necessary to discover who did this and where she went."

Finn wasn't sure if Meyer would reveal that they thought they knew the who but wasn't sure it made sense. The chancellor and his daughter weren't the kinds of people to have any exposure to Holden or his crew—other than as a target.

"I understand that you're distraught. Losing one's daughter is—"

"I did *not* lose her," she said. "She's missing. All while my husband is here to deal with the Alainsith. The king should have handled them long ago. Now we're forced to come to this place and bargain with them?"

Meyer tipped his head. "We think we know who took her." Meyer hesitated, as if he were expecting Mistress Jarvis to look relieved. She gave no reaction. "Was she traveling anywhere in the city recently where she might have been spotted? Perhaps with your husband or—"

Her face soured. "Of course she was spotted with him. We traveled here, didn't we?" She shook her head. "If this is the level of service we're getting from the inquisitors in the city, then I will have to speak to the king myself. I know him well."

"I'm sure you do," Meyer said. He smiled, though it was strained and forced. "Anything that you might be able to offer would be beneficial."

"We've given your Archer a portrait of her already. Isn't that enough? A copy, though we weren't giving anyone the original. Horshach himself painted it." She looked at Meyer, who gave no reaction to the comment. Finn suspected Horshach must be a famous painter in the capital. "Find her, Mr. Meyer, or the king will have your head."

She stepped back and closed the door.

They headed out to the street, where Meyer paused a moment before letting out a long frustrated sigh.

"Her threats aren't going to make us find her daughter any faster," Finn said.

"Of course not, but she feels empowered by her husband's position. And she's worried about her daughter, as any parent would be."

Meyer started off, shaking his head. When they reached the end of the street, Finn looked back at the physician's home.

"I wonder if the king knows his chancellor's feelings on the Alainsith," Finn said.

Meyer glanced at Finn. "His feelings matter little if he fulfills his duty to the king. Much like mine—and yours— don't matter. Always remember that, Finn. But she's not wrong. We must find her daughter. I'm going to look into where Elizabeth Jarvis disappeared. I need for you to push Holden for answers."

CHAPTER FIVE

It was later in the day, and the shafts of sunlight cutting through the rare windows inside Declan didn't provide much light. Most of the light came from the lanterns along the walls, giving off a dim glow that didn't fully illuminate the inside of the prison.

He came alone.

Meyer would help him keep watch on the prison, but the questioning was his task.

This time, he avoided going to the warden. He needed to limit the number of people who knew his business until he had a better understanding about what leaks might be present within the prison.

Here he had thought they didn't have any. That was until Holden.

Finn marched through the halls, nodding to the various iron masters, glancing at them as he tried to gauge their reaction to his presence. He didn't see anything from the first man that would suggest that he didn't expect to encounter Finn.

"Do you need me to escort anyone to the chapel?" Rogel asked.

He was an older guard and had served in the prison for the better part of a decade. It was hard work at times, and Finn couldn't imagine serving as an iron master as a career, but there were several men who had been there a long time. They were the ones he didn't *think* he had to be as concerned about, though he didn't really know.

"I will take care of it today," he said.

Rogel nodded as Finn moved past.

He headed down into the deeper part of the prison. The more dangerous prisoners were kept in the lower levels, not only to ensure they remained confined but because it carried with it a more ominous feel. There was something about taking the journey down into the bowels of the prison that intimidated most men.

When he reached the lower level, Finn paused.

Another pair of iron masters stood watch.

Finn glanced at both of them. Jalen was not much older than Finn and had served his post for the last few years. Shiner was only a few years older than that. Both men were clean-shaven—their way of looking different than the men they guarded—and had short, dark hair.

Neither showed much in the way of surprise at his passing.

"Who you here for today?" Jalen asked.

"Holden. Why don't you help me escort him to the chapel?"

Jalen nodded, pulling his keys from his pocket and rattling them briefly.

Finn followed him along the row of cells. These days, he didn't come down to the cells as often. The guards were more than happy to bring the prisoners to him, and Finn preferred that to coming down there and smelling the awfulness of this level.

He passed by a series of cells, looking into each one briefly before moving on.

The prison census was lower than usual these days. A few of the cells were empty.

When he reached Holden's cell, he found him settled on the ground near the back of the cell. He looked up when Jalen rattled his keys.

"What's this… you."

He looked over to Finn. In the dark light of this level, it was difficult to tell whether Holden was surprised or not. It might only be his disappointment at having to go to the chapel for questioning again.

"Come along. Looks like the Hunter wants to ask you a few questions," Jalen said.

"The Hunter?" Holden didn't get to his feet. "I've heard he goes by other names."

"That right? What would you call him?"

Jalen entered the cell, heading toward Holden.

"Someone once told me he was known as Shuffles when he worked the streets."

Holden looked over, darkness in his eyes.

Finn saw something there.

"Jalen," he warned.

It was too slow.

Holden lurched forward.

He was quicker than Finn would have expected, given how long he'd been in prison. He jumped to his feet and wrapped his arms around Jalen's throat, already starting to squeeze by the time Finn got to him.

"Shiner!" Finn shouted as he raced into the cell.

Pain twinged in his back where he'd been stabbed, a memory of the night before.

Finn reached Jalen. His eyes were starting to bulge.

Holden kept his arms wrapped around his neck. He jerked from side to side.

Holden kicked as Finn attempted to move around him. Finn slipped off to the side, ignoring the attack, and jabbed out with a quick strike. The blow caught Holden in his flank.

It would be a painful shot. If his aim was accurate, it would hit Holden in the kidney.

Holden still squeezed.

Shiner reached the cell. "What in Heleth's name..."

He grabbed for his short club and slammed it into Holden's arm, battering at it.

"Careful," Finn snapped.

He punched again, this time striking him in the other kidney. Still Holden held on.

Most men would have collapsed under strikes like that.

Finn had targeted them with surgical precision.

Shiner slammed his baton down again. This time, there came a *crack*.

Holden released Jalen with that arm but still clung to him with the other.

Shiner jerked him forward, freeing Jalen, who went staggering to the entrance of the cell. Once freed, Shiner turned his attention to Holden and began to beat at him, slamming his baton into him again and again. It took only a few blows for him to fall unconscious.

"Stop!" Finn shouted.

Shiner still struck him.

Finn grabbed Shiner, pulling him back and pushing him toward the far side of the cell. "Stop. He's down."

"The bastard nearly killed Jalen! He's going to get what's coming to him."

Finn looked down at Holden. His face had been bloodied. The swelling would be significant. A massive gash on one side of his head oozed blood. The arm that Shiner had struck now bent at a strange angle, the broken bone pushing up against the skin.

It would be painful. If he were unconscious, Finn would lose precious time searching for Rachel Herns, time he didn't think he could afford.

And worse was that it would be visible.

"He is going to get what's coming to him, and he would have gotten it sooner if you had managed to hold back."

Shiner rounded on him. "Hold back, Jags? I had to get

him off Jalen before he choked the life out of him. What were you doing to him?"

"Something that wouldn't be visible," Finn said. "Dressed in the Sinner's Cloth, none would even be able to see it. This"—he motioned to the fallen form of Holden—"will now need time to heal before he goes before the Blood Court."

That was the worst part of all of this for Finn—and the part that he suspected Holden had wanted.

There were often prisoners who understood the workings of the Blood Court and how people were supposed to be brought to their final sentencing. They were to come intact. At least by appearances. There had been plenty who'd gone for their sentencing bruised and injured, something that both Jalen and Shiner would know, but with someone like Holden, they would have to be intact.

Which meant healed.

Finn had to mend the bastard's broken arm. It would need a few weeks to set. Not heal completely, just long enough that it wouldn't flop around on the way to the court. The bruises now covering his face would need time to fade away.

All in all, it would take much more time than what Finn wanted.

And it had to be what Holden had intended.

"Jalen isn't seriously hurt." Finn could tell that from a cursory exam, though he might need to get closer to know if he needed any healing. "Get Holden to the chapel," Finn said.

Shiner looked over to Jalen. He had gotten to his feet and already started to rub his neck. The redness in his face was better. Every so often, he coughed and winced.

They moved forward, grabbed Holden, and dragged him.

Finn looked around the cell when he was gone. There was nothing else there.

That wasn't uncommon. Prisoners in Declan weren't given much in the way of possessions. They weren't allowed visitors. They were fed once a day. Declan was a hard prison, for hard prisoners.

Why does it look like there was a small metal stake on the ground where Holden had been?

Finn leaned down and grabbed the stake, lifting it and holding it up to the light. The silver metal gleamed. Either this had been dropped by one of the guards—which was certainly possible—or Holden had it on him.

He pocketed the stake.

Finn looked around the inside of the cell but didn't see anything else.

He followed the guards out and up to the chapel.

They'd dropped him into the chair and were starting to strap him in when Finn arrived.

"You'll have to pull him out of the straps," Finn said, heading to the far side of the room. His first thought was on how to set the bone, but that would be the easiest of the injuries. Those on his face were going to be more difficult. Finn wanted them to heal as quickly as possible, which meant that he'd have to apply some sort of poultice to them.

"You sure about that?" Shiner asked.

"He's not going anywhere now." Finn looked down at Holden. At least, not while he was unconscious, but it wouldn't take much for him to come around. When he did... "Why don't you strap his legs together? That way, he can't run even when he comes around."

Jalen grabbed the leather straps from the chair and began to wrap them around Holden's legs. He pulled them tight—tight enough that Finn wouldn't even need the boots —and then bound them.

It would work.

Finn found a splint in one of the cupboards along the wall. They kept supplies for this sort of thing there. Finn didn't need to use them often, but with the types of questioning they used, there were times when they were necessary afterward.

Returning to Holden, he wrapped the splint around Holden's arm. The fracture was angulated, and he had to pull on his wrist in order to pop the bone back into alignment. Holden grunted, but Finn ignored it.

"That's all you have to do?" Shiner asked.

Finn looked up and saw both iron masters watching. "For a break like this, you have to stabilize it to let the bone mend. It can take a few weeks, which is why we try not to break bones on those who are going to the Stone. In his case, we just need the bone to mend. I'm less concerned with how straight the end result would be."

"What would you do if you cared?" Shiner asked.

Finn shrugged. "I'd make sure the alignment felt right."

He traced his hand along his forearm. What would it hurt to demonstrate what he would do normally? "When you do it, you can feel the way the bone runs. If you've got it aligned well, you won't feel much of a deformity. Still some. There's not a way of healing bone like that quickly." Without hegen magic, he realized. He frowned as he looked down at Holden. That would be an option, though he wasn't about to get tied to the hegen just so Holden could go to the gallows faster than he would otherwise. "In his case, I just want it to look straight."

He wrapped the splint around Holden's arm. The splint consisted of a series of metal bars slipped into leather. Finn could remove some of the bars to adjust for the size of the splint. He pulled it tight, cinching it around Holden's arm.

When he was done, he headed back to the cupboard.

He had to make the right poultice.

There were several compounds that should help with swelling. That was going to be the most important. If he could reduce the swelling, it was possible they could even bring Holden to the Stone with his arm broken like this. He wouldn't need to expose the splint.

Finn looked around and found the supplies he needed, pouring them into a small bowl Meyer kept here for just this purpose.

After mixing it into a paste, he turned back to Holden.

Shiner stood over him, glaring down at him. Jalen stood off to the side, holding his neck.

Finn looked to Jalen. "Are you hurt?"

Jalen looked up. "Not too bad. Bastard didn't do anything I can't recover from."

Finn noticed that Jalen's voice was hoarser than usual.

"That may be, but I'm going to give you something to drink before we leave."

"You buyin' me ale, Hunter?" Jalen asked, forcing a smile.

Finn laughed softly. "I'd buy you ale after what you went through, but that's not what I mean. I want to make sure you don't have too much swelling in your throat." He should have considered it before. The type of pressure that Holden had applied to his throat might be enough that it would cause even more swelling. That kind could be difficult to suppress. "It'll be a powder. You put it in water. Or ale. Doesn't make much difference. Should help make sure he didn't hurt you any worse."

Jalen nodded.

"I was trying to get him off you," Finn said.

"I know," Jalen said.

There was a hint of something in his eyes that left Finn wondering if he believed him. After what Jalen had gone through, he wouldn't blame him for accusing Finn of not having done enough. His concern had been getting Holden off of Jalen, but he'd also been concerned with ensuring that Holden would be able to go to the Court intact.

Finn crouched down next to Holden and started smearing the paste onto his face. He applied it liberally, adding it to all of the places that looked as if they were swelling, and to others that looked as if they might swell. He made sure to give extra attention to the gash on his scalp.

Finn thought that he could stitch that and make it look a little better than it did now.

"I never understood why we cared how they look when they go to the Stone. No one can really see them, anyway," Shiner said.

"The gods can see them," Jalen said. "Men gotta be given a chance to repent."

"This bastard isn't going to repent. Look at him. He wanted to kill again."

Finn couldn't even argue with that. There were times when he thought that it would be much easier if they were able to bring the prisoners to the Stone in whatever condition they were in. There weren't too many sentences delayed because of injuries, though when they happened, it was almost as if the condemned somehow cheated their sentencing.

In the case of Holden, he wanted to have the man sentenced so that he didn't have to deal with him anymore. That wasn't the right reason for a man to be sentenced, but with Holden, Finn couldn't help but feel that way. The bastard deserved what he got.

"What's that going to do?" Shiner asked as Finn continued to smear the poultice on Holden.

"It should reduce any swelling. It doesn't always work, but if nothing else, it can take away some of it so that we can get him to the Stone faster."

"Faster is fine with me," Jalen said.

Finn stood, holding on to the poultice before turning back to the cupboard. He needed to find something for

Jalen.

Meyer kept jars full of different powders in the chapel for just this purpose. It had almost become an apothecary.

He sorted through the various jars until he found one that would work and tipped a bit of the arenad powder into a separate vial. In powder form, it was somewhat caustic, but when mixed with water, it became something of an anti-inflammatory.

"Take this. You have to mix it into water. A full glass. It won't taste the greatest, but it will eliminate some of the swelling you might experience."

"You sure about this?" Jalen asked.

Finn nodded. "Quite sure. This will work. You just need to drink the entire thing." He looked down to Holden. "Get him into the chair now."

Jalen took the powder and stuck it into his pocket, and he and Shiner lifted Holden and bound him to the chair.

"I'll let you know when he's ready to return to his cell."

They nodded and left Finn alone with Holden.

He studied him. With the injuries he'd sustained, Finn would have to modify any sort of questioning he might traditionally use on Holden.

Going to the basin nearby, Finn scooped some water out of it and brought it over to Holden, where he poured it down the back of his neck.

He jerked around, coming awake quickly.

Holden strained against the bindings for a moment before easing off. He looked at his injured and splinted arm and started laughing. "Bet you didn't like to see that," he said, looking up at Finn.

There wasn't anything in his gaze that revealed to Finn whether he was surprised to see him or not. Just like there hadn't been anything in his gaze while down in the cell. If Holden *were* surprised, he hid it well.

"We're going to talk a little bit more today."

Holden leaned back, looking up at him. One eye was swollen, making it difficult for him to be able to see much out of. The other had a faint bruise forming around it. The gash on his forehead still oozed with blood.

"What if I don't want to talk?"

Finn stood before him, his hands clasped. He didn't want the anger at what happened to him the night before to get the best of him. He knew better than that. Meyer had taught him better than that. Still, it was difficult to ignore what had happened.

"I think you and I both know that you will be spending more time within Declan over the coming weeks." Finn looked down at the injured arm. "Perhaps that was your intention, or perhaps not."

Goading one of the guards into attacking wasn't a good idea, regardless of how much it might delay an execution. Were Shiner to have gone a little too far, there would be few repercussions. He would be censured. Perhaps docked pay. Finn doubted it would be more than that, especially when it was discovered *why* Shiner had acted the way he had. The iron masters had a hard job, but they were paid reasonably well and protected by the magister.

"Either way, since you'll be spending time with me, I'll be able to take my time with you. There's no need for me to rush."

"Other than you wanting to find the delightful Rachel Herns."

Finn cocked his head, frowning. "You think we haven't?"

"You wouldn't be questioning me again if you had."

Finn forced a smile. "Perhaps not." He turned back to the table of implements. He could still use the boots, but Holden had proven that he didn't necessarily care about the pressure from the boots. That surprised Finn, though not as much as it surprised him that Holden still managed to hold out without providing any sort of information. "Today I want to know about Elizabeth Jarvis, so why don't we try a different approach today?"

He saw no reaction at Elizabeth's name.

"Your approaches won't do a damn thing. You won't be fast enough to save them."

Finn glanced over his shoulder, looking back at Holden. "You're probably right. As much as it pains me to admit it, they're likely gone." He'd given it quite a bit of consideration since the attack, and it was the only answer that really made sense. If they weren't going to ransom them, it would be unlikely that he would have kept them alive. It just didn't make sense.

He still had to find what he could of the chancellor's daughter.

"Why don't we talk about your crew?"

It was a different line of questioning from what Finn had used before.

He watched Holden and was pleased to note that he reacted the way that he had hoped: he tensed.

It was a slight shift, but when Holden had been talking about Rachel Herns, there had been something carefree to him, as if he knew that regardless of what Finn asked, he wouldn't share something that he didn't want to share.

That was even more evidence for Finn that Rachel was already gone.

His crew was a different matter.

Finn didn't know if Holden even cared about his crew. The King hadn't cared about all the members of *his* crew. He'd viewed them as useful tools. All but Wolf.

There would have to be someone on the crew that Holden cared about.

That was what Finn would go after.

He grabbed a few slender needles and carried them to Holden.

"You've gone quiet. That's not what I expected from you. Don't you want to tell me all about how we won't be able to find her?" Finn crouched down in front of Holden. "Your crew is a different matter. Seeing as how you know my old nickname, you'll know that I have my own connections to the streets. Finding your crew is something I *can* do."

He took one of the needles and shoved it under the nail of his big toe.

Finn tried to tell himself he didn't enjoy tormenting Holden. That wasn't a part of the job. He served the king.

The city. He served those within the city. By using these techniques, he prevented crimes where others suffered. With Holden, he found that it was harder than he expected to ignore that he *wanted* to hurt him.

Holden tried to kick, but with his legs bound the way they were, he couldn't do anything to Finn.

"We're going to have this conversation. You can share what you know. I will find out what I want regardless." He looked up at Holden. "It will go much easier on you if you do."

Holden didn't say anything more.

Finn smiled tightly and held out the fistful of needles he had clutched in hand. "That is your choice."

When Finn stuck another needle under his toenail, Holden wasn't able to ignore the pain. He cried out.

"I will stop when you share with me details of your crew."

"You're a bastard."

"No. I believe that's your nickname."

Finn pressed another needle into Holden.

CHAPTER SIX

The lantern in the kitchen glowed softly, and Finn sat twisting an iron pan, trying to work out the kinks in his arms while strengthening them. A mug of tea steamed near him, and he breathed in the aroma. After the previous day spent in Declan, he wanted to smell something different. He didn't know how much more of that stench he'd be able to tolerate.

"Will it be a difficult day?"

Finn looked over to see Helda standing in the doorway of the kitchen. One of his sister's oldest friends, she had taken to coming around more lately, spending time with Lena. A hint of perfume drifted from her, the lilac familiar.

"Some days are harder than others," he said, getting to his feet.

Helda watched him with her deep brown eyes. She had on a tan cloak that covered a white dress, with a pouch strapped to one hip. "Your sister said you were hurt. The way she described it made it sound as if you were worse than this."

Finn looked down at himself. It was easy to forget how badly he'd been injured considering how quickly he'd recovered, but every so often, there would be a twinge of pain that served as a reminder of it. "It was worse than this."

Helda pressed her lips together. After a moment, she opened her mouth as if to say something, before clamping it shut again. She clutched her hands up to her chest. "Do you know if Lena is here?"

"I thought you were with her."

"I stopped by to visit her. Master Meyer told me to let myself in; otherwise, I wouldn't have—"

"I didn't mean anything by that," Finn said.

Helda shook her head. "We're going to the market today. She has a few items she needed to purchase."

Finn regarded Helda. She had grown up in the Brinder section like him and Lena, which meant that she would be as poor as them. She managed to make it look as if she belonged somewhere else, despite how she still lived in that section. Unlike Finn and Lena.

Helda had been Lena's friend for as long as Finn could remember. He'd always admired her for her loyalty to Lena. That was rare in Brinder. Helda had not yet gotten out of the section, though her father was a bit wealthier than most in that section.

"I can check if she's in her room," he said.

"Would you? Master Meyer has welcomed me to his

home, but I don't feel comfortable wandering around as if it were mine."

Finn grinned. "I don't have any such difficulty."

He slipped past her, breathing in the hint of the lilac perfume she'd always worn, as if to hide that she came from Brinder, and glancing over at her as he did. Helda really could be lovely. Reaching the stairs, Finn hurried up them to find Lena's door closed.

He knocked and waited. There wasn't an answer.

It was early enough that she should be up, but he would have expected for her to be down in the kitchen at this time of the day, not hiding in her room.

"Lena?"

He knocked again, waiting a moment before opening the door.

Lena had a much larger room than the one Finn occupied. It had once been Meyer's child's room. The bed was neatly made. The wardrobe was closed, and only a single dress hung outside of the wardrobe, as if Lena hadn't wanted to leave anything amiss. He stood in the room for a moment, sweeping his gaze, before noticing something on the small table next to the bed.

He didn't have to get too close to know what it would be. He had seen them often enough that he recognized the hegen card immediately.

Finn lifted the card and held it up.

His hegen card might be blank now, but that wasn't common when it came to the hegen. They usually had something on them, some signal for what the hegen would ask of the bearer. This card had a small candle with wax dripping down it, a flame that practically seemed to dance along the card. Whether by magic or some trick of the eye, he couldn't say.

What would that even mean?

He turned and started toward the stairs when he ran into Meyer.

"Your sister left early this morning," Meyer said.

He had on dark pants and jacket and a hat tipped askew on his head.

Finn held out the card. "Did it have anything to do with this?"

Meyer took the hegen card and looked at it. "I wouldn't know. Your sister wouldn't be the one to tell us, either. Knowing the hegen, it's possible that this will be only a minor request."

Finn looked over to the card. The hegen wanted his sister to do something on their behalf, which was troubling enough. Lena was capable. That she had been willing and able to bring him to the hegen when injured suggested that she wasn't afraid. That wasn't even the first time that she'd gone to the hegen. When their mother had been sick and dying, the hegen had helped. That had bought them another few months with their mother, time they wouldn't have had otherwise. She had recovered, at least as much as one could recover after her lengthy, terrible sickness. They'd had a few more months with her, time where she'd been able to interact, time where she'd been able to live, time where...

"I worry about her," Finn said softly.

"Your sister is quite capable," Meyer said.

"I know that, but it doesn't mean that I won't worry about her. She doesn't deserve for anything to happen to her because of me."

"Knowing your sister, she would say that was a price she would be willing to pay. She cares about her family."

Finn squeezed his eyes shut and nodded. Lena did care about him. And he cared about her. They were all each other had remaining. With their father gone, imprisoned somewhere far from there, and now with their mother gone, they were the only family they had left. He didn't want to lose her —and he suspected she felt the same way about him, which was probably why she had gone to the hegen when he'd been found bleeding and dying on the street outside Meyer's home.

"I know she does," Finn said.

Meyer handed him the card back, and Finn slipped it into his pocket. It wasn't his card, but since she'd become indebted to the hegen because of him, he figured he had some tie to it.

"What did you have in store for the day?" Finn asked as they headed down the stairs.

"I'll be visiting each of the wardens."

"All in one day?"

They reached the main level and Meyer headed to the kitchen. With Lena gone, Finn took the opportunity to cook. He wouldn't make quite as delicious a breakfast as his sister, but Meyer wouldn't complain.

"All in one day. I need to borrow some of the iron

masters for the search for the missing women. You must keep pushing. We need answers, Finn." Meyer looked over to Helda standing near the doorway. "Ms. Helda. You're welcome to join us for breakfast."

Helda squeezed the fabric of her dress. Unlike so many, she didn't look away from Meyer. She never had. "I would like that."

Helda joined Finn at the stove as he cracked an egg into the iron pan. He frowned at her briefly. "You don't have to help," he whispered.

"I don't mind."

There was a comfortable silence between them as they worked. Finn worked at the eggs, while Helda pulled out some bacon along with bread Lena had baked the day before, toasting that in the bacon fat. When it was done, they set the breakfast on the table.

"Why do you need to visit all the wardens in one day?" Finn asked in between bites.

"The king wanted me to ensure that I reminded them how they served."

"I don't think many would forget how they serve the king," Helda said softly.

Meyer finished chewing a bite of the toasted bread. "You'd be surprised. There are quite a few in the city who don't remember. They don't see the king, so they don't think of themselves as ruled. Some even think they don't need the king."

Helda looked down. "Maybe they don't."

Finn smiled to himself. Helda probably felt the same way that Finn had felt. Perhaps the way he still felt.

Growing up in the Brinder section, isolated as they were there, as *poor* as they were there, there wasn't much. They didn't have a chance to thrive the way those in the central sections did. Knowing that some of the money they earned went to a king they never saw, whose influence they never really knew, was difficult.

Finn had heard plenty of people complain about the taxes over the years. His father had done so, though once he had gotten in thick with Oscar, there hadn't been quite as much complaining. It was easy to avoid paying taxes when a significant portion of your income came from other means.

"Maybe they don't," Meyer started. "Can't say I haven't had the same thought." Finn looked up. That was a surprise coming from him. "I suspect all men think about that from time to time, thinking they might be better off without having to serve." He took a bite and chewed it slowly. "Of course, without the king and his rule, we'd likely as not fall into darker times. Men fall toward their baser instincts. I've seen it too often. That's why I have a job."

Helda twisted her hands together. "I don't mean to offend, Master Meyer. You've been kind to me these years, and I—"

"I don't take offense to someone asking the questions. It's the same as those who question the role of the gods." He didn't look to Finn, but he knew he directed the comment at him. "They think that just because we don't see the gods, we don't have to follow their lead. Still, the gods show themselves in ways we can't always see, much like the king shows his rule in ways we can't always see."

"Even you?" Helda asked. "I thought the master executioner would be privy to the king's plans."

Meyer smiled slightly. "Perhaps a bit more than the average citizen, but not so much that I'm involved in his plans." He finished eating and pushed his plate forward. "There are other protections the king offers besides those within the city. Were it not for the king and the army, the Alainsith people would have posed a greater threat over the years. We don't have to fear them, even out here on the edge of the kingdom."

She took a small bite and nodded slowly.

Finn didn't speak up, but they had trouble with the Alainsith regardless of the treaty the king had with their people. He'd already been a part of one attempt made to disrupt the agreement, though none had been harmed in it. Worse, it wasn't even the Alainsith who had wanted to break the treaty but others who thought to benefit from it.

The silence around the table lingered while Finn finished eating. When he was done, he looked up at Meyer. "Would you like me to accompany you?"

"Not for this. There's too much still to be done. I'll make the visits to the prisons and you gather the supplies we need." He paused. "Will you get answers from Holden?"

Finn glanced to Helda, but she kept her attention down on her plate, not looking up at them. "I don't know." He hesitated. "I'm pushing—"

"If you need me to intervene, I will."

Finn shook his head. "That's not it." He could do this. "But there's something else. He will need a few weeks before he meets with the magister."

He worded it carefully so as not to offend Helda, though he didn't even know if it would.

"What happened?"

"He tried to choke Jalen."

Meyer shook his head. "They didn't go in a pair with that one? They know he can be so—" Meyer looked over at Helda, who seemed to have tensed. He took a breath. "That is unfortunate. Probably what he wanted, anyway."

"That's what I thought, too. It's unlikely we're going to be able to get the other answer we want, so I changed my approach."

"To?"

"His crew."

Meyer nodded. "That would be a reasonable approach. You've got others working on different aspects of the investigation." Meyer got to his feet. "Thank you for breakfast, Ms. Helda."

She nodded.

Meyer placed his dirtied dishes in the basin and then left the house, leaving Finn and Helda sitting across the table from each other. For a time, neither of them spoke.

Finn had been around Helda often enough with his sister that he wasn't really uncomfortable with her, but usually it was with Helda looking for his sister and not because she was with him. Not that she was with him.

He pushed those thoughts away.

"I didn't know that you investigated the prisoners."

"What did you think we did?"

"I don't know. I guess I thought most you had in prison were guilty."

Finn shook his head. "Not all. Quite a few of them are, and though there are some we come across that aren't guilty, they know something. It's our responsibility to find those answers. Meyer takes it seriously, so I guess I take it seriously."

"You don't worry about having an innocent man in prison?"

Finn looked up, meeting her gaze. "To be honest, that doesn't happen too often. Most of the time when we have people in prison, they've done the very thing that they're accused of."

"What did you mean by *questioning*?"

Finn didn't look away, but he could feel that she wanted him to be honest with her. "I meant questioning."

Her brow furrowed. "Do you hurt them?"

Finn took a deep breath. "There are times when we need to get answers from someone who isn't willing to provide them. Most of the time, men are more than willing to share what happened so they can get a reduced sentence. Admitting to a theft can turn a lashing into a chain detail. There are other times when men are less than inclined to admit their crimes."

Helda still worked at chewing her bread. "Wouldn't they admit whatever you wanted to hear to get the torment to stop? What if you're only punishing an innocent man?"

Finn didn't have an answer. He knew what Meyer would say. The questioning of even an innocent man was done to protect others within the city. Such things were necessary, so that they could continue to carry out the king's will.

It was something that he had compartmentalized, not wanting to think too deeply upon it. Partly that was because he had come to see how most of the men they had captured were guilty of their accused crimes, and partly because he'd come to learn how to read a man, to see the slight shifting of their expressions, and was able to know whether they were telling him the truth or not.

"I like to think that I know when a man has lied to me."

"And if you're wrong?"

Finn shook his head. When he'd first started working with Meyer, he'd questioned it more than he did now. These days, he'd found most men were guilty of something. He uncovered the truth quickly enough in those who weren't. "I don't know."

She finished with her bread and set her hands down on the table. "What did the man you're questioning now do?"

"You don't want to hear about it."

"Is that because you don't want to tell me?"

Finn smiled. "It's because it's horrific."

"How bad could it be?"

Finn inhaled deeply. "When I first started working with Meyer, the thing I feared the most was the actual execution. I didn't know if I would ever be capable of being the one to carry out the sentence. Killing a man seemed something I couldn't do. It's strange, thinking back on that now. It's not something I do lightly, and it's not something that I relish, but I no longer have the same fear."

"Because you believe the man to be guilty."

"Or woman."

Helda pursed her lips together. "There aren't many women sentenced to death."

"Not many, but there have been a few." The few that Finn had been a part of had been particularly heinous crimes. Murder, for the most part. Once a dead child. That had been hard on Finn, especially the investigation of it.

"What do you fear, then?"

Finn let out a breath. "There are parts of the job that have been easier. I've enjoyed learning anatomy and healing. That didn't surprise me, but it did surprise me how much of the job involves that aspect. It was questioning the guilty that's been the hardest. Knowing there are men like that in our city who are willing to do some of the things they do, that they have *justification* for the things they do." Finn shook his head. "Men like that shouldn't live among us."

Helda tilted her head. "What did this man do?"

"He captured a young woman named Rachel Herns. We don't know where. All we know is that he claims she's still alive."

"And you're trying to find her."

Finn nodded. "Trying. Failing. I don't even think she *is* alive. Not anymore. That wouldn't fit with the kind of thing Holden is known for doing."

"I didn't know you did that sort of thing."

"There are many parts of this job that are difficult. That's just one of them. Mostly because I get to see how dark men can be."

"Does killing them shine a light, then?"

Finn shook his head. "I think if you asked the magister and the jurors, they'd say the purpose of the sentencing is to punish the one responsible for the crime and to deter others in the city from thinking they could attempt something similar." Finn shrugged. "I'm not so sure it does that. When I was working in the crew, we knew the risks, and we still took the jobs. I don't know that we would have been less inclined were the punishments harsher."

"If you don't think the punishment serves as a deterrent, then why do we need it?"

"You're asking the wrong person. I just serve on behalf of the king." They sat in silence until Finn finally got to his feet. He could sit and debate with Helda most of the day, but that didn't get the work done. "Thank you for helping this morning, Helda. I've got to get work done."

"More questioning?"

"Not this morning." That would be later in the day. "It's more about visiting a few places for supplies." He set his dishes into the basin and took Helda's as well.

"Would you mind if I came with you?"

"Why would you want to do that?"

She looked up at him. "I planned on shopping today with Lena, but if she's gone... I don't want to go back yet."

What would it hurt to have Helda come with him? She was pretty enough, and though she might look at him every so often as if his job were distasteful, Finn really wouldn't mind the company.

"If you want. I need to get to the general store and to the apothecary this morning. That one might take a little longer than the general store."

"Because you need so many supplies?" she asked as they headed toward the door.

Finn pulled the door open and stepped out into the early morning sunlight. There wasn't much warmth to it today, but he enjoyed the bright sun. "It's not so much about the supplies I need. Wella likes to test how much I've learned from Meyer. Sometimes, she takes it upon herself to try to teach me more about the various compounds she has." He smiled to himself, shaking his head.

"That doesn't sound so bad."

"Just wait."

"Is that what you do most mornings?" Helda asked as they headed through the street. She paused at one point to adjust her boot.

Finn caught the flash of silver, smiling to himself. She kept a knife tucked away, protected as well as she could be, like a typical Brinder woman. Tough.

Finn guided them toward Tahn's general store. They needed more oil along with a few other supplies. Meyer had left a list of what he thought they needed, though Finn had already identified most of them. Tahn's wasn't that far from them. Near enough that he wouldn't have to carry supplies for long, but Tahn would even deliver what they needed back to Meyer's home. That was the advantage of going with a store that knew Meyer as well as Tahn did.

"Some mornings. I have to visit the apothecary most weeks. The general store not as often. I prefer Wella's apothecary, though there are some supplies she isn't able to acquire, so I have to visit Deran. There are a few different general stores that Meyer likes, but I've been comfortable with Tahn. He likes to spread his business out a bit." Finn chuckled, shaking his head. "He thinks it's better not to play favorites. Plus, that way, they can continue to stock what he needs."

"And maybe keep prices down," Helda said. When Finn looked over, she just shrugged. "If you focus too much on one store and one supply, they can ask whatever they want from you. If you don't have any choice but to go to them..."

Finn nodded.

It made him think of the hegen. There wasn't an alternative to their magic. Even if there were others who had that kind of magic, he wasn't sure that they would be any better. From what he'd seen, the hegen used their monopoly on magic and the kind of things they could offer to draw more and more out of a person.

At one point, a man whistled at Helda. She shot him a quick glare, and he quieted.

Considering what he knew of Holden and his crew taking women, Finn studied the man. He scurried away from them, disappearing into the crowd before Finn had a chance to do anything. Not that he thought there was anything he *could* do.

"What is it?"

He forced a smile and turned his attention back to her. She didn't need to know what he'd been dealing with, regardless of how he wanted to chase the man down. "Consider me impressed."

"By what?"

"I don't know if I should say. After what I've seen lately, I'm glad you have that knife. I just don't want to be on the wrong end of it."

That elicited a smile from her. "Then don't do anything to earn it."

He laughed again. "What if *I* whistle at you?"

"That depends."

They reached the general store, and Finn glanced over. "On what?"

"On what you intend."

As he looked at her, he couldn't help but wonder what it might be like to spend *more* time with Helda, but sighed and pushed those thoughts away. He'd gone through the difficulties of trying to find romance as an executioner. Besides, Helda deserved better than him.

He looked over to her. "Why don't I introduce you to Tahn? I think you'll like him. I'm not quite as certain about Wella."

CHAPTER SEVEN

Finn brushed a flake of pastry off his usually tidy cuff as he looked toward the closed door of the chapel, feeling a hint of a smile come to him despite the questioning. He'd bought Helda lunch, and the two of them had spent much of the early part of the day together, which had left him happier than he would have expected.

Until he'd come back to Declan.

He still hadn't gotten anywhere with Holden today despite pushing him as hard as he felt comfortable. There was an art to the questioning. He had to play the reluctant side, making Holden think Finn really didn't want to proceed, while at the same time making it clear that he would.

With someone like Holden, Finn wasn't even sure that tactic mattered. He resisted Finn's questioning. He'd screamed this time, the most emotion that Finn had seen from him, but hadn't been willing to answer any questions.

Finn needed to push but had hesitated going too hard. Partly, that had to do with how he hadn't been convinced that it would make a difference, but partly, it had to do with the conversation that he'd shared with Helda. After having spent the morning with her, she stayed on his mind more than she ever had before. Always before, he'd been able to push away thoughts of her since she was only his sister's friend. Seeing the inquisitive way she'd questioned Tahn and gotten him talking about his suppliers, and then how she had been willing to visit with Wella and keep her talking more than even Wella normally did... Finn couldn't help but smile at the memories. He'd always admired her loyalty to his sister. Now he saw her mind.

He replaced the implements that he'd used on the table, rinsing them first. They were given a good washing in between prisoners. Finn hadn't understood why that would matter, but Meyer had made a point of telling him that it wouldn't do for the prisoners to get an infection from someone else because they weren't careful in their techniques. Finn had no idea if other executioners were as careful as Meyer, but it seemed like a reasonable approach.

When he stepped out into the hall, he thought through what else he had to do for the day. He'd taken care of supplies and now questioning, which left him with checking in with Oscar and Annie. Oscar might be more difficult to track down, and he didn't know how Annie would respond to him after the way that he'd gone to her.

Finn nodded to the iron master outside the door. Pedran was thin for one of the guards, as if he were underfed, but

Finn had seen him handle unruly prisoners before without any difficulty, so he was much stronger than he looked. He had a hint of a beard forming, probably about as much as any of the iron masters would let grow, given their desire to look different from the prisoners, and his wavy brown hair was combed over to the side.

"Did he cause any trouble getting him back into the cell?" Finn asked.

Pedran shook his head. "That one won't cause much trouble no more."

Finn arched a brow.

"We don't beat him, Finn."

Finn snorted. "I'm not accusing you of doing anything."

"I see the look. If he's not giving us trouble, we're not going to cause any trouble for him. You know how it goes."

Finn nodded. "I know how it goes."

"Say. The warden heard you were here and wanted you to visit."

"Did he say why?" It might have something to do with Meyer's visit earlier in the day, though Finn didn't really know what Meyer had asked of the warden. If James tried to pressure Finn into sharing something, he wouldn't have any answers.

"You know the warden. He doesn't tell us anything. We're just the muscle."

Finn patted Pedran on the shoulder as he moved past. "I don't know if I'd call *you* the muscle."

"Careful."

Finn grinned. "Take care of yourself."

"You do the same."

Pedran resumed his patrol through the halls, and Finn headed toward the warden's office. When he reached it and knocked, he tried to think through what James might want with him. It might be nothing more than to explain what happened with Holden, though as Finn had been present and had been the one to have tried to fix him up a bit, there wouldn't need to be any reason for him to meet with James about it unless the warden considered punishing the two guards involved. Finn hoped that wasn't the case.

When James shouted for him to enter, Finn pushed the door open and stepped inside. The warden wasn't alone. That was unexpected. Stranger still was the man sitting across from the warden.

He wasn't one of the guards. The cut of his jacket and pants suggested someone of wealth, though that would be strange as well. Visitors weren't permitted at Declan. Other than those who worked in the prison and Finn and Meyer, the only other people who came were the priests.

"Finn. If you would give me a moment?"

Finn nodded and stepped outside, pulling the door mostly closed. He listened, though there was only a murmuring of voices from the other side.

A shuffling sound came, then the door came open. The well-dressed man paused and looked over to Finn, his eyes narrowing a moment, and then he headed past.

Finn entered the office. "Who was he?"

James waved his hand. "Ah, that was someone here on a personal errand. Nothing to do with the prison at all."

"You're letting him go through without an escort?"

James looked up at Finn. There was a flicker of irritation in his eyes but then it passed. "He's not going to go anywhere but out of the prison. No one wants to go deeper into the prison."

Finn stood there for a moment, debating whether to say anything more. He wasn't the warden. As executioner who helped oversee the prisons, it was his place to say something, but he didn't need to annoy James for something that was relatively trivial. Not that Finn thought that someone dressed like that man would head through the prison and try to break someone out, but there was the concern that they might pass something along to one of the prisoners. Considering that he'd found the strange metallic stake in Holden's cell, Finn didn't want anything to happen to any of the guards.

"Pedran said you wanted to see me."

James nodded. "I did. Take a seat."

Finn settled into the chair. James sat behind his desk, a stack of papers piled on it making it feel more formal than the last visit. More formal than most of his visits to the prison. From the way James watched him across the desk, using it almost as a way to create distance between them, it seemed to him that James wanted it that way.

"What happened with Holden?"

He reached out and rested one hand on a sculpture Finn suspected was meant to depict Fell, though he didn't know with certainty. James had called him there to talk about Holden?

"An accident. He caught Jalen and nearly choked him out. Shiner had to dislodge him so that he didn't kill him."

James leaned forward, resting his elbow on his desk. The stack of papers seemed to obscure the surface, scattered across it with less organization than Finn was accustomed to seeing from him. "What was Jalen doing, getting close enough for Holden to be able to have an opportunity to jump him, anyway?"

"He had to be brought to the chapel for questioning."

James leaned back, waving his hand. "I never really understood why you couldn't ask your questions in the cell."

"The chapel is a more controlled environment."

It was strange that he'd be making comments like that, especially since James knew the reason they used the chapel. Accessing the chapel for questioning made it so that everyone could be safe. It ensured that the prisoner didn't cause trouble for the guards or for the questioner.

"Disappointing that Jalen would let himself get caught like that," James said.

"Not as disappointing as having Holden here for as long as he's going to have to be here."

"How long do you anticipate that will need to be?"

Finn shook his head. "I can't be sure. Another month. Possibly longer. And that's *if* he doesn't attempt something more so that he can stay even longer."

"Maybe the gods just take this one as he is." He looked over to another of the sculptures.

"You know how they feel about that."

"There was a time when I thought about becoming a

priest, but…" He looked up, smiling, as if sharing some hidden secret with Finn. "I realized the gods don't care about those without the power to honor them. Certainly not about the condemned. Only those who remain and have the ability to praise them." His hand went to the statue of Fell again.

Finn said nothing, just nodding. Were he to tell the truth, he would say that the gods didn't necessarily care about even those who were left behind. The gods—if they were real, and Finn hadn't seen any sign of that in his time —didn't really care about anyone.

"Then the priests and the jurors care," Finn said. "Regardless, it's tradition that those condemned are brought to their sentence as healed as they can be."

James waved his hand. "We've had men like him before."

"I know," Finn said softly.

James leaned forward, smiling. "Sometimes, I forget about that. The Executioner's Right. You know that hasn't been claimed in decades?"

"I know," Finn said.

Longer, actually. What Meyer had done for him had not been done for a long time. Claiming the right for Finn, and saving his life, had been a blessing to Finn. It had given him a chance at a new life. It had given him the opportunity to become something more than what he would have been before. It had given him the chance to finally *be*.

"There were rumors after he claimed you."

"Were there?" Finn would have expected some rumors. In a city like Verendal, that wasn't altogether surprising.

"You know there would be. They're the kind of rumors any man would love to have spread."

"Not me."

"No? You don't want people to think you can't be killed?" James chuckled. "Gods—Meyer probably helped to seed some of those rumors. I've been around him long enough to know that he can be a tricky one."

"You have no idea."

"Do you know that some think Meyer was in on whatever your crew planned all along?"

"Then they don't know Meyer."

"Can't say I know him all that well, either, though it doesn't seem like the kind of thing that he'd be a part of. He comes across as too..."

"Ethical," Finn said.

James grunted. "Maybe that's what it is. Ethical. Not that it's a bad thing to be like that, only that I can't believe our executioner is."

"Wouldn't you want to make sure the man who's responsible for carrying out the king's justice isn't corrupt?"

James only nodded. "I'm not complaining, mind you. Just saying what I've seen."

Finn studied him. There was something more to what he intended to tell him, though Finn couldn't tell what it was. "Was it only about Jalen?"

James looked past him, his gaze going to the door. "Not only about Jalen, though I did want to know from your perspective what had happened."

"They're good men."

"I know they are," he said, waving his hand as he leaned back, "but even good men can be corrupted."

Finn frowned. "I wouldn't have taken either Jalen or Shiner to be that kind."

James inhaled deeply. "Hopefully not. It can be difficult to know." He turned to Finn, flashing a wide smile. There was something unpleasant in the way that he looked at Finn, leaving Finn slightly uncomfortable with him. "There's another man here that I think you need to question. I've been waiting for the chance to talk to you about him."

"The man you brought in a few days ago."

"That's right."

"You told me you were still processing him."

"We were. Are. We haven't been able to get anywhere with him. He knows something, Finn."

"You haven't even told me everything about what he's accused of."

"He's accused of theft. Torture. The usual. This was outside of the city, though, so I suppose it's not *quite* the usual."

They didn't often deal with prisoners from outside of the city. There was enough crime within the city, and they had a hard enough time keeping up with everything as it was. There were other arms of the king's justice that handled the activity outside of the city.

"What are you concerned about?"

That had to be the real reason that James had asked Finn to come. Whatever he'd uncovered had been enough that the warden was uncomfortable with the prisoner. Most of the time, Finn and Meyer were responsible for the questioning of prisoners, though there were times when they wouldn't be able to get to everyone.

"I don't really know. Only that when we had him questioned, he kept repeating the same phrase. It didn't make much sense, which is why we wanted you to come."

"Don't keep me in the dark. What's the phrase?"

"I wish I could tell you."

Finn smiled. "You can't?"

"Oh, I could tell you what I *think* he's saying, but the problem is that I'm not exactly sure what it was. He repeats it over and over. The problem is that none of what he says really makes any sense to us."

"Where's he from?"

The warden shrugged. "Can't get him to share that, either."

"So, you have a man accused of theft and torture who doesn't speak the language. He's repeating the same phrase over and again that you can't understand. Still, you're convinced of his guilt?"

"The report of how he was found is solid, Finn."

"I'd love to hear it."

"Then I'll have to share it with you. First, I want you to meet with him and see if you can come up with anything. Do you mind?"

"That's the job, warden."

James smiled at him. "That's what I hoped you'd say, but I never know with you types."

"What types are those?"

"You know. Like you and Meyer. Whenever I've asked him to question someone, he always goes about it in his own away."

Finn sat back, not sure how much to say. He didn't want to anger James, but at the same time, Finn thought that he had a responsibility to ensure that he knew that neither he nor Meyer would be coerced into anything.

"We have a particular way of questioning. There's no doubt about that. We serve on behalf of the king, and that carries with it the responsibility to ensure that anything that we uncover is accurate."

James waved his hand at him. "That's not what I'm getting at, but there are times when I wonder if it's even necessary. There are plenty of men who come here and we know what they've done."

"And the magister sentences them quickly when that's the case."

What are we doing, having this argument now?

It troubled him that James would be pushing him like this. Of all of the wardens, Finn had the best rapport with James, though he had grown to have a good rapport with most of the wardens. That was one of the earlier lessons Meyer had wanted him to learn. Partly, that was because as the executioner, they would serve in a supervisory role, but partly, that was because an irritated warden could make life altogether unpleasant for them.

"I think I know what you're trying to tell me about your concerns," Finn said.

James looked up at him. "You do."

Finn tipped his head. "I think so." He forced a smile that he didn't feel. "Why don't I go and visit with this prisoner now and see what I might be able to learn from him? Then we can get him off your hands."

James nodded. "That would be perfect. Any of the boys can have him brought to you, though like I said, you might as well just go and see him in his cell. He'll probably not tell you anything different in either location."

Finn got to his feet and nodded to James. "You'll have to let me buy you a mug of ale soon."

"I'd like that."

When he left, Finn hesitated with his hand on the door for a moment, frowning.

He considered what James had been getting at, but it still didn't make much sense to him.

It wasn't uncommon for wardens to want prisoners to move through more quickly. For prisoners like Holden, that was to be expected. They could be difficult, and having a difficult prisoner put a strain on the guards, making it hard for the warden to keep his men safe. Declan should be different. The prison was known for the difficult prisoners. They didn't have much hope of getting anyone easier.

Then there was the man who'd been visiting with James. Finn wondered about that as well. He should have brought it back around to Meyer. The executioner would have been there earlier today—which might be the reason that James brought Finn in.

That had to be it.

Whatever Meyer had said to James had him irritated.

Finn would have to see what the old executioner had said to the wardens to find out if he was going to be having a similar conversation with others, or if this would only be James. James he could handle. They *did* have enough of a friendship, such as it was, that Finn thought he could ultimately get to the bottom of what he tried to tell him.

He made his way through the halls and caught up with Varden. "The warden wants me to question your newest prisoner."

Varden was one of the oldest in the prison. When Finn had started working with Meyer, he had come to recognize him from his time as a prisoner. He treated Finn well enough, but he'd always looked at him as if he were still a prisoner at times. Not that Finn minded. The keys he carried got him in and out of the prison, and the clothes that he wore made him feel as if he were something different, regardless of what someone like Varden might think.

"He said that to you?"

"Sounds like he's an interesting case."

"If you think a man covered in shit and piss is interesting. We've dunked him a few times, trying to get the filth off of him, but the bastard still reeks. Smells like he's been living in his filth his whole life."

"Not the way too many highwaymen tend to smell."

"What do I know? I've lived in the city my whole life."

"And served under your king that entire time."

Varden nodded. "Damn right. It's been an honor. Most of the time. There are plenty of times when I get caught up in the bastards like this one that make me question it, though."

"Bring him to the chapel?"

"He's not going to tell you much."

"That's fine. I still need to meet with him and see what he knows."

When Varden grunted, annoyance plain in his voice, Finn turned away from Varden rather than listening to him complain. It was better for both of them. Finn might make the mistake of saying something, and he didn't want to do that and run the risk of angering him.

Keeping the iron masters on his side was a delicate balance. He needed to keep them aligned with him almost as much as he needed to keep the warden on his side. The guards could make his job just as difficult—more so. He spent more time around them than he did the warden.

When he returned to the chapel, he waited until Varden brought the man into the room. He didn't have to wait long.

Varden arrived with Pedran helping, carrying the man into the room.

The prisoner was lean—as if he'd been in a cell for years already. A thick graying beard looked to have bits of grass or leaves in it. Hollowed eyes stared at the floor.

The guards tossed him into a chair to question him and started to strap him in when Finn shook his head.

"I don't know if that's necessary."

"You starting to think you're like the hangman now?" Varden asked.

"He *is* the hangman," Pedran said. "Last festival I went to, the Hunter was the one who pulled the rope. That seems to be a hangman as much as anything."

Varden grunted and stepped back.

"If he jumps you, we're not taking the blame for it."

Finn frowned at him. "Have I ever had you take the blame for anything?"

Varden shook his head, muttering softly while leaving Finn.

"Don't mind him," Pedran said. "He just gets bothered by men like this."

"Because he smells?"

"Nah. They all smell after a while. Story about him is that he was caught having his way with a merchant's wife after he killed the man. Said he stripped the flesh from him before leaving the body. Supposedly forced the wife to watch."

"How would he have heard any of that?" Finn asked, eyeing the prisoner. There wasn't any way for him to pass judgment without having a conversation with a prisoner. Finn had learned that long before as well. Men he thought looked to be too prim could have some of the worst crimes. Others who looked like this man would often end up as the salt of the earth. Of course, they could end up just as likely guilty of the crime they were accused of. "That would be hard to claim, seeing as how he hasn't spoken anything useful, from what the warden told me."

Pedran shrugged. "Got me. That's the report we were given when the Archers brought him in."

"I'll see what he tells me."

"Need me to stay? I don't mind if you do. I get it with men like this. Need to have an extra set of hands."

"I think I'll be fine. It might be best if I get the chance to question him without anyone here."

"Got it. You holler if you need something. I'll stay nearby."

When he was gone, Finn made his way around the front of the chair and looked down at the prisoner. He was slumped in the chair, one arm draped over the side, his legs kicked out, barely holding himself up.

Finn fetched the small stool from the far side of the room and brought it over before taking a seat on it, just outside of the man's reach.

Finn's approach with him would have to be different than what he'd done with Holden. With this man, Finn thought that he'd need to be careful. Slow. That was if he would be able to get anything from him, anyway. It was possible that the man didn't speak any language that Finn would be able to understand.

"My name is Finn Jagger. I just want to ask you a few questions."

The man lifted his head. The dark hollows of his eyes met Finn, but there wasn't anything within them that seemed as if he recognized Finn. It was almost as if he looked *past* him.

"You're in the Declan Prison in Verendal. You've been accused of"—he debated telling him *how* he had been accused before deciding against it—"crimes against the king."

It was better for him to keep things vague. Doing so offered the accused a chance to reveal more than giving them something to deny. There had been plenty of times when Finn had questioned men, knowing what they had done—at least, thinking that he knew what they had done—only to have them admit to something completely different. That was why his job as questioner was one of asking questions but also of giving the accused a chance to share and incriminate themselves.

The man said nothing.

He looked at Finn.

There wasn't anything in his gaze that seemed as if he understood what Finn said.

Nothing other than the slight twitch when Finn had said *king*.

"You will remain here until we understand why you would commit the crimes that you're accused of." He left unsaid that it would be difficult, remaining in the prison. Any prisoner here would know that after even a few days. "What I'd like to know first is your name. Can you start with that?"

The man looked at him, the hollowed glare continuing to stare out at Finn. There was a darkness in his eyes. Perhaps Finn would have been intimidated by such a look earlier, but now he recognized the way the man sat, the difficulty he had of keeping his back straight, the slumped manner he had as he hung his arms over the side of the chair.

He was weak.

Probably too weak to do what he was accused of doing. That didn't mean he was innocent.

Crimes like the man had been accused of had a way of getting inflated. A telling and then a retelling could often lead to exaggeration, so it wasn't surprising that he would have heard from Pedran that the man was responsible for killing a merchant and raping his wife.

Was it true?

The dead merchant might be true. The rape might be true. Even the stealing might be true.

The question was how much of the crime this man had a part in, and how much of a part someone else had. What if this man had a crew?

Finn didn't have much experience outside of the city. Crimes within the city were at least familiar to him. Not all, but there were plenty that he understood the way they would unfold—and who to chase as responsible. Outside the city was a different matter. The crimes weren't necessarily different—they had theft, rape, murder along with a host of other crimes within Verendal—but at least within the city there was a feel of everything being more closed off.

"Your name. That's all I'm looking for. Can you tell me who you are?"

Finn leaned forward.

The man lurched toward him.

It was quicker than he would have expected, given how thin and frail he appeared, but when he lunged, Finn made a point of not moving. Instead, he held out his hand.

The man toppled onto him.

He stank, the filth exactly what Varden had claimed.

Pain surged in Finn's back and stomach from his injuries, the freshly healed flesh pulling despite how magic had been used to seal off the wounds. He tried to roll the man off of him, but he was surprisingly heavy for how thin he'd looked.

Not again.

Finn grunted, shoving with everything that he had within him.

The man's breath was hot in Finn's ears.

He muttered something. A phrase.

"Na'alani es ite prosh!"

He pressed on him, trying to force him away, but the man pushed him down.

"Na'alani es ite prosh!"

"I don't know what you're saying!"

Finn shoved again. The man rolled away and Finn got himself freed, getting to his feet and backing away from the man.

He stayed on the ground, not trying to come toward him, though if he did, Finn suspected he would have little difficulty reaching him.

The man twitched, and Finn stayed ready.

Too fast.

Suddenly, the idea that this man could have been responsible for the murder of a merchant, the rape of his wife, made much more sense. Not much else did.

"Pedran!"

The door came open quickly and Pedran darted in,

putting himself in between the man and Finn. "What happened?"

"He attacked. He's faster than he looks."

"This one?" Pedran asked, peering briefly over his shoulder before turning his attention back to the man. Pedran widened his stance.

"That one," Finn said. "He moved... well, faster than I would have expected."

He would have to take that as another lesson. Prisoners might look weak and diminished, but that didn't mean that they were. Even those like this man could pose a threat.

Finn backed toward the far wall. He wasn't scared. That was what he told himself, but in the moment that the man had crashed onto him, the only thought in his mind had been about the knife in his back. His belly.

"Do you want him back in the chair?" Pedran asked.

"I think I'll let him return to his cell. I can visit with him another time."

"Did you find anything?"

"Just the same thing the warden warned me about."

"Do you recognize what he said?"

"Not at all. Whatever he's saying is some other language."

"Or not one at all."

"Why would you say that?"

"Never heard a man speak like him. I *have* heard men who've lost their minds begin to speak in tongues. The priests want us to believe they're touched by the gods, but I know better."

That might be all that it was. It could be that the man

had been touched in the head. There certainly were enough men he'd seen like that. Most of them weren't held in Declan. The city had another place that was better for them. The only thing that didn't fit was how the man had moved. The men who were touched like that generally didn't move like they were gifted by the gods.

"Thanks for your help," Finn said.

Pedran looked over as he grabbed the man and dragged him out of the room.

Finn watched, making sure that Pedran wasn't in any danger. There was the risk that the man would lunge at him the way that he had with Finn. With his head hanging down, his eyes on the ground, he looked as if he wasn't any threat, but there was a flicker in his eyes that left Finn wondering if there was something more.

He followed Pedran out of the chapel and watched as he headed along the hall until he dragged him down the stairs. One of the other guards joined, slipping his arm around the prisoner. Finn felt bad about that, considering how badly the man smelled, but he noticed an occasional stiffness to the man's spine.

It wasn't until they had disappeared completely that Finn tore his attention away, closed the door to the chapel, and headed out of the prison.

CHAPTER EIGHT

Finn lingered outside of the Wenderwolf, waiting for
Oscar, wanting to know more about Holden's men.
There had been no sign of Oscar so far, though that wasn't
altogether unusual. Oscar didn't necessarily come through
the tavern every night.

That didn't matter. He had questions for Annie as well.

At one point, three men made their way into the tavern
together. One of them was short with a shaved head and
close-set eyes. Another was about two feet taller than the
other's height and muscular—the bruiser. The third had
longer hair and a hint of gray to it. There was something
about his eyes that strangely reminded Finn of what he'd
seen in the prisoner's eyes.

Another crew, though it wasn't one that Finn had seen at
the Wenderwolf before.

It didn't surprise him that there would be a new crew,
but the timing of it was what bothered him most of all.

Crews came and went, especially here after the King had lost his place, but since Oscar had made his play and taken over, there hadn't been any pressure upon his territory.

"What are you watching for?"

He turned and shook his head. "You should be careful, Oscar."

"Why? Because the executioner is hanging outside the tavern I frequent?" Oscar regarded him for a long moment. "You're looking better than I would have expected."

"Thanks to you."

Finn didn't know how Oscar was going to react or what he might admit to him.

"I couldn't very well let you bleed out."

"Thank you."

Oscar looked past him. "I hear you paid Annie a visit earlier. Sounds like it was an official visit."

Finn nodded. "Meyer wanted to make sure that she didn't have anything to do with the attack. With Holden."

"What did you decide?"

"I don't know. She's hiding something from us." There was no point in keeping that from Oscar. He needed Oscar to be a part of what they were doing, so sharing with him that he believed that Annie kept something from him was a way that he could accomplish it. He didn't necessarily like that it felt like he used Oscar, but then, he had a feeling that Oscar used him here as well. Maybe it could be a mutually beneficial relationship, the way it once had been. "I'm not sure if she knows anything about the attack, but seeing as how it happened after I left here and had been talking with you…"

"Anyone could have been listening there. You know that."

"I know."

"You still felt the need to come to Annie." Finn didn't say anything and Oscar grunted. "I see. This was *his* decision. And he made you ask the questions."

"I'm in training."

"He's pitting you against the people who care about you."

"People who once cared about me. And he's not pitting me against them. He's asking me to do the job." Finn glanced toward the tavern. There were a few more people who had gone in, though none more like the crew that he'd seen.

"You don't think there's anyone left in the Wenderwolf who cares for you?"

"I didn't say that."

"Sounded like you did."

"Come on, Oscar. The attack came after I'd talked to you. Annie is known to have ears throughout the tavern. And when I questioned her…"

"What?"

"I saw something."

Oscar watched him and then started laughing. "That's it? You *saw* something? Damn, Finn. I thought maybe she'd revealed something to you that you used to piece together with some other information you have. You've got the reputation now, you know."

"I know," Finn said softly. *The Hunter.* Not one that he thought he deserved, but it was a far cry from the other things that he'd been called around here before. "I can read people. I'm sure you don't think that's true, but it doesn't matter. Meyer has me learning how to watch for signs that someone isn't telling the truth. We use that to dig a little deeper. Find something more. Then we keep digging."

"When do you stop digging?"

"When the answers stop."

"So, that's how you do your torturing? You throw out a piece of information and then use that to torment a man until he gives you what you want?"

Finn hadn't realized that Oscar felt that way about it, though he shouldn't be surprised. There were a lot of people who felt that way about the kind of work that he did.

"It's not about tormenting. Questioning."

"You don't have to try to use that tone with me, Finn. I've known you your whole life. And I've lived in this city long enough to know if the hangman starts to ask you questions, you'd better be ready with the answers."

"You don't think people tell me the truth."

"I think people would tell you whatever they think you want to hear so they don't have to suffer. Truth or not. A man has limits, Finn. When you keep pushing, you get to those limits and you—"

"Stop. That's what we do. We get to the limits and we can tell we've reached them. That's the kind of thing that Meyer teaches. Find when a man is telling the truth and when he's lying."

"What if you're wrong?"

"Then I'm wrong."

Oscar regarded him for a moment, the corner of his lip peeling back in a bit of a smile. "Damn. I guess I didn't realize how hard you've become."

"It's not a matter of being hard."

"It's not soft, either. Not many men have the stomach to push someone to their breaking point." Oscar looked away and Finn followed the direction of his gaze. He didn't see anything there, though knowing Oscar, he'd probably turned that way as a distraction. "Do you like it?"

"It's a part of the job," Finn said.

"That's not an answer."

"It beats the alternative," Finn said, and Oscar looked over to him. "When I got pinched, I'd made peace with my time. I made a walk through the city following the Blood Court. Thought I'd be swinging. Climbed the gallows. All that time, I never said anything about anyone in the crew. I protected them. For nothing. None of the crew—none—came to rescue me. Then Meyer offers me an out. Gave me a chance for something different." Finn looked toward the Wenderwolf. It was strange how spending any time around Oscar made him flash back to those days. It was part of the reason he didn't like to come around him. He followed from a distance, learning about his rise and how he'd pulled his own crew. The jobs he was suspected of taking. All without pushing him. "Liking it doesn't matter to me. It's what I do. Besides, I get to help people this way. Help the city." Though with his current case, it didn't feel like it.

Oscar held his gaze. "You can admit that you like it. Nothing wrong with it."

Finn looked away. He told himself that he didn't like the questioning part of the job, but there wasn't any use denying that there were times when he felt that it was necessary. He'd saved the king. Stopped an attack on Verendal. That mattered.

Most of the time, that was when there were men like Holden who he *knew* had done something heinous and he had to uncover what they had done so that he could ensure that those who'd been hurt by him wouldn't have to continue to suffer.

"You know that's not it," Finn said.

Oscar grunted. "Do I?"

Finn needed to change the topic. "There was a new crew in the Wenderwolf," Finn said.

Oscar looked over. "What crew?"

Finn shrugged. "Not sure. Saw them heading into the tavern before you decided to sneak up on me. I'm still looking for that missing girl."

Oscar patted him on the shoulders. "I know. And not a lot of sneaking necessary when it comes to you, Finn. Not these days. You've lost your touch."

"I don't know if I ever had much in the way of a touch when it came to sneaking through the city."

Oscar's smile shifted a little. It was as much of a smile as Finn was going to get from him. "True enough. It's probably better you ended up doing what you do now. You wouldn't have been able to keep at it otherwise."

"I didn't necessarily have to be a lookout like you wanted me to be."

"You have to start somewhere. We all start at the bottom."

Finn tipped his head toward the tavern. "Whoever is in there looks like they're a full crew. At least the start of it." Finn glanced to Oscar. "You lose your standing in the tavern?"

"You think I'd admit it if I did?"

"Probably not. Still wanted to ask."

Oscar patted him on the shoulder. "Glad you're back in one piece. I'd hate to think I was losing you again."

That much, at least, felt like an honest admission from Oscar. Having nearly died before, Oscar had been the only one who had made any effort of coming to see him when he'd been brought toward the gallows. The others might have been there, though Finn doubted that they were. It was much more likely that they had avoided it, probably because it would remind them of the dangers they placed themselves in when it came to the kind of jobs they took.

"You're going to make me do something to pay you back."

"You don't own me nothing, Finn. I told your father that I would make sure you and your family was taken care of."

It had been a long time since he'd given much thought to his father. He wasn't connected well enough to other cities or to any other prisons for him to have much hope of finding where his father had been imprisoned.

"I hope the hegen didn't ask much of you."

Oscar tipped his head. "You know I can't talk about that."

"Is that what they told you? Because I'm fully aware that the hegen would have asked you for something for helping me."

"Is that right? Your experience with the hegen is now so great that you know exactly what they're going to do and what they'll demand of someone? For all you know, they owe me."

"They don't owe anyone."

Oscar watched him for a moment, and Finn thought that he might head into the Wenderwolf, but he turned his attention away and looked at Finn. "What do you really know about the hegen, Finn?"

"I know about the same as anyone, I suppose."

"That's not entirely true. Not too many have owed the hegen, and even fewer have owed them more than one time."

"You get in with the hegen and they're going to do whatever they need to do to keep you working with them."

"Only if you're useful," Oscar said.

"And if I'm not?"

"Then you pay whatever they ask of you and move on. That's the end of the transaction. There are plenty of folks who've worked on behalf of the hegen and haven't had to do anything more than the initial ask."

"I'm sure they see me as something more."

Oscar shrugged. "Probably. Getting their fingers into someone like you would give them the chance to have real influence."

"I don't have any influence."

"Your access to the prisons isn't influence? Your ability to move through the city without raising any questions isn't influence? I think you're underestimating the role you play, Finn. Someday, you'll end up as the master executioner. Think about how much influence you're going to have then."

"Meyer has a while before he retires."

"Are you sure about that? He's served the city for a long time already. There comes a time when everyone has to pass the torch on to the next."

Finn started to smile. "Who do you plan on passing on your torch to?"

The hint of a smile on Oscar's face faded. "I had someone in mind, but then they went ahead and got themselves pinched."

"I'm sorry about that."

"Who said I meant you?"

"I'm sorry either way," Finn said, trying to suppress his smile. "For whoever you intended to pass your torch on to." He nodded to the Wenderwolf. "You want to come in with me? I should find out what Annie discovered."

"She's not going to like me coming with you like that."

He started toward the Wenderwolf without waiting for Finn.

Finn hesitated a moment. The timing didn't feel quite right to visit Annie. She would probably welcome him, but there was a risk in coming late like this. At least his coming earlier in the day could be overlooked. There wouldn't be as much in the way of questions from others in the tavern. Coming at night ran the risk of others alerted to the fact that the executioner had questioned Annie.

That might be what he needed, though.

Finn followed Oscar.

When he reached the tavern, Finn paused at the door as he surveyed the inside. The last time that he'd come at night like this, he'd ended up on the wrong side of a knife. Not that there was a right end of a knife, only that he didn't want to find himself gutted near the Wenderwolf.

The tavern was busy, the way it was many nights. The Hand had taken a seat in a booth near the back of the tavern. Another man sat next to him, the shadows of the Wenderwolf making it difficult for Finn to see much about him. The booth was otherwise empty, though one of the waitresses had already headed over to the table and leaned close to speak to Oscar. Tara had a wide smile that matched her wide hips.

Finn shifted his gaze, sweeping it toward the other booths and considering the other crew members that he'd seen. They occupied one of the tables near the center of the tavern. That was unusual for a crew, though even more unusual was the way that people seemed to avoid them, as if fearful of getting too close.

Not everyone within the Wenderwolf came there for criminal reasons. There were quite a few who simply came because Annie was known to have quality ale and always hired the best musicians.

Finn didn't see Annie.

She'd have to be there. There had never been a time when he'd come to the tavern and not seen her. As the owner of the tavern, she watched over it like a mother bear watching over her cubs, and could be just as vigorous when it came to defending it.

Finn slipped through the tavern. Oscar glanced in his direction, though he tried not to make it too obvious. Finn nodded to him briefly, but Oscar had tipped his head away so that it looked as if he weren't paying any attention to him.

Finn knew better. Oscar probably saw everything that happened in the tavern. From where he sat, he'd be able to watch the inside of the tavern and be able to find anything that set off alarms for him.

When he reached the far side of the tavern, Finn leaned against the wall and made a show of listening to the musicians, tapping his foot.

Gina found him, dressed today in a low-cut dress of a deep blue that drew his gaze. She chuckled when he looked up. "You haven't been much of a looker these days," she said.

Finn shrugged. "Have to play the part, don't I?"

"That's all this is to you? Playing?"

Finn glanced behind her. A table of men tossing dice had gotten a little loud. One of the men thumped his fist on the table, a flash of anger darting through his eyes when Tara made her way to him, offering another mug of ale. That would either placate him or cause tempers to flare even more as he got drunker.

"Not playing." He fell silent a moment. "You're busy tonight."

"We're busy every night."

"I suppose that's true enough. Makes Annie happy, I bet."

"You would bet?"

Finn met her gaze. "Is she here?"

"You could have just asked."

"I am asking."

She chewed at her lip a moment. "Annie isn't here."

"That's not like her."

"I don't know what to say. She didn't come tonight. Left word that she might be gone for a bit. We were to carry on without her."

Finn looked around, now with a different interest. If she was gone, it likely had to do with what he'd asked of her, though why wouldn't she have been able to find those answers and return before the tavern got as busy as it did?

"Do you know what she's been up to?"

"All I know is that she had to visit with a man named Packer."

Finn frowned. He knew the name. Packer was a minor thief, though his crew didn't pull many jobs in this section. Why would Annie have gone to him?

"You know more than that."

Gina looked up at him. "I told you what I know. I know better than to keep anything from the executioner."

"I'm not the executioner."

"No. That's right. You're his Hunter." She sighed and

turned to look into the tavern, leaning up against the wall and resting her shoulder against his. "Why did you do it?"

"Do what?"

"Come and question her." Gina looked over to him. "She didn't do anything to you, Finn. Annie wanted us to leave you alone."

"What?"

Gina shrugged. "After what happened with the King, she wanted us to leave you alone. It was a long time ago now, but there were a few who were angry. They liked the King and felt like you didn't get what you deserved for betraying him."

Finn noticed Oscar watching him. The mug of ale in front of him was mostly untouched, and his gaze lingered toward this side of the tavern.

Finn shook his head. "It doesn't matter what you heard. All of that was so long ago that it doesn't matter."

It felt like ages ago, though could it really have been only five years?

In that time, he'd become a different person. He'd learned lessons Meyer wanted to teach. He'd learned how to read people and how to question, along with how to heal. Through it all, he felt as if he were actually making a difference, something that he hadn't realized he would even care about.

"Do you really feel that you betraying the King doesn't matter?"

Finn turned to her and realized that she'd taken a step away from him and looked beyond him. He didn't have to follow the direction of her gaze. He knew where she looked. Toward the other crew.

"What are you doing, Gina?" he asked.

"Did you really think there would be no consequences? You come back here like it don't matter. Like all that time don't matter. Then you dare to question Annie about all of it, the one person who had protected you through it."

Gina nodded.

Finn turned, realizing his mistake too late.

He was near the back of the tavern without any way for him to move.

Trapped.

And the three men he'd watched enter the tavern were headed right toward him.

CHAPTER NINE

It had been a long time since Finn had fought anyone. He'd never been much of a fighter, but life spent in the streets had at least given him a chance to learn some of the techniques. Since he'd become the executioner's apprentice, there had never been the need to fight.

That didn't mean he was weak.

One of the things that he'd been forced by Meyer to do was to improve his fitness and his strength. The executioner had to be nearly perfect. It wasn't always easy, but they had to ensure that they were able to complete the job without any sign of trouble. It allowed the jurors to look as if they were carrying out the gods' will.

When the three men came toward him, Finn eyed them carefully.

He didn't want to end up in a fight. Not against three men.

Was this because of Gina—or were these members of Holden's crew?

"Call them back," he said softly.

Gina was still near him, having moved away though still close enough that he could feel her presence. He'd thought they had been on good terms, but perhaps that was his mistake. One made because he wasn't a part of this world anymore. How could he be on good terms with her?

"Call them back. I'll let it go this time."

Would I, though?

Finn had thought he'd been attacked because of Holden, but maybe that had been wrong. If it was because of Gina and her perceived need to get revenge for what she believed that he'd done to the King, a different answer fit.

"You won't be letting anything go. Neither will I."

"Trust me that you don't want to push this."

"Trust you. That's rich, coming from someone like you."

She slipped away from him, heading toward a table on the far side of the tavern, where she took a seat. Gina intended to watch.

Gods.

A gleam of metal caught his attention.

Finn would have to act.

He didn't have any weapons other than a short knife, and that was more decorative than useful. Finn hadn't needed any weapons.

He could imagine Meyer's disappointment to learn that he'd been jumped a second time in a week. All because he'd wanted to find Rachel Herns. The missing women. Now the chancellor's daughter.

Finn pushed that thought away.

What would Meyer do in this situation?

Probably wouldn't find himself in a situation like this, so it was difficult for Finn to even be able to guess.

He wouldn't show weakness.

Neither would Finn.

Finn raised his hands and straightened his spine. "I don't know what you think you intend, but as an executioner apprenticed to the master executioner of the city, in service of the king—"

He didn't have a chance to finish.

One of the men lunged at him.

He was the smaller man he'd seen coming into the tavern.

Finn kicked at a chair near him.

The chair went flying toward the man, who got tangled in it.

It bought him a moment. He turned toward the other two who approached. The bruiser was the one he knew to be concerned about, but the other man—the one who looked like he was the crew leader—was the one that Finn had to get to end it.

"What do you think you're going to accomplish here?" he asked.

The men approached him slowly. They didn't need to move quickly.

The chair toppling over had made some noise, but it did

little to disrupt the sounds inside the tavern. The music and the voices were loud enough that they covered up anything else.

Approaching slowly the way they did, they didn't look particularly threatening, though he knew better.

They hemmed him in.

Even the man he'd tripped up with the chair didn't need to get untangled all that quickly. He could take his time, get back to his feet, and come at Finn.

Which is what he did.

Finn twisted, turning so that he could see the three men in front of him, positioning himself in such a way that he wouldn't allow them to get off to either side of him. The door to the tavern was behind him, and the music still played with a fast clip in the back of the tavern.

The only hope that he really had of making it out of this alive was Oscar.

The bruiser made it difficult for Finn to even see Oscar.

"This is your last chance," Finn said.

The crew leader started to smile. "Our last chance?"

He shifted his cloak, and a longsword sheathed at his side became visible.

Were they really going to unsheathe and attack me in the middle of the Wenderwolf tavern?

He'd seen fights. The gods knew that he had been a part of several fights over the years, though he'd never found men willing to so openly attack.

The tavern wasn't one where the Archers would patrol.

He wouldn't have any chance of anyone coming to help him.

The bruiser lunged.

Finn reacted, grabbing for the table near him, positioning it so that he placed the table in between himself and the bruiser. The bruiser tried to get closer, but Finn held the table in front of him.

The bruiser glared at Finn.

The crew leader smiled. "You and I both know that this isn't going to end with you walking out of here. You might have survived the last one, but you won't survive this."

At least that answered Finn's question about whether or not these attacks were related.

He surveyed the tavern.

He could shout. It was possible that if he shouted loud enough, and with enough frenzy, that those within the tavern who weren't a part of it might be suddenly inclined to offer a bit of help. It was equally possible that they would see a servant of the king and ignore him.

In this section of the city, there was no love lost for the king.

He hoped that by waiting just a little bit that he might be able to get Oscar moving.

Only, Finn didn't see any sign of that.

Where was Oscar?

He had been sitting at the booth, but now he was gone.

The three members of the crew used that opportunity to move closer to him.

They went slowly.

He was trapped behind the table, forced behind it because of his own foolishness.

Finn considered tipping the table and running behind it.

All he needed was to disrupt the bruiser and buy him a moment of reprieve. With that reprieve, Finn thought he would be able to get out of the back of the tavern. From there, he could get to the street and, if lucky, find Archers.

That was if everything worked out for him.

He didn't have any choice. Finn kicked the table.

It popped up. It was a square table, not very large, but still heavy enough that kicking it sent it toward the bruiser.

The crew leader grinned.

Finn slammed forward, crashing into the crew leader.

The sudden change of direction caught the crew leader off guard. Finn used that opportunity, and he staggered back.

They fell, getting tangled up.

The man stank.

At first, he reminded Finn of the stench of the prisoner that he had interrogated earlier in the day, but that man had more of a wild odor to him. This crew leader stank as if he had worked the slaughterhouse.

Finn stayed close. He rolled to the side, forcing the leader to go with him.

Finn continued to roll, trying to force the crew leader off of him. He reached for his belt knife, but he could already tell that he wasn't going to be fast enough.

The crew leader jabbed something into Finn's side.

Finn winced, but other than a twinge of pain, he didn't find the searing heat that he expected.

Either he hadn't pierced Finn's side or the excitement of the attack prevented Finn from feeling it.

He tried turning so that he could move away from the attacker, but something caught him.

A hand grabbed him by the back of his shirt, started to lift him.

The bruiser.

That was the advantage of having a bruiser on the crew. A man like that would be able to handle someone like Finn with relative ease. This bruiser pulled Finn off and tossed him, sending him flying back against the wall.

Finn slammed into it, pulling his head in to keep from crashing against the wall. If he were to slam into it, he would be knocked unconscious, and any chance of escaping this with his life would be over.

Finn struggled, trying to get to his feet.

The bruiser was there, lifting him again.

He pulled Finn up so that they were practically face-to-face. He breathed out, his breath hot. A waft of ale and tobacco hit Finn.

"Your breath stinks," Finn said.

The bruiser slammed him back, forcing Finn back against the wall.

He tried to engage his mind. He had to get away from the bruiser, but then he would have to get around the crew leader as well. That might be too much for him to ask.

The bruiser slammed him again, and Finn timed it, kicking at the same time as his back crashed into the wall.

His foot caught the bruiser in the groin, and he grunted. Even a big man couldn't stomach a blow like that. The bruiser doubled over, and Finn used that opportunity to kick again.

His second blow struck true, and the bruiser moaned, writhing on the ground.

Finn scrambled to his feet, looking around the tavern for any sign that anyone might offer any help. The other patrons in the tavern didn't seem to notice.

Figures.

In a tavern like this, he wasn't terribly surprised that they would ignore anything around them. It was better that way. Better to avoid the appearance that they were paying attention to something they shouldn't be.

Finn scrambled forward.

The bruiser was down now, but he wouldn't stay that way for very long. Any bruiser worth his pay had been in a few scrapes before, and most would have suffered a kick to the groin more than once. They were painful, but breathing through it would permit anyone to tolerate the blow.

As Finn attempted to scramble past the crew leader, someone caught his leg, and Finn went stumbling forward. He struck his head. A flash of light warned him that he was injured, a bright glowing that surrounded everything.

Finn tried to ignore the throbbing in his head. He lurched forward, struggling to get moving.

Something held on to his leg, and Finn kicked.

His leg came loose.

Finn scrambled forward, darting away.

He reached the booths. When he did, he glanced over to where he had seen Oscar. The Hand rested, slumped over on the table.

Damn.

The crew knew Oscar would help. They knew to target him.

As far as Finn knew, Gina had poisoned Oscar. He had to know what it was so that he could know what to treat him with. He had to get Oscar out of there.

He wouldn't have time for that, though. He had to get free, then he could come back for Oscar.

Finn scrambled toward the door, throwing it open and stepping out into the cool night air. He paused in the doorway, glancing back at the crew as they came toward him.

The other people in the tavern finally seemed to realize something was taking place. The music had halted, and several had turned their attention toward the door.

Finn waited until he was sure the crew followed him, and then he stepped out into the night. He backed along the street.

When the crew appeared in the doorway, Finn let out a shrill whistle.

The crew leader watched him, eyeing him with a dark expression on his face. "Do you think that will save you?"

"All I need is for one Archer to come," Finn said.

Finn watched as the crew leader unsheathed his sword.

The city Archers weren't soldiers. They were glorified

guards. Little more than iron masters, only their prison was the city. If the crew really did intend to attack with swords, any Archer would be overwhelmed. They might not even come.

Finn whistled again.

The bruiser lumbered toward him.

He was a large man and yet moved far more quickly than what Finn would've expected, given his size.

Why did it always seem that bruisers had speed to go along with strength?

Finn tried to dart off to the side, but a burning pain along his flank slowed him.

So much for his hope that he hadn't been injured. It seemed that they had cut him. How badly would it be this time?

The bruiser neared him, and Finn braced for impact.

The bruiser stumbled, falling to the ground in front of Finn.

Finn glanced down at him for a moment before jerking his head around to see if there were any Archers nearby that might've helped, but didn't see any sign of them.

The other two members of the crew stared at the fallen bruiser.

The bruiser started to get up, but blood spilled down from a crossbow bolt in his gut. He had his hands clenched around it, and the blood pooled around them.

"An injury like that is going to need stitching," Finn said. "You need a surgeon."

The bruiser was up, and lumbered toward him again.

Finn evaded, stepping off to the side, and the bruiser stumbled, his feet tangling together, and he fell forward.

It would only force the bolt deeper into his stomach.

He turned his attention to the crew leader and the smaller man.

The smaller man was likely his scout, though given how he had been the first one to attack, Finn wondered if perhaps he had some other role within this crew. Finn whistled again, this time letting out two sharp whistles, the cry piercing the darkened night.

"The Archers are already on their way," Finn said. "If you want to get pinched, that's fine by me. I try not to take much pleasure in questioning my prisoners, but I would make an exception on your behalf."

The crew leader marched toward him, seemingly unmindful of the downed bruiser.

Finn took a moment to glance around the street.

There didn't seem to be anybody else around him, though someone must've been there. Whoever had taken out the bruiser would have to be nearby.

He could run, though without knowing how injured he was, he didn't know if he would be able to outrun the other two. The last time he'd attempted to run, he'd been run down. Finn didn't want to risk it again.

He kept the crew leader and the smaller man in view.

The smaller man darted.

Finn was ready and he reached for his knife, pulling it out.

He flashed it toward the smaller man, sweeping around

to try to intimidate him, but the small man glowered at him, lowering his shoulder, and prepared to barrel into Finn.

He stopped suddenly, grunting and grabbing his shoulder.

A crossbow bolt jutted from it.

"I told you the Archers would be here soon," Finn said.

He didn't know who this was, but it wasn't Archers. No Archers he knew used crossbow bolts, though maybe they should. Whoever this was had helped him, though Finn didn't exactly know why.

The man grabbed the bolt in his shoulder and jerked on it.

He tossed it to the ground.

Here, Finn thought the bruiser was the one to be concerned about, but any man who was able to yank a crossbow bolt from his shoulder without making any sound was a person to fear.

He turned his attention back to Finn, then came racing toward him.

Finn jammed his knife forward, catching the attacker in the gut.

The small man knocked him back. Finn reached for the injured shoulder, squeezing his thumb into it and pinching.

The man cried out.

Finn kicked, and he rolled so that he could get out from underneath the small attacker. He had to get up before the crew leader got to him.

He rolled again.

The smaller man grabbed for him, but Finn moved out of the way.

He scrambled to his feet, barely to his knees when the man grunted and fell forward. Another crossbow bolt stuck out from his back.

Where is this mysterious helper?

Finn looked, but he didn't dare spend too much time searching around the street for whoever might be helping him. He needed to pay attention to the crew leader.

He stood about a dozen paces from Finn.

"If you don't want the same thing to happen to you, you had better go," Finn said.

The crew leader snorted. "I don't know who's helping you, but you made a mistake."

"Did I? You're the one who has lost two-thirds of your crew. I don't have any problem with having the Archers bring you down as well."

Finn whistled.

The crew leader tensed.

It was the first time Finn had seen him hesitate at all.

He turned, casting a glance from side to side, before focusing on Finn once again.

"There aren't any Archers. You have someone helping you."

"It doesn't matter if they're Archers or not. I'm the executioner's apprentice. Either way, I'm serving the king, and anyone who is helping me is serving the king!"

He raised his voice at the end, wanting to make sure that

whoever was out there knew that Finn would offer whatever protection he could.

Perhaps it didn't matter.

Whoever was out there *was* helping.

Finn whistled again.

The crew leader jerked his head around before backing toward the tavern.

"This isn't over," he said.

"It is until you get a new crew."

The crew leader glared at Finn, turned, and disappeared down an alley.

Finn knew where the alley led. Had he any known support, he'd chase him down, but without knowing who was out there helping, he didn't dare.

And there was still the issue of the two fallen men.

He might be able to help them and still get answers.

Finn turned his attention to the two men. The smaller one had been shot in the shoulder and the back. Neither injury was particularly dangerous, though he had seen men take wounds to the back that could be fatal. Anything that struck the lung had that possibility.

The bruiser wasn't likely to get up. He'd taken one to the stomach and had been lying motionless for a while. If he was going to get back up, it was going to be a while.

Before checking on either of them, he had to see who might be responsible.

"You can come out," he said, turning in place and speaking to the darkness around him. "The crew leader is gone. These two aren't going to pose any further danger."

Finn hesitated, and realized whoever had done this wasn't afraid of them. They *might* be more concerned with what *he* would do. "I'm not going to report you to the magister."

He looked around, watching the shadows around the small square.

There wasn't any movement. He studied the fallen bruiser before turning to the other man. He might be able to figure something out from them. From the direction the bolts would have needed to come, Finn had a pretty good idea *where* they had come from.

The Wenderwolf.

There wouldn't have been anyone in the tavern who would have helped.

Oscar was already out—he had to get back to him and see if he needed help—and the other man in his crew wouldn't have been likely to help. Gina had been in on it with this crew, so that didn't leave much in the way for Finn to know who might have participated.

There wasn't anyone he could see, though he believed there had to be someone there.

"It's safe for you to come out now," he said again.

There wasn't an answer.

Finn stared at the Wenderwolf. Though he *thought* that whoever had helped had been near it, he wasn't entirely sure.

Whoever it was didn't want to show themselves.

Finn looked down at the bruiser and crouched to check for a pulse. There wasn't any. He'd bled too much. With a bolt to the belly it didn't surprise Finn that it would be fatal.

The smaller man coughed.

He still lived.

Finn would start with him.

Boots thudded toward him.

Finn looked up to see a pair of Archers approaching. He didn't know either of them, but that didn't matter as much anymore. "It's good you're here," he said. He was tempted to tell them that it took them long enough, but snapping at them like that would only make it less likely that they would come the next time he needed them. "I was attacked by these two and their crew leader. Not sure who fired on them. This guy"—he motioned to the smaller man—"is still alive but needs help. Bring him to the nearest prison and send for Master Meyer."

"Who are you?" one of the Archers asked.

"Quiet, Shald. Don't you know that's the Hunter?"

Finn nodded, turning toward the tavern. He *was* the Hunter. Now it was time for him to hunt.

CHAPTER TEN

The Wenderwolf looked as if nothing had happened. The musicians had started up their song, the crowd sang and danced along, and the tables that Finn and the crew had tipped over had been righted.

Gina wasn't anywhere to be seen.

Finn hurried to the table and checked on Oscar.

He lived. His breathing was slow, as was his pulse, but he was still alive.

Finn grabbed the mug from in front of him. There was still a little liquid in it.

He had an empty vial in his pocket and he poured a bit of the ale into the vial before capping it and sticking it into his pocket. Slipping his arm around Oscar, he dragged him from the booth. He was heavy, but Finn was strong enough to carry him.

Or he would have were it not for the sudden pain in his side.

Finn had forgotten about his injury.

It hadn't been so bad that he hadn't been able to move, but now that his heart wasn't pumping as fast and he could calm down a bit, all of the fighting energy that he had faded, leaving him much more aware of the pain in his side.

"Dammit, but you're heavier than you should be," he whispered.

He dragged Oscar toward the door. He wasn't going to be able to carry him all the way to Meyer's home, and Finn wasn't sure that he trusted anyone to get him help otherwise.

Once he was out on the street, the Archers looked over to him. They were still working on the smaller man, getting him ready to carry to the prison.

"I'm going to need one more Archer to help me with this man," Finn said.

"That one going to the prisons too?"

Finn shook his head. "Not the prisons. This one is going to Meyer's house."

"You're bringing him straight to the hangman?"

"He's a witness."

That would be believable enough.

"I won't be able to carry him. Got stabbed during the attack," Finn explained.

The nearest Archer's eyes widened. "They clipped you?" He kicked the fallen bruiser.

Finn just nodded. Had they been around during the attack, he wondered if they would have been so brave against the bruiser, though decided that he shouldn't blame them for not being there when he'd been hurt. They wouldn't have known. The Archers didn't patrol constantly.

His side continued to throb. Oscar was getting too heavy. He sank to the ground, lowering Oscar to the ground near him.

"You need help?" the Archer asked.

"I'll be fine. Just call for more men."

The bearded Archer ran off, disappearing. He was gone for a while, though Finn lost track of how long. He focused on his breathing, noticing that it was slowing. He checked his pulse and realized that was slowing as well.

Had the knife the crew leader stabbed him with been poisoned?

Finn didn't have a lot of experience with poisons. That wasn't something that Meyer ever had to deal with much. Mostly they talked about them in terms of trying to understand what might have been used during murders, but even that wasn't always possible.

Another pair of Archers appeared along with the bearded man who'd gone running off. Finn knew one of them.

"Derry," he said, looking up.

Derry had been an Archer for the last few years and had been friendly to Finn. From what Finn knew of the man, he was one of the good ones. Finn wasn't naïve enough to think that all of the Archers took the job for noble purposes. It was a stable pay, but they also enjoyed a certain freedom in the city that others did not. Having that freedom attracted the wrong sort of men sometimes. They were the sort of men that *shouldn't* be given authority, but it was often difficult to know who would turn out that way until they were given a chance.

"What happened here?" Derry asked, offering his hand.

"I'm not entirely sure just yet. Got a man I need help getting to Meyer's home."

"What about you?"

Finn took a deep breath and tried to focus his mind. If he could just get to his feet, he thought that he could keep moving. "Help me up."

Derry reached out and grabbed Finn's hand, helping him to his feet. He looked down at Oscar. "That's the Hand!"

"I know."

"You gonna put him away?"

Finn shook his head. "He's a witness."

The first two Archers that had appeared had already grabbed the smaller man and were dragging him off. "Which prison are you taking him to?"

"Declan is closest."

Of course it would be.

"I'll have Meyer meet you there. Bring him to the chapel. The iron masters will guide you."

They'd probably take over the moment the Archers brought the man to them. Finn doubted the iron masters would be too eager to have any Archers wandering through the prison.

Derry was lifting Oscar with the help of the other Archer. "Damn, but he's heavier than he looks."

"That's what I said," Finn told him.

He started off, heading toward Meyer's home. It wasn't a long walk, but given the way that he felt, it seemed as if it would be too far. Every so often, he'd glance back and see the Archers dragging Oscar along with them. Finn worried that they weren't going fast enough. With whatever poison had been used on him, he ran the risk of his heart slowing too much or his breathing stopping altogether. Either would mean the end of him.

The farther he went, the more his mind started to clear. He could feel it as it seemed to open up, as if with each passing moment that he could think more easily.

"I'm going up ahead. You bring him to Meyer's as quickly as you can," Finn said to Derry.

The Archer nodded.

Had it been two Archers he didn't know, Finn might not have been willing to leave Oscar with them, but this was Derry, and he'd known him well enough.

Finn jogged forward.

His side hurt but not so much as it had before. The movement *did* seem to help his mind, and he started to clear even more. When Meyer's home came into view, the bright lantern light in the windows drawing to him, he hurried faster.

Until he saw shadows slip around the fence.

Finn paused and looked over his shoulder. *Could someone really be chasing me down again?* The crew leader. That was the one person Finn wouldn't be surprised to see coming after him.

Finn pulled out his knife. He was glad to still have it but

wondered if it would be necessary. With the Archers coming along the street, there wouldn't be need for him to do anything.

He just had to wait.

The Archers didn't come.

The shadow around the house continued to move, slipping in the darkness. Finn watched a moment, curious what the shadowed form might do, but then it disappeared.

It was unusual for anyone to target Meyer.

Dangerous for them, too.

Where was Derry?

He didn't want to leave Meyer's house if someone was going to try to break in, but he also wanted to know what Derry had done with Oscar.

He wasn't about to leave Oscar, either.

The shadow moved.

That decided it for Finn.

He darted forward.

Staying low, Finn glanced behind him, wanting to see if there would be any movement that might draw his attention but not making anything out. The Archers that were there—they *had* to be coming—still hadn't revealed themselves.

The shadowy form that he'd seen had looped around the wall.

That was where he had to go. His sister was there. Meyer. He had to go inside and get them help.

First, he had to see who thought they could sneak around Meyer's home.

There wasn't any sign of the attacker, though Finn thought that he should be able to find them. He circled around the outside of the wall, still finding nothing, before heading back around.

There hadn't been anything there.

He headed to the gate.

He felt as if there was something near him.

Finn dropped to the ground, looking toward the street. He felt foolish, but if there was someone coming, then he wanted to know.

He didn't see anything.

Finn got to his feet and headed inside the gate.

He looked around.

Maybe he was paranoid, but he didn't think so. Not after a night like he'd had.

When he reached the door to Meyer's home, he looked back. There was still no sign of Derry or the other Archer. They should have been nearby now. They weren't that far behind him, though maybe they had gotten slowed.

Finn looked around before pushing the door open.

"Master Meyer!"

His voice sounded off.

Maybe he was more injured than he had realized. Finn pulled up his shirt, looking to see where the knife had gone into his side. He didn't see anything, but that didn't mean that there wasn't still an injury there. He felt along and brought his hand up to look.

"What is it?"

Meyer stepped out of his office at the end of the hall and

Finn let out a relieved sigh. Meyer was there. He would make sure that nothing happened to Finn.

"Another attack."

"Holden's men?"

Finn shook his head. "I don't think so. Don't know, though. They poisoned Oscar, or I think they did. Derry and another Archer are bringing him here now. There were three in a crew who came at me. Two were brought down by someone with a crossbow, and the third got away. Might be prowling around your home."

Meyer grabbed Finn's shirt and pulled it up. "Looks shallow. Should be able to bandage you." He leaned close, inhaling near the wound. "Might be something in it, though. I'd bind it with pultin and grishan."

"I'll do that. One of the survivors was brought to Declan. He's going to need help. Has a bolt in the shoulder and another in the back."

"That's not the Archers' work."

"I don't know who helped. I didn't have time to figure it out, and they didn't reveal themselves."

Meyer nodded.

"Any suggestions for Oscar when they bring him here?"

Where was *Oscar? He should be here by now.*

"Sedated, you said?"

Finn pulled the vial of ale from his pocket and handed it to Meyer. He took the cap off and sniffed it before bringing it to his lips and tipping it back and sipping, then spitting it back out.

"Not an obvious sedative. Could be loratath or even erasth. Doesn't have much of a taste."

"Oscar would have noticed otherwise."

"Good point. Why don't you try to give him a mixture of silverleaf and therinberry? That should give us a bit of time to see if there's anything else he might need. Most of these toxins will wash out of the body if we give him enough time. If it wasn't immediately fatal, then we should have time."

Finn nodded. Meyer grabbed his cloak from the closet and then took out a walking stick.

"Are you feeling unwell?" Finn asked.

"This is to protect me. We've got men in the city who think they can attack a servant of the king. Twice."

Finn nodded. "If you see Derry out there…"

"I will make certain to tell him to hurry along."

Finn nodded.

Meyer ducked out into the night.

Finn headed to the office and gathered the supplies that Meyer had suggested. They weren't compounds that he was accustomed to working with, but they made sense. They were all compounds that he had helped Meyer acquire over the years, and Finn could easily imagine Wella guiding him on where to find the various compounds in her store.

When he had them together, he mixed the two medicinals Meyer had suggested for him and smeared them into the wound. It was a cooling sensation, and Finn breathed out a sigh of relief.

After dressing his wounds, he started to make arrangements for what he'd need for Oscar.

Where was *Oscar?*

Finn would have to go back out after him.

He didn't like that he might have to do it, but he also didn't like the idea that something had happened to him in the short time after leaving him.

When he reached the door, a knocking sounded against it.

"Who is it?"

"Derry. We've got your witness. Got a bit tied up. Some bastard thought to try to tangle with us. Scared him away, but it took a little longer than we would have liked."

Finn pulled the door open.

Derry and the other Archer stood there with Oscar dangling between them. His skin looked paler than it had before. The two Archers looked unharmed.

"Do you get attacked often?"

"These days, we do. The last month has been full of crazy."

"What do you mean?"

Finn motioned for them to follow and guided the Archers through Meyer's home and back to the office near the back. They settled Oscar on the cot in the room for that purpose, though it wasn't often that men came to the office drugged like Oscar. Most of them had minor wounds that could have gone to a surgeon, but they preferred someone with Meyer's skill.

"Just that we've had more activity over the last month. Happens like that from time to time. You spend enough time in the city, and eventually you're going to find that there are some real troublemakers out there." Derry motioned to the other Archer. "You need anything more?"

"Not tonight. Thanks for your help."

Derry nodded, slipping out of the office and heading down the hall before closing the door behind them.

It left Finn alone with Oscar.

He started with the two powders that Meyer had suggested. He didn't know which of them would work, nor did he even know what ratio to use. Most powders like these were mixed in water, though not all of them would be.

He would have to try something.

That was the only thing that Finn could do. Try. Hope for the best.

After checking Oscar's pulse, noting that it seemed even slower than before—as did his breathing—he didn't want to take much longer with all of this. He needed to do something.

Finn mixed the silverleaf and therinberry together, sticking to a one-to-one ratio, before adding a bit of water. The next trick was getting it into Oscar.

Slipping his arm beneath his neck, he propped his head up enough so that he could try to get him to drink. Oscar's neck flopped a bit more than Finn thought that it should.

Meyer had always been around when there was a healing that *really* mattered. Finn was able to take care of minor things, and when it came to what he'd dealt with in the prisons, most of those were minor enough. Meyer had even given him a chance to work with some of the clients who came to Meyer's office seeking medicines, but he hadn't ever been faced with someone like Oscar whose life depended on him.

"Master Meyer?"

Finn looked back to see his sister standing in the doorway. He hadn't seen her since she'd disappeared the day before, though she didn't look any worse than she'd been. She had high-necked gray dress with a hint of lace along the sleeves. A new scarf wrapped around her neck. "It's just me, Lena. Do you think you might be able to give me a hand?"

She hurried into the room and looked down. "That's Oscar Richter."

"It is. I think he was poisoned, though I don't really know what it was. Some sort of sedative that's slowing his heart and his breathing. Meyer suggested silverleaf and—"

"Therinberry," Lena said, looking over to the shelves of powders that Finn had pulled out. "That would be a bit of a stimulant."

"Right. Now I just have to get it into him."

She lifted Oscar's head. "I used to have to do this with Mother when she was sick. The key is tipping the head back and opening the mouth. If you stroke the throat, you should be able to stimulate a swallow. If you can't, then we have to try something much harder."

"Like what?"

"Like something that I never tried before. So, we'd better hope that this works."

Finn lifted the concoction to Oscar's mouth and tipped it back while Lena held his head. Finn stroked Oscar's neck, and thankfully, he swallowed. As he poured a bit more of the concoction into Oscar, he let out a pent-up breath.

"Why did he get poisoned?" Lena asked.

"I think because they knew he might help me."

"Who knew?"

"Someone who's angry I lived and a man named Leon Konig did not."

"I know that name."

Finn nodded. "I'm sure I've mentioned it before."

"Why do they care about what you did with him?" Lena asked.

Finn shook his head. "I'm not entirely sure. When I get the chance, I'll ask her."

"Her? Don't tell me this is one of the women you used to—"

"I didn't used to do anything," Finn said, "so you don't have to worry about what it is or isn't."

They finished pouring the liquid into Oscar's mouth, and then Lena laid his head back, resting it on the cot. His color hadn't improved.

Finn tested his pulse but found that hadn't changed much either. His breathing might be a little quicker than before, but it was still too slow. Almost painfully slow.

"It's not working," he said softly.

"You need to give it a little more time. From what I've learned about these compounds, it can take a little while for them to begin to work. In the case of something like this, you'll likely need to give it a few minutes to see if it's going to make a difference."

Finn glanced to the two bottles of powder that he'd mixed into the water. Maybe the ratio was wrong.

"Do you think we needed to give him more than what we did?" he asked.

"I don't know. It's possible he might respond to a higher concentration, but then you run the risk of overdosing him. I don't know if you *can* with these, mind you, only that if you were to do it, he would find himself with a racing heart. Possibly damage."

Finn looked around the inside of the room. There were plenty of other medicines that he could try, but without knowing what they were dealing with, he wasn't sure that it was safe to do so.

Meyer hadn't known the compound. He'd guessed.

"I need to know what was used on him," Finn said.

"What changes when you do?"

"We might be able to find the right counter for it."

"Maybe," she said slowly. "It's possible that there won't be an easy counter for it, though. I don't know as much about poisons as Master Meyer, but what I've read suggests that treating them is mostly supportive."

Finn touched Oscar's wrist. His skin was cool and clammy.

It seemed a cruel twist of fate that he'd be responsible for trying to help Oscar so soon after Oscar had helped him. He could go to the hegen for help. There was little doubt that Esmerelda would have something she could offer to heal Oscar, and he would pay it for his friend.

There was another possibility that might keep him from that.

"I'm going to see if Wella can help," he said. And if she couldn't, he'd have no choice but to go to the hegen.

"Will she even be open at this time of night?"

"I don't know, but if there's anyone who might know something that could help, it would be her. Meyer won't be back for a while, so she's the only one I can think of who might be able to help."

That was if she would even answer her door at this time of night. And if Finn could make it without getting jumped again.

The other crew leader was still out there.

He would come for Finn.

"You'd rather go to her than to…"

"I have to see if she knows something that can help. It's better than risking *them* again."

Finn watched her, wondering what she might have been asked to do. Her cards were her own, much like Finn's cards were his own. That was, if he were to even have a card. With the blank card, it would be a simple matter for them to demand something of him. When they did, Finn wasn't sure how he would respond. He'd never attempted to deny the hegen what they wanted. He wasn't even sure if that was possible. When he'd been given a card representing Oscar before, he'd done what he thought was needed, but it had turned out to be exactly what the hegen had wanted.

"Go. I'll take care of him while you're gone."

Finn patted Oscar's hand and then headed out of the

room, down the hall, and out into the night. Unlike Meyer, he didn't have a staff to bring with him to protect himself. He supposed that he could bring Justice, but that felt... wrong. The sword was meant for executions, nothing else. Anything more than that and Finn would feel as if he were betraying the purpose of the blade.

He stepped through the gate and paused for a moment. Had the night been this cool earlier? A soft breeze gusted along the street, leaving a chill washing along his skin, though Finn wondered if that was just because he had been sweating while trying to keep Oscar alive.

Racing through the streets, he tried to remain focused on his destination. Every so often, it seemed as if footsteps followed him, but then the sound died off, leaving Finn thinking that he'd only imagined it.

When he reached Wella's street, he slowed. It was dark, and in this part of Olin, there weren't many streetlights. The air had a damp smell to it, one that mixed with a hint of rot. Finn tried not to think of what that might come from.

No lights illuminated Wella's shop.

Finn knocked anyway.

He waited.

It was unlikely that she would answer. He was clutching for hope the gods would be unlikely to offer, but it was the kind of hope that he had to try. If this failed, the only other option he had was heading out to the hegen and seeing if Esmerelda would help.

It might even be exactly what she wanted.

Finn knocked again.

There was still no answer.

He sighed, turning his attention to the city wall and the distant gate. It was late enough that it would be difficult to get through, though he thought that with enough persuasion, he might be able to convince the Archers that he needed to be let out of the city. Even if he did, he wondered whether they would accept his explanation or whether they would question why he had to go to the hegen at this time of night.

Finn frowned to himself. When *he'd* been attacked, it had been late at night. Oscar and Lena would have needed to bring him from the city in the darkness, which would have meant making their way past the Archers at the wall and out of the city. What would they have said to be able to do that?

Questions for another time.

Finn knocked again.

A light flickered on in a nearby home.

It might be a mistake for him to knock this loud.

In the Brinder section where he'd grown up, neighbors wouldn't watch out for each other. In Wella's part of the city, he suspected it was different. There would be more neighbors who would keep an eye out for her, probably even sending word to the Archers—or worse, taking care of intruders on their own. The only hope that he had was that Wella had people coming to her at strange hours at other times.

He contemplated turning away when the sound of movement stirred from the other side of the door.

The door came open. Wella looked little different from how she did in the daytime, almost as if she slept in the same rumpled clothing that she wore all day. She eyed him slowly, blinking before pressing her mouth into a tight line.

"Finn? What on earth are you doing here at this hour? Is something wrong with Henry?"

Finn shook his head, reaching into his pocket and pulling the vial of tainted ale, and handed it to her. "Not Master Meyer. He's preoccupied at the moment, but even he wasn't quite sure what was in this."

Wella unstoppered the vial and brought it to her nose, inhaling slowly and deliberately. She tipped the vial from one side to the other before wrinkling her nose. "Where did you find this?"

"It's the ale from someone I know. A friend. He was poisoned so he couldn't help me when I was attacked."

Wella stood for a moment, watching him. "That's quite a lot to take in all at once. Who attacked you?"

"A crew. I think hired by someone angry about what happened with my crew."

"That was years ago."

"Years ago, but apparently, she held on to it." Finn nodded to the vial she held. "Is there anything you can do?"

Wella swirled the liquid around and it sloshed up the sides of the vial. "I know what it is, but I'm afraid I'm not going to be able to help you. I suspect your friend is sedated?"

Finn nodded. "Slow heartbeat. Breathing. Color is fading. If I don't help him soon, he's going to die."

Wella looked at the vial again, holding it up to the faint moonlight before bringing it back down. "He's not going to die. Not immediately, at least."

"What do you mean? If his heart slows too much—"

"What you've detected is probably as slow as it's going to go. His breathing too. If he didn't die already, then it's not going to kill him."

That was similar to what his sister had said.

Relief swept through him. Oscar would live.

Finn hadn't known, and when Meyer hadn't been able to help him, Finn's fear for his friend had intensified. Knowing that Oscar *would* live let his mind finally start to slow, and he could begin to think more clearly.

"We tried silverleaf and therinberry, but it hasn't made a difference," Finn said.

"A reasonable stimulant. Henry has paid attention over the years." She smiled slightly, swirling the liquid again. It seemed as if it reflected the moonlight more than what Finn would have expected. "Unfortunately, in this case, the two compounds will be unlikely to make a difference for your friend. While they have a stimulating effect, that's not going to work for him."

"Are you sure?"

"Quite."

"What is it? What happened to him?"

Wella lowered the vial and handed it back to Finn, who took it reluctantly.

"It's magic, Finn. Your friend was poisoned by magic."

CHAPTER ELEVEN

F inn didn't sleep well that night. Lena stayed with him, both of them resting with Oscar in the office; he was thankful for the company. Oscar didn't mean as much to Lena as he did to Finn, but she recognized that Oscar had been their father's friend, and Oscar had helped Finn when he'd been injured, which meant that he was someone to both of them.

When morning came as a streamer of light drifting through the windows, Finn looked up as the door to the office came open. Meyer looked in, dirt staining his hands, his eyes darkened and weary.

"You're here," he said.

Finn sat up, looking over to Lena. She was draped in a chair, her head resting along the wall. It was the most she had slept so far. "The silverleaf and therinberry didn't help."

"I'm sorry, Finn. If those didn't work, I'm not sure what else to try."

"I went to Wella." Finn shifted on the chair, looking over to Oscar. His color hadn't changed. He looked just as pale as he had before. As he watched, he tried to determine how quickly he breathed, but didn't find a regular pattern to it. Either he wasn't breathing regularly at all, or it was too shallow for Finn to tell. "She said there's nothing that we would be able to give him to help."

"She recognized it."

Finn looked up. There was something in the way that Meyer had said it that suggested he knew more than what he'd told Finn.

Why should that surprise him? Meyer had tasted the liquid, whatever it was.

"You knew."

Meyer inhaled heavily as he looked over at Oscar. "I suspected."

"How?"

"There's a distinct taste when magic is involved. Unfortunately, I've come to know it all too well."

"A taste?"

"Perhaps it's more of a smell. It's hard for me to know. Taste and smell are so interconnected, it could be either." He breathed out, tipping his head toward Oscar. "It's a strange draught. He must have consumed enough to be rendered unconscious, though it does surprise me that it would affect him so much."

"Is it hegen?"

"It's magic, or at least I suspect it is. Wella saying the same thing makes it more likely to be so. But not all magic is hegen. Not all hegen have magic. There is a spectrum, as you have seen. Some of the hegen are traders. Some are craftsmen. Some are cooks or teachers or—"

"Witches."

"Call them that if you must, but there are some who have magic."

Finn looked over to Oscar. The hegen wouldn't have poisoned Oscar. "I don't understand why Esmerelda would let him be targeted after what he did for me. He would owe them."

"This is probably not her magic."

"Would the hegen work against each other?"

Meyer looked at Finn, saying nothing. Normally, Meyer would have an easy time masking his emotions. Whether it was fatigue or something else, he failed hiding his concern.

"They wouldn't," Finn said.

Meyer shook his head.

Which meant Finn was going to have to visit Esmerelda. They needed answers.

"Did you find anything from the man I sent you?"

Meyer grunted, pulling a chair out from behind his bench and taking a seat. "Other than whoever your mysterious helper is has incredible aim."

"Why would you say that?"

"The shot in the shoulder looked to be centered in the meat of the muscle. It would hurt and would make it hard to lift his arm. The second shot in the back didn't hit any vital organs."

"So, you kept him alive."

Meyer nodded. "He won't be answering many questions for a while, but he lives."

"Why won't he be answering?"

"The Archers did a number on him on the way over."

Finn swore softly.

"Don't get like that. We don't know what they were dealing with. It sounds as if he came around while they dragged him to Declan and they had to get him to settle down."

"We need to know more about that crew."

"I'm not so sure 'we' need to do anything."

"What's that supposed to mean?"

Meyer took a deep breath. "It means you will do this." He looked over to Oscar. "Why don't you go find the answer to your questions. I will be waiting here when you return."

Finn nodded slowly. Meyer *wanted* him to go to the hegen.

That surprised him, though it might be because Meyer knew that Finn wouldn't be held back from going. He needed to know more about what happened to Oscar and to find out if there was anything that they'd be able to do to help him.

"Will you let Lena know where I've gone when she wakes? I don't want her coming after me."

"I'm sure you don't."

Finn frowned, but he was too tired to try to work through what Meyer was getting at. Perhaps now wasn't the best time for him to be going to the hegen. When he visited with Esmerelda, he felt as if he needed to have his mind clear, but Finn didn't feel that way at all right now.

He paused in the kitchen and brewed a mug of tea. When it was ready, he tested it before drinking it as quickly as he could tolerate. He needed to wake up.

The air outside Meyer's home was crisp. Finn pulled his cloak around his shoulders and headed out into the street. It was early morning, though there was activity out now.

Finn glanced in the direction of the Wenderwolf, but he needed answers about Oscar. He wasn't going to get those by going back to the tavern. He would have to go to the one person who might be able to explain what had happened to Oscar.

The Teller Gate was open, and Finn hurried through it. He nodded to the Archers, feeling his mind begin to clear, the longer he was out. By the time he passed the Stone, he had begun to think through how he would question Esmerelda.

It would have to be a relatively cautious approach. She wasn't the kind to take well to a forceful questioning, though she would be more likely to spin any such forceful questioning to her favor, anyway. He paused as he neared the Stone. With the sunlight coming up today, it reflected off the gallows. The wood seemed a bit damper than he would have expected. The gallows hadn't been rebuilt all that long before, but even now, he thought that it would need to be revisited. Something more to speak to Meyer about when he returned.

Nearing the hegen section, Finn slowed. Though there

were people out in the main part of the city, there weren't many out in the hegen part at this time. A child with a scrawny-looking dog. A woman carrying a basket who turned away at the sight of him. Two others that were far enough away that he didn't get to see if they were men or women. With the hegen, it could be difficult to tell from their clothing.

Then he reached Esmerelda's home. It was no easier finding it in the day than it was at night. At either time of day, it seemed as if the streets were designed to make it difficult to make his way through. In the daylight, he was able to see the city behind him, the massive palace rising up on the hillside, and even the upper part of the wall from certain vantages.

Finn paused at the door before knocking. He should have brought the card she'd given him, not that it would have changed anything.

Even before he had a chance to knock, the door came open and Esmerelda stood before him. She was dressed in a long flowing blue gown that stretched almost to the ground. Her lips were a vibrant shade of red. After having spent the night watching men get shot and bleed in the streets, he found the brightness of her lips a little unsettling.

"Finn Jagger."

"Esmerelda. You were expecting me."

She smiled. "Was I?"

Finn regarded her, wondering how much she would admit to him. In his few interactions with her, she had only shared what she'd needed, and never more than what she thought he needed to know.

He pulled the vial of tainted ale from his pocket and held it out to her. She was now the third person he'd offered it to. Hopefully, he would find out what kind of magic this was from her.

"What is this? A gift? You don't need to offer me a gift, Finn."

"Not a gift. At least, not for you. This was gifted to Oscar Richter."

She started to smile but must have seen something on his face, and she pulled the top off the vial before bringing it to her nose and breathing it in. She swirled it similarly to the way that Wella had swirled it, though she didn't hold it out to the light. "Where did you get this?" She asked it softly, her voice taking on a different tone, and one that was completely unlike the sweetness that he'd seen from her before.

"Oscar was poisoned with it last night. It took me a while to realize it was a magic poisoning. He's still alive. I came here for answers."

Esmerelda looked beyond him, toward the city, frowning deeply. "You will come in."

"Fine. If I come in, you're going to agree to share with me what your people did to Oscar. And you're going to tell me how to help him, because he didn't deserve to be poisoned." He would go after Gina later. As the one responsible for what had been given to Oscar, she would be questioned. More than that, she *deserved* to be in prison, though that wasn't entirely up to him.

"I will tell you what you need to know."

She stepped off to the side, waiting on him.

There was something about the look in her eye that left Finn a little troubled.

What I need to know?

What he needed was to know what had happened to Oscar.

Finn stepped into her home.

The scent of the incense he noticed the last time he'd been there struck him immediately. It was almost minty and left his nostrils tingling. He tried not to take too deep a breath, but there wasn't anything about the scent that seemed dangerous to him. In fact, it seemed almost pleasing. Refreshing.

"Can I offer you anything to drink?" Esmerelda asked.

"Will I need it for this visit?"

She tipped her head to the side. "This is different, Finn Jagger."

Finn held her gaze before nodding. "If that's the case, then I would take something to drink."

For all he knew, she would give him something similar to what had been given to Oscar, though when she returned from the stove, she carried two mugs, and she sipped at one.

"Have a seat."

Finn looked at her. "You didn't have anything to do with what happened to Oscar, did you?"

She shook her head. "I wouldn't have poisoned the Hand."

Finn breathed in the smell of the drink she'd given him. It was like the tea that he'd had earlier, though this carried with it some of the minty aroma of the incense. When he breathed it in, he could feel his thoughts starting to clear even more. Considering how tired he was from the night before, it surprised him that he would start to feel this much better.

Esmerelda guided him to a sturdy-appearing wooden chair at the table near the center of the home. Like so much else in the home, it was mismatched, though when he took a seat, the wood seemed much more comfortable than he would have expected, as if it conformed to his back.

She sat across from him, resting her drink on the table, watching him. "Tell me what happened."

"That's not how I do things."

She frowned. "Tell me what happened and I will answer three of your questions."

That wasn't really how he did things, either, but he had a feeling she was troubled by what had taken place. "Five."

"There will be no negotiation. Three is the offer."

"Fine. Three questions. No holding back on the answers."

She nodded.

Finn started to think through what he could ask. He had so many questions about the hegen, but perhaps that wasn't going to be the best use of the questions.

"The agreement has been made. Now you will tell me what happened with the Hand."

Finn told her about the attack in the Wenderwolf the night before, not keeping any details from her. It was his experience with the hegen that they would know if he did, anyway, so it was better for him to share as much as he could. By sharing with her, he had to hope that she would reveal more with him.

"You found him along the table?" Esmerelda asked as he finished.

"He was slumped over. The mug of ale was in front of him. I gathered a sample because I didn't know what he'd been given but thought it might be necessary for me to know how best to help him."

"You did well."

Finn sniffed. "Oscar is usually better with this sort of thing. I was surprised that he would have allowed himself to get caught like that."

Then again, were the ale poisoned with magic, Oscar might not even have known. It was possible that he wouldn't have been able to sniff out the poison.

Esmerelda held the vial up and swirled it. It seemed there was something more in the vial that she could see, as she tipped it from side to side.

"He wouldn't have known," she said softly. "He should have been protected."

"If it wasn't you, then who was responsible?"

Finn didn't want that to be one of his questions, but if Esmerelda required it of him, he would have to take it. He needed to know so that he knew who to go to in order to question. Finn would need to find Gina, and then he would need to find the crew leader. Finding both would enable him to really get started with helping Oscar.

"I'm sure Master Meyer has explained there are other magics in the worlds."

"He doesn't really like to talk about magic."

"Most men don't, but that one more than others."

Finn started to smile. "Meyer can be practical, though."

"It has nothing to do with practicality. It has everything to do with how he sees the order of the world. Your Master Meyer views himself as directly serving the king, who in turn serves at the behest of his gods. In a way, Master Meyer serves the gods themselves." Esmerelda leaned forward. "Is that why you serve?"

Finn met her gaze. "Meyer might be devout, but that doesn't mean that he doesn't recognize the way you use power."

"I did not say it did, only that the hegen don't fall into his order for the world. He tolerates us, which makes him better than many. There are so many who believe we use dark magic to harm those without it."

"I think some of that stems from how you use your magic."

"What, exactly, do you know about how we use our magic?"

Finn shrugged. "I suppose I don't. You collect remains from the condemned and use them in your magic."

"There is power in death," she said.

"That's why?"

"There is power in life as well. Much of what you would call magic is merely drawing the power out of the transition. There is nothing inherently dark in death. It is as much a part of life as eating and breathing. All creatures die, Finn Jagger, and so we use that energy and repurpose it."

"You don't only use the power of death."

Were that the case, there would be more limits to their power. As there didn't seem to be that much in the way of limitations, then Finn thought there had to be more to what they did. While the city held its Blood Court often enough, there couldn't be so many dead and condemned that it would power everything the hegen did.

"Not only the power of dead. You are right. There are other ways of accessing and redirecting power."

Finn wondered when she would tell him that he'd used his three questions. He felt as if she'd been more forthcoming with him now than she had been before. Much more than what Meyer had ever been when it came to understanding magic.

"Who is responsible for what happened to Oscar Richter?"

Esmerelda leaned forward. She smelled of cinnamon and radiated a kind of heat. With her leaning as close as she did, Finn felt a stirring within himself. It was probably magically influenced, though Esmerelda was beautiful enough without magic.

"Is that your question?"

"My first," he said.

She smiled. "You do better than most," she said softly. "As to who is responsible, I'm afraid that I won't be able to answer that for you."

"Not hegen."

"The magic is not hegen in origin," she said. "And none of the hegen would have attacked Oscar Richter."

There was something about the way that she said it that left Finn watching her, curiosity flaring within him.

Why wouldn't they attack Oscar?

Finn knew he had some sort of relationship with the hegen, though Oscar had never revealed that to him. When he'd been given his card before, he'd needed to do something on behalf of Oscar, coaxing him into helping, or harming. Finn had believed they'd wanted him harmed, though even then he wasn't sure if that had been true. Esmerelda might have wanted him to be protected.

"If it wasn't hegen, then who attacked Oscar?"

"Why do you believe the attack was meant for Oscar?"

Finn frowned. "He was at the table. They used it to prevent him from helping me."

Esmerelda watched him. "Then it may not have been an attack meant for him."

Finn leaned back. The tea sat untouched on the table, and he lifted it, sniffing briefly and letting it clear his mind. His thoughts raced. "Was it meant for me?"

"I cannot say that, either."

"What can you say?"

She smiled, tapping the table. "You reach the end of your three questions, Finn Jagger. Is that how you would finish?"

He was irritated but could only laugh softly. She had allowed him to question her, but when he had called for his first question, she'd begun counting.

Was that what I needed to know?

There was more taking place than he understood. It was tied to Oscar—or he'd thought that it was. If it were somehow tied to him, then it might be more complicated than he'd realized.

Everything had started around the time that he'd begun questioning Holden.

"That is how I would finish," he said.

Esmerelda lifted her tea and took a long drink, looking over the rim of the cup at him. "There are other magics in the world, Finn Jagger. Some of them are stronger than others. The hegen have but one kind, the kind of magic that can redirect the powers of the world. It can be powerful at times, but trust me when I tell you there are other powers that exist that are more powerful. That is what you must fear."

Other magics.

"You mean the Alainsith."

The chancellor was in the city for the treaty.

Could it be that?

Esmerelda tipped her mug back again before setting it down and looking over at him. "I mean there are other powers. I would caution you about how you ask your questions."

"They have a treaty with the king." Finn didn't know all the details about that treaty, only that it prevented war with the people to the west. They were powerful and were rumored to have strange magics that allowed them to conquer much of the land. It was only because of Dayden the Conqueror that they had avoided war.

"A treaty, yes, but that doesn't mean all feel the same about the treaty, much like all of your people don't feel the same about serving the king."

Finn shook his head. "I don't need to get caught up in magic. I'm just an executioner."

She smiled at him tightly. "I'm afraid that is too late. And you are not *just* anything."

"Why?"

She set her mug down. "Because you have been involved ever since you were reborn."

Esmerelda got to her feet and headed into her kitchen, disappearing for a moment.

Ever since I'd been reborn?

She meant when Meyer had exerted his right. That had somehow tied him into magic. Knowing what he did of Meyer, Finn doubted that he'd been used by the hegen, but what if it was because of the job that Finn had been pulling at the time? He knew it had something to do with magical artifacts of the hegen. Bellut had wanted them for some reason. When he'd disappeared from the city, Finn hadn't thought much of it. He had run away, sneaking off in the night, something that was probably for the best. That way, Finn wouldn't have to try to arrest him. As much as he might enjoy questioning Bellut, he also didn't want him in the city.

Esmerelda returned and handed him a leather packet. "Apply this to Oscar Richter's temples."

"What's the cost?"

Esmerelda smiled. "There is no cost. To you. This will help the Hand, but the effect will be slow. You will not have him back with you immediately."

"But it will remove the magical effect on him?"

"Over time."

Finn pocketed the packet and got to his feet. "Thank you for your answers."

She walked him to the door and he stepped back outside, breathing in the difference in the air between her home and the rest of the hegen section. Finn really didn't know all that much about the rest of the hegen, only that they weren't all magical users the way that he'd once believed.

"Safe journeys, Finn Jagger."

He frowned but didn't have the chance to ask what she thought he might encounter as she pulled the door closed.

Finn passed through the hegen section and out into the open landscape before reaching the city. The Raven Stone and the gallows loomed like a promise of something darker, a threat or a warning that he didn't fully understand as he made his way back in through the gates and to Meyer's home.

CHAPTER TWELVE

The hegen card had changed.

Finn shook his head as he stared at it. It was almost as if Esmerelda were taunting him. When he'd left that morning, the card had still been blank. He was almost certain of that. Now there was an image of a forest with a path leading up to it.

Pocketing the card, he found Meyer in the kitchen.

"You've returned."

Finn nodded and pulled the packet out. "She gave me this." Meyer's brow furrowed. "There wasn't a cost."

Meyer got to his feet. "There's always a cost. Go and see what you can do for him, then meet me outside."

Finn slipped to the back of the home. Lena rested, her head tilted at an awkward angle as she slept. Her hair spilled around her and a bit of drool drifted down from her mouth. Were it another time, he would tease her about the way she looked while sleeping, but considering that she had spent the night worrying about Oscar, Finn didn't think that was deserved.

Oscar rested quietly on the cot. He breathed steadily, his chest rising and falling, and his slow pulse still had Finn concerned about whether he'd be able to survive that for long.

He pulled the packet Esmerelda had given him and unfolded the leather flaps. It was a strange, pungent paste.

Finn dipped his finger into the paste and brought it to his nose. He had no idea what might be in it, though whatever she had given him smelled terrible. It had a strange cooling effect on his finger, tracing up it, before leaving his stomach cramping.

He smeared it onto Oscar's temples the way she instructed.

As he rubbed it in, Oscar's breathing quickened for a moment, but then it passed.

That was something.

He rubbed the rest of the paste on his other temple. When he was done, Finn wiped his hands clean on Oscar's shirt and stepped back.

Other than the odor from the paste, he couldn't even see that he'd applied anything, it absorbed so completely into Oscar's skin.

He folded the packet up and stuffed it into his pocket.

Now it was a matter of waiting.

It would take time, she said. Finn would have to be patient.

He didn't know how long it would take, and whether

Oscar would start to come around later today or the next day or if it would take even longer. Meyer might have a limit to how long he'd be willing to have Oscar lying there, though Finn had never seen Meyer turn someone away who needed help.

As he started to turn, Lena stirred and rubbed a hand over her mouth.

"Ow," she muttered, sitting up. She looked around, her gaze drifting to Oscar. "He's still alive. Did Master Meyer have any different suggestions?"

"Nothing more than what we'd already tried."

"Something seems different." She scooted forward and then leaned toward Oscar, taking in a deep breath. She tilted her head to Finn. "You went to them?"

"For answers."

"Why?"

"Because he'd been poisoned by magic. Wella and Meyer both knew it. There wasn't anything that we would be able to do for him. I just wanted to know—"

"What did you have to pay?"

Finn shook his head.

"Then he has to pay," she said, inhaling deeply. "He knew exactly where to go when you were injured. I remembered when I went to the hegen for Mother how difficult it was for me to find my way through. All I wanted was a healer who might be able to provide something more than what we'd done for her. I didn't know if it would work. Gods, I think I doubted that it could. That didn't change the fact that I was willing to try. I thought that I had to in order to save her."

"You did save her," Finn said.

"I didn't. Master Meyer did. For a time, at least."

"I think he needed the hegen help." Finn had never asked him about it, but he had that feeling that whatever the hegen had given their mother had made a difference. It *had* helped.

"When we carried you through that section, Oscar knew right where to go. I questioned him a few times, but he never answered. The woman who helped you—"

"Esmerelda."

Lena nodded. "She knew him. Knew *you*."

Finn sighed. "I don't know what he owes the hegen, but they didn't make me pay this time. She said it would take time for the healing to work. I don't have any idea how long that will be."

"I will keep an eye on him."

"Thank you, Lena."

She leaned forward, resting her elbows on her thighs. "Having him here makes me think of Father. Do you know how long it has been since I've thought of him?"

"Probably a while," Finn said.

Lena looked over to him. "I feel like I should worry about him more. He's not gone. Not like Mother. But I don't think about him the way that I do Mother."

Finn nodded. "I don't either. I suppose that makes me a bad son."

"Having Oscar here only makes me wonder what it would have been like had Father never been taken away. What might our lives have been like?"

Finn didn't know. He hadn't given it that much thought, and he certainly hadn't considered it lately. There was a certain contentedness to the kind of work that he did.

"Meyer needs me. Oscar needs you. Keep him well."

Lena looked over to him for a moment before nodding.

Finn headed out of the office, down the hall, and met Meyer outside in the small garden. Meyer wore his deep brown cloak draped around his shoulders, and he carried the same staff that Finn had seen the night before.

"Are you expecting to find trouble?"

Meyer shook his head. "I'm not expecting it, but given the events of the last few days, I can't ignore the possibility that it might find us."

"I feel like it's my fault."

"You can't feel that way. We haven't talked about this before, but one of the things an executioner must keep in mind is that there will always be vengeful people. You serve on behalf of the king. You must always remember that."

Finn smiled at the comment, thinking about what Esmerelda had said about Meyer. He was devout, and everything he did was on behalf of the king and, in effect, the gods.

That wasn't the way Finn felt about his service.

Not that he felt as if he didn't serve on behalf of something, only that Finn didn't feel as if he were serving some higher power other than the people of the city.

"It all started after I began questioning Holden," Finn said.

"I have noticed that connection as well. Which is why we are going to visit him today. I think it's time that we have a joint questioning."

Finn frowned. He'd been working independently these days, so this felt like him stepping back. "A joint questioning?"

"We will question Holden. We will question this man from last night, and perhaps we will find answers that provide us additional insight."

"Then we need to find what happened to Gina, the waitress who instigated the attack."

"I already have the Archers looking for her."

"I don't imagine that she'll be easy to find."

Meyer shook his head. "I don't either.

As they made their way toward Declan, Meyer tapped the staff along the ground every so often, the sound it made like a steady march guiding them to the prison. Finn looked over to him, noticing the weary look in his eyes. He had forgotten that Meyer had been awake for most of the night as well, though he had been busy with different activities.

"Esmerelda offered me three answers in exchange for my telling her what happened."

"That is unusual."

"I figured. I've never known the hegen to offer anything like that. I tried to get her to give me five answers, but she refused."

Meyer smiled slightly. "I am not surprised. Even three is

significant. She must have been quite concerned about what happened."

"That's the thing. I think she was concerned but she also didn't want to tell me *why* she was concerned. It has to do with the magic that was used on Oscar." Finn lowered his voice and looked around, but he needn't have bothered. There wasn't anyone out in the street who came near them. No one would bother Meyer and his apprentice. "She seemed to think the nature of the magic significant."

"Did she tell you why?"

"I used one of my questions to try to understand. I wanted to know what was taking place in the city. If it has to do with magic, I thought that we should know."

Meyer looked over to him. They turned a corner, and the prison was visible in the distance. This was the part of the city where few people tended to wander. The only times that Finn ever saw many people out there were during the Blood Courts. Then there would be a considerable number of vendors and a crowd, some of them wanting to get as close as possible to the condemned as early as they could, as if coming into contact with them before they reached the rest of the city was somehow a blessing.

"What did she tell you?"

"It was more about what she didn't tell me. I suspect the magic used was Alainsith."

Meyer stopped. "Did she tell you that or did you make the assumption? With the chancellor here, and the treaty to be finalized, this matters, Finn."

Finn shook his head. "I don't remember. When it comes to asking questions of her, it's easy to get confused. I think she told me, though. I asked her why Oscar would have been targeted and she said he wasn't."

"She thinks it was you," Meyer said.

"She didn't answer clearly either, but why?"

Meyer shook his head. "It doesn't matter."

He quickened his pace, heading toward the prison. When they reached the prison, he unlocked the door and stepped inside, nodding to the iron master there. It was Pedran.

Finn tipped his head toward him and Pedran frowned, glancing from Meyer to Finn.

"We would see the prisoner Holden," Meyer said.

"Of course. You want him in the chapel?"

"Eventually. I would have you bring me to his cell."

Meyer locked the door to the prison behind them, and Pedran guided them down to the cell. As they descended the stairs, the stench building around them, Finn heard a soft and mournful singing.

"Who is that?" he asked Pedran.

Finn didn't recognize the words in the song. It was as if the halls of the prison swallowed them, leaving only the haunting melody.

"That's the rapist."

"Rapist?" Meyer asked.

Finn nodded. "I haven't gotten far with him. He was brought here not long ago. A highwayman. Accused of killing a merchant and raping his wife. I didn't get much from him." He grunted. "To be honest, I wouldn't have thought him capable of it, but then he tried to jump me. He's faster than I would have expected."

"Is that right?" Meyer asked.

Finn nodded.

They reached the lower level, and Pedran guided them to Holden's cell. The last time that Finn had been down there, Holden had attacked Jalen. He didn't want the same thing to happen again, though Pedran was generally more careful.

Holden rested in the back of the cell, his head lolled back and pressing against the stone. The cell stank. His brace hung slightly askew, as if he'd been trying to pry it off.

"Damn," Finn whispered. "Not going to be able to get him sentenced if he keeps picking at it."

Meyer eyed the splint. "That would be good work for most. With someone who's determined to stay here, you need to make sure it can't be removed. You might need to use metal bands around it."

Finn hadn't tried that, though it made sense.

"Holden Grimes," Meyer said, approaching the bars. "I am Master Henry Meyer, master executioner for Verendal. I am here to question you regarding your crimes."

Holden rolled his head around, making it look almost as if he had no bones in his neck as he looked up at Meyer. "I don't have nothing to say to you. I've said all I need to Shuffles."

"Your attack on my apprentice has not gone unnoticed. You will answer my questions."

Holden started to smile. "My attack? What about your apprentice attacking me?"

Finn stared at him. He remembered the first time that a prisoner had accused him of misconduct. He hadn't been working with Meyer all that long at the time, and he had worried that Meyer would believe the prisoner and think he took advantage of his position.

That was no longer a concern.

"Any questioning done in service of understanding your crimes is done on behalf of the king."

Holden spat and looked toward the ground, ignoring them.

"Open the cell," Meyer said to Pedran.

"I can get someone to help," Pedran said. "I heard what the bastard did to Jalen. Damn near ripped his head off, he did."

"We can manage," Meyer said.

He tapped the staff once on the ground.

The sound rang out like a crack in the confines of the lower level of the prison.

Holden even looked up, his eye narrowing a moment, and there was a different expression on his face.

Could it be fear?

Holden wouldn't be the first person to dismiss Finn but respect Meyer. That was what a lifetime of service to the king, a lifetime of uncorruptible service, would do.

The door came open.

Meyer stepped forward.

Holden lunged.

Finn noticed a flash of metal in his hands almost too late.

It reminded him of the spike that he'd seen in the cell after the last attack. He hadn't said anything to Meyer about it, though in hindsight he suddenly realized that he should have.

Holden nearly managed to make it over to Meyer when the staff came up, then down atop Holden's back, slamming him down to the stone floor. Meyer squeezed. When Holden stabbed with whatever was in his hand, Meyer kicked it away from him.

"Fetch that," he said to Pedran.

Meyer held on to the staff, pushing it down into Holden's back.

Pedran stepped over Holden and the prisoner tried to twist to get to him, but Meyer rotated the staff down a bit, grinding the staff into his back even more. Holden grunted but didn't say anything. Considering how well he'd withstood questioning so far, that didn't surprise Finn.

"It's a little piece of metal. Strange thing, too." Pedran held it down near Holden. "Where'd you get this?"

Holden twisted so that he could look over at Pedran, hatred flashing in his eyes.

"That's the second time he's had something like that in his cell," Finn said, leaning to Meyer. "When he attacked Jalen, there was something like it."

Pedran stepped over him and Finn took the metal. It was

shaped like a spike, with a sharp end and a blunted end. The metal gleamed. It would make for a deadly weapon, especially there in the prison where no one should have anything.

"Did you have that for us?" Finn asked, leaning forward toward Holden.

He glared at Finn and then pulled his head back to spit.

Meyer twisted the staff again, grinding it into his back.

"Let's carry him to the chapel," Meyer said.

Holden stank from his time in the cell, but he didn't try to fight. Finn stayed behind him, keeping his injured arm twisted behind him so that he couldn't rotate and cause any more harm. Holden tried to writhe away, but Finn kept his arm pinned to his back and his attempts failed.

They guided Holden to the chapel, and Finn and Pedran strapped his legs into the chair. Holden thrashed against the bindings, and Finn had little remorse about twisting his legs and forcing him back.

When they were done, Pedran glanced over. "Do you need me here?"

Finn shook his head. "I think we'll be fine." He looked to Holden. "I've got to see how this bastard managed to get ahold of that metal. Someone should have searched him."

Finn wasn't going to tell him that he was certain that someone had searched him. More than once, most likely. And still Holden had gotten a weapon like that into the prison.

He looked down at the spike. When he'd taken the other one, he hadn't really considered it, though he should have. It wasn't entirely uncommon to find contraband within the prisons, though in Declan it was much rarer than in other places. It was harder to sneak it in, and the iron masters were generally more diligent about searching for it.

The metal had a strange shape to it. Triangular with a sharp point at one end. The blunted end looked like it had been hammered flat, which was why it seemed like a spike to Finn.

"Where did you get this?" Finn asked.

Meyer stood behind Holden, working at the table with all the questioning implements. Maybe Holden thought that he would be able to get off without answering any questions.

Holden looked at it, the darkness that he'd seen in his eyes lingering. "There goes Shuffles again, thinking that he knows so much more than he does. Dancing around in things that he knows nothing about." Holden looked up and met Finn's eyes. "It's that kind of thing that's going to get you killed again."

Finn looked over to him. "What was that?"

Holden started to laugh.

Finn glared at him.

Killed again?

Finn had come to believe that the attack was because of Gina. Because of what he'd done to Leon. Could he have been right from the beginning that it was tied to Holden instead?

Finn didn't have any idea how Holden would be able to communicate with his crew. There shouldn't be any way for him to do so while trapped in the cell. Not without having someone inside who worked on his behalf.

"We are going to start with a few questions," Meyer said, interrupting. He carried a piece of cloth and a bucket of water. "I'm sure my apprentice has discussed with you the various natures of the ways that we question, but I thought that I should repeat it, in case you have forgotten. Today we're going to use a water technique. I will apologize ahead of time that it will be unpleasant, but until you provide the answers I'm looking for, you will face additional questioning."

Holden eyed the bucket of water. Finn hadn't proceeded to water questioning with him yet. There hadn't been a need, though it wasn't because Finn was above using water in his questioning, more because he didn't believe that Holden would answer with it.

Finn didn't really know what technique would be effective against Holden. So far, Holden had managed to tolerate pain considerably well. Perhaps water would be a better strategy anyway. With water, it wasn't so much pain as it was a fear of dying. A fear of drowning. Against someone like Holden, that fear might be powerful enough to convince him to provide answers.

Meyer slipped the cloth onto Holden's head, tipping his head back. He began to pour water onto Holden's face, letting it run down, filling his mouth, his nose, and overwhelming him. He continued pouring, letting the water run out slowly. Through it all, Holden tried to jerk his head back, trying to spit, but Meyer was persistent.

After pouring for a little while, Meyer released Holden's head. Holden gasped for air, and he jerked against the bindings, straining to get himself free, but there would be no way for him to do so.

"Do you have any answers for me?" Meyer asked.

"You didn't ask any questions."

"All I need are answers," Meyer said.

"You don't have much time left, hangman. All of this will be over soon."

Holden jerked at the bindings again, straining with them, and Meyer grabbed him by the back of the head, tipping him back once more. He started to pour water into his mouth again.

Finn turned away, looking at the metal spike. He raised his shirt, pressing the spike up against his skin. The wound had been unusual. He had recognized it when he had been injured, noticing how oddly shaped the wound was, which was part of the reason he had bled so much. Even now, there was a faint pink outline of where he'd been stabbed. It was enough that Finn could see the shape of what had stabbed him, though it wasn't shaped like any knife he had ever encountered.

It was shaped like this spike.

If he were able to look at his back, he suspected there would be something similar there. Finn lowered his shirt, looking over to Holden.

He gagged, vomiting out the water as Meyer finished pouring it into his mouth and nose, coughing.

Meyer leaned close, lowering his voice. He was calm. "All I need are answers."

Holden jerked his head forward, as if to strike Meyer, but Meyer was prepared for that.

He brought the bucket around so that Holden smacked his head into the bucket, and he cried out again.

Meyer immediately grabbed the back of Holden's head and began to pour water into his mouth and nose. He went on like that for a while, repeating the torture as he attempted to get answers from Holden.

Holden never answered.

Finn had not expected him to.

In between the coughing and gagging and vomiting, Holden somehow managed to laugh, and at one point he even turned his head toward Finn, almost as if he were aware of where Finn was standing, and he cackled.

Holden wanted to get a reaction out of Finn.

With Meyer, there wasn't going to be any sort of reaction. Meyer was too calm and collected to react to someone like Holden trying to taunt him. Finn could hear it in the way that Meyer asked questions, and he could see it in the way that he pulled Holden's head back, holding firmly.

Had I not been nearly as collected?

Finn had thought he was, but perhaps he hadn't been.

That might have been why Holden had believed that he would be able to get to Finn.

After a few more cycles of water questioning, Meyer released his head again.

"I will let you sit here a little while longer. We will return to continue with your questioning."

Meyer set the bucket down and nodded to Finn.

They stepped out in to the hall. Pedran looked toward the door.

"Did you get what you wanted?" he asked.

Meyer frowned. "He is a challenge."

"He's a bastard, that's what he is," Pedran said. "Do you need me to bring him back to the cell?"

"Not yet. We will let him remain there a little while longer and then come back to question him again. Keep an eye on him."

"What do you think he'll do, bound up like that? Dance?"

Pedran smiled, but the comment had gotten no reaction out of Meyer.

They headed down the stairs and toward the lower level.

"I'm troubled by what he did tell us," Meyer said. "That all of this will be over soon. If they have the chancellor's daughter—"

"He said something like that to me before."

Meyer nodded. "We may be running out of time." A dark frown creased his brow. "Come."

"What now?"

"I'd like to see this other prisoner."

"The rapist?"

"If that's what he is."

Finn shook his head. "I honestly don't really know what he is. He might be guilty of the crimes they accuse him of, but when you see him, you'll understand my question."

They headed down the stairs, reaching the main row of cells. Two iron masters nodded to them as they passed through, neither of them saying anything.

The prisoner's cell was near the end of the row of cells. All of them were similar. They were small, barely large enough for the prisoner to stand, and only a few paces in either direction. Declan Prison was designed to be difficult and uncomfortable.

Finn nodded to the prisoner.

He lay curled up into a ball at the back of his cell. From here, he looked thin and frail, though that was the way that he had appeared when Finn had questioned him as well.

"What's his name?" Meyer asked.

"I didn't even get a name out of him. He wouldn't answer any of my questions. At least, he didn't answer any of them in any language that I understood."

"What do you mean?"

"Just that. He speaks in tongues. The guards think he's touched by the gods."

Meyer grunted.

He pulled his keys out from his pocket, jingling them softly as he stepped closer to the cell. He cleared his throat. "My name is Henry Meyer, master executioner in Verendal."

The man didn't move. He remained curled up in the back of his cell without doing anything more.

Meyer had started to turn the keys in the lock when the man twitched.

That was the only reaction that Finn noticed. It was enough.

He held his hand out, resting it on Meyer's arm.

Meyer looked over to him, frowning.

"Wait," Finn whispered.

Meyer continued to slowly turn the key in the lock, moving it deliberately.

The man twitched again.

The door started swinging open.

Finn held his hand on it, watching.

The man lunged.

When he did, it happened faster than Finn could see. The only way he had anticipated it was because he had expected that something might happen. The man had been lying motionless, facing away from them, then twisted and lunged toward the bars faster than an eyeblink.

Finn jerked the door back, and the man slammed into it.

Meyer staggered back.

The keys dropped.

Finn kicked them back toward Meyer, still holding on to the bars.

The man stared at him, meeting Finn's gaze with a strange, wild expression.

"*Na'alani es ite prosh.*"

That was the same thing he'd said the last time.

The man jerked on it. Finn almost wasn't strong enough to keep it closed.

He strained, holding with everything inside of him so that he could keep him from getting past, but somehow the man was stronger.

"*Na'alani es ite prosh.*"

"I don't know what you're saying," Finn told him through gritted teeth as he tried to hold on to the cell door and keep it closed.

"I do," Meyer said as he jammed the keys into the cell and twisted. "And I wonder why he's speaking in Alainsith."

The man held Finn's gaze as he jerked on the bars, before finally letting go and sinking back to the ground.

CHAPTER THIRTEEN

"Where are you going?" Finn asked as he followed Meyer through the city and away from the prison. They moved past a series of closed shops, and the people on the street they passed all moved away from them. Most seemed to recognize Meyer.

After having secured the man in the cell, Meyer had been silent. Whatever he knew about the man had not been shared. They'd asked Pedran to return Holden to his cell without even questioning him further. They hadn't even questioned the other man from the attack like Meyer suggested he would.

Whatever he'd heard from the strange man had him worried.

"You should return to check on your friend."

"What?"

"I need to know what he said. This is something I must do. Return and check on your friend."

When Finn attempted to go with him, Meyer gave him a warning glance.

Finn stopped, then left Meyer.

What about the strange man had troubled Meyer?

Finn would have to wait for Meyer to return and share with him. If he ever did.

That didn't mean Finn couldn't see what he might be able to find on his own. There might be more that he could learn, only he wasn't going to be able to learn it standing there. He could return to the home and see if Oscar had started to come around, but Esmerelda had warned him that it would take a while for him to do so, and Finn didn't expect that to happen all that quickly. Which meant that he had time.

As he started away from the prison, he caught sight of Warden James.

He wasn't alone.

James stood listening to a tall, thin man with thinning hair dressed in the black robes of the magister's office. Magister Yolath seemed to be better than Magister Fol—so far. Finn hadn't had a *bad* experience with him, though the man *was* distant.

They seemed to notice him watching, and James looked over, flashing a brief smile.

"Mr. Jagger," the magister said. "I understand you and Master Meyer haven't managed to elicit the confession requested of you."

Finn frowned, noticing the way that James watched him. *Was this about getting information about Elizabeth Jarvis?* Finn supposed that he shouldn't be surprised that the magister was aware of the need, though he hadn't expected that the magister would bring it up here, of all places.

"We're working with the information that we have on hand and hope to have something soon." It wasn't that he felt he *needed* to keep things from the magister, but habit was difficult to break. Finn suspected the magister understood exactly what had happened to his predecessor, even if they had never spoken of it. Maybe he and Meyer had discussed it. Finn wouldn't put it past Meyer to have gone behind him and shared with the magister what they'd been through in the past. "This prisoner has been somewhat difficult."

"Then find a way to make him more conforming," the magister snapped.

Finn frowned at him. With his thin glasses that matched his thin frame, there was something about him that Finn just didn't like. "I've been—"

"You should know that Mr. Jagger has been most aggressive with his attempt to acquire additional information from our prisoner, though he does have another that has posed additional challenges for him," James cut in. He looked over to Finn and smiled. "I can't imagine how difficult the role of the executioner can be, especially with all that's demanded of them."

Finn nodded. It was nice of James to defend him, though unnecessary. "Between Master Meyer and myself, we are more than capable of handling the demands placed on us."

If he weren't careful, he could imagine the magister suddenly deciding that they needed additional resources. That was something that Finn very much didn't want to have happen. Not without having some measure of control over what those resources might look like.

The magister frowned. "There is an urgency here, Mr. Jagger, as I'm sure you're well aware."

Finn bowed his head in a respectful nod. "I'm aware. We should have more information for you shortly."

The magister glanced from Finn to James before clasping his hands behind his back. "We will discuss the concern you've raised at another time," the magister said to James. "Good day to you both."

When he was gone, Finn turned to James and found him watching the magister depart.

"That one is a strange man," James said, sighing. "I think they can't help it, though. They get assigned out here in Verendal, knowing nothing but the heart of the kingdom, and tasked with supporting the king's laws in a place where they don't always match up the same as they do in other parts of the kingdom."

Finn frowned. "The laws are the same throughout the kingdom," he said.

"The laws might be, but the customs change. Different places have different expectations. I'm sure you've seen that in your journeys out of the city. Gods, we see that often enough with those who live here."

They fell into a momentary silence.

"Were the two of you discussing our prisoners?" Finn asked.

James waved his hand, as if dismissing the idea. "Only briefly. I asked him about an opportunity for myself." He smiled sheepishly. "There might be a way for me to leave the prison, but it involves having the magister's help."

"I didn't realize you were looking to leave the prison."

The job of warden was a difficult one, but it carried with it a measure of respectability. He would have expected James to have wanted to stay as long as he could in a job like that.

"Not necessarily now, but I wanted to discuss my options, as they were. Anyway," he said, turning back to Declan, "I should probably get back. I have a meeting later today."

A meeting in Declan?

Finn didn't say anything. James *had* defended him, after all, and who was he to question how he ran the prison, so long as he kept it in line with the king's expectations?

"And I have a few more errands I need to run."

James tipped his head toward Finn in a polite way, then headed toward the prison.

Finn could return to Meyer's home, but something had been troubling him for a while. There was something more than what he'd learned about the prisoners—especially the strange man who *might* have been speaking Alainsith. James might have been able to help, but Finn doubted he knew the answers.

For those, Finn would have to go to the iron masters. Thankfully, he knew exactly where to go. It was a place he'd been a few times, and had become somewhat comfortable. Not the same as he had been in the Wenderwolf, but there was at least a familiarity about the tavern the iron masters favored.

He wound through a narrow street just outside of the prison, heading along it until he came to the Treble Coat tavern. It was a smaller place, a little bit dingier than the Wenderwolf, but it was where the iron masters of Declan tended to congregate. As far as Finn knew, they had been going to this tavern for years. Partly, that was because of how close it was to the prison, but partly, it was because of the serving staff.

When Finn stepped in, a hazy smoke greeted him. There was always a bit of a haze in the Treble Coat. It came from the fire in the hearth along with the long pipes favored by some of the men who came in there.

He looked around until he saw a familiar face.

Faces.

Andrew and Grady sat at a table, a stack of cards between them. Both had enormous mugs of ale set in front of them. Another iron master, a tall lanky man named Burton, was in the back of the tavern with his arm around a woman whose dress barely covered her breasts.

Finn pulled a chair over and took a seat.

Andrew looked over at him first. His hand paused while reaching for cards. He was average height and incredibly hairy, with great tufts of it sticking out of the end of his jacket. "What can we do for you, Hunter?"

Grady frowned but said nothing.

"I need to know everything you know about the strange prisoner."

"The rapist?" Andrew finished grabbing his cards and flicked them up so that he could look at them before sorting through his hand and setting several others aside. "What's there to know? The bastard came to us smelling filthy. Still smells filthy. Doesn't talk, and when he does, he don't make any sense. Makes up the words, I think."

Na'alani es ite prosh.

The words set in Finn's mind. He needed to know what they meant. Whatever they meant seemed important enough to Meyer to have him go chasing out of the prison to find something.

"Right. The rapist. I need to know which of the Archers brought him into the city."

"What's that matter?" Grady asked.

"I just have a few questions for them."

"The kind of questions they aren't going to like?" Andrew asked.

"Nothing all that exciting. Just need to know where they found him. Who he was with. That sort of thing."

Grady watched him. He was smart. Of the two of them, he probably knew there was more to Finn's sudden interest than he was letting on. Whatever Grady knew would be important. If he knew anything.

"What happened, Hunter?"

"I need to look into him a bit more than we have," Finn said.

As he did, he realized how it had to look that he'd come to the tavern asking questions about the strange man. They would have to wonder whether there was more to him that they'd have missed, especially as he knew the warden had had them question the man already. He'd spent some time in the tavern drinking with the iron masters before, but this was different. And it felt different.

He forced a smile. "We need to know where he might have come from."

Grady leaned back and pulled his cards forward, looking at them briefly before setting them back down. "You don't think he's just touched?"

"Probably, but seeing as how he was found outside of the city, we have to look into the possibility he knows more than what he's sharing."

Andrew shrugged. "You could ask Fetch and Pecker. They were the ones who brought him to Declan."

"I know Fetch. Don't know Pecker."

"Ah, he's a young shit. Thinks he knows what's what." Andrew glanced over, smiling and showing off a mouthful of twisted and yellowed teeth. "Not that he does, mind you. He's just a city Archer."

Finn smiled along with him. There had always been a strange competition between iron masters and the Archers, at least those of the city. Not palace Archers. Those were a different animal altogether. They served in the army, trained with the king's guard, which made them more dangerous. Deadly.

"Thanks. I'll check with them."

Grady took a drink. "If you really want to know more about the bastard"—everyone in the prison was a bastard, according to the iron masters—"you'd go and see for yerself what he did."

"That's too far to travel," Andrew said. "Nearly to Warsen, that is."

Warsen was a small village a few days from the city. "That was where he was picked up?"

"Nah, that was where he did the crime. The bodies were found there. The Archers snagged the bastard closer to Verendal all covered in blood. Made the connection between the two when they found the remains."

"So, we don't have any real confirmation he did it?" As much as it troubled him to think of the strange man as potentially innocent, he couldn't assume that he'd done what he was accused of.

"He was covered in blood, Hunter," Grady said, irritation slipping into his voice.

There were some of the iron masters who felt that he went too far trying to understand. When they had a guilty man, they just wanted him sentenced, anything to get him out of the prison if that was where he was going to end up. Someone like this man who was accused of raping and murdering would end up swinging.

He just wanted to ensure what they did was right.

"I'm sure you're right," Finn said. "Perhaps I should just talk to Fetch and Pecker."

"They're working tonight. Saw Fetch on my way here. Patrol."

"Are they partners?"

"For now. Not that Fetch cares much for it. Pecker is too much of a…"

"Pecker," Grady finished.

Finn nodded. "Thanks for your help."

He got to his feet as a waitress made her way over. Much like the one near the back of the tavern with Burton, her dress had slipped, revealing more cleavage than Annie would have permitted in the Wenderwolf. Not that cleavage wasn't allowed in the Wenderwolf; it was more that Annie was about the seduction and the suggestion. She didn't want it out on display.

"You're not staying?"

Finn reached into his pocket and pulled out a silver coin, setting it on the table. "Not staying tonight, but let me buy the boys a round."

Andrew grinned. A silver would buy more than a round there. It might even ease Grady's irritation.

"Don't forget about him," Finn said, nodding to Burton. He didn't think there were any other iron masters in the tavern, but if he'd missed any, he'd have to make up for it later.

The woman rested her hand on his arm as if to stop him, but Finn peeled it away. He'd much rather have the seduction than have it thrown at him.

"I have to get going. Duty calls."

"What duty could be more important than staying here with me?" she purred.

"Hey there, Delilah. Don't go holding the hangman back," Andrew said.

She jerked her hand back, as if Finn were tainted. "Hangman?"

"Apprentice," Finn said, tapping the table. "Take care of them, would you?"

He headed out of the tavern and paused in the street.

Now to find Fetch.

The Archers didn't have a set patrol. They wandered wherever they were needed. In this section of the city, they could be needed constantly. There weren't enough Archers to patrol and keep the violence in the city down.

Finn started through the streets, feeling as if it were wasting time. He didn't know how long Meyer would be gone on his errand, but Finn wanted to get answers as quickly as possible. It was possible that was a mistake. Maybe he needed to find more patience. That was what Meyer would tell him, he was certain.

Finn paused at a street light and whistled, low and with a flutter at the end. He had learned the calls the Archers used to summon help, though he'd known some of them before. Having worked with Meyer, he had come to learn they rotated the whistle schedule, so that he had to know which night they were on in order for him to use the right one. If he didn't, then his whistling wouldn't do a whole lot of good.

Then he waited.

It felt as if he waited without any hope of the Archers finding him.

Finn looked back toward the Treble, but he didn't expect to see any of the iron masters coming out of it.

Whistling again, he waited.

It was a relatively moonless night. Dark other than the lanterns stationed throughout the city. From there, he wasn't able to make out too much, though at this time of night, there weren't many others even out in the street.

A shadowy form appeared at the end of the street.

Finn looked along the street, expecting another, but it was only the one.

Not an Archer.

They traveled in pairs, at least at night. It was safest for them that way.

This would be someone else. Given that they were out this late, he immediately began to wonder if they were out there on some nefarious purpose.

Finn slunk into the shadows, looking along the street as they headed toward him.

They were coming straight toward him.

Finn stared. Something about the figure struck him as familiar. It was the movement, mostly. The crew leader.

Finn stayed where he was. He was near enough an alley that he could slip along it and run, but that wasn't what he wanted to do. The crew leader needed to answer for what he did, though Finn doubted that he would unless he could somehow incapacitate him.

How would he have known Finn was there? The only one who knew that he was there were the iron masters. They wouldn't have triggered the crew leader to come for him.

Finn had only the knife on him. Nothing else to defend himself.

He backed along the alley.

He didn't want to whistle to the Archers again too soon. They would have to be there, though if he whistled for them, would they even come?

Fetch and Pecker. *Where were they?*

"I heard you might be out," the crew leader said as he neared.

Finn remained hidden in the shadows, but apparently not so well the crew leader couldn't see him. There was no point in denying that he was here. The man obviously had either seen him or had been sent to find him.

"No help is going to come for you this time."

"What makes you think I need help?" Finn asked.

The crew leader shifted his cloak, revealing a sword.

Finn wasn't about to get into a sword fight with a crew leader in a darkened street. "You can turn away. Otherwise, you're not going to like what happens to you," Finn said.

"Like what you did to Odon?"

"He your bruiser?" Odon sounded like a bruiser's name. Poor bastard.

"I've worked with him for years."

The crew leader smiled, taking a step toward him. He

moved with a confidence that spoke of his belief that Finn wouldn't be able to do anything against him.

He could run.

He hazarded a glance over his shoulder, looking down the alley. In this part of the city, Finn thought that he knew where to go to make it to safety, but all it would take would be for the crew leader to run him down and stab him in the back with his sword.

The crew leader seemed to know that. He smiled at Finn.

Finn had been injured, and he was tired. He didn't like the chances he had of being able to outrun him.

"Your other man lives," Finn said.

The crew leader frowned. "Mennal was never much good at dying," he said.

"You wanted him to die?"

"I wouldn't have been opposed. He could be a right bastard. He never had my back the way Odon did. Can't having him talking, if you know what I mean."

"I'll make sure he knows that."

"No. You won't."

The crew leader unsheathed his sword.

Finn reached for his knife, whistling for the Archers again.

He had begun to think that it wouldn't matter. The Archers, if they were out there patrolling, weren't coming for him.

"Who tipped you off that I would be here?"

The crew leader chuckled. "You thought they all served you, didn't you?"

"Who?"

"The iron masters. They know what you are."

"If they know what I am, then they would have known that there was no reason to betray me."

"Once a thief, always a thief," the crew leader said.

The crew leader darted toward him.

He was quick enough, but Finn had some experience with avoiding attacks. Having worked with prisoners over the years, he knew how to slip off to the side.

He glided to his left, darting down with the knife and trying to swing around. The crew leader caught the knife with the end of his sword, and the blade went spinning away from him.

The crew leader spun around, facing Finn.

Now he stood in the alley, darkness around him.

"If you want to run, go ahead. I'll even give you a start."

"I'm not running," Finn said.

It wouldn't do any good, anyway. He wasn't going to get very far before the crew leader caught up to him. His only hope was that the Archers would find him.

Finn whistled again, adding a trill to the end of it. More urgency. *Where were the Archers?* Of course, if the iron masters had betrayed him, it was possible the Archers weren't there, anyway. That implied the iron masters were in on this.

The crew leader lunged again, and Finn was ready, twisting. Without his knife, he wasn't going to be able to avoid the attack, but he had to hope that he could find a way to trip up the crew leader.

He stepped back, and the man spun again. Finn ducked. The sword whistled just over him, barely missing him. He wasn't going to be able to go on like this.

The crew leader seemed to know this. He darted toward him, stabbing with the sword, and Finn twisted again, once more barely avoiding getting skewered by the blade.

He needed to get to his knife.

A sharp blow to the crew leader's side and he might be able to slow him.

As he backed toward where the knife had fallen, the crew leader slipped over to the side, cutting him off, a dark grin crossing his face.

"Not going to let you do that," he said.

Finn had no weapon. Nowhere to go. And it didn't appear that any help was coming to him.

He shifted his hands. If nothing else, he would block the blow and see what Meyer might be able to do to heal him.

When he moved, he felt something in his pocket.

The spike.

He'd forgotten he still had that in his pocket. Finn fished it out while the crew leader turned toward him, and held it out from him.

A flash of recognition came across the crew leader's face.

"Ah. Too bad Holden didn't get the chance to sink that into your side."

He darted toward Finn.

Finn hesitated.

He couldn't move too quickly. He had to time this right.

When he finally twisted, he jabbed with the spike.

The sword brushed through his cloak, getting tangled. Finn jerked his arm down, trying to trap it, and then jabbed upward, driving the stake into the crew leader. It struck his chest.

The man staggered back. Finn kept his arm pinched down, holding on to the sword.

The stake had entered the right side of the man's chest. Blood spilled out around it. The stake was sharp, and the shape of it allowed it to pierce straight into him. The same way that it would have pierced straight into Finn.

He cupped the spike.

"That went into your lung," Finn said as calmly as he could. "You're going to cough blood."

As if on cue, the crew leader coughed, and a glob of blood came up, which he spit onto the ground.

"You'll find it getting harder to take a breath. A blow like that isn't instantly fatal. Had I wanted that, I would have stabbed you on the other side. This one is a more delayed reaction. Now, if you want to live, you'll drop to your knees so I can help you."

The crew leader backed away.

Finn shifted his arm, moving so that he could grab for the sword that he'd trapped under his arm, finally getting it freed. He didn't know if he'd been cut. It didn't feel like it.

The blade was a simple steel sword. Not too heavy, certainly not as heavy as Justice, and it felt strange for him to hold.

The man backed away from him. He sucked in a gasping breath.

"There it is," Finn said. "You see, you'll find that it's going to get harder for you to breathe. You won't be going far." He took a step toward him. "Which iron master told you where I'd be?"

The crew leader's eyes widened.

"Fine. I can leave you like this. You'll bleed internally. Then you'll suffocate. It's not a pleasant way to go out. The alternative..."

He stood in place, waiting.

The crew leader staggered back.

Then he dropped to his knees.

Finn hurried to him.

The man tried to punch, but with him suffering the way that he was, there wasn't strength in him to make much of a difference. Finn pinned his arm behind him and reached for the spike, pressing on it.

The spike pushed into his chest. It would be painful.

"No fighting. I'm going to escort you to Declan. Once we're there, I'll remove the spike from your chest and do everything I can to ensure you survive." Finn pushed on the spike again. "Then you'll answer my questions."

The man groaned.

He quickly searched him and found several more of the spikes like Holden had in his cell. At least he knew they were connected. Finn pocketed them, ignoring the man's groans, and jerked him to his feet.

He looked along the street. There was no sign of

Archers, which was surprising, given how many times he'd whistled. There should have been someone who would come.

If the iron masters were responsible for what had happened to him, Finn wasn't about to go back the way he'd come. He didn't want them to know he'd caught the crew leader. What he needed was to take a different path, but most other paths would take longer than what he wanted. The man wouldn't be able to survive too much longer.

The alley was the only other option that Finn had.

He dragged the man down the alley, pausing when he neared his knife, and plucked it off the ground and slipped it back into his belt.

The alley twisted and turned, and he followed a nearby connection that would guide him back to Declan. At one point, he thought that he saw movement in the alley, but he wasn't sure. Pausing a moment didn't show him anything, so he continued until he neared the end of the alley.

Another figure moved in the street. Meyer.

Finn hurried out of the shadows, heading over to Meyer. Meyer stepped back, bringing the staff in front of him until he realized that it was Finn.

"What are you doing here? You were supposed to have gone back to check on your friend."

"Well, I didn't. I wanted to know more about our mysterious prisoner, so I went to the Treble Coat. I spoke to Andrew and Grady, and they told me that Fetch and Pecker were the Archers who had brought him to the city."

"That doesn't explain what happened here."

"This is the crew leader who jumped me earlier. He came after me again after I left the tavern. Which makes me wonder if the iron masters alerted him."

Meyer's brow furrowed and he looked to the side, toward the Treble Coat, before turning his attention back to Finn. "I know this man. Loren Thilson."

Finn hadn't heard that name before. "Is he someone significant?"

Meyer looked up at him. "He has a history of attacking women. He'd been exiled from Verendal about a year ago."

Finn hadn't been a part of that sentencing, which surprised him. "Unfortunately, he had a sword, and—"

"And you decided to stick a stake into his chest."

"I had to slow him somehow," Finn said.

Meyer grunted, slipping his arm around the man, propping him up. "I will take him to Declan and see what I can do. You get back to the house."

"I can help."

Meyer flicked his gaze down the street before turning his attention back to Finn. "In this case, I don't think that you should. Until we know what's taking place, we need for you to stay hidden, at least a bit."

"We should stay together, Master Meyer. It will be safer."

"I am not the target, but it appears you are. Now go."

Finn knew better than to argue with him. Especially when it came to this. He turned, heading back to Meyer's home, and when he reached the end of the street, he glanced back to see Meyer dragging the man along the street, heading toward the prison.

There was a part of Finn that wanted to return to the tavern and find out whether it was Andrew or Grady, but Meyer was probably right.

He needed to say hidden, at least for now.

When he neared Meyer's home, there was a bright light glowing from most of the windows on the main level. He stepped inside the gate, pulled the door open, and nearly crashed into Helda.

"I'm sorry," he said, stepping back as he closed the door behind him.

She had on a deep green dress along with a silver necklace. Her lips were a bright red. She looked lovely. "Finn," she said, smiling. "Your sister thought that you might be back soon."

"Well, I'm here," he said. "What are you doing here?"

That didn't come out the way that he intended, but she didn't seem to notice. Helda smiled at him. That was unusual for her.

"Your sister was supposed to come with me to a dance tonight, but she told me she was unable to. Something about someone she's providing care to on behalf of Master Meyer."

Finn glanced down the hall, looking toward the closed door to Meyer's office. "That's probably true," he said.

"Would you like to go?" She twisted the fabric of her dress as she said it, holding his gaze before looking down briefly and then looking up once again.

There was a time when Helda couldn't stand to be around him. It didn't seem as if it were all that long ago, even. The day they'd spent together had shown Finn a different side of her.

"I..."

"Is that a sword?"

Finn looked down, having forgotten that he still had the sword clutched in one hand. Both were bloodied from the Loren Thilson.

"Your hands!"

Finn forced a smile. "As you can see, I'm a bit preoccupied at the moment."

She looked up at him. "I understand."

"If I weren't, I'd love to go with you."

She frowned at him. "You aren't playing with me, are you, Finn Jagger?"

Finn shook his head. "I'm not playing with you, Helda. Unfortunately, my responsibilities aren't finished for the day."

She glanced back. "Maybe with you here, your sister will be able to come with me."

"I can let her know."

He moved past her, pausing briefly when he was close, feeling the warmth coming off of her, the scent of the floral perfume she wore, and inhaled deeply. If only...

Then he continued on.

When he pushed the door open, Lena looked up. Her eyes were tired and her clothing rumpled and wrinkled. A tray of water and additional powders set around Oscar suggested that she had been trying other ways to help him.

He lay where Finn had last seen him, though didn't look any worse than he had been.

"You're back." She quickly noticed the sword and his bloodstained hands. "And bloody."

"I can explain later."

She shook her head. "I don't need you to explain."

Finn took a deep breath. "I can sit with Oscar. You can go with Helda."

Lena glanced to the door, her brow wrinkling briefly. "I'm too tired, Finn."

"I can let her know."

Lena got to her feet. "No. Let me have a word with her." She glanced to his hands. "You should clean up before you sit with him."

She headed past Finn and out to speak to Helda.

Finn went to the kitchen to wash his hands, looking along the hall as he did, noticing Helda looking in his direction. He smiled.

He lingered in the hall a moment before heading into the kitchen.

A lantern there glowed brightly. Lena had everything illuminated tonight, probably to offer another layer of protection. He scrubbed his hands in the basin of cool water, getting as much of the blood off his hands as he could, and then carried the basin to the back of the home and dumped it outside. He would refill it later.

When he carried it back in, Helda was gone.

"You could have gone with her," Finn said.

"I know that I could. I think she would rather..." She shook her head, glancing toward the back of the home.

"She would rather what?"

His sister shook her head. "It doesn't matter."

Finn wanted to grab her and tell her that it did. Instead, he stepped aside as Lena headed toward the back of the home, returning to her vigil standing watch over Oscar.

After emptying the spikes from his pockets and setting them on Meyer's desk for study later, he headed to the door to the home, standing and looking out through the small window as he stared into the night, waiting.

CHAPTER FOURTEEN

W hen the dark form of Master Meyer lumbered along the street, Finn felt as if he'd been watching for the better part of an hour. There was no need for him to stay where he was. He could have returned to the office and sat with his sister and Oscar, but he had remained where he did because he knew Meyer wouldn't be long.

The executioner pushed open the gate in the small wall surrounding his home and headed toward the house. At one point, he paused and turned, looking out into the night, as if he saw something worrisome, before turning his attention back to make his way to the house.

"What are you doing waiting here?" Meyer asked when Finn pulled the door open.

"I wanted to know what you uncovered." Meyer looked behind him briefly before turning and motioning for Finn to move out of the way. "Did he tell you anything?"

Meyer shook his head. "Nothing useful. It might be a few days before he comes around."

A few days...

"If he's working with any of the iron masters—"

"I have taken care of that." Meyer stopped and regarded Finn with a harsh expression.

Finn blinked. "Were they released from their jobs?"

Meyer shook his head. "Not yet. I don't know the extent of the rot, and we need the bodies searching for Elizabeth Jarvis. She hadn't been in the city long before she disappeared, which makes the search for her more challenging."

More than challenging. The only leads would come from Holden and his crew.

Had they known who she was, or had she simply been unlucky?

"They haven't asked for any ransom," Finn said.

Meyer shook his head. "Nothing. Which is even more troubling."

He didn't need to say it, but it likely meant she was already dead.

Meyer moved past Finn and headed to his office, pushing the door open and pausing briefly as he surveyed the way that Lena had left everything. He made his way to Oscar, resting his hand on him briefly before looking up at Lena. "What did you try?"

"There was a mixture of burgot root and granerth I thought would be effective at bringing him around," Lena said.

"Interesting," Meyer said, lifting one of the bottles near

the table. "What prompted you to think of that particular combination?"

"The burgot is generally a sedative, but given in the right mixture, there can be a stimulating effect. The granerth should augment that effect."

"I had not considered that. Did you come up with it on your own?"

Lena lifted an old, leatherbound book and held it out for Meyer. "I wish that I could take the credit, but it was described in the Regelar text."

"One of my oldest books," Meyer said. He took the book from her, flipping open the pages and running his hand along the page. "The apothecary who wrote this is widely considered one of the greatest experts of his time."

"It's not an easy one to get through," Lena said.

"It isn't. There aren't even many physicians who have read it. Probably because they don't think there's much to learn from an apothecary." His tone suggested what he thought of that, and Finn had been around Meyer enough over the years to know exactly how he felt about the physicians in Verendal.

They were skilled—there was no doubting that. Training in the university in Evelar made it so that they were incredibly knowledgeable, but they were also difficult and believed they were the only ones who had the kind of knowledge they studied. Finn had seen apothecaries with incredible knowledge. Even a few surgeons who were more skilled than he would have expected. While their guilds protected them, they still were considered less than the physicians.

Then there was Meyer.

Before Finn had come to work with him, he wouldn't have understood just how skilled a healer he was. His work as an executioner and a questioner was only a part of what he did. The main part of his work, and what Finn suspected Meyer would consider the most important part, was the healing that he offered to those who came to him, a healing that was so much *more* than what Finn would have expected.

"If you would prefer that I not read it…"

Meyer smiled at Lena. "If you can work through it, then you should read it. I have a few others like it, but I wonder if I will soon run out of works to challenge you."

"I'm sure you'll find ways to challenge me," Lena said.

Meyer smiled at her, though there was a hint of sadness in his eyes. "Were it only possible for me to help you get into the university. You have a mind for it. You would have made a wonderful physician."

Lena looked up. "There are two problems with that, Master Meyer."

"Only two?" Finn asked.

She ignored him. "I don't have the money to pay for the university," she started. As Finn looked over to Meyer, he wondered if that were the barrier that Lena believed it to be. It was possible that Meyer would be willing to fund her education. "And they don't take women."

Meyer's brow darkened. "Fools for it too. They think the

only capable healer is a man. If the gods have gifted you, then they've gifted you. It doesn't matter what bits you have." He took a deep breath. "I need to have a conversation with Finn."

Lena flickered her gaze to Finn before nodding. "Of course."

She gathered a few things to herself and then headed out of the room, glancing at Finn as if he had done something wrong.

When she pulled the door closed, Meyer looked over at him.

"Is this about Loren Thilson?"

Meyer motioned for Finn to sit, and he took a seat on the other side of his desk. "Thilson is troubling but not so surprising. It was only a matter of time before you drew the attention of a crew that would decide they could intimidate you. Have they?"

Finn rubbed his stomach without thinking. "I wouldn't say they've intimidated me."

"What would you say?"

"I don't know. It didn't feel too good getting attacked the way I did."

"I'm sure it didn't."

"And I don't care for the fact that the iron masters allowed that to happen." It was more than that, though. The iron masters had not only allowed him to get attacked, but someone had been sneaking the metal spikes in to Holden. He could have hurt someone other than Finn.

"Did you think them your friends?"

"I…" Finn hesitated. Hadn't he thought that way? When it had come to his experience with the iron masters, he had tried to be friendly with them. He'd gone to the tavern with them before, shared ale. It was the same as he had done when trying to solidify other friendships. "I guess I did."

"Do you know what an iron master makes in a year?"

Finn shook his head. "I suppose I don't."

"It's a steady job; there's no doubt about that. And there is some honor in serving the king, so you have men who will take the work for that reason only. They likely think they can progress to something more, though it's rare for the wardens to come out of the guard pool." Meyer looked up at him. "Most iron masters make a few silver drebs a year."

"A year?"

Meyer nodded.

Finn made that in a month. When he was further along in his studies, and when he was able to charge for the healings, then he would make even more. Meyer had made it clear to him that an executioner was a well-paid position. A position that had more honor to it than he ever would have believed.

"How do you think they see you?"

"I guess I hadn't considered it."

"Do you prepare for how the prisoners will perceive you when you bring them to the chapel?"

"Every time."

That was part of Meyer's training. He had to be ready for how the prisoners would receive him. He was young, and he wasn't Meyer, so there were always those who thought they might be able to treat him differently than they did Meyer. He'd seen it recently with Holden. When Meyer had arrived, his demeanor had shifted, ever so slightly.

"Do you do the same with the guards?"

Finn shook his head. "I suppose I haven't."

"You *are* different. That's something you'll have to come to your own terms with. It's why I don't socialize with the guards. Or the wardens. As the master executioner, I have a supervisory role with many of them, and I wouldn't be able to carry out the obligations of the office if I were to treat with them like that."

Finn nodded. "I understand."

"Good."

"So, if you aren't concerned about the iron masters who were bought"—and Finn was, regardless of whether Meyer was—"what *are* you concerned by?"

"Your prisoner. The one who spoke in tongues. I recognized the language. I went to see what it meant."

Finn sat up in the chair. "Where did you go?"

"There aren't many who know the Alainsith language."

"Do you really think he's Alainsith?"

Meyer shook his head. "I don't even know. It's possible. Likely, even. I wouldn't have expected it, but with the chancellor here and the treaty..."

Finn knew so little about their people. Much like he had known so little about the hegen. Some of the Alainsith had magic. That much was known. Perhaps not all, though

Finn didn't know if that were true or not. "What did he say?"

"Do you remember the words?"

"*Na'alani es ite prosh.*"

"Very good. There aren't many men who would be able to speak them after hearing them once."

"I've heard them more than once. The crazy man in the cell made certain of it. What did he say?"

Meyer took a deep breath, clenching his jaw briefly. "He said: 'Release me or face war.'"

Finn's heart felt like it skipped a beat. "Could he have been the one who was sent to meet with the chancellor?"

"I have sent word to the palace but have not heard. Worse, if he *is* guilty of these crimes, then the king may have no choice but to sentence him."

Finn leaned back, thinking through what Meyer had told him. *Na'alani es ite prosh.* Release me or face war. "You went to the hegen to ask."

Meyer held his gaze and then nodded.

"Did they make you pay anything?"

Meyer leaned forward. "As you've experienced, there are times when the hegen will make a different bargain."

"She wanted information."

Meyer nodded again.

"You traded for it."

"When it comes to the hegen, you have to come to them in a position of strength, even when you want something from them. When you do that, you will find that they will be much more revealing than otherwise."

If Esmerelda had helped him understand what the Alain-sith man had said, then Finn suspected the translation was right.

Which was even more troubling.

"Did she say whether we really had to be concerned about war?"

Meyer smiled at him. "That's your concern?"

"I suppose he could be some random Alainsith beggar, but if he's promising war—and the way you're looking at me—that suggests it's something else. If he's Alainsith, and someone who can carry out his promise, then we're holding prisoner someone who might precipitate a conflict that we haven't had in…"

"Over several centuries," Meyer said.

Finn took a deep breath. "We could release him."

"Could we? We know little about the crime he's been accused of committing. We are the only ones who suspect he's Alainsith. The Archers, along with the guards at Declan, believe he's nothing more than a crazed man who committed a heinous crime outside of the city. Until we know…" He sighed. "We have the merchant's wife who shared explicit details of what happened. She's the one who brought the Archers to the remains of her husband. I plan on speaking with her"—that answered Finn's next question —"and then we have the man who was found with blood on his hands and body, along with one of the merchant's fingers."

"What will happen?"

"Word will go to the king. It will buy us time but may

impact the treaty. We must find the truth as quickly as we can."

He had never heard of one of the Alainsith getting sentenced. Not in Verendal in the time that he'd been working with Meyer, though he thought that he would have heard about it were it to have happened before then as well.

"Do you think him guilty?" Meyer asked. "You're the one who had time with him in the chapel. I have not. The magister and the jury have sentenced him, so I'm not sure that I will have that opportunity, especially if my requests are denied."

"You've told me not to make decisions based on how I feel about a person."

"Do you feel he is guilty?"

Finn took a deep breath. "When I first had him in the chapel, I would have said no. He didn't strike me as the kind of person who could do that crime. But then he moved." Finn thought about what he'd felt when the man had attacked him. There were a speed and a ferocity there that Finn hadn't seen before. "I don't know."

Meyer scratched at his chin. "Perhaps he *is* guilty. If so, then he must be sentenced no differently than any of our citizens, regardless of what threats he makes."

"You don't know, though."

"I don't know, and considering that you don't either," Meyer said, watching Finn for a moment as if waiting for confirmation of that, "I don't feel particularly comfortable about this."

Finn waited for Meyer to go on. There was something

more to what Meyer wanted to tell him than what he already had. That was the point of this conversation.

"Given that your situation within Declan is tenuous at the current moment, I think there is something more that you could do for me right now."

"What is that?" Finn asked.

"I need for you to investigate this man."

"You want me to talk to the merchant's wife? I thought you planned on doing that."

"I do. There is much going on here, Finn, and I think we must split our focus."

"I was already looking for the Archers who brought him to the city. Andrew told me it was Fetch and Pecker, which was where I was going when I was attacked by Thilson."

Meyer nodded. "I will speak with them. And I will break Holden."

"Then what do you want me to do?"

Meyer took a deep breath. "What I need for you to do is to see what you might be able to uncover about this crime. We must do so carefully. The chancellor and those with him must not learn how we are looking. It will be best for you to do so under the guise of having you gain experience." He leaned forward, resting his arms on the table. "It is time for you to take a pilgrimage."

"A what?"

"A rite of passage for many journeymen executioners. You have been apprenticed to me for a long time now, and it's time for you to take your pilgrimage."

"Master Meyer?"

"This will permit you to leave the city. A pilgrimage doesn't have to be a long journey. Simply an opportunity for the journeyman to gain experience on his own. I think a week will be sufficient. When you return, you will be tested to pass to journeyman status."

That seemed as important as anything else Meyer offered, but he didn't have time to think through the offer. "Now? We have to find the women—"

"The Archers will continue their search."

"And there's Holden's threat."

"I will continue to get through to him."

Finn didn't have much choice. That much was clear. "Where am I to go?"

"The villages of Torthen and Ferd have sent word that they have need for an executioner's skills. They are on the border of Alainsith lands, and the road you must travel is where this merchant had been."

"What is my involvement?"

"You will go, perform the duties and responsibilities of an executioner, and you will return to the city when your pilgrimage is complete."

Finn nodded. "I see," he said.

"Do you?"

"I do. I will take my pilgrimage and gain experience as my master demands."

Meyer leaned back, crossing his hands. "Do not take longer than a week, Finn. That is all the time we have before the chancellor is to sign this treaty. I don't know if any of the Alainsith have arrived already, but if they have, we cannot take any longer than that."

"I understand."

A week would take him away from the search for the missing women.

It would take him away from all of it.

Meyer had effectively distanced Finn.

"In the meantime, I will see if I can't uncover the depths of the corruption within the prison and find these women."

"And Gina—"

Meyer raised his hand, nodding to Finn. "I am fully aware of what needs to be done, Finn."

Finn inhaled deeply. "It just feels like the wrong time for me to be leaving the city. With everything that's going on, and everything I could help with, I feel like I need to be here. What if Holden and the corruption within the prison are tied to whatever is happening with this man?"

Meyer watched him for a moment. "You feel you need to be here because of the connections that you suspect. Those very connections are the reason that you need to take your pilgrimage."

"But you need your apprentice within the city, especially when everything is…"

Finn almost said *going to shit*, but he was careful not to curse around Meyer.

"Chaotic," he said.

"You are right. It would be beneficial for me to have my apprentice at a time like this, but it might be even more beneficial for me to have someone else."

"Who?" Finn asked.

"I need the Hunter, out there, chasing what others cannot."

Finn shook his head. "You know the truth about that," he said, glancing over to Oscar.

"I know what you try to tell yourself is the truth, but I also know the actual truth. You are dogged in your approach to understanding complicated cases. There aren't many who would take that approach to keep pushing and searching for information even when it's not obvious. That makes you valuable. Not only to the kingdom but also to those who have been impacted by these crimes."

"What if I can't find what you need?"

"If you can't find what I need, then perhaps this man is as guilty as he is assumed to be." Meyer leaned back, staring straight ahead. "And if he is guilty, then we cannot deny the city and its citizens the sentencing of such a man. If he is not guilty, then we need to ensure that we find the truth. Regardless of how difficult that truth might be."

Finn leaned back, and he looked over at Meyer.

He had been on his own within the city. Meyer gave him the autonomy to act on his behalf within Verendal, but Finn had never truly been on his own.

Under other circumstances, he would have relished the opportunity to leave and see what it felt like for him to serve as a truly independent executioner.

Not that he was eager to carry out sentences, but eventually, he would have to prove his capability, even if it was to himself.

"When would you have me go?"

"Considering how you have now been attacked several times in a short period of time, I think it is important that you leave soon."

"I doubt Holden would have his people attack me again so soon."

"Perhaps not," Meyer said. "Or perhaps he would. I don't know, which is reason enough for me to want to have you get to safety."

Finn grunted. "I'm not so sure leaving the city is getting me to safety."

"You might be safer there than you have been here. Take whatever supplies you feel you need to for a week's journey."

Finn started thinking about what he might need on a journey like that, and what supplies might be necessary, and realized that there was something he lacked.

"If I am to carry out the king's sentencing, there might be something I will need."

Meyer regarded him for a moment. "You are right. Come with me."

Finn got to his feet, following Meyer out of the room. He closed the door behind him and thought that he heard a faint stirring, but when he looked over to Oscar, he didn't see any sign of movement from his friend.

Meyer guided him to the end of the hall and to a closet. He opened it, pulling out a bundle.

"You will need this."

"You would let me take Justice?"

Meyer shook his head. "Not Justice. That sword serves the city. This, on the other hand, will belong to you."

Finn took the bundle, and he began to unwrap it. When he had it fully unwrapped, he realized there was an executioner's sword bundled within the burlap. The hilt was not nearly as ornate as that of Justice, but the blade was solid and appeared sharp.

He unsheathed it carefully, noting the writing etched along the blade.

"Where did you get this?"

"I had it made," Meyer said, studying the blade with Finn. "You showed promise early on, and I knew that eventually you would need to take your pilgrimage. An executioner can't take a pilgrimage without an executioner's sword. Garston made this blade. Once you become a journeyman, this will be yours."

Finn looked up. Garston was one of the most skilled blacksmiths within the city.

"It doesn't have the same age and history to it as Justice, but you can give it its own history."

Finn held the sword, noting the blunted end, the blade guard, and the massive hilt that required two hands. It was weighted very similarly to Justice, though not completely the same. He would need a few practice swings to ensure that he would be able to use it adequately.

"Thank you," Finn said.

"You are not only taking your pilgrimage because of what has happened recently. You are ready, Finn."

Finn took a deep breath, letting it out slowly. He might

be ready, but he didn't necessarily feel as if the time was right.

Unfortunately, that wasn't going to be up to him. Meyer had decided.

Finn would do as Meyer required.

Perhaps he would even learn something. Perhaps he would be able to uncover whether this man was really guilty of the crime as it seemed. And if not, then perhaps Finn would be able to uncover what really happened.

He only had a week.

Not long enough; at least, he didn't feel like it was long enough, but it would have to be.

"I will leave in the morning," he said.

"I think that is for the best," Meyer said.

Meyer turned away, leaving Finn alone in the hall, holding his new sword.

It would need a name much like Justice had a name.

He didn't know what that name should be but hoped that it would reveal itself to him in time.

CHAPTER FIFTEEN

Finn looked back at the city. From here, he could see the palace rising above the wall, stretching toward the sky. The heavens, according to the priests within the city who believed the king served at the behest of the gods. The various churches around the city were almost visible as well, though they didn't have the same prominence as the palace. For places that *did* serve the gods, that seemed an amusing contrast to the palace.

With the sword strapped to his back and a pack of supplies strapped to the horse he rode, he had all that he needed to take his pilgrimage.

It felt strange leaving the city like this. Stranger still that he would be going on his own with so much taking place within the city.

There was the concern about Holden and the attacks on Finn. There was Gina and her involvement in them. There was even the Alainsith man, if that was what he was. Then the deadline Holden had suggested. All of it felt as if Finn should remain to help Meyer.

Lena had understood, though she'd looked at Finn with concern. She didn't tell him not to go, but he'd seen that same concern after his attack, so he knew the reason.

It wasn't him he was worried about.

A week wasn't a long time. Not for him to do what Meyer asked, though it was long enough to get to the two small villages that needed an executioner's services. He had traveled for a while, the city behind him, trees sweeping on either side of hm, when he started to have an uncomfortable feeling.

At first, Finn thought it was only his imagination, but the farther he went, the more he started to wonder if perhaps he truly *did* feel something behind him. Following him.

The roads north of Verendal were generally safe, though the farther he went from the city, the less the protections of the city extended, no longer offering the same safe passage. He was a single rider, which would make him something of a target for highwaymen. Finn had enough experience with the crime in his part of the world to know that men wouldn't hesitate to take advantage of a single traveler.

There wasn't any sign of anyone following him, only the strange feeling that he had.

It was midday when he noticed the riders behind him.

Finn had been looking around every so often, unable to shake his concern. When he came across the movement behind him, that of the riders, he realized that he hadn't been imagining it, though they were still quite a ways back.

He kicked the horse faster.

Finn wasn't a skilled rider. He handled the horse about as well as he could, but the horse didn't care for his ignorance and seemed to take pleasure in shifting so that he slipped off to one side, nearly falling. Finn imagined the horse dropping him to the ground and then running off.

Every so often, he would look behind him to see what the riders behind him were doing but wasn't able to see whether they were giving chase or whether they were simply following the same path as he did. He wanted to give them the benefit of the doubt, but it was difficult.

After a while, Finn decided to veer into the neighboring trees.

The trees surrounding the road weren't so dense as to mask his movement, but he hoped they would be enough for him to get away from whoever followed him and let him see what they were doing.

He guided the horse deeper into the forest, staying there for a bit as he looked around, waiting for the oncoming riders to appear.

They never did.

His heart skipped.

Had they followed him into the forest?

He looked around, realizing he wouldn't be able to do much to stay away from any rider in the forest. Anyone with skill would be able to catch him easily.

Finn patted the horse. It might be best to get back on the

road.

They had started toward the road when he saw a figure moving in the trees around him. For a moment, he thought they followed him, but the figure disappeared, blending into the blanket of the forest.

Finn sat upright. If there was someone there after him, then he would have to look as confident as he could so that they didn't come at him.

That was hard when he didn't *feel* confident.

He continued moving toward the road.

The movement followed him.

They hadn't headed that far off the road, but now that he was there, he didn't know if he would be able to get back to the main road before whoever followed him reached him.

The horse lurched to a trot, as if concerned about what was out there. Finn clutched the reins, trying to hold on as tightly as he could. They neared the road. When they returned to it, he looked behind him but didn't see anything.

He kicked the horse to a fast gallop.

They wouldn't be able to maintain this pace for long, but hopefully it would be long enough that they could put whatever followed them behind them. Maybe he hadn't even been followed. For all he knew, it was nothing more than his imagination, but he didn't think so.

He turned as he rode, looking behind him, but found nothing. Could they be following him from within the trees?

Finn looked to the sides but didn't see anything.

Gradually, he began to slow the horse. There was no point in pushing the animal unnecessarily, though he wasn't entirely sure it had been unnecessary.

They continued at that pace. Not a gallop but something more than a gentle trot. It forced Finn to hold tightly to the horse, clutching the horse with his heels, keeping his hands squeezed on the reins. Already he could feel his muscles rebelling against how hard he held on. He would be sore when the day was done.

Finn didn't want to stop too soon. When he camped for the night, he wanted to ensure he didn't encounter anything. There wasn't going to be any way for him to make certain that he was safe.

As he continued, he again started to feel like he was followed. This time, Finn didn't see whoever it was, though he could feel something. The day passed without any further sign, only the vague feeling within him that he was chased.

As the sun began to set, he knew he'd need to camp for the night. Meyer had warned him he would need to, and he had planned for it, but he didn't want to take the break he'd need. Shadows began to move strangely around him.

That was *certainly* his imagination. He felt as if they were moving, as if they were alive. The horse seemed spooked as well, moving quickly, jumping every so often. It made it difficult for Finn to stay in the saddle. It was harder for him to keep control of the horse.

What he needed was a place to stop that he might be able to defend were it to come down to it. He doubted that he'd make it to the first village, even if he were to travel into the night. Meyer had suggested that he camp and come into Torthen in the midmorning, though would it matter if he came through at night?

The people there might be startled by his arrival. That was a concern. He was supposed to come as a representative of the king, coming so that he could prepare the king's justice. Having an executioner arrive wasn't common in some of the outer villages, though there were other journeymen who were able to travel and handle these tasks.

The forest tapered a little, and Finn slowed, looking around him. There still wasn't anything near where he felt comfortable stopping. When he did stop, he wouldn't be able to rest.

It might be better to keep moving. When he got to Torthen, he could explain he'd been forced to come straight to them. He could find a place to rest. It would be less likely that anyone would attack the closer he got to the village, anyway.

Having decided that, it made Finn feel a little better.

He leaned forward, holding on to the horse and trying to focus on the ride. He didn't want to worry about anything else. Just getting to Torthen. From there, he could...

There was a gusting of air from behind him.

Finn spun, looking behind him. He didn't see anything, though he felt something there.

Get to the village.

That was the thought in his head.

It seemed ridiculous he'd be nervous traveling like this.

He'd once wandered the streets of Verendal at night, pulling jobs and not feeling nervous about any of them. Why would he suddenly feel so nervous about coming out on the road like this?

The village wouldn't be all that far from there. All he needed to do was keep going. If he were able to maintain this pace, he should be able to make it by midnight, if not a little bit earlier.

Perhaps he could even get the horse moving faster and get there sooner.

His mind worked, racing through the thoughts of everything happening around him. It seemed surprising there would be highwaymen out so close to Verendal. The city itself should offer a certain level of protection, and that it didn't left Finn still surprised. Of course, the merchant and his wife would've expected a certain level of protection around the city as well, and with what had happened to them...

If he was already pursued so close to the city, how did he expect to be able to investigate the crime?

He rode for another hour with the ongoing sense of something behind him. Finn could feel it, even if he didn't see anything. That came from instinct honed on the streets, but he wondered how much of it was real.

Lights gleamed in the distance.

The village.

It wasn't too far from him. He thought he felt movement. Finn kicked the horse to go faster. If he was this close to the village, he wasn't going to slow.

He might even be able to reach it at a reasonable time, not coming in so late as to upset the locals. Finn glanced around him.

He had no idea why he felt so troubled. It wasn't only him, though. The horse had been spooked as well.

Finn breathed out as he stayed low, holding on to the horse as they raced toward the village. He had no idea what time it was, only that he didn't think it was midnight. Yet.

As he neared the village, the strange feeling he'd of being followed began to disappear. Finn even considered waiting, camping outside of the village overnight, but decided against it.

The entire point of hurrying like he had was to get to the safety of the village as quickly as he could. Now that he was close, he wanted nothing more than to reach Torthen and have a night in a warm bed. Gods, he would take a mug of ale and a plate of hot food. Anything to take his mind off the strangeness that he'd detected.

As he neared the village, Finn slowed. A shadowy shape outside of the village caught his eye. A gallows.

Torthen has its own gallows?

That seemed strange to him. Unless they'd erected it knowing he was coming. Even that seemed a bit strange.

He passed by it, no longer thinking about what he'd detected out in the darkness, now thinking more about what he'd be asked to do once he got settled into the village. The reason he was there was to be the sword of justice, to serve as the executioner, and he had to get his mind right.

That wasn't the only reason that he'd left Verendal, but

he still had a ways to go before he neared where the merchant had been murdered. Finn would need to find whatever he could about the merchant, but that would be beyond Torthen and closer to Ferd.

He climbed down from the saddle as he entered the village and began to lead the horse. There were still a few lights on in the village, though not so many as to make it easy for him to see where he was heading. It wasn't a large village. There were a few smaller homes on the outskirts, what Finn suspected were farms. They were spread a bit more widely than some of the homes he found as he got farther into Torthen. Most of the buildings were small, with thatched roofs. A hint of smoke drifted in the air, fitting given the cool night.

As he got deeper into the village, he came across a larger building. This was all stone, with a slate roof. For a moment, Finn thought this might be an inn he could stay in, but no lights illuminated the interior. As he looked at it, he realized that it was more likely to be an administrative building, probably the village hall. If that wasn't the local inn, then...

He found it almost directly across the street.

The building was two stories, smallish in appearance, but had a few lights still glowing in the windows.

Finn stabled his horse in the small stable outside the tavern before heading to the door and pausing to listen. He had experience with the taverns of Verendal, but what would they be like in a place like this?

There was a part of him that was eager to find out, a part

that was all too willing to forget about what he'd felt on the ride to Torthen. He hadn't *actually* been chased, and since he'd not seen anyone, he had to wonder if maybe it had all been only his imagination.

As Finn waited at the door, listening, he didn't hear any sounds from the other side. It was late enough that he wasn't sure if he should even try going into the tavern. He might startle them. Still, given that there was a gallows built outside of the village, somebody must have expected his arrival.

He tested the door, finding it unlocked, and headed inside.

The tavern was mostly empty. A fire still crackled in the hearth along the far wall. A few lanterns lit the inside. Tables were scattered, in various shapes of repair. He noticed one table with two men playing cards at it, reminding him of the iron masters at the Treble Coat. No one else was inside. He saw no sign of waitresses, tavern owners, or minstrels.

Finn headed inside and took a seat at a table near the door. He shifted, trying to get comfortable, before remembering that he had the long sword strapped to his back. Finn removed it, setting it next to him. He looked around the inside of the tavern and waited. If nothing else, finding a tavern with people still up was a boon.

Surprisingly, the door to one of the back rooms opened, and a waitress came out, frowning when she saw him, then headed toward him. She had on a tan dress that matched her wavy brown hair, and pale blue eyes that seemed to catch everything she looked upon. She carried a tray with two mugs of ale that she paused briefly to set on the table with the two men playing cards. When she reached him, she stopped, looking him up and down, and noting the sword resting on the ground.

"A visitor?"

Finn nodded.

"It's a bit late for a visitor to suddenly appear."

"It is a bit late, but I wasn't too eager to camp out on the road tonight."

"Why not?"

Finn shrugged, glancing over to the two men playing cards and the ale resting on their table. "I prefer a bed indoors."

She grunted. "We only have one room left. It's not the nicest."

"How many rooms do you have in general?"

"Three," she said. "Those two men took the other two."

"They aren't from here?"

She shook her head. "Anyone from Torthen has already gone to bed. Gods, I would have already gone to bed had those two not still been here. Master Bennington wants to make sure they're served." She shook her head. "That's what coin will do, though."

"How much for the room?"

"You'll have to talk to Bennington."

"You don't know?"

"It's his last room."

"I figured you would know."

"You would think so, but he likes to make arrangements like that on his own. He don't much care for me to do so. I'm just the hired help, you see." She leaned back, resting the now-empty tray on her hip. "Can I get you anything?"

"I don't suppose I can still get food."

"You can. I can't say that it's going to be fresh."

Finn smiled. "What about ale?"

"That's a bit fresher, though still…"

"Not good?"

"I mean, if you're thirsty, it's fine, but Bennington doesn't always get the highest quality. No need to, out here. He is looking for what he can get for cheap and sell for as much as possible."

"No different than any other proprietor I've ever met."

"Wait until you meet Bennington."

Finn grinned. "I'll take food and drink."

"Are you sure?" She arched a brow at him, shaking her head. "Like I told you, I can't speak to how fresh it's going to be."

"I understand."

She shrugged. "Your choice."

She disappeared back into the kitchen, and Finn sat watching the two men.

They were quiet, barely saying anything as they played out their game. Neither of them paid much attention to him. It was almost as if they didn't see him sitting there. Either that or they didn't care that he was sitting there.

Probably more that.

Finn leaned back, resting against the chair, letting his eyes drift closed for a moment.

When the sound of footsteps over the floorboards came, he blinked his eyes open. He sat up with a start, looking down to make sure that he still had the sword, before noticing the two men still playing their card game.

The waitress headed back toward him, carrying a tray with ale and a plate of food. It was a hunk of meat, maybe venison, though it was gray, and a pile of what appeared to be mushy onions and carrots. She set them both down in front of him, nodding to it. "I'm not going to charge you too much for these. Bennington is going to make sure he gets your coin anyway."

"Thanks," Finn said.

"What brings you to town?"

"Work," Finn said.

She chuckled. "What kind of work brings you out to Torthen? Are you a soldier? You must be a soldier with that sword."

Finn grabbed for the ale, pulling it toward him as he took a slow sip. "Not a soldier."

The ale was a little bit stale, and he appreciated her honesty with it. Considering what she'd said about the food, he wasn't anticipating that it would taste that great, either.

"If you're not a soldier, then why have a sword? Are you some sort of mercenary?"

Finn shook his head. "Not a mercenary, either."

She waited for him to say something more, but Finn didn't want to.

"I see," she said.

"Where can I find Bennington?"

"I already tried to kick him out of bed to let them know that you needed a room."

"Tried?" Finn asked, flashing a smile.

"Well, when it comes to Bennington and his sleep, he's a bit partial to it. Can't say that he's going to scurry down to meet with you."

"So, he doesn't want to rent the room?"

"Oh, I'm sure he does. He's probably lying there in bed, debating whether he wants his sleep or the coin. Knowing Bennington, it's a great debate. Maybe because the night is half-over, he'll give you a bargain. Then again, he might see the opportunity to gouge you. Probably think you're desperate, but then you *did* say you didn't want to sleep under the open sky."

"Is that what you told him?"

She flashed a smile. She was pretty. The kind of woman he'd once been drawn to back when he was still working in the crew. He supposed that he was still drawn to her, though the kind of work that he did now meant that there weren't too many women who were willing to spend time with him.

"Well, seeing as how I work for Bennington, I have to tell him the truth about the kind of patron he's got, don't I?"

"I suppose that's true," Finn said.

"We've had some shitty men come through here recently, and he puts it on me to screen them."

"Is that right?"

"You know, the kind of man who carry swords but are part of the army and don't admit that they are mercenaries."

Finn grinned at her. "Not a mercenary."

"No?" She nodded to the two men playing cards. "Those two bastards claim they are patrolling the King's Road. Not that I believe it. I can't imagine the king would have men like that guarding his road."

"Why not?"

"They've been drinking for the better part of the evening. Not a lot of guarding getting done in the morning, if you know what I mean."

"I suppose not." Finn took another sip of his ale before looking up at her. "Have you much need for guards like that?"

"The road has been a bit more dangerous these days, so I suppose it wouldn't be the worst thing for the king to hire extra help."

"How has it been dangerous?"

He wondered how much she might be able to help him learn about what had happened. He was the Hunter, after all, and though he had come to serve his pilgrimage and to provide the city with the king's justice, he also had come to try to investigate and see what else had been going on. Meyer wanted him to help determine if the Alainsith man was really responsible for the rape of the merchant's wife and his murder.

"Oh, not *so* different than usual."

Finn arched a brow, taking another sip of ale. "If it's not

so different than usual, then why would you need to have soldiers patrolling?"

Of course, *he* had been followed. The road *was* dangerous.

"Who said we needed it?" The waitress grinned, watching him. "Some fools are dumb enough to believe they're going to be jumped. I suppose this far out in the kingdom, with only Verendal before the edge of the king's land and the beginning of the Alainsith people, you might need a bit of protection. Not that I ever get out there to see."

"You don't leave the village?"

"My place is here. Bennington wouldn't let me leave, anyway. And if I did, chances are good he'd have hired my replacement by the time I ever returned." She glanced over to the table with the two men gaming, shaking her head slightly. "It's good enough work. Stable. Bennington might be a pain in my ass, but I can work with that. Especially when I get mercenaries in here who don't want to admit that they are mercenaries." She flashed a smile and nodded to the door opening near the back of the tavern. "That must be Bennington. See? I told you he'd be trying to decide whether he wanted sleep or the coin. Guess which won out?"

"Thanks for your help," Finn said.

"Help? Gods, I gave you food made yesterday and ale that probably has been sitting in that cask for the better part of a year. When morning comes, you're going to be cursing my name."

"I didn't even get your name," Finn said.

"No? That's probably because I don't want you to curse it."

Finn chuckled.

"Are you harassing my clientele, Bev?"

Bev shrugged. "Someone's got to while you're upstairs sleeping. Gods, it doesn't even help, Bennington. I mean, you claim you need beauty rest, but then you come down here looking like this."

Finn looked over to Bennington. He did look a little disheveled, with his graying hair standing up on end, glasses shoved up on his nose, though one side was a little askew. He had pulled on a long shirt, and had fleece pants and slippered feet.

"Well, when my clientele arrived after midnight—"

"After midnight? It's barely ten bells, Bennington. You just don't like to admit you can't stay up like you used to."

"A man my age needs his rest, Bev."

"Ah, you needed your rest even when you were a decade younger," she said.

"How would you know? You weren't even working with me then."

"I wasn't, but my mother told me how you could barely stay awake through the evening rush. You always made her work her nails to the bone because you couldn't."

"I never did anything of the sort," Bennington said.

"You did. Now you have her coming in first thing in the morning so that you can have your breakfast."

"She does make the best rolls," Bennington said.

"I know she does, but now I have to come here if I want to eat them."

"I don't charge you that much for them."

Bev glanced Finn. "See what I said? He even makes me pay for my mother's cooking."

Finn found himself smiling at the two of them. When she'd been talking about Bennington, he wasn't sure what to expect from the man, but she clearly cared for him.

"Bev wasn't willing to tell me how much you would charge me to rent a room for the night."

"Well, if it's only for the night, I'll have to charge you a bit more than I would if you were staying here for a few days. Cleaning fees and all."

"Cleaning fees?" Bev asked. She jabbed at Bennington with the tray. "Since when have you started charging cleaning fees?"

"I've always included a cleaning fee."

"If you have, you haven't paid the one doing the cleaning any of that fee."

"You get more than your share," Bennington said.

"Do I?" She jabbed him again.

Bennington raised his hands, fixing his glasses before grabbing at the tray. Bev jerked it back and he grasped at empty air.

"Fine. Maybe I could give you a little bit more."

"A little bit?"

"There are other people in town who would be more than happy to take a little bit," Bennington said.

"Do those other people have mothers who would also

move on? I'm sure my mother would be happy to sell her rolls somewhere else. Seeing what you charge for them, I'm sure we could open our own bakery. It might be easier, anyway. She's getting up early for you; she might as well get up early for herself."

"You wouldn't."

"I don't know. Maybe I would. If it's just a little bit."

Bennington shook his head. "Can we have this discussion another time?"

"You can be assured that I'm going to make sure we have this discussion," she said.

Bennington waved his hand, and Bev grinned. "Go and see if those two men need anything more."

"I'm going to see if those two men would go to bed," Bev said.

"We have ale to sell."

"I'd be careful calling it that," she said.

She sauntered away, leaving Bennington with Finn.

"That Bev. She's something."

"She seems fantastic," Finn said.

"She is. A fantastic pain in my ass." Bennington looked over, warmth in his eyes as he looked at her. "She tells me that you need a room for the night?" Bennington looked him up and down before his gaze settled on the sword resting next to the table. "Another mercenary?"

"Not a mercenary. I'm here to provide the king's justice."

Bennington's eyes widened slightly, and he pulled his glasses off his face, rubbing at his eyes. "The executioner. We knew you were coming. Didn't know when. The court doesn't share those details, only that they will make sure that an executioner comes out here to carry out the king's justice."

"I saw the gallows outside of the village."

"We had our best men erect them."

"Really?"

Bennington waved his hand, pulling out a chair and taking a seat across from Finn. "We don't keep up the gallows out here in Torthen that often. Not much need. Of course, when we get a crime like we did, the village council meets and needs to pass a sentence."

"I will be meeting with them in the morning."

"Why wait?"

"I don't need to awaken any of them."

"You already did," Bennington said.

"I presume then that you're on it?"

Bennington nodded. "Not many want to serve on the town council. It's not a glamorous position. Necessary from time to time, but in Torthen, we don't really have much to do most of the time. Not until cases like this come up."

"What happened?"

"I suppose you heard about the murder."

Finn stared at Bennington. Was he going to come to Torthen and suddenly find the answers that he had wanted to uncover so quickly? It seemed unlikely, but was that what Bennington was getting at?

"Why don't you tell me about it?"

"The poor bastard thought he could get away with it. Not from here, you know. That's the only time we really get crime like that. It's unusual with the locals. We've lived together most of our lives, and we understand the challenges of living here at the edge of the kingdom."

Finn suppressed a smile. They were isolated, that was true, but they weren't really at the edge of the kingdom. Verendal wasn't that far away.

"I can understand," Finn said.

Bennington looked up at him. "Where did you say you were from?"

"I didn't," Finn said.

"Last time we called somebody from the court, they came from Charen. Gods, but that's a long way from here. Figure it's easier to get someone from the court from Holaf or even Verendal, but it has been a while since Verendal has had the means to send someone to perform the king's justice."

"I guess you're in luck," Finn said. "Because I'm from Verendal."

Bennington regarded him before nodding slowly. "Ah. Then you're the apprentice. Heard about you."

Finn tensed. "What did you hear?"

"Oh, rumors of a new hangman. I guess there was a man in the city a while ago, but he got caught up in something."

Finn nodded. "He was my predecessor."

"Good thing you haven't suffered the same fate. Astonishing that somebody would decide to attack a hangman."

"You'd be surprised," Finn said.

"Why is that?"

"We aren't necessarily beloved."

"Who needs to love their hangman? It's a job, though. No different than mine. Or Bev's. A job means pay. More honorable than some," he said, looking over toward the mercenaries.

"Can you tell me anything about them?"

"What's there to say? We get crime along the King's Road. It's a bit more common than crime here in Torthen. Never really had much in the way of mercenaries out here. That's something new."

"I see."

"I'll be honest, I didn't think much of it. Thought they might've been overreacting. Then we ended up with Leland Volt."

"That's who I'm here for?" All the details Finn had were the towns he was to visit, not names. That was typical for these journeys, from what he'd seen with Meyer.

"Right. The bastard thought to come to Torthen and continue his little crime spree." Bennington sat up, shifting his shirt. "Didn't expect that we'd be the ones to stop him."

Finn didn't say that he couldn't blame anyone for not expecting that they would be stopped in Torthen. It would be unusual for anyone to expect to have trouble in a place like Torthen. The village wasn't very large, and it would be easy enough to hide evidence of any previous crime by coming to the village.

"You haven't said what you'd charge for the room."

Bennington rubbed his eyes before slipping his glasses back onto his face. "I'm sure Bev told you all that."

"She made it clear that you're the one who decides whether the room would get rented, and at what rate."

"Is that right? She really does listen." He glanced toward where Bev stood in the back of the tavern, watching Finn and Bennington. "I have the one room left. We don't have much in Torthen, but what I've got are fairly nice. I'm sure you will find the accommodations to your liking."

"How much?"

"You're here in service to the king, so I can give you a bargain. One silver for the night."

Finn leaned toward Bennington. "Seeing as how I'm here in service of the king and to offer sentencing for the criminal Leland Volt, I will pay no more than half that. You're lucky I'm willing to do even that much."

Bennington shifted in his seat and started to sit up. "I'm sure you won't have much luck finding alternative arrangements, especially at this time of night."

Finn got to his feet and he started toward the door.

Bennington held up his hands. "Don't go, Mr. Jagger. I'm sure we can work out a bargain. A half-silver. I think that's reasonable."

Finn nodded. "Very good. You can take that out of my fee."

"Your fee?"

Finn frowned, tilting his head to the side. "You didn't think I worked for free, did you?"

Bennington watched him.

Finn didn't know what was reasonable to ask for payment, but Meyer had made it clear that he *would* be paid for coming out. He claimed that during his apprenticeship he could often make more in one week traveling the countryside than he could in several months. Finn had seen how much Meyer charged in previous visits.

That gave Finn a little idea about how much the services were worth. Enough that he had a starting point. Seeing that he had a member of the town council in front of him, he knew that he would have an opportunity to get paid.

"How much do your services cost?"

"Five silvers per."

Bennington sputtered. "Five? The last executioner we summoned..."

Finn watched him. "Yes?"

Bennington started to smile, though there remained a hint of irritation. "I suppose your fee is warranted. A man like yourself must have training."

"I must," Finn agreed.

"Very well. Five silvers. Minus your room cost."

Finn nodded. "Thank you. I assume Bev will show me to my room?"

Bennington got to his feet and motioned to her. "You said Master Meyer is your mentor?"

Finn wasn't sure that he had, but he nodded anyway.

"Figures."

"Why is that?"

"He always believed that he was worth more than the others too."

"We're worth what you'll pay," Finn said. "Much like your room."

CHAPTER SIXTEEN

Finn stood outside of the tavern, looking up at the overcast sky. He wasn't as well rested as he would have liked, but having a bed to sleep in was better than the alternative. There was some activity in the village this morning. An energy. It was familiar to him, though a little bit different from what he would have felt in Verendal.

The Blood Court.

Word of his arrival had spread. Even though it was early, somehow word had gotten out that he had come to the village and would be exacting the king's justice today. He shouldn't be surprised, especially in a small village like this. Even in Verendal, word got around quickly.

Finn returned to the tavern and took a seat at one of the empty tables. There were many. Only two other people were up and seated in the tavern at that time of the morning, neither of them the mercenaries that he'd seen the night before. Bev was probably right that they wouldn't be getting up all that early.

An older woman smiled at him. She had a stooped back and a faded brown apron tied around her waist, but her eyes flashed with the same amusement that he'd seen from Bev. Though she was older, she had the same wavy brown hair and pale blue eyes as Bev, and there was no doubt that they were related.

"You must be the executioner," she said.

Finn nodded. "And you must be Bev's mother."

"Did she tell you that?"

"There was a discussion about the quality of your rolls."

The older woman smiled. "Bev has always loved them. Bennington too, though he doesn't like to admit that."

"Why wouldn't he admit it?"

"He thinks that sharing would only increase my cost to him. Probably concerned I'd start my own bakery."

I wonder where he would get that idea.

"I'd love to try them if you have any this morning."

"Ah, for a man coming to exact the king's justice, I can make sure you have whatever you need. Can't have you running out of energy when you're supposed to be working."

She tottered off and Finn settled in at the table, looking over briefly to the two others in the tavern. They were well dressed, both men in jacket and pants, hair neatly combed. It was too early for them to be there, he suspected, which left him thinking they were part of the village council.

He didn't say anything, rather just sitting at the table and waiting until food was brought out to him.

"I didn't catch your name," Finn said when she placed the tray in front of him.

"I'm Mariah. Most around here call me May."

Finn could smell the sweetness of the roll. A delicious-looking frosting coated the top, and she'd set two hard-boiled eggs alongside it, with two smaller sausages. His stomach rumbled immediately at the plate.

She left him to his breakfast and Finn ate in silence, enjoying the flavor of the food. Mariah really was a good cook.

When he had finished his plate, one of the men from the nearby table got to his feet and made his way over to Finn, stopping about three paces away, his hands clasped in front of him. He had a thin beard and mustache that he'd oiled down, as if it would make it look less ridiculous.

"You're the hangman?"

Finn looked up and forced a smile. He *had* come intending to work, so he might as well get to it. This was as much a part of the reason that Meyer had sent him from the city as investigating the murder along the King's Road.

"Finn Jagger," he said. He got to his feet.

"I'm sure you've heard all about the criminal."

"Some," Finn said. "I would prefer to have a chance to question him myself."

"Yourself? You do understand he's been sentenced by the council."

Finn had expected a reaction like that. Meyer had

proven to him that it wouldn't be uncommon for there to be a bit of resistance to the idea that he would ask his own questions.

Partly that was because many of these villages had to enact their own judgment, and they weren't accustomed to having somebody working on behalf of the king coming and asking additional questions. Finn still worried that if he didn't ask his own questions, he wouldn't feel comfortable with everything that he uncovered. It was simply part of the job.

Finn nodded to the man. "I am fully aware that he has been sentenced. That is why you have requested the services of the king's executioner."

"Indeed," he said. "Is it typical for you to question a prisoner yourself?"

"In Verendal, I perform most of the questioning," Finn said.

"Interesting. You don't have your magister do that?"

Finn could only imagine how the magister might react if he were expected to perform the questioning of all of their prisoners. The new magister, especially. He probably wouldn't do well with it.

"He has a better use of his time," Finn said.

"I suppose that's true. In the larger cities, there is no need to waste the time of one's betters."

Finn frowned. *Betters?* Perhaps he had misread this man. Maybe he wouldn't end up liking him.

"Would you like to bring me to your prisoner?" Finn asked.

The man watched him for a moment, and to his credit, it seemed as if he realized that he had said something that offended Finn, though even recognizing it, he still didn't show any remorse.

The man bobbed his head. "Of course. I will take you to him."

Finn looked around the tavern, though the other man who'd been sitting at the table with him hadn't gotten up. Finn had thought that they worked together on the council, though maybe he'd been wrong.

He followed him out of the tavern and along the street.

"Have you been to Torthen before?" the councilor asked, guiding Finn away from where he'd come into the village the night before.

Finn glanced in that direction, wondering if his imagination would bring a renewed threat to him this morning, or if there was truly nothing there for him to be concerned about.

"I have not."

"You'll find that we are a pleasant people. We like our quiet. Of course, that's why so many of us stay here rather than in Garamand."

Finn frowned. *The capital rather than Verendal?* That surprised him. There wouldn't be much reason for the people to think of Garamand first. It was far enough away that it would take the better part of two weeks to reach by horseback. Not at all like Verendal, which was only a day.

"Is that right?" Finn asked.

280 | D.K. HOLMBERG

"We do appreciate it when we get visitors from that way, of course. I'm sure you feel the same way in Verendal."

Finn started to smile. "Have you been to Verendal?"

The councilor glanced back, his nose wrinkled. "There is no need for me to visit Verendal. Not when everything that I need is right here or in Garamand."

The comment amused him. *Could the people of Torthen really believe themselves above the people of Verendal?*

"You haven't visited even when the king comes through?"

"Ah, well, there is some appeal in trying to see the king. We catch glimpses of him here, you know. Near the King's Road, his caravan comes this direction, but he keeps it well guarded when he travels, preventing anyone from getting too close to him."

Finn nodded, making it seem as if he knew.

They had turned a corner and were now heading down a wide street. The edge of village loomed into view. He didn't see anything else beyond it.

"You have your prison on this side of the village?" Finn asked.

"Of course. We don't want our prisoners to have the opportunity to run along the King's Road if they were to escape."

Finn glanced back. It wasn't as if this side of the village offered *that* much in the way of protection. Whoever was imprisoned would be able to easily sneak out and around, and from there they could disappear into the forest.

That would be what he would do were he captured.

"You have the gallows on the other side of the village."

"We wouldn't want to deprive the people of the festival," he said.

Finn grunted. Even there, they wanted a gallows festival.

He followed the councilor as they made their way along the street, heading to the outskirts of the village. When they reached it, Finn recognized the prison—if that's what it could be called—at once.

It was a simple building. Small and made of stout stone, and even had there not been a man standing guard, sword sheathed at his hip, Finn would have recognized it as the prison. They had iron masters even out there. Maybe they would betray him the same way that the iron masters in Verendal had betrayed him.

Finn pushed those thoughts away.

The man leading him nodded to the guard. "Toby has been with us for many years. He has served the town quite diligently," he said. He nodded to Toby.

Finn looked over to him. Toby was balding, a little pudgy, and with eyes that seemed too closely set together. There was nothing intimidating about him other than the sword he carried. Even in that, Finn doubted he had much skill with the blade.

"Everyone needs to have their way of serving," Finn said.

"Indeed," the councilor said. "Toby, if you don't mind, would you do us the favor of unlocking the door?"

Toby fished out a ring of keys, and he slipped it into the lock, twisting it. Finn suppressed a smile.

He wasn't sure what to expect, but inside the building

was a row of wooden bars. A man on the other side of the bars looked up, his eyes wild. He had a thick beard and shaggy black hair. He was dirty and he stunk. The stench hit Finn the most.

"You haven't tried to clean him?" Finn asked.

"There is no need to clean him."

"All men get the opportunity to come to the gods as redeemed," Finn said.

He doubted they would even recognize the slight.

"We will get him cleaned before he goes to his sentencing," the councilor said.

"Hmm. You have a priest? Someone who serves Heleth?"

"Is there a need?"

Finn nodded slowly. "When did you say the last execution that you've had here was?"

"We didn't, but it has been a little while."

"How long is a little while?"

"About ten years ago," he said.

Ten years.

Ten years wasn't so long that they shouldn't know the tradition. They should still understand that they had an obligation to offer the condemned a chance at redemption.

"Do you have any priests?"

"Well…" the councilor started.

"We have one," Toby said.

Finn looked over to Toby. "Go fetch your priest," he said. Toby looked to the councilor for confirmation, and Finn just shook his head. "Go."

Toby marched off.

"Are you sure that's wise?"

Finn approached the wooden bars, studying the man inside. "You can pull the door closed. If you would like to stand watch, you certainly may."

"This is most unusual," the councilor said.

Finn grunted. "All of this is most unusual," he said.

The councilor pulled the door closed, sealing Finn inside.

He would prefer not to have the stench to deal with, but it was better to have the councilor outside and not in the room with Finn. He didn't care much for him.

Finn studied the man.

"What's your name?"

The man looked up, watching him.

Finn avoided taking a deep breath, thinking through what Meyer would have wanted for him. Meyer had wanted Finn to represent the king's justice honorably. That meant doing the same job that Meyer would have done, were he there. Finn had plenty of experience questioning men, so he didn't feel uncomfortable with what was expected of him, only he didn't have the necessary equipment there, were the man to refuse to answer.

"My name is Finn Jagger, executioner for King Porman. I am here to carry out your sentence."

"Then do what you must," the man said.

He had a deep, almost scarred voice. There was an accent to it that Finn couldn't place.

"What is your name?"

"They didn't tell you?"

"They told me. I find it best to ask the questions as well."

The man grunted. "You believe you will find out something they did not."

"Yes."

He looked up at Finn, and his brow furrowed in a deep frown. "You won't find what you're looking for."

Finn glanced to either side of him, finding a small wooden stool, and pulled it over to take a seat on it. "How do you know what I'm looking for?"

"You want to convict me."

"You believe yourself to be innocent?"

"Don't all men?"

Finn started to smile. "No. Many know what they've done. When it comes to the end of their days and to their sentencing, most atone for their crimes and look to the gods for forgiveness."

"The gods don't offer forgiveness. Even if they did, I don't want what they have to offer."

Finn shifted on the stool, watching the man. It was a surprising conversation to have with him. "Tell me what you would want for them to offer."

The man shuffled on the ground, moving his legs around. "Release."

"Release from what?" He turned away from Finn. "Do you deny your name is Leland Volt?"

"That's what they tell me."

"You don't know?"

He looked up. A flicker of a question skimmed across his

eyes, but then was gone. "What is there to know? I have gone by many names."

"Which one were you given?"

"All of them."

Finn studied him. How would he get the answers he needed? Shifting the conversation might help, but he wasn't entirely certain it would.

"Which one do you claim?"

"All of them."

"Then you are Leland Volt."

"If you must have a title. What is yours?"

Finn shrugged. "I've gone by many, but I try to use the name given to me upon my birth."

"I don't know mine."

"How is it that you don't know the name given to you at your birth?"

"I don't remember anything from my birth," he said.

"No one decided to tell you the name you were given?"

"They may have told me, but what if they are wrong?"

"You think your parents would lie to you about your name?"

"Yes," he said. "What purpose would there be in telling the truth?"

"I suppose they would want to tell you the truth so that you could know who you are meant to be."

"And how do you know what I'm meant to be?"

Finn regarded him, shifting the stool.

He had a feeling from this man that he would be able to get answers from him without needing to resort to a different sort of questioning, but would they be the answers he wanted? He couldn't tell. He didn't know if this man was merely trying to waste his time or if this truly was who he was.

"Do you know what you are accused of doing?"

"They didn't tell you?"

"I find it best to ask the accused," Finn said.

"Do you believe I will tell you something more than what they told you?"

"There are many reasons for asking you myself," Finn said. "Partly, you may have a different understanding of what you did than what they have accused you of."

"That's not why you are asking me," he said.

"Why am I asking you?"

"You want me to convict myself."

"You think that you would by sharing with me what you are accused of?"

"I think you will try to warp whatever I say to fit whatever narrative you've decided upon."

"I haven't decided upon any narrative."

"You wouldn't be here if there wasn't already a narrative about me."

"Perhaps," Finn said. "It doesn't change the fact I still need to make up my own mind."

"When you do, what changes for me?"

"It's possible I would choose not to carry out the sentencing the village council has recommended."

"How often does that actually happen?"

"I don't know. I haven't been sent outside of the city very often."

"This is your first execution?"

Finn shook his head. "Not my first. Outside of the city," he said. Alone, at least.

"Then I truly am blessed," he said.

"I cannot say I don't have the necessary skill, nor does it mean I don't have the necessary experience. I've been serving as a king's executioner for the better part of five years."

"And do you believe that those five years has made you an expert?"

"It has made me enough of an expert I'm permitted to carry out the king's justice."

He grunted, shaking his head. "What happens if I don't recognize the king's justice?"

"It's your prerogative. You prefer not to tell me what you are accused of?"

"As I've said, it won't change anything."

"Possibly not," Finn said. "I won't lie to you and tell you that you sharing with me what you are accused of having done will sway me. What I will tell you is that I have quite a bit of experience speaking to men such as yourself."

"Men in prison?"

"In prison. In other situations," Finn said. "And I have found that often the story is not quite the way it's initially presented," Finn said.

"You wouldn't believe my story," he said.

"Are you so certain?"

"Certain enough to know it's unlikely you'll listen."

Finn stared at him for a moment. "Unfortunately, if you don't speak on your behalf, the only testimony that I have then becomes that of the village."

"Is that enough to convict?"

"Generally, I would say no, but seeing as how the king saw fit to send me here to carry out his justice"—Finn wasn't sure if he would be swayed by that line of argument, but it seemed appropriate to try—"there is at least some suggestion that the testimony against you is valid. Unless you offer something that might refute that, I am afraid I have little choice but to go along with what little information I have."

Leland turned away. "Then do what you must," he said.

Finn slid the stool closer. The stench within the room didn't seem to be coming from Leland. It seemed that they had forced him to soil himself, leaving refuse piled within the small cell. Why would they torment a prisoner like that? It was an added insult, and it left Finn thinking even more poorly of the captors within the village.

"I would prefer to have an opportunity to hear your side of the story."

"I doubt that," he said.

"You may doubt it, but I tell you the truth."

Leland looked up, holding Finn's gaze. "Is this always how you go about questioning your prisoners?"

"No. In Verendal where I typically work, there are other aspects of questioning."

"Torture."

"Sometimes. It is an unfortunate necessity of the line of work that I take part in, but not always. There are times when simply asking the right questions gives the information I need."

"The others thought they needed to torture," Leland said.

"And as I have tried to make clear, I am not the others. I have brought no enhanced questioning tools with me."

He chuckled. "Is that what you refer to them as?"

"It makes me feel better," Finn admitted.

"I'm sure. It doesn't make me feel any better."

"Unfortunately, if you are subjected to enhanced questioning, there is no way to make it feel better."

He watched him, frowning. "You say that almost as if you have experienced it yourself."

"Perhaps."

He grunted again. "I imagine that would be a story worth hearing."

"If you share yours, I would be willing to share mine."

Finn's story was no secret, at least not in Verendal.

"I suspect that's more of a bargain for you than it is for me."

"You don't think my story is an even trade?"

"I don't know. You would argue it is, but you're looking for me to share something that might end with me swinging from the end of a rope."

Finn nodded. "I can't deny it might. At the same time, you're likely end up at the end of the rope either way."

"So, I should believe your story is worth my life?"

"I'm not going to tell you what to believe."

Leland looked past him, glancing over at the door. "They probably accused me of murder."

Finn said nothing.

"And they're right."

"Really?"

"If that's what they want to accuse me of having done, there isn't any way for me to deny it. I've done what they accused me of doing."

"You're not helping your case."

"I doubt anything I'll tell you will help my case. The most I can hope for is an honorable death, though the council has made it clear I won't even be offered that."

"You would prefer the sword?"

"Wouldn't you?"

The question left him thinking of when he'd been brought to the Raven Stone, the way he'd been guided through the Blood Court, and how he had felt when he had nearly died. There had been the conviction that he would die. That he would hang. Then there had been the surprising desire to speak to the gods looking for forgiveness. That had been the last time that Finn had really spoken to the gods.

"I suppose I would," Finn said softly.

"I came across him while making my way to Verendal. I'd been on the road for the better part of a week. Assaulted three times, and had managed to fight off each attempt to rob me." He shook his head. "If the king cared so much for his people, he would try to do more to protect them on his road, rather than letting us suffer. Do you know how many people I encountered that were attacked the same way that I was attacked?"

"I don't."

"More than you would believe," Leland said. "You don't have the look of someone who has much experience on the road. Not that I can blame you. If I had a nice place in Verendal, I'd probably stay there too."

"Why don't I have the look?"

"You're too soft." He shrugged. "Men on the road, they get hard or they get dead."

"Why would you spend so much time on the road?"

Leland glowered at him. "What choice do I have?"

"There's always choice in the matter," Finn said. "Find a village. A town. A city. Stay there."

"They don't want men like me."

"What kind of man is that?"

"The kind who don't have much in the way to offer. I've come to terms with it. It's just the way it is. You get tied into a grind, and getting out isn't easy."

Finn understood, having gone through something similar. There came a point where even if he had wanted to get out, there wasn't much of a way to do so. He'd been bound to a lifestyle without any hope of getting freed from it.

"What would you have done otherwise?"

"It doesn't matter."

"That was the question asked of me."

"When?"

"When I was about to hang."

Leland watched Finn then grunted out a laugh. "Now you're just mocking me."

"Not mocking. You wanted my story, and that's it. I was a thief. Got pinched breaking into the viscount's manor, sentenced to hang, and saved by the executioner."

"Why'd he save you?"

Finn shook his head. "I don't really know. He never said."

"Usually when someone saves you, they want something from you. Either that or someone else does. If you haven't found out, you'd best get looking."

Finn inhaled deeply and then wished that he wouldn't have. "I went looking for those answers, but there aren't any. Meyer wanted to help me. He's never said why."

"Sounds to me like you didn't dig."

"I dug at it," Finn said.

"He saved you and made you his apprentice?"

"Called it the Executioner's Right."

"Is that what you're going to do with me?"

Finn shook his head. "Unfortunately, I don't have the pull needed to do that. Nor am I convinced that you're as remorseful as you would have me believe."

"Why is that?"

"I've talked to men accused of murder. They either are defiant or they proclaim their innocence. Occasionally, they're innocent, though in my experience, that's not nearly as often as they would have me believe. You're something else. You're someone who admits to what you did, but you don't see the crime in it."

"The man deserved what he had coming to him."

"Why would any man deserve to die?"

"A hangman would ask that question?"

"I serve the king's justice. The gods' justice. I don't take it upon myself."

"What are you doing here, then?"

Finn actually enjoyed the banter with Leland. It reminded him of Helda. With her, she challenged him to make sure that what he did was for the right reason, and not because he was told what he was supposed to do.

"I'm here to ensure you're brought to justice for what you've done. Seeing as how you've admitted your guilt, I don't see much of a choice in what must follow."

"What if I told you I didn't do it?"

"Then I would have to ask what you did. You've admitted to killing a man."

"A man raping a woman. Wouldn't you kill someone?"

"Did you know either of them?"

Leland stared at him before shaking his head. "I didn't, but a man can't let something like that stand."

Finn frowned. He couldn't tell if he were telling the truth or not. "The lawful act would have been bringing him for justice."

"Not the way he was doing it," Leland said.

"Where was this?"

"They didn't tell you?"

"I find it best to uncover what I can from the condemned."

"Just outside the village. Bastard had his pants down to his ankles, the woman's dress hiked up. She was screaming bloody murder. I came along... and, well it's not a hard thing to stick a knife into a man's back."

"That's why you attacked him?"

He shrugged. "What kind of man would I be if I let him hurt a woman like that? I did it and can't say I regret it."

Leland fell silent a moment. "What do you say now, hangman?"

Finn watched him for a moment more before getting to his feet.

"You've decided?" Leland asked.

"You admitted your guilt. It's not a man's right to kill another. By taking his life, you've removed the chance for the crown to get justice."

"The crown takes too long," he muttered.

Finn breathed out, then nodded. "That might be. I won't deny there are times when I wished we were able to act more quickly, much like I won't deny that there are times when justice isn't what we think it should be. That doesn't mean we get to take it into our hands."

"So, I get the rope. Just like they wanted."

Finn paused at the doorway, his hand resting for a moment. "You'll get the sentence you deserve."

CHAPTER SEVENTEEN

A crowd lined the streets of Torthen, far more people than Finn would have expected to be present. There were hundreds packing the streets, and even a few street vendors, making it feel almost as much like a festival as what he experienced in Verendal. A real gallows festival.

He'd tried to find more about the raped woman and the man Leland had killed, but none had shared anything of use. The woman was a traveler who'd kept moving east, and none knew the man. A stranger wearing clothes that suggested he came from one of the larger cities. Most suspected Vur. The only reason they'd held Volt was because he'd come into Torthen covered in blood. Otherwise, Finn had to wonder if they would have let it be.

Finn met the councilor near the prison on the edge of the village. Finn had changed into the only other clothing that he'd brought with him, the formal leathers he wore during executions, the longsword Meyer had given him now strapped to his back.

Toby was there, the only jailor that Finn had seen in his time in the village. A younger man wearing the brown robes of the Church of Heleth stood nearby, a book clutched in hand. He looked up as Finn approached.

"You don't need me for this," the priest said.

"What's your name?" Finn asked.

"Dirk Preston," the priest said.

"How long have you served Heleth?"

He glanced over to the councilor as if he needed to get permission to answer. The councilor looked at Finn for a moment before waving his hand.

"I've served for two years. I've never been privy to an execution, though. We don't get too many of them out here."

"You know how to pray with a man?"

"What?"

"Do you know how to pray with a man?" Finn asked again.

"Of course."

"All you need is to offer him an opportunity at redemption."

"There isn't going to be redemption for a man like him," the councilor said.

Finn shot him an annoyed look. "Every man is given a chance at redemption in the eyes of the gods, especially in their final moments. If you pray with him, you can offer him that opportunity. Whether he takes it is up to him."

The priest licked his lips and nodded nervously.

Had Finn been presented with a priest like that when he'd made his walk along the Blood Court, he wasn't sure he would have been able to find the faith he had. It was because the priest had prayed with him, speaking the words of absolution during his march along the streets, that Finn had found a measure of peace.

He'd been with many other men on their march since then. Almost all had found a desire to speak the words during the walk. Only one had not, though he'd spoken different words, as if the priest didn't represent his god.

Finn turned to Toby. "You can escort the condemned."

The guard unlocked the cell and headed inside.

"I still don't think the extra cost was necessary," the councilor muttered.

"What extra cost?" Finn asked.

"To dress him."

"He won't go to meet the gods dressed in filth." Finn had been adamant about that. It had taken quite a bit of urging for the councilor to offer Leland Volt a new set of clothing. He hadn't realized that it was the cost that had been the greatest deterrent. Why make an issue about the extra clothing?

"It's a waste, is all."

"A waste to you but not to the gods," the priest said.

Finn smiled to himself. At least the priest had found a bit of himself. Finn wasn't going to be able to serve as priest and executioner. Serving as the one without Meyer present was strange enough.

Toby walked Leland out of the cell.

He had changed into the simple brown clothing the council had arranged on his behalf. The Sinner's Cloth. Surprisingly, the cut and the quality of the fabric were nicer than what Finn had been given, though it might be that was all they'd been able to arrange.

His hair was slicked back, and though he looked haggard, there was a determination to his face. Leland locked eyes with Finn briefly before turning away.

"Leland Volt. You have been sentenced according to the king's laws. You have admitted to your crimes. You will now face punishment before the eyes of men and the gods."

The others had fallen silent.

"Is there anything more you'd care to say before we begin our walk?" Finn asked.

Leland looked over at him. "Make it quick."

Finn smiled tightly. "I will offer you an honorable death."

He started along the street.

The councilor marched alongside him, looking in his direction, but Finn ignored him.

This wasn't about the councilor. Even the council. This was about the man who'd been condemned and what he owed.

Finn made his way through the streets, past the crowd who looked from him to the condemned, his heart heavy as it often was when traveling toward a sentencing, though knowing that Leland was guilty of the crime he'd been accused of committing.

Behind him, he heard the priest speaking softly, his voice rising over the murmuring all around them. Finn could hear him offering the prayers of Heleth, the protection of the Mother, and an offer for him to find his salvation. After a while, Leland began to speak the words along with him.

Finn wasn't terribly surprised.

They reached the far side of the village far more quickly than Finn was accustomed to during the Blood Court in Verendal. Normally, he had an opportunity to steel himself for what must be done, but with what he did today, there wasn't the same chance to prepare.

When they reached the gallows, Finn stopped and waited for the councilor to join the rest of the council who were arranged there. Bennington was there with them, and the crowd shuffled so that they could get nearer, as if they wanted to be as close as possible following the execution. Would any of the hegen be there? In Verendal, the hegen came out after the execution to claim their prizes, though he didn't know if the same would happen here.

He stopped before the council, sweeping his gaze over each of them. "I, Finn Jagger, acting on behalf of King Porman to enact his justice, present the condemned Leland Volt for his sentencing. He stands accused and convicted of murder, and has confessed his guilt to me."

There was a steady murmuring all around at that.

Bennington stepped forward. "Then we trust you to carry out the sentencing."

Finn looked behind him, looking to Leland.

"As he has confessed his crime, and given the circumstances surrounding his crime, I would appeal to the council to permit an honorable death."

It was a stretch, and one Finn didn't know whether the council would even permit. Most in the village wouldn't know the difference between what Finn proposed and what the council had proposed, but those who did would have questions about *why* he had altered the sentencing. More than that, he didn't know if he even had to ask permission, but he suspected the sentencing would go easier if he did.

"Honorable?" The question came from the councilor who had been with Finn during his time in the city, a man whose name Finn hadn't learned. "Murder deserves an honorable death? Perhaps in Verendal, but not in Torthen."

There was a murmuring of agreement.

Finn would have to get a handle on the crowd now. That was a lesson Meyer had instructed him in, though in Verendal, it was rarely necessary. The crowd never got all that out of hand. They had the jurors and the magister present and there was always an air of formality because of it.

"Leland Volt admitted to the crime of murder. A heinous act, and one the king has clearly deemed a capital offense. Leland Volt committed the act after observing the rape of a woman traveling along the King's Road."

Such horrendous crimes were not uncommon outside of the city. Even in the city, they were not altogether uncommon.

The councilor scoffed at him. "And you believe him?"

"He admitted to his guilt. There is nothing to gain otherwise."

"Other than your mercy."

Finn stepped toward the councilor, lowering his voice.

"The rope or the sword. Either is death." He held the councilor's gaze until he looked away. "If this was your wife, and Leland Volt had murdered the man responsible, would you want him hanged or offered a more honorable passing?"

The councilor backed away.

The village had fallen silent.

Finn looked to Bennington but wasn't able to read anything from him.

"As the representative of the king, seeing as there is no further objection, I will carry out the sentencing."

He expected there to be more of a response from the council, but there was none.

Finn approached Leland. "Have you made your peace with your gods?"

"Is there peace with gods?"

"Only you can decide that," Finn said.

Leland looked up. "I don't regret what I did."

"I understand."

"I don't regret killing the other, either."

Finn tensed. Had he acted too quickly? "What other?"

"The bastard who watched. Wretched thing. Stood in the forest near that stupid hut. I had to chase him down, and he almost reached a little pond. Drove my knife into him, as well. Someone had to stop it."

Finn considered rescinding the honorable death and using the noose. The crowd would approve, especially now that he admitted killing two people.

A faint murmuring built.

He had to keep control. Changing the sentencing would take control from him and give it to the villagers.

Finn nodded. "Step forward."

Everything seemed to slow for Finn.

He had carried out the beheading of only a handful of men. It was a different execution, one that required timing and strength and skill. It was why Meyer had him practice as often as he had.

Leland knelt before him.

Finn looked around him briefly before forcing out the thought of anyone else in the village. He focused only on Leland. Only on the task at hand.

He unsheathed the longsword and held it at his side.

Pausing for a moment, Finn half-expected that there would be some from the council who would think to try to stop him, but no one said anything.

He lifted the sword, setting his feet the way that he'd practiced, and raised it.

In that moment, he was all too aware of how he was by himself. Not only did he not have Meyer with him for guidance on the execution, but he'd argued with the council to change the sentencing.

Finn forced those thoughts out of his mind.

He focused on the blade.

On a clean strike.

Provide the honorable death.

One blow. Nothing more.

Steadying his breathing, he swung.

Finn sat in the tavern, a mug of ale in front of him. His pack rested next to him, the sword bundled up with it. He was tired, though it was an unusual tiredness.

The tavern was busy this evening, though most of the people within the tavern gave him a wide berth. Those who glanced in his direction did so quickly and briefly before hurriedly turning away.

Finn would have to get moving soon, though he hoped to have another night in the village before he headed out. He didn't want to have another experience like the last one.

Bev headed over to him, carrying a meal and a plate. She paused, setting the ale down, holding on to the plate, watching him for a moment.

"Not much of a mercenary, are you?"

Finn looked over, shaking his head. "I told you I wasn't a mercenary."

"You can't blame me for thinking that you were. Not too many men come in here with swords who aren't with the military or mercenaries."

"I suppose you don't get many executioners here," he said.

"None that I can recall." She glanced over toward the kitchen, shaking her head. "Bennington thinks you did the right thing."

"And what thing was that?"

"Offering him an honorable death." She leaned closer, setting the tray on the table. "He knew a girl who went through something similar, you see. He always wishes he'd been able to do something more for her. The man got away, escaping from the king's justice. I suppose in Bennington's eyes, what Leland did was justice of a sort."

Finn understood that perception. He also understood why Leland had been willing to carry out the murder the way that he had. He even wondered if he would have done something similar if it would have been his sister. Had somebody come after Lena, Finn could easily imagine what he might be willing to do.

"Knew her, cared about her. She had once worked here. In between my mother and me, that is."

"You believe Leland?"

"No reason not to believe him, now, is there? Like you said, he was condemned either way."

Finn nodded. "He was."

"Some of the men are a bit disappointed they didn't get to test the gallows. When they summoned the executioner… well, *you*… they all thought they were going to have a chance to see whether the gallows was adequate."

"They did good work with its construction. There's no shame in not needing it."

"Tell that to them. They think that they needed to prove themselves."

Finn grunted, taking the ale and drinking. It was cool, and just the right bitterness. "I appreciate what you have done for me here."

"I haven't done anything for you here. Other than put you into contact with Bennington. You know, I think he's still a bit irritated he didn't get to charge you as much as what he wanted for the room."

"I could have included it in my fee," Finn said.

Bev straightened, wiping her hands on her apron. "It seems to me you did." She winked and spun away, leaving Finn. He picked at his plate. The food was good, warm enough, and tasty, and he dug into it.

When he was done, he started getting to his feet when a commotion within the crowd near him caught his attention.

"You don't need to say anything, John."

"You're damn right I need to say something," the man named John said.

He was a larger man, his head shaved, and had a scar along one cheek. One eye narrowed more than the others, and he had a bit of redness within the wider one.

Bloodshot, or possibly infected.

Finn wasn't there to do any healing. He was there for a different purpose, and even if he wanted to do any healing, he doubted that the people there would be all that eager to permit it from him. Especially not after what happened today.

"What do you need to say?" Finn asked, grabbing his pack and holding the sword.

John eyed the sword up and down, before turning his gaze to Finn. "You let him off lightly."

"You think death is a light sentence?" Finn asked.

He was tempted to drop his pack, to hold on to the sword in a more threatening manner, but there was no need for that.

John wanted justice. That was all, at least as far as Finn suspected.

It was how he wanted justice that troubled Finn a bit.

"That bastard deserved to be drawn and quartered," John said.

"And why is that?"

"You might've believed him when he gave you that sob story about why he killed the man, but we know better."

"And what exactly is it that you think you know?" Finn asked.

"We saw what he did to the man."

Finn frowned. "Did to him?"

"He carved through his guts. Pulled out his intestines. Draped them around his neck, wrapping them around his legs. That's not a crime of passion."

Finn stared at him. It wasn't a crime of passion. It was a crime of vengeance.

John and these others didn't see it that way. Finn wondered if they could.

"He's faced his sentencing," Finn said. "Justice has been served."

"Your justice, isn't it? Not ours."

"My justice is the king's justice. Which means that it's the same as your justice."

"That's not my justice," John said.

Once again, he glanced over to Finn's sword, and Finn wondered whether or not John was going to do or say something more, but he turned away, heading back to the others with him.

Three men pulled John back toward them, moving him away from Finn's attention.

Finn just shook his head.

He headed up to his room. As Bennington had claimed, the room wasn't much. It was small, about as comfortable as he could hope to expect in a small village like that, but the sheets had been clean. The food in the tavern had been decent. The people there had been kind, and Finn had wanted to offer them the services that he had come for.

Propping the bag and the sword in front of the door, he blocked anyone from getting in. He sat on the bed for a moment, resting his elbows on his knees, staring straight ahead.

There was a soft knock on the door.

Finn got to his feet.

"Can I help you?"

"I thought you might want some company."

Finn pulled the door open. "Bev?"

She stood with a mug of ale on the other side of the door, a hint of a smile on her face. "You don't have to take it, but…"

Finn stepped back, moving aside for her to come into the room.

She set the mug down on the narrow table at the end of the room and looked up at Finn before closing the door. "After a day like today, I figured you needed to talk."

"I've done this before," Finn said.

"Have you?"

He nodded. "I've been an apprentice for the last five years."

She took a seat on the bed and Finn considered for a moment before taking a seat next to her. "Does it get any easier?"

"Over time."

"What's it like?"

Finn closed his eyes a moment before opening them and staring at the door. "The first time was the hardest, even knowing the man deserved it. Taking a life... there's no coming back from that."

"Plenty of men take someone's life."

"I suppose so. In war, we think of it as honorable. Fight for your king and country. Kill those who don't." Finn had spoken to a few men over the years who had fought in wars, and had found that they either tried not to think of what they'd done or got bogged down in it, never able to move past. He wasn't sure which was healthier.

They fell into a long silence. "How do you justify it with your belief in the gods?"

Finn glanced over at her. "Depends on who you ask."

"I'm asking you."

"Then I would say I'm not sure what I believe about the gods."

She regarded him. "I saw you. When you were walking through the village, you were reciting the words of Heleth."

Had I?

Finn didn't remember, and with the procession, it was

possible that he had been. If he had, it would make him wonder if he had done the same with other executions.

"I've probably said them so many times that I don't even think about it anymore."

"Seems to me that you'd only say them if you were concerned about what Heleth had in store for you."

"I've stopped thinking that way."

"Why?"

"Because I don't have a choice in what I do."

"All men get a choice."

"All?"

She shrugged. "Maybe not all. It seems to me that any man who serves in the kind of role that you do would have a choice."

"Not me."

She didn't push. Finn didn't elaborate.

"Where do you go from here?"

"There's another village not far from here that I was asked to visit."

"Let me guess. You're going to Ferd."

"How did you know?"

Bev smiled slightly, and it made her look pretty, innocent. She shifted where she sat on the bed, somehow scooting closer to him without it seeming as if she tried.

"We live in Torthen. Word comes through here. Lots of travelers along the King's Road. Makes it interesting, but it makes it dangerous, too. The word out of Ferd is they got someone who was robbing men near town. Maimed one man. Cut off his hand. Another lost an ear. Another a foot.

All pretty gruesome." She shivered. "I'd almost rather have someone like Leland. At least I can understand what he was doing."

"Thanks."

"For what?"

"For giving me an idea of what I'm getting into. I didn't know."

"How could you not know?"

"I was only told that I needed to come to Torthen and Ferd, not what the people I came for had done. Usually, it doesn't matter. I'm going to question them myself."

"That's how you found out about the rape."

"That is."

"There've been others."

"Rapes?"

She nodded. "Rapes. Murders, even. None has been caught. The council has sent word to the king, asking for more protection along his road, but we haven't been given any. At least not yet. We suspect that he'll send it eventually, but with the rumbles of war..."

"What war?"

She frowned at him. "How is it you live in Verendal and you don't know?"

"We don't get pulled into the politics that often. We're situated too far to the west for that."

"I'd have figured that with the stirring coming from the other side of the forest, you would have heard something. Gods, it sounds terrifying! We haven't had a war with the Alainsith in..."

"Centuries," Finn finished. "What do you know about it?"

"Nothing more than rumor. I would've figured that you would have heard more from Verendal. Maybe the king don't want you to be worried. Verendal would be the first impacted, you know." She took a deep breath. "You'll be leaving in the morning?"

"I have to."

"Will you stop through on your way back?"

Finn might stop, though he'd been gone for two days and still hadn't uncovered anything that would help him know what they needed to do for the strange man in Declan. Two rapists and rumors of a thief who cut off body parts. Any of them could have done the crime the man in Declan had been accused of committing. What Finn needed was proof.

But he also needed something that suggested the Alainsith.

There *was* that strange promise.

Finn hadn't known what to make of it. Even now, he still wasn't sure what to make of that promise, uncertain whether he could do anything about what he had said.

If he could, what did it mean for Finn?

What did it mean for the rest of them?

War, possibly.

"I will do my best to stop here on my way back" Finn said.

"I'm sure that Bennington would allow you to stay," she said.

"I'm sure," Finn said, chuckling softly. "And I'm sure he would have a particular fee in mind."

Bev laughed. "There's no doubt about that," she said.

She looked at Finn for a moment. Finally, she took his hand. "I didn't only come here to see if you wanted company," she said.

"Bev—"

She pulled on his hand, looking up and meeting his eyes. "After what you went through today, I figured you needed some company."

Finn allowed himself to be pulled down. When he had performed executions before, he had never really had anyone make such an offer to him. Even now, he wasn't sure how he felt about it. Perhaps a little guilty, were he honest.

There was almost a longing in her eyes. She leaned forward, kissing him.

Finn kissed her back.

"Maybe I will stop through here on my way back."

CHAPTER EIGHTEEN

Finn guided the horse along the road. They moved quickly, heading toward Ferd, and yet, he found himself looking back, wondering what it might feel like were he to remain. Bev had welcomed him in a way that he hadn't felt welcomed in a long time.

Serving as an executioner was difficult, not only for those he had to sentence but also for himself. He was isolated, and Meyer didn't make it seem as if executioners were given the opportunity to spend time with anyone. As far as Finn had seen, there was nothing for Finn to look forward to.

Maybe he would only have moments like this, moments where he was outside of the village, away from people who viewed him as somehow less than the others within the city. If that were the case, then he needed to take advantage of these opportunities when they came to him.

And Bev…

Bev certainly had been willing.

Finn pushed those thoughts out of his mind. He had to focus on the next assignment.

From what Bev had told him, he had to be concerned about someone taking body parts, maybe even like the hegen did for magic. He'd been careful not to say anything to her about that, concerned about what it might mean and who might be involved. Something like that could be hegen, though that didn't seem to him anything that the hegen typically did. Of course, Finn's experience with the hegen was inside of Verendal, not outside. Perhaps outside of the city, there wasn't nearly the same opportunity for hegen to acquire the necessary parts of magic. If that were the case, then the hegen might resort to taking things they should not have.

He should have asked more questions of Esmerelda.

There was nothing of Alainsith, though.

Nothing to help figure out why Meyer had sent him from the city.

Nothing.

Finn didn't feel as if there was anyone following him the way that he'd felt when he'd been traveling toward Torthen. Perhaps his time away from the city had given him a different feeling for things so that he didn't feel quite as jumpy as before.

A small building caught his attention. Finn looked over to it. Set back into the trees, it couldn't be much more than a small hut. Leland had spoken of a hut.

He steered the horse off the road and toward the hut. It

was set into a small clearing, with a few fallen branches around it. The trees there were all towering pines and oaks, the ground littered with detritus and the air stinking of dampness.

Could this have been the hut?

Finn frowned.

Leland had chased the man through the woods from the hut. He'd almost reached a small pond...

Finn circled through the woods and came across the pond. There was no doubt in his mind this was it.

Where was the body?

This would have been the other person Leland had admitted to killing, someone else who had watched. As he looked around, he didn't see anything. The people must have buried the body.

Finn headed back to the hut, climbing from the saddle. The door had strange carvings on it, almost as if someone had tried to decorate it with symbols. The inside was sparsely appointed. There was a cot tilted up against one wall. A small trunk that was empty when Finn checked near the cot. A cookstove with pots stacked atop it. Nothing else. Dust covered everything, so whoever owned the hut hadn't been there in some time.

He glanced toward the road.

He didn't know how long it would take for him to get to Ferd, but he didn't want to linger. He'd already felt the nerves of taking too long on the journey once before, and he still had to see what he could uncover about the man in Declan for Meyer. Turning back to the King's Road, Finn found himself looking back along the road toward the hut every so often.

It was late in the day when the trees began to thin out around him.

The change happened gradually. Finn had scarcely been aware of how much tree cover there was when it began, leaving only a few trees with a grassy plain stretching out before him. There wasn't anything other than the road stretching before him.

As the day progressed, Finn realized he wouldn't reach Ferd before dark.

He didn't know how much farther he was going to have to go to get there, but he had expected to come across some sign of it by now. There wasn't even any evidence of other travelers out. It had just been him.

Thankfully, the road was easy to follow, and it was wide enough he could travel quickly along it, but without any real light by which to see, he wasn't going to have an easy time. Which meant that he would have to camp for the night.

Finn wasn't eager to camp. He wouldn't be able to sleep well without feeling as if he had to keep an eye open at all times. Perhaps he should have gotten someone to come along with him, though who would he have brought out on this journey? There wasn't anyone in the city who would have come with him. Maybe Lena. Oscar might have, were he well enough. That was about it.

As the sun started to set, he sat upright in the saddle,

looking along the road to see if there might be any sign of the village, but saw nothing.

He would have to start planning for where he would camp. It couldn't be on the road. Given what he'd heard within Verendal and what he'd heard since leaving the city, Finn didn't think it was a good idea for him to be too close to the road, were he to camp. That meant he'd have to move off the road.

A small copse of trees nearby would provide some shelter. He had the necessary supplies to camp for the night otherwise. He wouldn't want to start a campfire, but there wouldn't necessarily be any need. He thought his cloak would keep him warm enough, he didn't need the fire to eat, and fire would draw attention.

Guiding the horse off the road, he headed toward the trees. When he reached them, he tied the horse off, then made a circle around the trees, looking for anything that might pose a problem while resting. He found nothing.

Finn pulled his pack off the horse and settled to the ground, leaning his back up against one of the tall oak trees. There wasn't much light remaining.

Chewing on some dried meat, he looked around him. Would it really be so bad for him to have a *small* fire? With a small fire, Finn could sit and read. He'd brought several books with him, though they predominantly dealt with healing. It would be a better use of his time. There wasn't much else for him to do.

After gathering a few fallen branches, he carefully worked to start a small fire.

He kept the sword at his side. It was protection.

After pulling out the books, he sat near the fire and read.

He lost track of how long he spent reading. Darkness fell in full, and sounds of the night, those of insects and the hoot of an owl, and even the distant sound of a mournful wolf crying in the night carried to him. This was a more advanced work on medicines, and it would have been better for him to study where he had a place to take notes, but even without that, he thought it was helpful. Not that Finn would ever think to become a full-time apothecary—at least, not until his service as an executioner was completed —but having that knowledge meant that he could help others. Balance the darkness of the job with the only light that it offered.

A soft rustling came to him.

Finn looked up. It might only be the wind, though he hadn't been bothered by the wind where he was. Within the trees, he was protected, shielded from most of the night, and the wind didn't reach him. There *had* been some rustling, though. He was certain of it.

He stuffed the books back into his pack and grabbed the sword.

It was a foolish gesture, he was certain of it, but Finn felt better having it with him. As he got to his feet and started looking around, he didn't find anything. He looked over to the horse. It seemed unconcerned.

Wouldn't the horse be worried if there was anything out there for me to be concerned by?

Patting the horse on the side, he looked out into the

night. With the small firelight, it was difficult for him to see much. That might have been another mistake in lighting a fire. His eyes were adjusted to the light rather than to the darkness around him. There was a danger in not being able to see anything near him.

Finn started away from the trees, putting some distance between him and the firelight. It had to be an overreaction, but there *were* dangerous people who traveled the road. Finn was determined to make sure that he knew whether or not there was anything out there.

Darkness. That was the only thing that he came across.

As he made a small circle around the copse of trees, he saw nothing. The fire was visible, practically a beacon that called anyone who might be out there toward his campsite. He had thought he had sheltered it better than that.

He paused near one of the trees, looking all around him. There was nothing there. It really was just his imagination. As Finn prepared to settle back down, he thought he heard a rustling again.

It was quiet.

Whatever was out there, it didn't make much noise. He looked around and realized he was going to have to step farther away from the trees in order for him to be able to figure out what was making any noise.

Finn moved into the darkness, searching for the source of the soft rustling, but didn't find anything.

He thought about what he had encountered on his way to Torthen. There *had* been movement behind him, chasing him. It was that feeling that had driven him to keep going all the way to the village when he had no interest in doing so.

Finn wandered a little bit farther from the copse of trees, looking around for anything. As he did, the fire from his campsite remained visible. It was far too visible even from a distance.

He circled a ways out before making his way back.

As he neared the campsite, the horse pranced softly, shuffling his feet.

Something was off.

Finn had no idea what it was, only that he felt that there was something different. He headed to the horse, patting him on the side, and realized there was somebody else there. A shadowy form sat next to the fire. Finn approached, holding on to the sword, studying the person now seated at his fire.

"I can see you standing there," a voice said.

It was soft, with a hint of an accent, and surprisingly familiar.

Finn stepped forward, clutching the sword, looking around briefly before turning his attention back to the seated figure. They appeared comfortable. They had a pale blue cloak, with a hood pulled up over their head. There was no weapon near them. No sign of any traveling supplies. No sign of horse.

They had come by foot.

Somehow, they had done so without him seeing anything.

"Pull back your hood," Finn said.

The figure chuckled. "Are you always this concerned with visitors?"

"I am in the middle of the night and out on the King's Road," Finn said.

They chuckled again. "If it suits you."

The figure turned toward him, pulling back the hood of their cloak.

Dark hair spilled out, and the face that looked up at him was familiar, and Finn suddenly understood why he had recognized the voice.

"Esmerelda?"

She tilted her head. "Finn Jagger. Out here alone on the King's Road. I thought perhaps you could use some company."

"It can be dangerous for you to sneak up on somebody out here like this."

"Can it?"

Finn looked out into the darkness again, searching for anyone else. *Esmerelda wouldn't have come alone, would she?* He didn't see any other hegen, though with their magic, it was possible that he wouldn't even be aware of it.

"Who else is with you?"

"Why must there be someone else?"

"You wouldn't have come here by yourself," he said.

"You have."

Finn made a steady circle around the campfire, moving behind her for a moment before heading onward and back around to face her once more. "I am out here to serve the king's justice."

"If that were the only reason that you were out here, then I would have no interest in finding you. As it is, I think you and I both know that is not the only reason that you are out here."

"What other reason am I out here?"

"To find the answers you think might be here."

Finn looked around once more before taking a seat, slipping the sword back into its sheath. It wouldn't have been of much use to him, anyway. Not only wasn't he much of a swordsman, but the sword was designed for a very different purpose.

"What answers do you think I came for?"

"I suppose they are the same answers that Henry Meyer came to me looking for. And the ones I told him needed to be found outside the city."

He took a seat across from Esmerelda, looking over the fire at her. The flames crackled, and shadows danced all around her. In the darkness, she had an even more exotic beauty than she did in the light.

"You're the reason I was sent on my pilgrimage?"

She smiled slightly. "I suggested he might look beyond Verendal for answers."

"What do you know about this?"

"Only what the cards suggest," she murmured, pulling one from her pocket and flipping it briefly before sliding it back.

"Are you alone?" Finn asked.

"Would it worry you if I was?"

"It would worry me for your safety."

"That is quite kind of you, Finn Jagger. You don't need to concern yourself with my protection, though."

"Which means you aren't alone."

"I didn't say that, either."

Finn laughed. Strangely, even though he normally felt uncomfortable around Esmerelda, always feeling as if he had to be prepared for what she might do or say that would position him to serve her in some way, sitting in front of the campfire left him feeling a little bit differently about it. He wasn't in her home, which meant she wasn't in control in the same way that she was when he came to the hegen section.

That didn't mean that Finn thought she wasn't still in control. He wouldn't be surprised if she were able to manipulate him. She *was* hegen, after all.

"I understand that you offered a different sentencing in Torthen," she said.

"Is that why you're here? Did you follow me or did you come to collect from the condemned?"

She regarded him a moment. "That would be reason to come. There is some benefit in venturing beyond the city, as there have been fewer condemned within Verendal recently."

"Does that disappoint you?"

"I don't long for men to die."

"It's not only men who are sentenced," Finn said.

"Not only, but predominantly."

Finn slid closer to the fire as a chill washed through him. He looked over to Esmerelda, wondering if she had anything to do with that or whether it was only him. She didn't give him any sign either way.

"Why did you come looking for me?" Finn asked.

"What makes you think I came looking for you?"

He smiled. "You had Meyer send me on a pilgrimage and now you followed me out here." He frowned, regarding her for another moment. Could it have been her—or the other hegen—that he'd detected the very first day after leaving Verendal? He doubted that she would tell him if that were the case. "There must be some reason you came out here."

Her gaze drifted to the sword resting next to him. "I see Meyer has gifted you a blade of your own."

The change in subject surprised him, though he knew it should not. With Esmerelda, he was accustomed to her changing topics quickly like that. "Does it trouble you?"

"The sword or what it represents?"

"I suppose both."

"I have lived most of my life understanding the king has his own ideals of what his justice means. You are merely an agent for that justice."

Finn leaned back, watching Esmerelda. "Why would you have left Verendal?"

"There are many reasons I would leave the city."

"Do you leave often?"

She smiled softly. "No."

"Then it has something to do with the Alainsith."

"What makes you say that?"

"There was the issue at the prison, then there was Meyer going to you for answers about what the man had said. I'm sure it troubled you. I wouldn't have expected it to have troubled you enough to feel the need to leave the city for answers of your own."

"Perhaps I came to assist you in finding the answers you seek."

"Did you?"

She smiled slightly and reached into the pocket of her cloak before pulling out a small bundle of waxed paper. As she unfolded it, Finn realized that it was food she'd brought with her that smelled quite delicious, despite it being packaged for traveling.

"Would you care for a bite?"

"I don't know what it would cost me."

"A trade. That is all."

He reached into his bag and pulled out some of the dried meat that he'd brought with him. "I can offer you this."

She took it, her nose wrinkling slightly.

"I won't be offended if you don't care for it. I needed something that would travel well."

"I am not certain this is what you should have brought with you. You would have been better off eating one of these branches."

"If you don't want it…"

Esmerelda held on to the offered meat and bit into it. Her nose wrinkled even more. "I find this quite unpleasant."

Finn took a bite of the bread she offered him and wasn't at all surprised that it was as good as it smelled. Probably some hegen magic in it, as well. He ate slowly, enjoying the food as he did, watching Esmerelda. There were strange spices mixed in it that he didn't recognize, and he noted she didn't have any meat packed with her supplies—just the bread and some dried berries.

"Thank you," he said.

"For offering you something more than the nearly inedible food you offered me?"

"You can thank Meyer for that."

"I think he's trying to carry out your sentence."

Finn fell silent. The flames crackled and the sounds of the night around him intruded. A soft wind gusted, blowing through the trees, carrying the hint of cold.

"That was poorly said on my part," Esmerelda said.

"You don't have to apologize," he said, realizing she hadn't apologized. "I'm past the sentencing."

"You are indeed." She tore off another bite of his jerky and looked over at Finn for a moment, before shaking her head.

"Are you going to tell me if the Alainsith brought you out of Verendal?"

"He should not have been there."

"In the city or in the prison?"

"Either place."

He wasn't sure how much Esmerelda would share with him. Before he'd left the city, she'd shared more with him than he would have expected, and he questioned whether she would be compelled to do the same again. Maybe time outside of the city would make her more likely to share. Finn doubted that she'd be compelled to provide him with the chance to ask three questions again, but even without that, he thought he might gain some insight.

"For one, he should not have come to the city."

"You say that as if you would think that he'd be incapable of reaching the city."

"It's not a matter of not reaching. It's a matter of the danger to him in doing so."

"Even though he was captured along the road outside of the city," Finn said. "And the king and the chancellor had come to secure the treaty."

"I think that it would be unlikely for one of the Alainsith to have traveled the King's Road. The forest provides a barrier between the Alainsith and this kingdom. For their people to have traveled along the King's Road, it would suggest the protection of the forest has shifted."

"I traveled through part of the forest when I was heading to Torthen."

"Part of the forest, though not a portion of the forest that provided a level of protection from the Alainsith."

"You're still concerned. Why? What role do the hegen play within the kingdom?"

"What makes you think we play any role?"

Finn leaned forward, resting his elbows on his knees, smiling at Esmerelda. "You intervened."

"Did I?"

"You intervened when it came to Oscar, and you've intervened when it came to me." He frowned, thinking back to a question that he'd been asked recently. *Could the hegen have intervened when it came to Meyer having exerted his right?*

"There had to be some reason behind it. You wanted to prevent Bellut from acquiring the hegen items."

She nodded. "There are others who would benefit from the kingdom rejoining war with the Alainsith."

"Others beyond Yelind?" She nodded. "Which others?"

"Dangerous ones."

"And the hegen offer protection against that?"

"My people have attempted to ensure a level of protection, of a sort."

"A magical protection," Finn said.

"Is that not protection?"

"I suppose it is."

"There are many ways to protect the kingdom. The Archers within the city, and within the palace, are but one. The king's army is another."

"And the hegen?"

Esmerelda smiled at him, saying nothing.

There was silence between them for little while, and she continued taking bites of the dried meat, chewing slowly as she did. Finn finished off the hegen bread that she had brought, savoring each bite.

"What are you concerned about?" Finn asked.

"I am concerned about why one of the Alainsith would be found on the King's Road. And I am concerned about the presence of magic I've been able to detect," Esmerelda said.

"Like the magic used on Oscar."

"That and others."

"You said that before, but what others are there?" Finn asked.

"Within the kingdom?" Esmerelda asked, and Finn nodded. "There is witchcraft, but that is rarely seen."

"Because of the hegen?"

"Yes," she said.

"And what about the Alainsith? Meyer is concerned about him. Especially after speaking to you."

"I believe Henry Meyer was concerned for different reasons," she said.

Finn frowned. The wind gusted again, whipping through the trees, rustling the branches high overhead. It seemed as if the temperature was dropping rapidly now. He was thankful for the fire, and he looked around, wondering if perhaps he should gather more branches to strengthen the fire so that he could stay warmer overnight.

"Meyer was concerned because of the man we had in the prison."

"That wasn't the reason for his concern," Esmerelda said.

"No. I suppose he was more concerned about what the man said to us."

She nodded. "He promised war. When it comes to the Alainsith, I have come to believe much of what they say."

"If he's threatening war, then maybe there's a reason behind it."

"I suspect there is."

"You don't believe he committed the crimes he was accused of committing."

Esmerelda watched Finn, shaking her head. "The Alainsith can be many things. Cold. Cruel. Powerful. I find it unlikely that one of the first men of the Alainsith seen in such a long time would be responsible for murdering a simple merchant and raping his wife." She regarded him for a moment. "But then, I suspect you have already come to that same conclusion."

Finn inhaled deeply. "I don't really know," he said. "It's possible he did what the Archers accused him of doing. At the same time, something about it doesn't feel right."

"Is that the only reason you're troubled?"

Finn sighed. "No. Everything happening within the city has left me troubled as well."

"The attempt on your life?"

"That. Holden and his crew. Loren Thilson and the others with him. All of it is troubling to me."

"It seems to me you overlook one other aspect that should bother you. The very thing Henry Meyer was working on."

Finn frowned. "He's been working on the same as me." At least, it was similar to what Finn had been doing. They'd both been looking into the disappearance of the women, though Meyer's search had focused on the chancellor's daughter. "What do you know?"

Esmerelda smiled at him. "I'm afraid you know that isn't how it works."

"You want to trade for something."

"I would. Tell me about the man that you sentenced in Torthen."

"What's there to tell?"

"Why did you change his sentencing?" Her gaze dipped down and looked at the sword resting next to Finn.

Finn stared at the fire, feeling the wind as it gusted around him. "I changed it because he deserved an honorable death."

"Is there such a thing?"

"Were it up to the council, he would have been quartered." Perhaps not the council, but enough of the people within the city might have been willing to let that happen to him. They didn't care about the *why*. It was all about what they believed him guilty of doing.

"Have you been a part of such a sentencing?"

Finn shook his head. "I have not."

"You don't sound disappointed."

"Have you mistaken me for someone who wants to inflict pain and suffering?"

"I have figured you for someone who is willing to do the job that he's been asked to do, whether or not he agrees with what he's asked to do. If that involves a sentencing you don't agree with, I suppose it doesn't matter. I would expect for you to carry it out."

"And I would."

"Then I would also expect for you to need the necessary experience with which to complete a task like that."

Finn looked over at Esmerelda. She watched him intently, the flames flickering in her eyes, dancing there. Her full lips were pressed tightly together and a hint of a smile curved their corners. "Meyer has many books that describe the more esoteric sentences."

"You would learn how to carry out a sentence like that in a book?"

"I learn many things from books. Sentencing. Anatomy. Healing. I can learn all of those things and not have to experience them firsthand."

"There's a difference between what you've read and what can be experienced. Does the book tell you what your prisoner would look and sound like? Would they describe the nervous energy of the horses? The smell of the earth? The hint of shit, both man and beast, that permeates everything as you're tying his limbs together? Would it tell you how you feel, the sweaty nature of your palms, the way your heart is racing, the nausea rolling up through you?"

"You sound as if you have some experience with it."

"I have experience with many things."

"With quartering a man?"

She watched him. "Have your books helped you understand the right way to mix the powders and the leaves and roots together so that you can find the right combination for the particular patient you have before you?" She leaned forward, and the flames seemed to dance even more in her eyes. "What about your study of anatomy? Has that helped you know just how to twist a fracture, making certain the limb heals straight?" She smiled at him. "There are many things you can learn from books, but I would caution you that it's what you cannot learn that is of as much value."

Finn rubbed at his eyes. It was getting late and he was getting tired. Now that Esmerelda was there, he thought that he might even be able to get a little sleep.

"He caught a man raping a woman and drove a knife into his back," Finn said.

"That makes him honorable?"

Finn opened his eyes and looked at her. "Maybe not honorable, but it makes it understandable."

"How do you know he was telling you the truth?"

Finn sighed. It was the same question that he'd been asked in Torthen. "I suppose I don't. If you're wondering if I questioned him the way I would question people in Verendal, the answer is no. I didn't have any supplies with me for such a thing, and it didn't seem necessary."

"You believed you could tell when he told you the truth."

"I believe he wanted me to challenge him. I believe he felt no remorse for what he did. And I believe he did it because he thought it was necessary." Finn paused. "I've seen men like that before, men who have done things in the past, men who have taken the law into their hands. Leland Volt was such a man."

"Why would that make him honorable?"

"I don't know that it does. It makes him... relatable."

She smiled at him. "Then perhaps the sentencing was justified."

"I don't know if I made a mistake." Finn looked down. "I'm trying to do what Meyer taught me, but without him here..."

They sat in silence for a little while, the wind still drawing through the upper branches, leaving them swaying and rustling high overhead. The horse whinnied at him, and Finn looked back, realizing again that she'd come on foot.

"Why did you come alone?"

"Do you think I need another with me for protection?

Perhaps you think I need a man such as yourself to watch over me."

Finn started to smile. "Actually, I was hoping *you'd* watch over *me* so I could rest since you have magic. That's something I lack."

She sniffed. "That you know of."

"I'm quite certain I would know if I had magic."

"Would you? Most wouldn't believe such a thing was possible."

Finn found himself smiling at her, and watched as Esmerelda leaned forward and dug into a small bag that she had with her. He didn't know if she would pull out another piece of the tasty bread, but instead she had a book that she flipped open, and began to thumb through the pages.

She didn't look up at him.

He rested his head back, looking up at the sky. Through the swaying of the trees, he could make out a few stars. Clouds drifted across the sky, making it more difficult for him to see them clearly, but when he did, he stared, trying to make out the patterns that were there, wondering if the gods were up among the stars and looking down upon him the same way that he was looking up. He didn't know, but he hoped that was the case.

CHAPTER NINETEEN

Finn rubbed the sleep from his eyes and sat up. Dawn had started to break, and as he looked around him, he started to wonder if the night had been something of a dream. Esmerelda wouldn't *really* have joined him in the middle of the darkness, sitting by his fire while he rested.

He found her leaned up against one of the trees. In the growing sunlight, her black hair had a luster to it that left him longing to run his hands through it. There'd probably be a cost in that as well. Her eyes seemed closed, and she breathed regularly. Finn found himself admiring her a moment. There was danger in doing so when she was awake.

Three different small ceramic items were situated around her, resting on the ground.

One of them looked familiar to him, and he wondered if he might have stolen it sometime before, though had he stolen it, he doubted that she would have left it out like that.

Maybe she would have. It would probably amuse her to remind him of the kinds of things that he once had done before meeting Meyer.

He sat back. The day was already beginning in full, and the wind whipped in with more force, cold and biting. He wrapped his cloak around his shoulders and got to his feet to check on the horse, patting his side as he neighed softly.

Esmerelda opened one eye and looked over at him. "You're awake. I've been waiting for you to come around. You sleep heavily."

She sat up, running her fingers through her dark hair and somehow managing to make it look as if she had brushed it. Probably magic, though if that was how she used magic, it would amuse him.

"I sleep heavily? You were still out when I got up."

"Only this time," she said.

"Was there another time?"

She started to smile. "Where to today, Finn Jagger?"

He patted the horse again, loosing the reins around the branch as he untied him. "Ferd. That's where I'm headed today. That was the second village I was asked to visit during this pilgrimage."

They started walking, heading away from the copse of trees and toward the road. Esmerelda stayed with him. He hadn't been entirely sure that she would, wondering if perhaps she would veer off and perhaps travel with other hegen.

"You really did come alone," Finn remarked as they neared the road.

"I am perfectly capable of managing on my own," she said.

"That's not what I was getting at," Finn said.

"Then what did you imply, Finn Jagger?"

"That the road has been dangerous."

"Who says?"

"Those who've been traveling it."

She quirked a smile at him. "Exactly."

She walked, which led Finn to remain walking. He would have ridden, and he considered having her sit astride the horse with him, but decided that might be much closer to Esmerelda than he was willing to get. Even walking alongside her left him... unsettled. Strangely, he thought the way she unsettled him was appealing. Not that he would ever tell her that. Esmerelda would likely find some way to use that against him.

"Would you prefer to ride?" he asked.

"Would you?"

"I would if you weren't here."

"Don't let me keep you from your pilgrimage."

"You plan on heading to Ferd as well, don't you?" Her arrival wasn't coincidence.

She was searching for something.

Would she find it in Ferd?

She turned to him, cocking her head slightly and offering a hint of a smile.

They remained silent. The sun continued to rise, though it did nothing to push back the chill in the air. It was cool, almost cold. Clouds in the sky spoke of weather moving toward them, though there was no other sign of a storm.

About midday, they crossed a small stream and Finn paused to let the horse drink.

"Do you know these lands?" he asked as he found Esmerelda staring into the forest. There was an intensity to her that he couldn't quite place.

"I know many lands," she said.

"Where are the hegen from?"

"You've seen the hegen section, I believe. The hegen aren't from anyplace else these days," Esmerelda said.

"Where are you from, then?"

"Why, the kingdom."

She turned away from where she studied the forest, crouching over the stream, dipping her hands into the cool water and cupping it to her face. As she drank, she looked down into the stream as if she were seeing something that Finn had not.

"Can you tell me more about the Alainsith people?"

"What would you have me tell you?"

"I am curious to know more about them. All I know from within the city are rumors."

"Rumors have a way of being true." She stood, wiping her hands on her cloak, and turned toward the King's Road. She waited for Finn to join her, and they started off, heading along the road, moving at the same steady pace.

Finn had no idea how long it would take him to reach Ferd at this pace. He ran the numbers in his head about how long he had been outside of the city. Long enough he would need to return soon. He'd been gone for the better part of three days now. That left only four more days for him to return to the city.

Would that be long enough for him to find the answers he sought? All he needed was either proof of his guilt or something that would suggest that they made a mistake in sentencing him. Finn had no idea whether he would find either. Meyer had wanted the Hunter, though Finn started to wonder if that was who he could be.

"The Alainsith have magic that keeps us from entering the forest, but are they truly faster than our soldiers?"

"Faster. Stronger."

"I suppose you would say smarter, too."

She started to smile. "I wouldn't say it, but I imagine they would."

"How have we managed peace, then?"

She frowned. "Why would you ask that?"

"If they're faster and stronger, why is it they haven't attacked?"

"Not all search for violence as an answer." Her gaze flickered to the sword at his back before she looked over to him. "And you have seen how the kingdom has managed peace." She glanced to the forest. "There are some who would prefer to see the treaty challenged. They would rather the kingdom and the Alainsith find reasons to fight. I fear they believe they would gain from such an arrangement. It's possible they have already planned for the possibility the kingdom would attack the Alainsith, though I would hope the king recognizes the folly in such a venture."

"Why would it be a folly?"

She slowed, which forced Finn to slow to avoid shooting past her. "You have seen magic firsthand, Finn Jagger. You understand there is more to the world than what you once knew. You should be able to understand that because of that magic, there are certain things others should not challenge. Doing so would be dangerous to them."

"Then how is it that we've been safe from them? Why would there even be a treaty..." Even as he said it, Finn thought that he understood. He'd seen the reason. That reason was all throughout Verendal. From the viscount's manor to the palace to the people situated outside the walls of the city. "What role do the hegen play in protecting the city?"

He'd seen it, though. From the very first time he'd gotten involved with the hegen.

He looked over at her, but she didn't meet his eyes.

They walked a little farther, staying silent.

"Does the king know?"

Finn tried to work through what he knew about the hegen, about the king, and even about the Alainsith.

It was possible that the king *didn't* know what they did.

He might believe that he had instigated a treaty and the Alainsith abided by it.

"Why would you help the kingdom in that way?" he asked. Esmerelda had moved ahead of him, and he needed to run to keep up with her. The horse jogged alongside, whinnying. Probably annoyed with Finn for moving so slowly.

She stopped and turned, reaching into her pocket. When she pulled her hand out, she had a collection of cards in hand. She turned them over, one at a time. They were all cards Finn had seen before. The blood hand. The crown. Even the blank card. All were tied to him.

Esmerelda continued flipping through the cards, and as she turned them over, the images on the cards shifted, changing into something else.

"Is it tied to the cards you give me?"

"I did not give you the cards," she said.

"I don't understand. You gave me the card."

She continued to flip them, and he saw them change. "What you see as me providing it was something I see as quite a bit different," she said. As she continued flipping the cards, Finn watched, wondering what she was getting at.

"If you didn't give me the card, then who did?"

"Perhaps that's the question, isn't it?"

She motioned for his hand, and Finn held it out. She motioned for the other, and he placed it alongside the first, cupping his hands together. She began placing cards atop his palms, one after another until the cards covered the surface of his palms.

"You recognize this one," she said, flipping over card that showed the bloody hand. "What about this one?" It was the crown.

Finn nodded to both. "Those were the cards you gave me originally."

"I believe this was the card I gave you originally," she said. She flipped another card, and this one was blank. It lingered there for a moment before it started to shimmer. It was almost as if ink began to appear on the surface, swirling in a pattern that began to take shape slowly. She flipped the card over, and it was once again blank. She turned it to the other side, and the ink continued to move, forming a spiraling sort of pattern until it took on the appearance of a sword.

"I haven't gotten a card like that yet."

"No." She turned another card, and this one was also blank. The ink started to swirl, but rather than starting to take shape, it remained swirling, a pattern that formed. "This one has not decided which way it would go," Esmerelda said.

"The card decides?"

"In a sense," she answered. "You probably believed we were in control of it."

"It seemed the most likely."

"The most likely for you. Yet it's what you find on the cards I'm most interested in."

"Why?"

"Because it helps me decide what must be done."

She turned another card, and it remained blank.

Finn looked at the others in her hand and noticed that many of them had symbols on their surface. They were not blank.

"What about those?"

"Those are cards I think I understand."

"You *think* you understand?"

"There is much about the cards that has yet to be

learned," she said.

Finn shook his head. "When you gave me the card—"

"When I gave you the card, it was blank. Much like these. The card decided how you would be used."

Finn started to smile. "That doesn't make any sense."

"Nor should it. Not to you. As you say, it is magic, and it is the kind of magic that does not belong to Finn Jagger."

"No. Hegen magic."

"Unfortunately, that is not hegen magic."

"I've seen hegen magic."

"You've felt hegen magic," Esmerelda said. "You have not seen it. This is not it. These cards are not hegen magic."

"Then what are they?"

"Our way of trying to understand."

"If they aren't yours, then whose are they?"

He thought that he knew what she was getting at, but he wanted her to tell him. If they *were* Alainsith, then he would have to try to understand why he was used by them.

All along, he had thought it was the hegen. Maybe it really was. Perhaps it was a hegen more powerful than Esmerelda. He didn't know that much about the hegen, so he suspected there would be someone among their people who was powerful enough to manipulate the cards like that, though the question remained as to what purpose there would be in doing something like that.

"They are tied to something greater."

"The Alainsith. That's what you don't want to share with me."

She tipped her head, nodding slightly. "Where you see

the touch of the hegen, I see a different influence."

"But they're your cards."

"The cards might be ours, but the magic used to touch them is not. It is ancient. Powerful. Tied to something so different that the knowledge of it no longer belongs to my people. The power we add into the making of the cards touches upon that ancient magic, gifting us insight we would not have otherwise."

"How do you make the cards?" She didn't answer, so Finn cupped his hands together, grabbing the cards that she'd placed there. "They're your creation, even if the magic within them is not yours. How do you make them?"

"I have already shared with you the secret of that," she said.

"The executions."

"There is power in death, much like there is power in life. We harness that power. It's what allows us to try to understand the way the Alainsith intend to influence us."

"Why would they allow you to know?"

"I'm not certain they do. Or if they do, I'm not certain they can do anything to stop it. Either way, by studying the cards, by trying to understand the message upon them, we have been able to maintain a level of peace with the Alainsith."

Finn flipped over the card. The bloody hand took on a different meaning. When he'd first seen it, he had thought the hegen had wanted him to hurt Oscar. He hadn't been willing to do it, and by his unwillingness, he believed that he'd gone against the hegen.

What if going against the card had been what she'd wanted from me?

It seemed possible.

"Why do you use the cards?" he asked softly. They still hadn't moved, though Finn wasn't sure that it made sense for him to move anywhere until he had a better understanding. He felt as if he were close. All it would take would be for Esmerelda to reveal a little more and he thought that he might finally start to understand the hegen. That was worth a delay. "In the city. Why do you use so many cards?"

"The more that we understand, the more we might begin to know just what it is that the Alainsith intend."

Finn continued flipping through the cards. He paused at the one that had the strange ink swirling around it. The ink was dark, almost black, though as he held up the light, he realized that wasn't the case at all.

It was maroon.

Blood.

That couldn't be a coincidence.

Not with the way the hegen used the cards. Not with the nature of the power that they summoned through them.

"What if this isn't the Alainsith at all?"

"We would know," she said.

"I'm not so sure you would. You believe these cards represent the Alainsith, but what if they represent some other power that has been using you?"

"We try to understand," she said.

"I understand you do. I can see you're gathering these cards." And it made sense why the hegen would suddenly be willing to help. It made sense why the hegen would trade favors.

It was the only way that they would be able to accumulate cards like this, cards that connected them to something different. Some other connection to power.

"We do what we must."

Finn sorted through the cards, seeing if there was anything that he'd be able to learn about them, but there was not. The one with the swirling ink didn't change at all, just continued to spiral, creating the strange, undulating pattern.

"What now?" he asked.

She took the cards from him. "Now we continue our search."

"Why are you concerned about the man in the city, then?"

"He should not have been there," she said.

"You've said that, but you haven't told me why."

"Finn Jagger, I'm sure that if you think about it, you can come up with the reason why."

"Because the Alainsith are from the other side of the forest."

She nodded.

"Unless they've decided to begin moving."

She said nothing.

"That's what you're concerned about."

Esmerelda looked over. "I'm concerned about the possibility that the protection we offer is no longer effective."

CHAPTER TWENTY

Ferd nestled in a small valley, so that when they came to it, the village was nothing more than a dozen houses and a stout central building that spread out before them. It was later in the day; a few hours until dusk.

He and Esmerelda had made small talk. Nothing more. She'd asked about his family, and Finn had shared. When he'd asked about hers, she had balked until he pushed and she revealed a little about them. He'd learned that she had a younger brother, though he didn't have magic as she did, and that her parents lived far from Verendal. It had been comfortable, and Finn found himself relaxing around her, having a conversation without thinking about what he would owe in exchange.

They had veered off the King's Road, heading farther to the north and west, closer to the dark forest that seemed to follow them. Esmerelda had known where to go and had guided them onto a less-traveled road. Finn hadn't objected.

He had a vague idea of how to find Ferd and thought that what she'd told him was right. Even if it wasn't, he'd been curious about where she would lead him.

When they reached the rise leading down into the valley, Finn had stopped and studied the village. If this was Ferd, as he had hoped, he started running through the time that would be needed to get him back to Verendal. It would require that he ride quickly. Hopefully, what had to be done there could be done as rapidly.

Smoke curled from chimneys. The few houses were small and quaint, with thatched roofs and wooden sides. There were a few people out in the streets, perhaps all the village held. They hadn't encountered many people on the walk, either. One man heading toward Torthen who'd looked at them, leering at Esmerelda until seeing Finn's sword, and a small caravan of travelers, mostly men with a few women, who had passed them by without even nodding.

"It does not look as if there should be a sentencing here," Esmerelda said, pausing as they looked down toward the village.

"Why not?"

"Many reasons, though perhaps the simplest is that it will change the energy here." She looked to the sky, pulling her cloak around her. "Imagine it when the snow falls. Blankets of white draped over the buildings. The smell of the smoke drifting from the homes warm and welcoming."

"I can imagine it. That doesn't mean this kind of place doesn't see violence." Assuming that was why he'd been summoned there. Unlike in Torthen, there was no gallows already erected. Whatever the reason for his summons, Finn had yet to learn it.

"I suppose not," she said softly.

She started forward and Finn followed.

Unlike within Torthen, where it seemed to teem with a strange energy, this village felt quiet and calm. Almost lazy. It was a place where he could imagine relaxing and not worrying about having to perform a questioning and carrying out a sentencing.

"Where would you have us go, Finn Jagger?"

They followed the main road through the village and he nodded toward the central building. "The village hall, I suppose. I would question the condemned." He turned to her. "What about you? What would you do now?"

She shrugged. "Perhaps I would watch."

"You would collect your prizes."

"There is no shame in that."

He didn't know whether having her with him would pose a challenge for him or not. It was possible that the hegen would raise questions within the village. They would be questions that Finn wouldn't necessarily have an answer for, either.

The small, squat building was situated in the shadow of a tiny church—probably intentionally—and made of stone. A wooden door was set into the center of the building without any other marking, and a few windows along the face of the building would allow light inside, though he didn't see any shining out of them.

Finn tied off the horse and headed to the door, glancing over to Esmerelda as she followed him. When he knocked, he stepped back and waited.

It didn't take long for the door to open. An older man with a balding head, graying hair at his temples, looked from Finn to Esmerelda. "I'm afraid this is not an inn. If you're looking for a place to stay, may I suggest Maggie's. She is welcoming to travelers and will put you up in a spare room for cheap."

He had started to pull the door closed when Finn grabbed it, prying it back open.

"Is this the village hall?"

The man cocked his head to the side. His eyes went to Finn's sword. "This is."

Finn took a deep breath. "I am Finn Jagger, a king's executioner from Verendal. I was dispatched to Ferd to carry out the king's justice."

"You seem young to be an executioner."

Finn nodded. "Perhaps that is true. Where might I visit with your condemned?"

"Visit? We sent word that we needed a hangman, not someone to question the poor sop. We've already done that enough."

"You will excuse me for my persistence, but I must ensure the sentence is just."

"You don't think we know how to apply the king's laws?"

It was more than just the king's laws. There were the local laws and customs that Finn had to account for. Many of them were different from those of the king, which meant that many of the crimes in places like this would be different from those the king would assign.

"I would make no claim as to that," Finn said. "Only that it is customary for the executioner to question the condemned."

The man stared at him before waving his hand. "Very well. Come along."

He stepped into the hall, and Finn hesitated.

He hadn't expected them to have kept him within the hall itself. When he followed, he glanced back, but Esmerelda was gone.

"What happened to your woman?" the man asked as they traveled.

"She must have decided to see the rest of your village."

He grunted. "Can't say there's much to see here. We don't get much trade here. Too far off the King's Road for that, I suppose. Those who come here do so because they intend to come here. Either that or they're hiding."

He reached a stone stair leading down and motioned for Finn to follow.

Lantern light lit the way, though it wasn't nearly as bright as what Finn thought he would need.

"You have a prison here?" Finn asked.

"Prison? Gods, no. We have a cellar. Figured that was the best place to keep him. Don't have anything else that's secured."

The man hurried ahead, making his way down the stairs, leaving Finn to follow.

When he reached the landing, he looked over to the man. "I didn't catch your name."

"Rory Oldam. Been the chief councilor here for... oh, well, I suppose going on twenty years. Folks get used to having a bit of the same, you see. Not that I would change anything. I'm more than happy to serve Ferd in this way."

They stopped in front of a small doorway. Rory tapped on the door before fishing in his pocket and pulling out a ring of keys. "Least these closets lock," he muttered. "Otherwise, we don't have much of a way to keep him tied up here. Not that Jarnel is going anywhere. Bastard slaughtered a man up on the hill and practically bathed in his blood, he did."

Rory pulled the door open and stepped aside.

There wasn't that much lantern light in the hall by which to see, but Finn didn't know that he needed all that much. He could smell the stench. It wasn't nearly as bad as what he'd smelled when it came to Leland Volt, but it was still foul. That wasn't what really caught his attention, though. It was the way Jarnel's leg seemed to be angled.

"You broke his leg," Finn said.

"Damn boy thought to run from us."

"You didn't think to try to set it?"

"What for? You're just going to hang him anyway. No need to get him all prettied up before he swings."

Finn turned to Jarnel, ignoring Rory for a moment. "Jarnel..." He hesitated, looking to Rory. "What's his surname?"

"Sarken. Came to the village a month back to help with

the harvest. Should have turned him away, but needed the help."

"Jarnel Sarken. I am Finn Jagger, king's executioner." Finn nodded to Rory. "You can leave him to me."

"Leave you? What do you intend to do with him?"

Finn frowned. "I intend to ask him a few questions." He stared intently at Rory until he finally turned away.

Finn sighed. It had gone easier in Torthen, though how much of that was because of the nature of the crime that had been committed? He'd heard the rumors in Torthen. Was Jarnel the one responsible for cutting people up?

Rory left the door open as he headed along the hall, leaving Finn alone with Jarnel. There wasn't much light drifting into the room. Only enough for him to make out Jarnel's outline, barely much more than that. He could easily see the way that his leg had been bent, and he wondered what they had done to him. An injury like that would be incredibly painful, though he didn't have the sense from Rory that they much cared. Finn did. He didn't like that he would have a prisoner he was expected to carry out a sentence upon who would go to the gallows—or the sword, he decided—without having a chance to recover. That was Meyer's influence on him, he supposed.

"Would you care to tell me what happened?" Finn asked.

Jarnel just grunted.

Finn crouched down. It was hard for him to tell just how injured Jarnel was. In the darkness, he could have any number of injuries. The smell could be from his injury, or it could just be the foulness of the cell.

He leaned forward, straining so that he could better understand just what had happened to Jarnel, but in the faint light of the cell, Finn wasn't able to see much.

Jarnel hadn't moved.

He moaned every so often, enough that Finn believed that he was awake and, better yet, still alive, but that was it.

"I need to know what happened," Finn said.

Jarnel grunted again.

Finn leaned forward, checking on Jarnel. His face was bruised, the assault leaving his mouth and jaw all twisted. Jarnel wasn't going to be able to tell him anything.

Finn let out a frustrated sigh.

He had come here intending to carry out the sentencing, but with what had happened to Jarnel, Finn didn't think that he would be able to do so.

Would the villagers understand?

Most people didn't really understand. Of course, when it came to carrying out a sentence, most of the time within Verendal, the sentencing was done by the magister and the jurors, and the people of the city knew nothing about it until the sentencing occurred.

How many of the villagers knew that Jarnel was there, awaiting sentence?

Finn stepped out of the room, closing the door behind him.

Jarnel wasn't going anywhere. He didn't even need to worry about locking it, though perhaps he should be more concerned than he was.

He ensured that the door was closed tightly before

THE EXECUTIONER'S BLADE | 355

heading back along the hallway. When he reached the stairs, he started up them slowly, and at the top, he found Rory waiting.

"You knew I wasn't going to be able to learn anything from him," Finn said.

"What would there be for you to learn, anyway? Told you what he did. Not much is going to change those facts."

"Every man has an opportunity to share their side," Finn said.

"We gave him a chance to speak," Rory said. He glanced behind Finn, looking toward the stairs. "We learned what he did. Probably came here just for that reason. And now he's going to swing for it."

"Not like this, he isn't," Finn said.

"What?" Rory sputtered.

Finn just shook his head. "You have a man who is in no shape to even answer questions. He isn't going to hang until he has the opportunity to do so."

Rory crossed his arms over his chest. "You aren't going to carry out the lawfully given sentence?"

"Lawfully?" Finn shook his head. "I'm not sure it was lawfully given."

"What are you saying, hangman?"

"What I'm saying, Mr. Oldam, is that your prisoner has been beaten. His face bruised, his jaw likely broken, along with his leg. No prisoner will be presented to the gods in such a manner."

Rory cocked his head, frowning. "Presented to the gods? What are you going on about?"

Finn stared at him. "How many men have you sentenced to die in your time serving the village?"

"Why, none. We don't have problems with this kind of thing that often. It was a horrible crime, it was. Murdering the poor man in the forest, coating himself in his blood..." Rory just closed his eyes. "The gods know that Jarnel deserves whatever fate befalls him."

Finn looked back along the stairs. *That* was what Jarnel had done? He couldn't imagine that man having murdered anyone, though he'd been around enough criminals over the years that it wasn't altogether surprising that someone would commit such a heinous act that he wouldn't have expected of them.

"The prisoners are given a chance at redemption. All prisoners, regardless of their crimes. They should have a priest visiting with them, giving them the chance to speak to the Mother—"

"We have no priests here. There will be no redemption. Didn't you hear what I had to say?"

No priests even though he'd seen the church?

What was going on in this village?

"I heard you," Finn said softly.

"Gods! Had I known what you were going to say, we would have strung him up ourselves."

That reminded him of what Volt had said. "You would have faced the king's punishment."

Rory waved his hand dismissively. "It would have been worth it."

Finn would have to decide whether he would violate

custom—and that was all it was—in order to carry out the sentence. He would have to decide if he *could* carry out the sentence. Which meant understanding whether Jarnel was guilty of what he'd been accused of doing.

"Show me where you found him."

"Where we found who?"

"Jarnel."

"What would that do for you?" Rory asked.

Finn glared at him. "It would allow me to know if you've followed the process of the law."

Rory met his gaze for a moment before turning away.

They headed out of the village hall. The sun hadn't set yet, though it was getting low in the sky. Colors streaked in the distance, a mixture of blue and orange and red, all as if a painter were sweeping a brush through the sky. There was no sign of Esmerelda, which made Finn smile. Of course she would disappear.

Rory stormed forward, not bothering to see if Finn would follow. They reached the edge of the village, and from there they took a narrow trail that led away from the village and toward the tree line. They climbed up the valley, and when they reached the top, Rory paused, finally looking behind him toward the village in the distance.

"I've always enjoyed the view from here," Rory said.

Finn looked behind him. From there, the village looked quite lovely, nestled into the valley. He could tell how it was longer than it was wide, and the church rising up from the middle of the village seemed to offer a protection, as if they were straining to reach for the gods.

"You have a beautiful village."

Rory shook his head. "It used to be. Lately, we've had trouble," Rory said. "We've seen bandits come riding through. They don't stop—we wouldn't give them a chance to stop—but they tear through the village, heading toward the forest."

"Bandits?" That didn't make a whole lot of sense to Finn, though there had been what Bev mentioned. Beyond Ferd wasn't anything but the forest. He understood traffic along the King's Road. It stretched from Verendal at the edge of the kingdom all the way to the capital itself, and then beyond, to other cities that Finn had only heard of. Murich. Dawarn. Altorn. All of them supposedly the size of Verendal and all on the far side of the kingdom. They were places that Finn imagined his father would have wanted to visit.

"Recently. Mostly in pairs, sometimes riding in larger groups. Thankfully, they've had no reason to try to stop in Ferd. Not that we would be able to do much if they thought to attack my people. We're not fighters here. We're simple folk, just wanting to live our lives."

"What do they look like?"

Rory frowned. "Why? You think you've come across them before?"

Finn just shrugged. He wasn't going to tell Rory that he hadn't been out of Verendal before recently. He had a sense that Rory wouldn't care for that.

"They're probably from closer to the capital. Riding sleek horses—likely stolen, mind you—and wearing strange colors. Green cloaks that blend into the forest. Bandits."

Rory turned away and motioned to the forest. "They didn't do nothing to us, so not sure why Jarnel decided to kill one of them. Maybe he knew him before he came. Terrible thing, it was. Saw him with the knife in hand, the blood all over his body. Do you know how long that took to scrub off of him? Poor sop was moaning the whole time. Couldn't talk, of course. Got hit during the assault, we think. Made it so he couldn't say nothing."

Here, Finn had believed that Rory and his people had been responsible for what had happened to Jarnel, but if they hadn't...

"Where did it take place?" he asked.

Rory looked at him for a moment before motioning for Finn to follow.

They reached the edge of the forest. The air changed immediately, shifting from a cool breeze to something even colder. The bite was unpleasant, even with the cloak he wore. Finn shifted it, pulling it around him. The trees weren't the usual pine and oak he'd been passing through on his way toward Ferd. These were older. Massive trunks stretched up high into the air. As he looked into the darkness of the forest, it seemed to him that the trees got even larger, if such a thing were possible. Some of the roots of the trees protruded from the ground, running along the surface and curling into another tree's roots, like strange long fingers intertwined.

"Here?" Finn asked in a whisper. That whisper felt right, for some reason.

Rory nodded. "Right about here. Somewhere just inside

the border. If you need to find the exact spot, I'm sure I could help you in the morning. I'm not going into the forest at night."

Finn realized that while he'd come close to the trees, Rory had stayed beyond the edge of the forest, as if afraid to get too close. He eyed the trees with a strange suspicion. Finn smiled, but Rory continued looking at the forest as if it might suddenly do something to attack.

"Why not?" Finn asked.

Rory looked over. "Strange things happen in the forest at night."

"What kind of strange things?"

Rory opened his mouth as if he were going to answer before clamping it shut again and shaking his head. A mournful howl echoed from within the trees.

"If you want to stay out here, you can be my guest, but I am going to return. As I told you before, you can probably find lodging with Maggie. She has offered it to travelers before. Look for the mark of Heleth on her door."

Rory turned away suddenly and hurried back toward the city.

That was strange.

Finn looked into the darkness of the forest, breathing in the forest's scents. He could feel that there was something different about the forest, but it *was* just a forest.

Why would Jarnel have attacked the bandit? And then coated himself in blood?

Finn started into the trees.

In his time working with Meyer, he had visited many

different crime scenes. Some were strange, homes or businesses or one time out near a farm where old Mr. Jorgen had thought to kill his apprentice and feed him to his hogs. There hadn't been much of the boy remaining. Some bones. A few limbs that Finn suspected Meyer had sold off to the hegen, and blood. Lots of blood. It had mixed with the mud, creating a muck that had stained his boots. It had taken Finn hours to scrub the boots clean. Not only his but Meyer's as well. As his apprentice, Finn was blessed with getting the opportunity to ensure that Meyer's boots were cleaned.

As he stepped into the woods, he sank into the ground a little bit. The ground was damp, spongier than he would've expected, and the air held a bit of pressure within it.

That pressure was strange to Finn. It was cold, and somehow the wind blowing through managed to pull out his cloak, tearing it away from his grip so that it seemed to slither beneath the protective layer. He grabbed at it, wrapping the cloak around himself, and headed deeper into the forest, wandering between the trees.

He studied the ground, looking for anything that would suggest the location where Jarnel had slaughtered the bandit. A murder like that should leave bloodstains on the ground. Gods, it should even leave bloodstains on the trees.

Finn looked for anything but came across nothing.

Another mournful cry erupted from the forest. It was soft, muted, but he could hear it echoing through, leaving him with a chill that had nothing to do with the cold.

Finn turned in place, trying to see where the tree line

was. It was difficult for him to be able to see it at all. Having come into the forest, now Finn was not able to make out the border.

That had to be the reason for Rory's concern. He must have known it was easy to get disoriented within the forest.

Finn wasn't a woodsman. He didn't have the knowledge and skill to track through the forest and find his way to freedom. He was a city boy and could navigate streets and alleys and darkened places with the best of them—or at least he once had been able to. He had never had much interest in wandering within a forest like this.

He paused, feeling the cold wind blowing through his cloak and along his arms. He clutched it to him, focusing on the direction of the wind. He remembered the way the wind had blown when he had come in. It had gusted out of the forest, as if pushing through the trees and toward the village.

He turned so that the wind was at his back and used that feeling to push him forward, guiding him away. He took a few steps, making his way around one massive tree, before pausing so that he could look out and see if he could find the edge of the forest.

He saw nothing.

The only thing he noticed was the wind, and a strange ongoing pressure from within the forest that seemed to try to squeeze him, as if it were trying to contain him within the forest.

Finn cursed his stupidity. He should have returned to the village with Rory. There might be another way that he could find himself freed from the forest. If the wolf cried out again, he could follow that sound and let it guide him.

He leaned against a tree. The bark was smooth, almost soft. Unpleasantly so.

Finn turned, looking around him. In the time that he'd been in the forest, the darkness had fallen, leaving him feeling trapped.

Another sound echoed, though this was not the sound of a wolf. A cry.

It was close.

What choice did he have but to see what had happened?

CHAPTER TWENTY-ONE

The forest seemed to swallow him.

Finn tried not to think that way, but as he followed the sound that he'd heard, he couldn't help it. The trees grew closer together, the deeper he went into the forest, making it difficult for him to be able to see much of anything. The darkened shadows of the trunks loomed in front of him, massive enough that he could at least avoid them, but he worried that he wouldn't be able to avoid running into all of them.

The roots that had been tracing along the surface of the ground stuck up in places, and he had to step over them, though he stumbled from time to time. Once, he'd landed on his hands and knees, surprised by how hard he'd hit the ground, considering how spongy it had felt.

He had to pull himself free from where the root tangled around his foot. When he was back up, he decided to use the sword to help him probe his way forward. The idea of explaining to Meyer why the blade might be dulled amused him, though that amusement didn't last all that long in the darkness. There was only the feeling of the blackness of the trees around him, that and the cold wind.

The cry didn't come again.

Finn worried about that.

He should have gone for help when he'd heard the cry, but who would he have gone to and how would he have even found a way to get help? He was stuck there in the forest, so finding his way to freedom wasn't going to be easy.

As he slowed, looking around him to try to decide if he was still heading in the right direction, he heard the cry again.

It was closer than before.

He could feel a mournful quality to it.

Finn started forward again, using the sword to jab at the ground so he wouldn't trip again. At least it helped him avoid getting tangled by the roots. A faint greenish light in the distance caught his attention.

A chill washed through him.

Finn approached it slowly.

There *had* been a soft cry. Not an animal sound; that had been decidedly human.

The wind seemed to pick up, whistling through the trees, even colder than it had been before. The green light disappeared.

He tried to follow it, but as he made his way around a massive tree, he found himself disoriented. Finn had to figure out where that sound had come from. In the darkness, it was increasingly difficult for him to do. He'd followed the wind, but even that wasn't possible for him to do quite as easily now.

He stopped and looked around.

The cry had been real. When it came again, he jumped.

It rang out in the quiet of the night, filtering through the trees. The sound was muted, but it was loud enough that he was able to track where it had come from.

Not far from him.

Finn hurried forward.

The greenish light returned.

"Hello?"

The wind picked up, carrying his voice away.

He moved more carefully toward that greenish light. He could go slowly, just far enough that he could get past the edge of the trees, but then it seemed as if he hit some sort of invisible wall.

Finn jabbed at it with the sword. A spark flickered where the sword touched, as if it were connecting to something.

The cry came again. It was just in front of him.

He couldn't see anything, but he knew there was something there.

Finn jabbed with the sword again. As before, sparks flickered.

He pressed forward. The executioner's sword had a blunted end, not pointed like a traditional sword. The blade was sharp enough to cleave a head off in a single stroke, and it had been freshly oiled before he'd left. The only thing that had changed about the blade since he'd been given it was that he had actually used it, and blood had stained the blade.

The blade continued to spark.

What was going on there?

His heart started racing slightly. The only thing that came to mind was something he didn't want to acknowledge. Magic.

He worried he somehow dulled it by whatever he pressed against.

The cry came again.

There was an urgency to it. It set his heart fluttering.

If magic were involved, it would be better for him to turn away. Run. Head back to the village if he could. That cry left him wondering if such a thing would even be possible.

He had to get past the magic.

There didn't seem to be any way for him to do it. The only thing that he could think of doing was hacking at the barrier. He brought the sword up and then down, slicing at it as if he were attempting an execution.

Finn had practiced the stroke enough times he knew how to angle his body for the most effective strike. Normally, he had a target. When the blade struck the strange barrier, not only were there sparks again but he felt something split.

It was the same way that he'd felt pumpkins split when he practiced on them. The way he'd felt the cadavers split when he'd practiced with them. And the way it felt when he sentenced a man.

The greenish light flickered, then faded.

The resistance was gone. Whatever had been there and opposed him was no longer.

He started forward, sweeping the blade in front of him. He didn't want to end up trapped by it again.

Where was the source of the cry?

Whatever had caused it had to be near. Finn searched, looking all around him. There was nothing. Darkness. That was it.

"Hello?"

His voice came out halting, and it sounded a bit nervous to him. Finn *was* nervous. Coming there like this and facing the gods only knew what left him feeling on edge.

There was no answer.

Finn continued forward. Whatever had been here had cried out. He was certain of that. He *had* heard something. Someone.

"Hello?"

He said it louder, though as before, there was no answer.

Finn took another step. The trees seemed to open up. A soft burbling sound, that of a stream, was nearby. He noticed a pale light, a soft white glowing, directly in front of him.

Could it be a lantern or a fire?

Finn headed toward that.

Something seemed to grab at his ankles again, and he jabbed at it with the sword. He didn't expect it to do anything, but he wasn't about to get tangled by the branches there.

Finn fell into something soft. Mushy. Mud? At least, he hoped that it was mud. He crawled to his feet, making it a few steps, before falling forward again. A stream near him sent a spray of water.

He had dropped close to the stream.

Finn got to his hands and knees and looked around. There wasn't anything there—other than that strange light. There had been no further cry. Whatever had made that sound had fallen silent.

Had I been drawn there in some way?

Finn stood, wiping his hands on his pants. The light was near him.

As he approached, using the sword to balance, he probed with the end of the blade, pressing outward. Finn found nothing other than the spongy ground.

"Hello?"

This time, he called out a little more loudly. His voice sounded muted nonetheless, as if the forest attempted to swallow everything that he said. The pale light in front of him surged, just a little.

A figure lying on the ground caught his attention. Finn hurried forward. When he crouched next to the figure, his breath caught.

"Esmerelda?"

She rolled her head toward him. Her eyes had a strange glaze to them, and though there was a hint of light that seemed to come from everywhere, shadows swirled around her.

"What happened?"

He ran his hands along her arms, then her legs, feeling only slightly guilty about it. Meyer had taught him to assess for injuries, and right now he needed to see if there was anything wrong with her. He wasn't able to see much in the darkness, so he had to try a different approach.

No obvious injuries.

He checked her neck, twisting her head from side to side, but didn't see anything on her face. There wasn't any obvious blood when he ran his fingers through her hair—*it was so soft*—and he moved her cloak to see if he might find anything there.

Nothing. No injuries. Nothing obvious, that was.

That didn't mean she hadn't been hurt.

Finn didn't know enough about magic. There was the hegen magic. Power that came from life—and death. He'd seen it used before. Felt it used before. That power had saved his life. Then there was the magic that had targeted Oscar. It *might* have been hegen, though Finn didn't think so. And if not, then it meant some other way of accessing power.

What was Esmerelda doing out there, though?

She moaned softly, and he touched her on the shoulder, trying to calm her as best as he could.

"What happened?" he whispered again.

There was no answer.

Finn tried to move her before realizing that maybe he

should not. Moving her without knowing how injured she might be could be dangerous to her.

Instead, he carefully lifted her head and propped it on his lap. He checked for anything else that might be injured but didn't find anything. He sat with her, waiting for her to come back around but not knowing whether she would. With what had happened there, he didn't know what it would take.

After a while, the wind started to whistle.

It had done that when he'd first come into the forest, but now he heard it differently. The sound was steady, almost mournful, and as it gusted between the trees, he looked around.

"You shouldn't be here," Esmerelda said.

Finn looked down, relieved that she was awake. "What happened to you?"

She tried to move but winced and laid her head back in his lap. "I don't remember."

Finn smiled at her. "You forget I have experience questioning."

"What does that have to do with anything?"

"It allows me to know when you're not telling me the truth."

She tried to sit again and had more success than the last time. She still winced but managed to get up and look around. "I felt something out here. I came to investigate. That is all."

Finn scooted away from her. Now that she was sitting

up, he didn't want her to think that he was forcing himself upon her. "What did you feel?"

"I imagine it was the same as what you felt, Finn Jagger."

He grunted. "I didn't feel anything. I came out here to investigate because the man in the village accused of murder supposedly committed his crime in the forest."

"You thought you'd investigate at night?"

"It wasn't night when I started. I was trying to find my way back when I heard a cry. Yours, I presume?"

Her brow furrowed as she frowned. "I don't remember."

She got to her knees, still wincing. The soft white light that had allowed him to see her began to intensify. Magic, though it wasn't the same kind of magic that he'd seen from her before. This was diffuse, and he couldn't identify the source.

"What did you feel out here?" he asked.

"Probably the same thing that killed the man you came for," she said.

She got to her feet, swaying slightly.

Finn followed, standing alongside her, ready to catch her should she need it. She continued to sway in place, moving from side to side, and it took him a moment to realize that what she did was intentional—her way of calling upon magic.

"What are you doing?" he whispered.

"Finding our way out."

She started forward, swaying with each step.

Finn stayed with her, afraid to leave her on her own,

uncertain whether she would stumble and fall. She didn't, but he stayed close to her side just in case.

"What kept me from getting to you?" Finn asked as they walked.

"Describe what you felt."

"What will you offer?" he asked, smiling slightly.

He didn't know if she'd see it.

She turned to him. "We are past the point of bargaining, Finn Jagger."

He hoped she felt the same way when it came to him asking questions. "There was something that kept me from moving forward. I tried to get to you, at least to what I thought was there, but couldn't."

"How did you penetrate it?"

He tapped on the sword, a flush working through him. He felt foolish for having used the sword against magic, but it had worked.

"I used the executioner's blade."

Her gaze flickered to it, and she bit her lip. "Interesting," she said softly.

"Why would it work?"

"I would not have thought that it would, but... ah. Yes. I see."

"What is it?"

"You and I have talked about how there is power in death. Your blade has been used in one of your sentencings. That is how it worked for you."

Finn touched the hilt of the sword. "You're saying that

because I used the sword on Leland Volt, I somehow gave it power?"

"I'm saying there's power in death. Your blade harnessed that power. That is how you were able to penetrate the shielding placed around me."

She nearly stumbled, but Finn was there and helped keep her from falling.

Esmerelda looked over at him strangely before turning her focus back to the forest.

They neared the tree line.

From there Finn could see the open darkness. The wind continued to whip around them, attempting to rip at his clothing, but he ignored it. The cold bit through the cloak, more painful than he would have expected. Esmerelda seemed not to be bothered by it.

"When I came out here, I couldn't find my way back," Finn said.

"It can be difficult. This forest was once Alainsith."

She stepped out of the tree line as she said it.

Finn frowned, following her. "All of it?"

Esmerelda seemed strengthened the moment she moved out of the trees. "All of it here was once a part of the Alainsith. The forest, even the lands beyond, but it's the forest that still retains their touch."

Finn turned and looked at the trees. In the darkness, they didn't look like much other than darkened trees. Just the forest. Nothing more.

"That was Alainsith magic?"

"Residual, I suspect," she said. "Were you to encounter their real magic, you would have a different time with it."

"What if that was the magic that shielded you?"

Esmerelda shook her head. "It was not."

"Are you sure?"

"Quite."

They started toward the hillside, though Finn watched her, checking to make sure that she would be safe as she walked. He needn't be concerned. Whatever had influenced her while in the forest seemed to have resolved, so that she no longer struggled as she had, and she no longer swayed as she walked.

In fact, with each passing moment, it seemed almost as if Esmerelda further strengthened. She stood taller, her hands clasped in front, and there was an energy that came off of her. Whether that was magic or something else, Finn didn't know, and he didn't want to ask and risk angering her.

They reached the outskirts of the village. A few lights were visible in windows, though not so many that they were able to fully light their way.

"Rory suggested that we try Maggie," Finn said. He kept his voice pitched low. It felt right to do so in the darkness, though he didn't really know how late it was. It didn't seem as if they had been trapped in the forest all that long. "He said we'd know her door because of the mark of Heleth on it."

Esmerelda looked over at him. "I know that door," she said softly.

She guided him, veering off the main street. Finn

glanced toward the village hall and the church that were darkened shadows behind him.

"What were you looking for?" he finally asked, breaking the silence between them.

"There's a magic to this place," she whispered.

"You said it was Alainsith magic."

She shook her head. "Not Alainsith. Their magic has a distinct energy to it. This is something else."

"Hegen?"

"I would know hegen magic, Finn Jagger."

They hurried through the village, and Esmerelda stopped at a small cottage near the outskirts of the village. As Rory had said, the mark of Heleth was visible on the door, etched into the wood.

"It doesn't look as if she's awake," Finn said.

He didn't look forward to the idea of staying out in the darkness of night, but at least he wouldn't be alone. Not that he would admit his discomfort to Esmerelda.

"Perhaps not. Only one way to find out."

She strode forward and rapped on the door.

Finn looked along the street. Ferd had so few homes that he wondered if he could stop at any and request lodging. None of the neighboring houses had any lights glowing in their windows, but that didn't mean the people there weren't awake. It was possible they remained hidden in the shadows looking out at the darkness to see what might be happening in the street.

Esmerelda raised her hand to knock again, but the door opened.

The woman standing on the other side was young. Probably the same age as Finn. A heavy robe wrapped around her shoulders, and her brown hair was a wild mess.

"Maggie, I presume?" Esmerelda said.

Maggie nodded.

"We were told to come to you for lodging for the night."

She frowned a moment. "Come in," she said, stepping aside and motioning for them to follow.

Finn stepped into the darkened home, aware of how the air felt strangely cooler the moment that they did. It reminded him of what he'd felt when he'd stepped into the forest, the way that the trees had left the air much cooler.

Everything was dark around them.

He looked around, trying to get his eyes to adjust to the darkness, but struggling. It was darker even than what it had been out on the street. Esmerelda didn't seem to have the same difficulty. She had stepped away from Finn, and her hands were spread off to her sides, sweeping them around her.

"I assume the councilor suggested I might put you up for the night?" Maggie muttered. "A little extra coin *would* help, these days. I suppose you can come along." She headed past them, little more than a shadow in the darkness. She waited for them near an open door. "Now, I've only got the one room, but it's yours for the night. I don't charge much. A few coppers, whatever you can spare. I ask that you clean up after yourself, is all."

"Thank you," Finn said.

Maggie stepped aside so they could enter the room, and when they were inside, Finn closed the door.

Esmerelda stood by the door, murmuring softly. She had her hands pressed up to her face, though he couldn't make out what she was saying. The words were too quiet for Finn.

There came a flash of light, nothing more, but when it faded, Esmerelda sank to the floor. Finn was there, helping her back to her feet.

"What happened?" he whispered.

"We should be safe for the night."

With that, she closed her eyes.

CHAPTER TWENTY-TWO

Finn sat on the edge of the bed atop the striped blanket, not wanting to sleep until he had a better sense of just what was going on. Esmerelda rested on the narrow bed, breathing slowly and regularly. Unlike the last time, he at least thought she would recover. It seemed to him that she was only fatigued, not injured as it had appeared when he'd found her in the forest.

Finn didn't want to sleep.

He questioned what happened around him. He couldn't tell. There came an occasional tapping, but that might only be his imagination. His heart hammered loudly in his chest, and he tried to maintain his focus to make sure there wasn't going to be anything dangerous around them, but found it difficult to stay awake. He'd been up for too long the way it was.

For Esmerelda, he thought he needed to remain alert, at

least until he had a better sense of what was taking place. She had said there was power there, but what kind?

The feeling he had was similar to what he'd felt in the forest, which was part of what worried him. If it was the same, then there was a danger that whatever power existed there would be used against them.

Finn held the sword resting in front of him.

It was probably not necessary, but without knowing what had happened and what they might have to deal with, he felt more comfortable having the sword with him.

Every so often, he found himself drifting.

When he did, dreams of the trees came to him.

Finn was fully aware that they *were* dreams, and when he jolted awake, he worried that he would find himself back in the forest, but each time he came around, he was still sitting on the edge of the bed. The brief spells happened enough times that Finn began to wonder if he even dreamed that he was dreaming. He wasn't able to tell what he needed to do, only that he found himself drifting, his mind floating as if he were going toward the forest, reminding him of the strange sense he had when he'd been wandering in the trees, struggling to find his way out.

After a while, he awoke lying next to Esmerelda. The sword was still gripped loosely in his hand. He looked over to the door. A tapping had alerted him, but it was a strange sort of tapping that he hadn't noticed before. This was soft, as if it were nails along the wooden floorboards.

He sat up, not wanting to disturb Esmerelda.

Leaning on the edge of the bed, he held the sword in

hand, staring at the door. She had claimed that they were protected, so maybe it wasn't even necessary for him to sit the way that he did, but unease had settled within him.

The soft tapping—or clicking—came closer.

Finn stood and headed toward the door.

He leaned toward it, waiting.

There wasn't any other sound.

He tipped his head toward the door so that he could listen better but still didn't hear anything.

Finn squeezed the sword.

When he glanced behind him, looking over to Esmerelda, he found her lying the way he'd left her. Her black hair spilled around her, the sheet barely up to her stomach, and her chest rising with each breath. She'd probably be angry if she caught him looking like this.

It felt a strange coincidence he'd be there with her now, though he knew it to be something other than a coincidence. She had planned it. She had probably planned a great many things when it came to influencing him.

The clicking came again and he turned back to the door.

There *was* something out there.

Finn shifted the sword.

It felt strange holding it like he did, prepared to use it as a weapon, but he had proven that it would work against magic. And the blade *was* honed to a razor edge.

The clicking sounded as if it were right outside of the door.

Finn leaned forward, trying to listen for any sounds on the other side of the door, but didn't hear anything.

He reached for the door handle. He needed to know what was on the other side of the door.

"Don't."

He glanced back to find Esmerelda sitting up and looking toward the door. "Why not?"

"You don't want to open the door. Not yet."

"What's on the other side?"

She shook her head. "I don't know."

The clicking—or scratching, he realized—persisted, and he waited, holding on to the sword for a moment, then stepped back toward the bed and took a seat next to her.

"What is this?" he asked softly.

"As I've made clear to you, I don't know."

"How don't you know? I thought you had magic."

She smiled at him. "Having magic and knowing that of others are different things."

"If it's not hegen, and it's not Alainsith, then what is it?"

Esmerelda moved so that she wasn't confined in the sheets anymore. She tossed them off to the side, scooting over the edge of the bed, where she sat next to Finn for a moment.

"I mentioned how there are differing kinds of magic in the world. It is much like you have differing kinds of gods."

Finn looked over to her. "You're saying the magics are bound to the different gods that we worship?"

She shrugged. "I'm saying there are other magics in the world. Nothing more." She stared at the closed door, and there was worry in her eyes.

"What do you fear?"

"That my magic will not be strong enough," she said. "And that I do not know why it would attack."

They sat together, silently. Finn holding the sword, Esmerelda saying nothing, though he suspected that she held on to some magic while sitting there. The steady clicking from the other side of the door persisted, the sound a rhythmic constant.

Finn wanted to know what caused it, but at the same time, he didn't want to see what would make Esmerelda nervous—and what might be capable of overpowering her magic.

"What did you place around the door?" Finn asked when they'd been sitting for a while.

"A protection."

"And that protection took everything out of you?"

"It took as much strength as I could spare."

"How do you use your magic?"

She glanced over to him. "Would you like to learn?"

"I…"

She smiled, patting him on the hand. "Don't worry, Finn Jagger. You would find that hegen magic is different enough that you would have a difficult time with it. With your access, though, you might be able to grow more rapidly than most of us."

"My access to death?"

She nodded.

Finn almost shivered.

Not many things unsettled him these days. Time spent with Meyer, questioning and carrying out sentences, made it so that he wasn't nearly as squeamish about such things as he once would have been. Talking about magic that he could master from the bodies of the dead somehow did.

"I would've thought I needed to be one of the hegen in order to access magic."

He spoke softly, his voice little more than a whisper, not wanting to alert the creature—and it had to be some sort of creature—on the other side of the door to their conversation. He also wanted to better understand what Esmerelda might be willing to share with him.

"The kind of power we access is different than what you might consider otherwise," Esmerelda said. "We access power trapped within each of us, released through death."

There was a time when Finn would have thought that her description of magic would feel too fantastical to believe. He had always known that the hegen claimed to have power, and he had known several people who had gone to the hegen for help, but knowing that and seeing their magic firsthand were very different things.

"But you healed me. That was only your connection to death?"

"That was redirecting power," she said.

The clicking continued. It seemed no louder and no softer than it had before, as if something were scratching on the other side of the door, attempting to claw its way in. It didn't happen consistently, nor did it happen persistently, but there was a rhythm to it nonetheless.

Finn flexed his hand, squeezing the sword.

Esmerelda looked down at him. "Perhaps you showed greater judgment than I would've expected," she said.

"Why is that?"

"By using your blade. You have empowered it."

Finn shook his head. "I didn't want to empower the sword in any way."

"Perhaps not, but still you did. Using it for your sentencing allowed it to penetrate the shielding placed around the forest."

"About that," Finn said, shifting so that he could better look at her. "If it wasn't Alainsith, and it wasn't hegen, and it wasn't the kind of magic that you know, how is it that you understand why my sword was able to carve through the shielding?"

She reached for the blade before staying her hand, not stretching any further. "Magic has many features to it, but a consistency is the power of life and death. Magic, in its purest form, the way that you view it, is life."

"I thought you claimed that you gained power through death."

"What is death but an absence of life?" She nodded to the sword. "The blood that stained your blade granted it a specific kind of power. Perhaps not intentionally. I doubt you would have done so intentionally." She looked up to him, and Finn nodded. "Even if you had, I doubt you would have been able to do anything more than what you managed to accomplish by chance."

"What about Justice?"

She nodded slowly. "That sword has been used for

centuries. According to rumor, it was once used by the king himself to conquer the Alainsith. A blade like that would necessarily be empowered by the magic of life."

Finn shook his head. "If that's the case, then it's powered by the magic of death."

Esmerelda sighed. "You haven't been paying attention, Finn Jagger. The magic of life and the magic of death are part of the same continuum. That power exists regardless of how you access it."

He traced his finger along the blade, feeling a strange thrill in doing so. He knew he shouldn't, and knew that if there really were magic involved, he should be more careful.

The scratching stopped.

At least, it seemed to have stopped.

Finn got to his feet, making his way to the door where he stood. "Why would Maggie have allowed us to stay here if she used some kind of magic?" he asked without taking his gaze off of the door. Was there still a soft clawing from the other side?

"It's possible she's not responsible," she said.

Which meant Maggie might be in danger. "Then I should open the door."

"Not at night," Esmerelda said.

"Why not at night?"

"I wasn't trapped until dusk. I suspect the same could be said about you."

Finn nodded slowly.

"There aren't any windows in this room," he said. "We won't be able to know when it is daylight."

"I will know," Esmerelda said.

"The scratching has stopped."

"Perhaps it's getting close to daylight, then."

He had no idea if he would even be able to open the door without her assistance. Even though his sword might be connected to magic in some way, it was possible that he wouldn't be able to break the seal she had placed around the door.

"How much longer would you have us wait?"

"Until I am convinced that there won't be any surprises."

"Surprises like what might have happened to Maggie?"

"Surprises," Esmerelda said.

Finn stood by the door, holding on to the sword, letting its blunted end rest along the floorboards. He waited. With each passing moment that he felt no additional scratching from the other side, he glanced over to Esmerelda, wondering whether she would permit them to leave.

After a while, she got to her feet, headed to the door, and traced her hand around the doorframe, murmuring softly.

He noticed something cupped in her hand. "What are you holding?"

"An item that helps me harness power."

"Like the sword harnessed power," he said.

"If you keep asking these questions, I will have to begin teaching you the ways of my people," she said.

Finn started to smile but realized that she did not. She nodded to him, stepping off to the side. He reached for the handle, and she touched him on the hand.

"Be prepared for the possibility that there might be something on the other side of that door," she said.

"Prepared how?"

She nodded to the sword.

Finn clutched the blade, lifting it, and jerked the door open.

He felt foolish doing so. He wasn't a swordsman. He could strike a target with precision, but a sword fight—at least from what he had seen of the Archers—involved more than just striking a target with precision. It involved movement, blocking, thrusting, all skills that he had never practiced.

There was nothing on the other side of the door.

The empty hall greeted them.

Sunlight streamed in through a window at the end of the hall. Finn headed toward the entrance to the home, suddenly feeling very foolish for his reaction to what had occurred the night before. There probably was nothing for him to have been concerned about.

The sunlight let them see everything with greater detail. The front room was a cluttered mess. Clothing was tossed wildly, and the table and chairs in the room looked to be old and worn. A bookcase was empty, though the belongings of the bookcase looked to be piled on the floor in front of it.

A body lay twisted on the floor. Finn didn't have to get too close to see that it was Maggie. She lay bent, partly broken, and her neck twisted at an unnatural angle. Blood pooled around her.

Throughout everything, there was a strange musky

smell.

Esmerelda guided him out of the house, where they paused, turning to look back.

"Why do you think we didn't notice anything magical before we came here last night?"

There wasn't anything to the outside of the home that looked strange in the daylight. The mark of Heleth on the door remained, though in the daylight he could see the outline of it clearer than he had at night. It was small enough that he wondered how they had even seen it in the darkness the night before. A slight scratch on it was new.

"I'm not sure that we were meant to," Esmeralda said.

As he headed toward the village hall, Esmeralda stopped at the next house.

She held her hand out, tracing something on the dark wood of the door.

"What is it?"

Instead of answering, she pushed open the door but didn't take a step inside.

She didn't need to. The stench from inside radiated out.

As she stepped away, making her way to the next house, Finn approached and poked his head inside. The entirety of the home looked sprayed in blood. He'd seen horrible crime scenes before, but this was something else.

Awful.

By the time he caught up to Esmeralda, he found her three houses farther along.

He had stopped at each, and each house looked the same.

"Whatever attacked didn't get to us," he said.

She shook her head. "We were protected. I am not entirely certain how."

They stopped at several more of the homes, each of them the same.

With each one, Finn wanted nothing more than to leave the village.

This wasn't something he could do anything about. This was a magical attack.

"Everyone is gone," he muttered.

"It seems that way."

She checked several more homes. Finn stopped looking inside.

By the time they reached the village hall, Esmeralda looked over to him, as if wanting him to be the one to open the door there.

Finn tried the handle. It was unlocked.

The village hall was dark, though it had been that way the day before. He headed toward the stairs and down, this time with Esmerelda along with him. At the bottom of the stairs, he paused. Something didn't feel right.

The air in the hallway smelled off. It had been off when he'd come the day before, but only after having opened the door. What he detected now was different. This was foul. Unpleasant. The kind of stench that left Finn feeling as if he wanted to take a bath.

"What is that?" Esmerelda asked.

Finn shook his head. He hurried to the door where the man had been and pulled it open.

And gagged.

The stench emanated from there.

Finn hadn't expected it to be quite so potent. Jarnel was curled up the way that he had been before, his leg bent and twisted, but even from the doorway, Finn could tell he wasn't breathing.

He was the first person they had seen in the village.

And he was gone.

"Was he like this when you came to him before?" Esmerelda asked. She stood in the doorway, a small curved item cupped in her hand, though she held it off to the side and swept it around in a small circle.

"Not like this," Finn said.

"The leg—"

"Was broken. Rory claimed they found him that way. Covered in blood at the edge of the forest and his leg broken."

She hurried forward, frowning. "That is unusual."

"All of this is unusual."

That was not even enough of a description for him.

It was more than unusual.

He'd say *terrifying* but didn't want to admit that to Esmeralda.

Crouching down next to him, she pulled a bottle from her pocket and tipped it into her palm. When done, she rubbed her hands together and held them above Jarnel, waving them in a small circle. Her eyes were closed and there was a tight frown of concentration on her face. After a moment, sweat beaded on her forehead.

"What are you doing?" Finn asked.

"It is obscured from me." She got to her feet and wiped her hands on her dress before stuffing the bottle back into her pocket. Finn stepped into the hall and was relieved when he closed the door behind him. It shut some of the stench inside.

"I need to see the place where the man was killed. I think if I do that, I will have a better understanding of what happened here," she said.

They made their way through the village, heading toward the slope on the far side that led up toward the forest. From above, it seemed a fog covered the valley the village was set into, leaving it layered and obscured.

When they reached the edge of the forest, Esmerelda paused and pulled something from her pocket. Finn swept his gaze along the edge of the forest. When he'd come there the day before, he hadn't seen anything, though he believed there was something that he would be able to find to explain what had happened with Jarnel.

Esmerelda walked slowly, working her way along the trees, staying on the outer edge of the forest as if she were concerned about what would happen were she to get too close. Finn studied the ground, looking for anything else he might find. Rory had mentioned that Jarnel had been found covered in blood, which was something that Finn *should* be able to find.

Finn turned away from where she worked, studying the village in the distance. From there it was difficult to see much of the village. The fog seemed even thicker than it had when they had headed up here in the first place.

Something about the fog felt *off.*

As he watched Esmeralda, he couldn't help but think about why Meyer had wanted him to come out there. This was a part of his pilgrimage, but had he known there would be something else? Maybe Esmeralda had warned Meyer that she'd join Finn, though he doubted that were the case. She'd probably just guided Meyer, the same way she guided Finn.

Because of magic.

It had targeted Oscar; now it was outside the city.

They were connected. It had to be—only he didn't know what it meant.

He turned to Esmerelda.

Whatever she'd been doing seemed to reveal a bright red stain on the ground.

"What is that?" he asked, joining her and looking down at the ground.

A trail, though it looked like blood. Every step she took revealed *more* of the trail—and more of the blood. She continued making her way around the edge of the forest, and Finn followed, noticing that as she walked, the trail continued to be illuminated. Whatever she did created more to follow.

The trail that they followed was faint. When he looked down at it, he could make out only a little of it, not enough that he was able to easily see it along the ground. As soon as Esmerelda had moved past by a few steps, the trail began to fade again, eventually disappearing.

It worked all the way around the edge of the forest.

"What does this mean?" Finn asked.

Esmerelda straightened and looked down into the village. "As I've told you, death has power. This is death in its purest form."

"Blood?"

"Yes."

"Why at the edge of the forest?" he asked.

She turned toward the trees, tipping her head back and breathing deeply. "This is an attempt to push back the Alainsith. Or influence. I'm not entirely sure. I would have thought there was no need to do so here. The Alainsith would not press beyond the trees..."

"This is what brought you out here?"

She pulled one of the cards out of her pocket, flipping it from front to back. The card was blank. "I am not entirely sure what called me out."

"The cards?"

She glanced up at him. "They guide us as much as they guide others."

"You saw something?"

She nodded. "And did not know what it meant."

Finn looked at the forest. "It's tied to the Alainsith?"

"Perhaps." She turned slowly, facing the village. Her nose wrinkled. "Or perhaps there is something else afoot. Dangerous and unexpected." She flipped the card, and for a moment, an image appeared before fading.

"Another threat to the kingdom?" he asked.

She tipped her head to the side. "Another magic."

CHAPTER TWENTY-THREE

They stopped at Maggie's home, standing before the door. Esmerelda had pulled out several of the items she carried in her pocket, all of them hegen artifacts he assumed would grant her magic, and looked as if she braced herself before heading toward the door.

Finn kept the sword unsheathed.

That had felt foolish in the village, but the longer he was there without seeing anyone else, the more he began to question whether or not there *was* something he needed to be concerned about. It was better to have the sword and not need it than to be unprepared.

"What do you expect to find?" Finn asked.

"There was something here last night," she said softly. "Now there is nothing in the village. That cannot be a coincidence."

"You think whatever we encountered somehow took the villagers?"

She looked over. "I've told you how certain kinds of magic works, Finn Jagger."

"If they took all the villagers"—and Finn wouldn't even be able to begin to think about how they would or what they would use them for—"and used them for some dark magic, then they would be..."

"Incredibly powerful," she finished for him. "You see my concern."

She took a deep breath and started forward.

When she reached the door, she threw it open and tossed something inside. There came a soft explosion followed by a gust of air, almost a breath that was expelled, and Esmerelda followed it inside the room.

The room looked the same as it had earlier in the morning. Everything seemed a mess, as if a tornado had whipped through, tossing everything around.

Esmerelda's magic hadn't changed it.

Only... it had.

The magic had seemed to *push* everything back up against the walls.

It revealed the floor. A pattern was there. Esmerelda stood at the edge of it before tossing another item to the middle of the pattern made out of some dark ink—possibly blood.

"What is that?"

"Witchcraft," she said.

"What kind?"

"The darkest kind."

The item she'd tossed onto the pattern exploded.

The pattern seemed as if it attempted to contain what she had done, bulging slightly, but then it wasn't strong enough. Esmerelda's magic managed to destroy whatever was there.

When it did, the strange energy in the air shifted.

Finn let out a heavy breath. He hadn't even realized he'd been holding it in before now, but as he let it out, he looked around the room, searching for another pattern like that.

"What would that do?"

Esmerelda shook her head. "A dark mark," she murmured. "Meant for disruption. I don't understand why it would be here."

"Why is that?"

"There should not be such witchcraft in the kingdom. This magic has a cost."

"More than the cost of the magic you perform?"

"Much more, Finn Jagger. There are times when such magic is easier or more potent."

"What kind of times?"

She hesitated. "Certain dates. Seasons. Circumstances," she said softly.

She headed down the hall, tossing whatever strange items she had as she went. Each time she did, there came another explosion. Anything in the way of what she tossed was thrown off to either side, leaving the floor open.

There was another pattern on the floor in front of the room where they'd stayed.

This one was smaller, compact, and long lines had been scratched in it.

Finn shivered.

"What do you think caused that?" Finn asked, pointing to the scratches along the ground.

"Whatever came at us last night," she said.

"It seems different than what these others are."

She leaned forward, inhaling deeply, as if doing so would somehow allow her to better understand what had taken place here.

"I don't know," she finally said. She traced a finger along it, her finger leaving a glowing trail that seemed to burn through it. "Patterns hold power. Disrupting them takes their power," she explained to him.

"Is this the kind of thing you deal with often?"

She looked over to him, and she shook her head. "Not often," she said.

"You seem comfortable with it."

"It's not a comfort with it so much as it is an understanding that there are things and powers outside of my understanding."

Finn just stood off to the side while Esmerelda continued her investigation, digging at the ground, scratching at the marking that had been made there. He didn't really understand what had happened, or what was there, only that whatever it was left him feeling unsettled.

He pushed the door open, glancing inside the room where they had spent the night.

Nothing had changed.

Not that he really expected it to. Finn thought that perhaps he might get a better understanding as to what had been going on there, only he didn't know if such a thing were even possible.

All of this was beyond him. All of this was outside of his area of expertise and comfort. It didn't seem to be beyond Esmerelda's, but even for her, he wondered if she found herself unsettled by what was taking place.

He looked around the room.

Maggie had given them a place to stay. That had been real.

Now she was gone.

Because magic had followed.

He turned, heading back into the hallway, reaching another door that he pushed on softly to see if he might find any magic on the other side of the door.

Finn jabbed with his sword, feeling a little bit foolish. He glanced over to where Esmerelda remained crouched on the ground, running her fingers along the symbol.

She placed something on top of it and murmured to herself. There came another gentle explosion, a burst of power, and the strange symbols suddenly disappeared. Finn watched what she had been doing, struggling to understand just what she did.

Finally, she got to her feet, and looked over to him. "I don't have any answers."

"I think I need to get back. My purpose in Ferd is done. Meyer wanted me to understand what was taking place with the Alainsith, but I don't know what to make of any of this." He looked around him. "The use of magic is beyond my understanding. And I believe I have found everything I can so far." He took a deep breath, looking toward the entrance of the house. "I'll report to Meyer what I found, but even with that, I don't know how this all interacts."

Or if it does.

He made his way to the front of the house.

When he got there, he looked around, noticing the coin he'd left still resting on the table despite Esmerelda having used the power that she had on the room. There was a considerable amount of energy that had been unleashed there, and somehow it had not managed to move the silver coin off the table.

Finn was tempted to take it back, but superstition made him hesitate. Instead, he stepped out of the home again. The fog that had layered over the village seemed even thicker than before.

"Esmerelda?" he called out to her.

She dusted her hands off as she made her way out of the house, though she seemed to do so reluctantly, as if she had no interest in leaving until she fully understood everything that had happened there.

"This fog—"

"Is unnatural," she said.

"I noticed it when we headed up to the forest, but it's only gotten thicker."

"Perhaps I've been too distracted," she said. She took a deep breath. "We should gather up your horse, if you can find him."

They made their way toward the village hall. The walk through the fog made it more difficult than it had been before to navigate through the streets and find his way. Finn had to use what he remembered. Maggie's house was on the outskirts of the village, and he knew that he had to head toward the center of the village to reach the hall, only without being able to see it...

"All of this is wrong," Esmerelda said.

Finn looked over to her. She had slipped on a large metal ring in the shape of a twisted spiral pattern. She held it out, her arm trembling as she did.

"What do you detect?"

"I can't penetrate the fog. This is something unlike anything that I've encountered."

"Witchcraft," Finn grunted.

She looked to the blade strapped to his back. "It's unfortunate that blade is newly made. There is little power stored within it. Were you to use it, you would likely exhaust the energy within the blade before it had an opportunity to complete the task."

Finn still resisted the urge to unsheathe the sword. There was nothing he could do with it, anyway.

He continued into the fog, plunging deeper and deeper through it, but began to wonder if he was even going to be able to find the village hall. He couldn't see anything well enough for him to know if he was even heading in the right direction. Esmerelda held her ring outward, but her arm continued to tremble.

Finn touched her on the arm. "We should turn back," he said.

"I think we need to reach that horse," she said.

"If your magic isn't strong enough to get us through the fog to get us there, I don't want us to put ourselves in danger."

He did worry about what would happen if he didn't reach the horse. He would have to get back to Verendal, and there weren't going to be all that many days remaining for him to do so. Without the horse, he would be forced to go by foot, a slow and time-consuming process, even if he were to jog the whole way.

Finn tried to plunge deeper into the fog but couldn't tell which direction to go. No matter what way they tried to travel, it didn't feel as if they made any progress. He looked over to Esmerelda, and her arm continued to sag.

"We should turn back," Finn said.

She didn't even argue.

He took her arm and held on to it. With the fog swirling around, it became increasingly difficult for him to see much of anything around him. He couldn't even make out the buildings. He looked down at his feet, trying to find the cobblestones so that he could follow that out of the village, but even the cobblestones were difficult for him to find.

It had been a mistake coming this far into the village. Perhaps he should have known that when he had begun to realize that the fog was thickening. He hadn't expected the fog to have grown that dense that quickly, though.

If Esmerelda was right, then the power of witchcraft came from the lives of the villagers. It felt as if he trudged through water. Or mud. Every step was difficult, and Finn forced himself forward, struggling to move against the fog.

"I think it's trying to coalesce around us." Finn looked over to Esmerelda, but now it was difficult to even see her. The fog had formed too thickly around them. "Is there anything you can do?"

"I have tried what I can do."

Finn reached for the sword. He had no idea if it would even work, but they needed to get freed. He pulled the sword from its sheath.

The blade crackled.

Finn swept the blade from side to side while holding on to Esmerelda. He didn't want to lose his grip on her hand.

The fog began to ease back as the sword touched it. The crackling became something palpable, and as he pushed it through the fog, he could feel the air changing. The pressure that had built upon them began to ease. He started spinning in a circle, using the sword to create an opening around them. The ground was barely visible, but enough that he was able to find where he needed to go.

A shape in the fog loomed close before passing.

Finn hesitated, but Esmerelda pulled on him.

"Keep going," she whispered.

The fog started to creep closer again. Where the sword had carved through it, now there was no longer the same effect that there had been before. It was as if the fog were growing stronger.

Or the sword was getting weaker.

That was more likely.

Esmerelda had said the sword wouldn't be able to over-power the magic that caused the fog. If it came from the villagers, then there would be too much involved. There would be no way for his single execution to be enough for him to overpower what had happened there.

Finn spun with increased urgency.

They hurried forward. Esmerelda hung onto his arm and they plunged into the fog. There was another time when he thought that he saw a shape in the fog, but she continued pulling on him, guiding him forward.

Then the fog began to thin.

Finn swung the sword a few more times.

He created a clearing around him that was enough to make out the ground. The road had ended, and they were on a grassy path, but they were able to move more easily now.

Finn still swept the sword around him, but it no longer had the same effect. The blade sizzled, as if it were damp and he stuck it into a flame, but there wasn't the same resistance that he'd noticed before.

"Keep moving," Esmerelda said.

She pressed her full lips together in concentration, and she held her arm up, as if to ward off the fog through some power of determination.

Finn pushed forward.

She stayed with him. He was thankful for that. What would have happened had she not been with him? The night before would have gone differently. He would have ended up a victim of whatever that strange scratching had been. Perhaps he wouldn't have been able to leave the forest, though as he thought about it, that might have been better for him. At least the forest didn't have strange creatures attempting to claw their way through a door to get at him. That he knew of.

The fog continued to lift. Now it was little more than wisps around them.

It was still difficult to see through, like he tried to peer through a thin veil. Everything had a haze around it.

Finn started to slow, and Esmerelda grabbed his arm, now pulling him.

He turned to her, but she ignored him, the look of concentration on her face telling him that she was determined to keep moving.

"How much further?" he asked.

"I don't know."

"We're almost past it, though."

"*Almost* is not *out*, Finn Jagger. I don't know the purpose of this fog, but even a little of it might be more than what we can withstand."

They started jogging.

In other circumstances, running from a fog like this would have felt foolish, but in this case, he thought it was necessary—and right.

Trees towered in front of them.

"Did we go the wrong way?" he asked.

"We did not climb the rise," she said.

Finn looked toward the trees. They appeared different from those on the edge of the forest as well. They weren't the same.

At least they hadn't headed from one magical danger to another.

He didn't know what sort of danger the forest might pose in the daylight. There had been the strange trail of blood that Esmerelda had found, so there was something there that they needed to be careful with, but he didn't know quite what it was. Alainsith. That was what she had said, though Finn didn't know what the Alainsith power might be, only that it *was* power.

When they reached the trees, it seemed as if the fog could no longer penetrate beyond it. He paused, leaning forward, trying to catch his breath.

They hadn't been running that long, but it felt like they'd been moving forever. Now he wanted to rest. Finn knew they couldn't.

Finn straightened and looked around him. He didn't know which side of the village they would have appeared on. The trees were closer together than he remembered coming through on the way to Ferd, but they were a different kind of tree than what he remembered from the far side of the village.

"Where do you think we are?" he asked.

"Outside the village. We will find our way from here." She looked over to him. "Where would you have us go?"

"Back, I think. Walking will take much longer than going by horseback, so I think we need to get going now." He hesitated. "That is, if you're going back as well."

She turned and faced the village. The fog was visible through the trees, though it wasn't nearly as prominent as it had been before. She inhaled slowly, clasping her hands behind her back, some hegen artifact in her hand. Finn noticed her twisting it, turning it in place as if to try and release whatever magic she had stored in it.

"What we've seen here is reason enough to return."

"Do you know which way we need to go?"

She closed her eyes, turning in a circle, and when she opened them, she pointed. "That way."

It wasn't the direction that Finn would have expected, but he followed where she suggested.

They made their way through the forest, and gradually the unsettled feeling he had from the fog and everything they had seen throughout the morning began to fade, burning off as the sun rose overhead. The trees thinned a little, but were still far closer together than what he remembered from when he had come through before. They had followed the King's Road, at least until it had split off, so now he didn't know if they were taking the same road back.

The day passed quickly, neither of them speaking much. They paused to eat, then halted again at a stream where Esmerelda forced him to wait while she did something to the water—likely testing it to ensure it wasn't magically contaminated—before allowing him to drink. By nightfall, they neared a village.

They still hadn't taken the King's Road, and yet they managed to make their way through the darkness toward the village.

"Which village is that?" he asked.

"You have been there before."

"Torthen?" He looked around him. "I didn't come at it from this way, so I guess I don't recognize the direction you had us come from."

"I had us come straight toward it."

"Why not return to the road?"

"I wasn't sure it was safe to do so."

Finn started to smile, though he didn't think she was kidding about it.

"The road was safe enough when we came along it before."

"That was before." She turned to him. "I do not fully understand what happened in that village, but I suspect all of those people are lost."

"All?"

She nodded slowly. "All. The fog we fought through"— her gaze went to the sword once again sheathed behind him —"could only have been created through magic. The power necessary to create it would be enormous."

"The whole village," he said.

She nodded. "That is my fear."

"Why then? What reason would they have for attacking then?"

"I do not know."

In Torthen, they'd mentioned the increased highwaymen attacks. While that *might* be it, it was also possible it was tied to the kind of magic that had attacked.

Esmerelda reached into her pocket and pulled out a card. "We must understand this magic."

He held her gaze a moment before shaking his head.

"That's not for me. I can't help with any of it. I'm just an executioner."

"Are you so certain?" She pulled out a card and it flashed with a brief image that he couldn't quite make out. "This would suggest otherwise."

"Just an executioner."

"Is that all you will be?"

Finn had given it thought. When Meyer had claimed him, he'd struggled with his purpose. Would that be all he could be? And if so, was it all bad?

It was not.

He served the king.

Served justice.

"I should get back."

Disappointment flickered across Esmerelda's face as she nodded.

CHAPTER TWENTY-FOUR

Finn stood at the edge of the village for a moment, looking at the lights and the sound of voices from somewhere deeper in the village, and the overall feeling of normalcy. After what he'd just been through, having this felt right.

It was the far edge of the village, where the prison had been. He was drawn to it, and headed toward the makeshift prison.

"Why here?" Esmerelda asked.

"This was where they held Leland Volt."

"Do you regret sentencing him?"

"I have carried out many sentences during my time with Meyer."

She looked over, smiling slightly. The moonlight reflected off her face, making her pale skin seem to glow. Esmerelda really was quite lovely. "That isn't an answer."

"I wish there was another way sometimes," he said.

"An executioner who would prefer not to execute."

"It's not as if I enjoy carrying out the sentences. I do it because I know that it is right and just. I do it because the victims need their restitution. And I do it so the criminals will not harm again."

"You did not fear that with this man."

"Not particularly," Finn admitted. "He had no remorse for what he did, but he also didn't commit the crime out of a desire to harm. He did it because he saw a wrong and he wanted to correct it." That might not have been all of it, though. He hadn't dug nearly deep enough. Now that he'd been to Ferd, he wondered how much more there might have been than what Volt had told him. "Meyer taught me to question the prisoners before carrying out their sentences. I... I didn't do as well as he would have wanted me to do, I don't think."

He pushed the door open and stood there for a moment, letting his eyes adjust to the darkness. The last time he had been there, it had been daylight, and he had been able to see Leland well. The stench of the room persisted, though Finn suspected that stench would linger for a long time.

Esmerelda joined him, and a soft glowing came from her hand. He looked over. "What's that?"

"A curiosity," she said.

"What sort of curiosity do you have?"

"Whether there is anything here that we would need to understand."

"Magic," he said.

She stepped forward, sweeping her hand around her, the

light illuminating the room. He suspected she looked for markings similar to what they had seen in Ferd, but there was nothing.

"What did this man tell you?" Her voice was soft and strained as she searched for whatever magic she thought might be here.

"He told me that he'd come across a man raping a woman and stabbed him in the back. Then he found another in the woods who watched and chased them before killing them."

She straightened. "Another rape." She looked over to him. "We've spoken about the power of life and death. There is another way to pull on power, though it's a different use of it. Darker, in some ways. Many likely think the hegen dark in the way we use those who have been convicted and sentenced by your king, but our magic comes from that of the world. The power that exists around us. Power drawn from those who no longer have use for the power that once flowed through them. There is another way to call power, though it is through pain. Suffering. Control."

She looked over to him.

"You think the rapes were tied to this witchcraft?"

Could what Volt have seen been a part of it?

Finn had seen the strange markings on the hut. That had to be tied in with this, only he didn't know how—or why.

"I would have said it was unlikely, but that was before. Now? I do not know."

She stepped back into the night.

Finn looked around. Here, he'd come and performed the sentencing, but if there *was* something more to it, they would never know.

Not there, at least.

There *was* a way for him to find out more, though.

It meant that he had to get back to Verendal quickly. The Alainsith might be guilty, but what was he guilty of having done? He wouldn't need to steal power through control.

Finn pulled the door to the prison closed behind him. "Do the Alainsith use that same kind of power?"

She shook her head. "They have power of their own. They do not need to borrow it from the world around them."

"Then they wouldn't have done what the man was accused of doing."

"Not for power."

That wasn't a denial, though.

"I think we need to know if the people killed used witchcraft." He looked at her. "Would there be any marker on them?"

"It's possible. I don't know that much about witchcraft, though, Finn Jagger. The kind of magic they use is different."

He had to find out.

Finn made his way through the village until he reached Bennington's tavern. He looked over to Esmerelda. He *could* have her wait outside, but that would open him to questions. Bringing her with him would open him to questions as well.

"I will look around the village for other signs of magic," Esmerelda decided.

"Can you find anything at night?"

"There should be a few signs of it if there is magic used here. I would be able to uncover something."

She touched him on the arm a moment before heading away.

Finn stepped into the tavern.

It was busy.

He looked around the inside of the tavern to see if he might find Bev. There were some villagers that he'd seen when he'd been here before, but he made a point of avoiding eye contact. He didn't want to create more trouble.

The door to the back of the tavern came open, and Bev came out carrying a tray and smiling widely at the three men who greeted her the moment that she did.

Finn waited until she neared him before stepping out of the shadows near the door.

"Finn?" she asked, turning to him. Her smile slipped a little. Enough that Finn worried what he might have interrupted. "I wasn't expecting to see you here."

"I'm just on my way back to Verendal."

Finn wanted to share what happened in Ferd. The people here would need to know about it, but explaining magic...

He wasn't entirely sure *how* to do that.

"I need to meet with the council." Bennington wouldn't be thrilled to see him, Finn doubted, but at least he could go into what he'd seen. The council could decide what to do about it while Finn returned to Verendal.

Then he would have to send word to the palace.

How would the king respond to a magical attack in the kingdom?

What if he blamed the Alainsith?

"Why do you need to see them?"

He forced a smile. "I still have questions about Volt."

She looked over suddenly, turning to some of the men standing in the tavern and flashing her wide smile, before turning back to Finn. "I thought you were done with him. He's gone, Finn."

"He's gone, but something similar happened in Ferd." Her eyes widened. "I don't know what's going on, but I need to have a complete understanding of everything that happened here. I think it might help me know how concerned the king needs to be about all of this."

"How similar?"

"People were killed. It's bad. That's why I need to talk to the council."

She looked as if she struggled with how much to answer. "I'll... I'll get Bennington."

"Bev?" She turned to him. "Where was the body left?"

It was one thing he hadn't thought of investigating when he'd been there before.

Normally, that wouldn't matter to him.

"The body?"

"Of the man Leland killed." Men, really, but maybe they didn't know about the other.

She frowned. "Gods, Finn. He's been dead for the last two weeks. He was buried—"

She cut herself off and Finn frowned.

Why wouldn't she want me to know about how the body had been buried?

That would be unusual, but many places had their own way of celebrating the gods. Within Verendal, most people who died were gifted to the Mother to allow her flames to consume them. It wasn't common for them to be buried, only because Lethael, the god of decay, was not celebrated nearly the same way that other gods were.

Why there, though?

"They were buried?"

"I shouldn't have said anything," she said. "Bennington and the council wanted to keep it quiet. Afraid of upsetting the gods, you know." He nodded in understanding. "But with everything that happened around here, they felt that best. A way of undoing some of the darkness, I guess." She inhaled deeply. "Not much else to say about it. Now, can I get you a drink? Some food? If you're going to stay, I'm sure you're going to want something to eat while I send for Bennington."

She hadn't said *where* they'd buried the bodies, but maybe that didn't matter. "That would be great."

She headed into the kitchen, leaving him standing in the tavern.

An older man sat at a nearby table. A narrow-brimmed hat covered his head, and long fingers picked at his food. "Is there a reason the hangman needs to know where they were buried?" the man asked.

He studied the man. "I just need to see the grave site. Part of being thorough."

He took a bite of food. "Not much to see. The place is outside of the village. Beran's Hill. An old grove. Some claim it's holy. A few gravesites in it, but like I said, not much to see." The man glanced at him, then shrugged.

A holy old grove.

What if that was another magic?

Finn looked to the kitchen. He *should* wait for Bev, but he needed to know before he talked with the council. That way, he'd have a better idea of how much danger they might be in. As it stood, Finn didn't really know.

Finn made his way out of the village. He remembered the small hill, though it was outside of the village by a short walk. He wrapped his cloak around his shoulders as he made his way toward it. The night grew cool, though it wasn't quite as cold as it had been even a little farther north in Ferd.

When he reached the hill, he started up it slowly. The air started to take on more of a chill. What he wouldn't give for Esmerelda's magic to light the way so that he would be able to make out where he was going. All he had was the moonlight, and it was faint tonight. Dark clouds streaked across the sky, leaving him with an almost-flickering light.

Finn reached the top of the hill and turned around to look toward the village. He couldn't see it all that well from there, though the lights of the village *were* visible; it looked as if he were looking through a haze.

A fog haze.

Finn began to tense.

Not here. Not already.

Fog. Witchcraft.

He had to find Esmerelda. He needed help before all of Torthen were slaughtered for magic, too. Finn unsheathed the sword and began to spin in place, looking around him.

There was something happening there, much like there had been something happening in Ferd.

Did that mean there had been witchcraft along the road leading toward Verendal as well? That might explain what had happened to the merchant. Killing him, raping his wife, would have led to magic.

Magic the Alainsith would *not* have been able to use.

Finn had to find the grave.

The man in the tavern had been the one to suggest he come there.

Finn looked around him. The growing fog made it difficult for him to see much of anything. He would have to either get moving or find the source of the fog.

He didn't see anything that suggested graves.

He should have waited. Come in the morning; that was, if they were still there in the morning. There wasn't any reason for him to be out there at night. He could have stayed behind and warned the village council before anything happened to them.

Which was what he still needed to do.

Finn had started down the far side of the hillside when he got tangled in a vine and stumbled. He rolled to his feet, trying to pop up as quickly as he could. He didn't want to be on the ground as that fog swept toward him. He looked to see what had tripped him up, but he couldn't tell.

Probably not a vine, though. There wouldn't have been a vine here.

What, then?

Finn swept the sword around as he tried to probe for what he might have tripped over, and came across a strange item protruding from the ground.

Getting to his feet and creeping forward, he tried to see better, though the moonlight seemed to have shifted again, making it even more difficult to see than before. Clouds had slid across the sky and obscured the moon. All he could make out was a mound of earth and a cold metal object buried in the ground.

A chill began to build around him.

Finn shivered.

He swung the sword around him. He'd gone the wrong direction.

If he really wanted to get to safety, he would have gone the other way. Back toward the village. Instead, now he was heading away from where he thought he should have gone.

Toward the fog, he realized. It was coming from the trees.

That's not quite right.

It was held back *from* the trees.

Finn ran toward them.

He didn't know whether the trees would be safer, but at least it wouldn't be the fog.

He reached the tree line just as the fog began to build even more. He spun around, looking through the trees. As he'd thought, the fog reached the edge of the trees and stopped.

The wind wasn't quite what it had been, either. Not with the same chill. Not a wind at all, really. Finn moved along within the trees, staying just inside the edge of the trees because the fog seemed to persist, pressing toward the trees but somehow unable to get any farther.

It was too much like in Ferd.

Finn wanted to find Esmerelda, warn the village, and then he wanted to head back to Verendal. He was done with magic.

He followed the trees around until they started to thin.

From there he could see how the fog persisted, pushing out and toward the trees. Finn paused and looked out toward the fog, but he didn't see anything about it that helped him understand whether there was a reason for fog to stop. With the trees thinning the way they did, he didn't know if they would provide the same protection as it did before.

Finn could see the outline of the village. The haze of the fog surrounded it, making it difficult for him to make out much more than the vaguest aspect of the village itself. A few lights were visible, but it was otherwise darkened. Had it been that way when he'd left? Finn didn't think that it had, but perhaps as it got later, there would be fewer lights in the village.

The fog looked to be little more than wisps here.

It was fading. As he waited, he watched as the fog retreated. Finn started to step forward.

"You should not do that yet."

He spun.

The voice had come out of the darkness behind him. Not Esmerelda.

"Who's there?"

"It isn't gone," the voice said.

It came from near a tree.

Finn took a step toward the voice, wondering if he were making a mistake. He had the sword to protect him, but whoever was out there didn't sound as if they were even from the kingdom.

"The fog? It's fading."

"Fading. Not gone. Dangerous to return to the village of man."

"Why is it dangerous?"

Could the village be responsible?

"It will follow. The village will succumb. All will be lost. It is untouched for now."

There was something accented about the words. Agitated. Familiar.

Finn had heard speech like that before, but where?

But then there was the comment about the "village of man."

"Who are you?"

The figure didn't move. They didn't step away from the tree, and as he tried to get closer, it seemed as if they faded deeper into the forest without even moving.

"You're Alainsith," Finn said.

That was where he'd heard that kind of speech. He was certain that it was similar to what he had heard from the man in Declan.

He might not have said anything that Finn would understand, but he had a similar way of speaking, the same sort of accent to the way he spoke.

The figure started to move.

"Wait."

They hesitated.

"What are you doing here?" Finn asked.

"Wait for it to disappear before going out. Or stay in the trees. You will be safer. Its power will fade at daybreak."

The figure spun and disappeared into the darkness.

Finn gave chase.

He didn't think that it was necessary, but he wanted to know more about the Alainsith. This one spoke his language. And had seemed willing to help. That had to matter, didn't it?

There was no sign of the Alainsith.

They had disappeared altogether.

Finn turned and looked around him. He felt like he had in the forest around Ferd. It left him confused about where he needed to go.

He had a sense of which way he had come, though, and he followed that, letting it guide him through the trees, and he found the edge of the forest, pausing there for a moment and looking at the fog still lying over the ground.

The temptation to step out on the road was there, but when he started to move forward, it seemed as if the fog surged, almost as if it were coming toward him.

The fog *knew* he was there.

And the trees offered some level of protection.

Finn took a seat, looking out through the fog.

He stared, losing track of how long he had been there. He would wait.

The fog didn't change. It remained layered over the ground. He might not even know what it was, were he not to have seen it before. If the Alainsith spoke the truth, it wouldn't reach the village. They'd be safe.

"There you are."

Finn turned and looked up at Esmerelda. A faint glow came from her, leaving her skin reflecting the pale light of the moon.

"We shouldn't go out there," he said.

"You see it."

"I see it. I was chased by it. A little, I think."

"Why are you out here?"

"One of the people in the tavern told me the bodies of the people that Leland had killed would be by a hill. I figured I'd come look before warning the council, but now I don't know if we can return." He pointed toward the distant hill, though he couldn't see the hill from there. The fog layered across the ground even more in that direction, which made it harder for him to make out much of anything. "When I got there, the fog started rolling in. Can you do anything for the village?"

"That is beyond me."

He looked toward the village. Get through the night. That was what the others had to do. If the fog would burn off with daybreak, then they could return and check on the village. It was time to return to Verendal, but he couldn't do that without knowing.

"There was an Alainsith." Finn motioned to the trees. "Out there. They warned me away from the fog." He had still started toward the fog, though he had known that he shouldn't. "I tried to catch them but couldn't."

"You wouldn't be able to catch one of the Alainsith in the forest. They are able to move more easily. They don't need much light to see."

Finn got to his feet. "He—or she; I guess I don't even know—told me to stay within the trees. That way, I'd be protected."

"You were given permission to remain in the trees?"

"I didn't see it like that. I guess they said I could stay here to stay away from the fog."

"They granted you passage," Esmerelda whispered.

"Why does that matter?"

"It is uncommon. The forest is tied to the Alainsith. It is the reason the kingdom doesn't spread beyond the forest. The trees have posed too much of a challenge for anyone to pass. The Alainsith make it difficult for anyone who is not granted passage to be able to get through."

Finn looked at the forest. "I didn't get the feeling they wanted to hurt me. They were offering me help."

"Then we should take it. It is time to get back."

The idea of not checking on the village didn't set well with him, but what *could* he do? Plus, the Alainsith had said the village was untouched.

"How? We take the forest back?"

"I think that would be the best. We cannot stay here. I'm not sure what is going on here, but I must return to search for answers."

He was curious *how* she would search for answers, but she didn't offer any hint.

They headed through the forest. By now, Finn was exhausted. They had spent the day traveling to Torthen, and he'd anticipated having a chance to rest at some point, but from the way Esmerelda sounded, she wanted to keep them moving.

"We can't keep this pace," Finn said.

"It's not a matter of the pace. We need to put distance between us and what was happening in that village."

Finn looked over his shoulder. They had been traveling through the forest and he wasn't able to see much behind him, though the trees were there, dark shadows that stretched up and around them. Had they been on horseback, he would have been concerned about running into the trees, but staying on foot that wasn't much of an issue.

There was no sign of the fog.

"We should rest, though." He looked over to Esmerelda.

"You said it yourself. The Alainsith have offered their help, such as it is."

"That is not what I said. I said they offered you safe passage."

"You're concerned that it doesn't extend to you."

She glanced in his direction, her head tilted, revealing her slender neck. The moonlight managed to filter through the trees so that he could see the pale reflection off her skin. "I have not had the opportunity to request the same safe passage."

"Would they grant it if you asked?"

"I don't know."

She continued forward, leaving Finn chasing after her. "We won't be able to make it to Verendal in one night. We'll need to rest. Now, we can either do that in the forest, or we can head back out to the King's Road and hope for the best."

Esmerelda looked over to him and frowned. "If you must rest, then so be it."

"You don't need to rest?"

"I would be able to keep moving, if it were necessary."

"I don't think it is."

She paused, looking around her for a moment before turning her attention back to him. "We may rest."

They stopped near a small stream, and after making a small circuit, Esmerelda settled to the ground. When she leaned back against one of the trees, she closed her eyes.

Despite her claims, she was tired.

Finn paused at the stream and leaned down. While cupping his hands into the water, he looked back at her. "Do you need to test the water to ensure that it's safe for us to drink?"

She opened one eye, glancing briefly to the stream before looking up at him. "Were they to want to harm you, it wouldn't be the water they use that would do it."

"What would it be?"

"Not the water."

Finn frowned before turning his attention back to the stream and taking a drink. The water was cool and had a coppery taste to it that wasn't unpleasant. He took a long drink before wiping his hands on his pants and turning back to Esmerelda. He couldn't tell whether she was asleep or not, though her breathing had slowed.

Settling to the ground near her, he closed his eyes.

He was tired.

Finn had no idea how long his eyes had been closed when he heard movement near him. He flicked open his eyes, looking over to Esmerelda to see if it was her, but she still rested against the tree. For all he could tell, she was awake, though her breathing was slow and steady.

Not her, then.

He *had* heard something.

Finn shifted, not wanting to move too much, but leaned away from the tree so that he could get a better look around him. There wasn't anything else moving. The moonlight seemed brighter than it had before, and he found it easier to see everything around him, though he wondered how much of that was from his eyes just adjusting to the darkness.

He listened.

The forest was quiet.

There was Esmerelda's steady breathing. Finn's own breathing. The pounding of his heart. The burbling of the stream. Even the sound of insects buzzing softly nearby. Every so often, he heard the soft hooting of an owl. There had been no sound of wolves howling, nor had there been any other creatures that he'd heard in the forest.

Nothing other than them.

And the Alainsith he'd seen.

Finn shifted again, looking around the forest as he did. He tried to lean forward, moving slowly so that he wouldn't draw any more attention from whatever was there, though he doubted that he was successful. Whatever was there probably already knew that they were here.

A soft shuffling came again.

It was a strange sound, almost like something were dragging along the forest floor.

Finn had to get to his feet.

As he stood, he leaned away from the tree a little bit more.

Then he saw a shadow through the trees.

It looked to be a wolf, though it was larger than any wolf that he'd seen before. The outline was wrong as well. Almost too stocky. It reminded him of the sculpture he'd seen in Wella's shop.

Finn reached for the sword and nudged Esmerelda with his foot.

She stirred briefly but didn't come completely around.

He didn't want to say anything for fear of having this strange creature come at him.

Finn nudged her again.

She still didn't move.

"Gods, woman," he whispered.

His hand found the hilt of the sword, and Finn started pulling it slowly from the sheath. The sound was loud in his ears, almost too loud. The wolf turned toward him, and light reflected from its pale yellow eyes. Finn shivered. Those were nothing like any wolf that he'd ever seen.

He nudged Esmerelda again; she still didn't come around.

Finn got the sword unsheathed and stood with it at the ready. He didn't know what the right way to hold the sword would be, especially were the wolf to decide to attack. He could use it the way Meyer had trained him, preparing to chop with the blade, but even were he to do that, he didn't know if he would have the aim that he needed to stop a wolf, should it attack.

Why would it, though?

Even approaching them was strange.

Finn wasn't about to make the first move with a creature that looked as if it didn't fear him. Instead, he watched. It seemed as if the wolf watched him as well.

"I would not harm it."

He spun.

Another figure stood near the stream, looking at him.

Alainsith.

"What is it?"

"It is one of the berahn."

"Not a wolf?"

The Alainsith leaned toward the stream, a long cylinder in hand. "Not a wolf. Normally, I would say they are difficult to kill, but with something like that"—the Alainsith nodded to Finn's sword—"you might be able to do it. Not that you should."

The Alainsith had a similar accent to the one he'd met near Torthen, though a soft and higher-pitched voice. Almost delicate, as if he—*she?*—were concerned about waking Esmerelda. Or upsetting the berahn.

"Will it hurt me?"

"You're still alive," the Alainsith said.

Finn grunted softly. He looked around, but the berahn hadn't moved. It stood watching him. "Did the berahn come with you?"

"It has followed me for some time." The Alainsith leaned forward, inhaling deeply. Finn still wasn't able to make much out about them because of the dark cloak that covered them.

"From your lands?"

"Yes."

"Why are you here?"

The Alainsith turned to him, watching him for a moment. Finn held on to the sword, feeling strangely uneasy. Perhaps it was knowing that these people had been able to kill so many of those of the kingdom without any real challenge.

Only, he felt no real sense of threat from them now.

Nor had he felt it before.

"The same as you, I suppose."

"I'm returning to my home."

The Alainsith tipped their head to the side, regarding him. "As am I."

"Where were you traveling?"

"East."

"Where is home?" Finn asked.

The Alainsith looked past him, and Finn turned.

Esmerelda stared at the Alainsith, her eyes wide.

"She won't hurt you," Finn said. "Neither of us will."

"You may pass through here."

The Alainsith stepped toward the water. Finn wanted to go after them, but he didn't want to upset them, either.

Instead, he waited.

In the distance, the berahn had disappeared.

Finn searched around the small clearing but didn't see any sign of the creature.

When he looked back for the Alainsith, they were gone.

CHAPTER TWENTY-FIVE

F inn sheathed the executioner's blade, sliding it into the sheath as carefully as he could, still concerned that he might find the berahn returning, though there was no sign of it. He made a quick circuit around where they had stopped for the night, but there wasn't anything other than Esmerelda.

"Did you see where it went?" Finn asked.

"I would not follow the Alainsith," she said softly.

He looked over his shoulder and found her standing near the stream, her gaze looking in the direction of where Finn suspected the Alainsith had gone, though he had no proof of that.

"Not the Alainsith. The berahn."

She gasped softly. "There was a berahn here?"

Finn motioned where he stood. There wasn't any evidence of anything having come through there, though without much light, Finn wasn't sure that he would be able to tell much, anyway. He couldn't see any footprints, though the forest was dense enough—and dark enough—that he might just have overlooked them.

"It was right here. It woke me from sleep."

"The berahn would not have awoken you."

Finn just shrugged. "There was something that woke me," he said.

She looked around her. "The berahn were once the silent killers. Men wouldn't know they were there until they had their hearts ripped out."

Finn licked his lips. The Alainsith *had* made a comment about how the fact that he was still alive meant the berahn wasn't going to harm him.

Was that *what he meant?*

"Why would they rip men's hearts out?"

She joined him, looking down at the ground. "I have never known anyone to have seen one of the berahn. The Alainsith will see them occasionally, but it is rare, even for them." She turned to Finn. "You have been doubly blessed on this journey, it seems. First you negotiated safe passage from the Alainsith, then you saw one of the berahn."

"I didn't necessarily negotiate for anything. I think the Alainsith just wanted to warn me."

"As I said. Blessed."

She crouched down and traced her fingers along the soil. She brought them to her mouth, tapping her tongue against them, before reaching into her pouch and pulling out a small bowl. She scooped a bit of earth into the bowl before setting it on the ground and whispering to it.

"What are you hoping to learn?" Finn asked.

"More about what the berahn would have been after."

"The Alainsith said the berahn had been following him."

"From where?"

"East."

Esmerelda straightened. "Are you sure of that? It wouldn't be uncommon for there to be a misunderstanding. Though the Alainsith can speak the Gerand language, they don't always do so in ways that men understand. There have been misunderstandings before."

"I'm pretty sure I understood him."

"Him?"

Finn shrugged. "I don't know. It could have been a her. It was hard to tell with the cloak."

"Did you see any weapons?"

"Weapons?" She nodded, and Finn shook his head. "It would have been difficult with the cloak, anyway. Why?"

"The Alainsith soldiers are mostly female."

"Really?"

"It's why the kingdom dismissed them as a threat early on. They learned otherwise."

Finn hadn't been able to tell if there were any weapons, but the person that he'd spoken to *did* have a higher-pitched and softer voice. It could have been female.

"I don't know. What are the males?"

He thought about the Alainsith man they had captured in Declan. If the females were the soldiers, he couldn't help but wonder what role the men played in that society. The man had threatened them with war, though. It suggested that he was a part of the military in some way.

"It depends."

"On what?"

"Many things, Finn Jagger." She started to pace. "Why would they have been coming through here? The north?" She looked at Finn and he nodded. "That would suggest they were traveling toward…"

She never finished the thought, and Finn waited, hoping that she would tell him more, but she didn't say anything.

"Toward what?" Finn asked.

"Perhaps toward Verendal." She shook her head. "It is possible they are after the one you hold." She breathed out slowly. "We should rest. Then we must get back as quickly as we can."

Finn had to get back as well. Meyer hadn't given him too much time, and it had now run out. That made it difficult, as Finn didn't feel like he had the answers he needed. And there was still Holden's timeline. Finn didn't know what the Thilson meant when he'd warned they had a short time remaining, but he suspected Holden hadn't lied about that. "Now you're not concerned about resting anymore?"

"I am permitted to be here."

"Are you sure? Because before, you weren't quite as certain about that. If you want, I can see if I can get the Alainsith to return—"

"That will not be necessary."

There was a hint of disappointment in her tone, though.

Whatever she might claim about the Alainsith, she *did* want to see them again.

That and the berahn.

Esmerelda took a seat near the base of the same tree where she'd been before, resting her back against it. Finn waited a moment, thinking that she might say something more, but soon her breathing began to become more regular and he could tell that she'd drifted off.

He settled to the ground, not sure that he'd sleep. When he closed his eyes, he figured he'd only be out for a few moments, but when he opened them again, daylight streamed through the branches overhead. Finn stretched, stiff from how he'd been sitting, and found Esmerelda already up and kneeling where the berahn had been.

"What are you doing?"

"I'm trying to determine if there is anything here that can be tracked."

Finn got to his feet and looked at where she knelt. The ground didn't appear trampled the way that he would expect, given that there was supposed to have been some massive animal through there the night before. There wasn't any sign that anything had been there. She had her small bowl out and dug at the dirt, scooping some into the bowl and swirling it around before tossing it back out. He couldn't tell if she detected anything using that technique or not.

"I didn't think you wanted to follow it."

"I need to find out what direction it came from."

"Have you found anything?"

She shook her head. "Unfortunately, no. I did not expect to, either. The berahn have not been tracked before, so it is not surprising that I would not be able to find anything, though I was hopeful that since you saw the creature the night before, we would be able to uncover some way of following it."

He inhaled deeply. The scent of the forest filled his nostrils, that of the fallen leaves, damp earth, and the wet rock of the stream. "The Alainsith said the berahn followed him, so maybe even the Alainsith can't follow them."

"That is probably true," she said.

She got to her feet, heading over to the stream, where she swirled some water around in the bowl before dumping it out and stuffing it back into her pocket. "We should get moving if your goal is to return to Verendal today."

"It'll be a long walk."

"It will, which is why we must get moving."

He grabbed his pack and followed her. Esmerelda seemed to know where she was going, though every so often, she would pause and look at the ground or reach into her pocket and pull something out, as if that would help her decide the direction she needed to take.

Late in the day, they came across another stream. She leaned toward the water, running her hands through it. The water swirled with a bit of green before that faded, and she cupped her hands to her mouth, taking a long drink.

Finn crouched next to her, tasting the water. "It's different than the last one," he said.

"The water comes from a different source."

"Are you sure? These streams crisscross through here. It seems to me they would all come from the same place."

"I can tell," she said.

She didn't elaborate and continued on through the forest, leaving Finn to take another drink before going after her.

It was strange that it had only been a day since he'd been in Torthen. A day even since he'd been in Ferd. It felt longer to him, long enough that everything that had happened to him had taken on a remote feel.

The sun had started to set when he noticed the forest thinning.

"We can't be to the edge of the forest yet," he said, mostly to himself.

"We have traveled a different direction than we would have, were we to have remained along the King's Road. That path winds through the trees, avoiding areas where the Alainsith have refused to budge."

Finn smiled at the comment but realized that Esmerelda seemed not to be joking with him. As they neared the edge of the forest, he could see the outline of Verendal in the distance.

He had been gone for less than a week, but it seemed as if it were a lifetime ago. When he'd left, he had known magic existed—it was the reason he lived—but knowing that it existed and seeing its effects were very different things.

"I'm going to have to see if I can get the Alainsith we have in Declan to talk."

What would happen if the other Alainsith were there to help?

He had promised war.

Could we be in real danger of war with the Alainsith?

She turned to him. Despite their days on the road, and sleeping next to a tree, she still looked as she did when he had first met her. "You have interacted with the Alainsith more than most, Finn Jagger. You will do what you must do."

They started toward the city.

By dark, as they approached the city, Esmerelda touched his arm, turning him toward her. "I hope your pilgrimage has been a fruitful one, Finn Jagger." She leaned forward and surprised him by kissing him on the cheek.

Esmerelda released his arm and turned toward the hegen section, leaving Finn alone on the road back into Verendal, the same as he had been on his way out of the city. His heart was heavy with what he'd seen, and fear lingered in him, concern for the witchcraft he'd seen and what it might mean for Verendal. He was tired and didn't know if his mind could even work through that enough to process.

His feet ached. His back was sore from sleeping on the ground. And all he wanted was to get to Meyer to share what he'd learned—and to check on his sister.

As he neared the Raven Stone, he looked over to the gallows. The stout wood of the gallows towered above the Stone. The air carried the slight stench near the stone as it often did; the reminder of the death that had been carried out in this place over the years. Not that Finn needed that reminder, but it served the city well.

When he reached Teller Gate, the Archers eyed him a moment before seeming to recognize him. None stopped him.

Finn made his way through the streets, heading toward Meyer's home. When he neared the gate, he paused. The lantern light illuminating this section of the city didn't seem quite as bright as it had been before. He looked around him, remembering his attack—and the near-attack that he'd missed before leaving on his pilgrimage.

There were still things that needed doing.

Iron masters in Declan needed to be dealt with, though Finn suspected that Meyer had done that already. There was the question of what to do with Holden, though he would have to heal before he could face any fate. First, there was the Alainsith.

That was what Finn still didn't know how to do.

Esmerelda had suggested he had the answers, though with what he'd seen outside the city, Finn didn't feel as if he did. What *had* he learned? There was witchcraft. That had always been spoken of in rumors, and though many believed the hegen used witchcraft for their particular kind of magic, what Finn had seen had been something very different. He'd met Alainsith, though neither of them that he had met had seemed at all like the man they had in Declan.

Why would that be?

Those thoughts stayed with him as he pushed the gate to Meyer's home open and headed toward the house. A lantern shone in the window, though not as brightly as he was accustomed to. When he stepped inside, he paused a moment, listening.

There was silence.

Was it so late that Meyer wouldn't be offering anyone healing?

That would be strange. Most nights, he was busy. There were always people coming to him, looking for whatever healing he might be able to offer them. As long as the lantern was on, people would come.

Finn set the sword into the small closet along with Justice. He would need to clean the blade, perhaps even sharpen it, but for now it could stay in the closet with the other. He pulled the door to his small room open and set his bag inside. He needed to clean up and change clothes, but first he wanted to find Meyer and let him know that he had returned.

Stopping in the kitchen, he found a small loaf of bread and cut off a section, chewing slowly, thankful for the simple normalcy of it.

When his stomach settled, he headed toward Meyer's office. He leaned his head toward it, listening for a moment. There was no sound on the other side, so he pushed it open.

A single lantern lit the room.

The desk was a mess. That was unlike Meyer. Most of the time, he was neat with his medicines. For him to have a mess like this suggested that he'd been busy in the time that Finn had been gone. Though that shouldn't surprise him. With as long as he'd been gone, all of the things that Finn normally would do would end up going to Meyer. He would have to run the small errands, stop and perform all of the questionings, carry out any executions that might have been sentenced in his absence.

Much like he once had done.

There hadn't been a mess when Finn had first come to work with Meyer, so why now?

He heard someone moving, and he glanced over to the cot. He should have looked there first.

Finn looked down at the cot, half-expecting to find Oscar still lying there the way that he had been when Finn had last been there, but that wasn't who he found.

It was Meyer.

Finn stared for a moment, trying to make sense of what he saw. His skin looked sallow, with his closed eyes seeming sunken. His hair had taken on a wispy quality that looked as if he had thinned and aged two decades in the week that Finn had been gone.

"Master Meyer?"

Finn's voice came out haltingly as he made his way over.

A sheen of sweat covered Meyer's forehead, running along his neck and leaving the sheets damp. He breathed slowly and erratically.

Finn touched his neck, feeling for his pulse the way Meyer himself had taught him. Unlike his breathing, the pulse seemed regular. For now. That might not be the case, were he to suffer for much longer.

Finn turned to the desk; the mess of medicines along the surface of it made a different sort of sense. Had Meyer been trying to find some way to heal himself? What of Lena? She would have been there, and he would have expected that she would be able to help, especially given what he knew she'd learned from Meyer, but there was no sign of his sister. She wouldn't have left him, though.

Then what of Oscar?

He looked at the items along the desk, searching for what had been tried. It would give him an idea of how sick Meyer might be. He found horeth seeds, elavander oil, daisel leaves, and saitl. All were nonspecific. A few other powders were unmarked. Finn sniffed at them but wasn't able to identify them easily.

Two bowls looked to have been used to mix various concoctions. Finn pressed his finger into one of them but didn't know what it might represent.

Unlike Meyer, who documented what he had tried with the people he cared for, there was nothing there to suggest that whoever had been mixing these compounds had done any sort of documentation.

The only thing on the desk was a slip of paper.

Finn stared at it.

Notes, made in Meyer's hand.

Directed to Finn.

The merchant's wife hadn't remembered anything more about her attack. Holden hadn't broken. Loren Thilson had mentioned a full moon. The other crew member had alluded to time running out to find all the women.

All the women?

There had been two—right?

Nothing about the iron masters.

There was one more word on the page, followed by a question: *Midnight?*

Midnight when?

The full moon.

But tonight was the full moon.

He turned back to the cot.

Finn would have to find his sister. That would be the only way that he might be able to know what had happened to Meyer and whether she had tried everything short of going to the hegen. Given his experience outside of the city, he would have no problem going to Esmerelda now. He figured they owed each other.

Stepping out of the room, he started up the stairs to see if his sister were resting in her room—though he thought it unlikely she would leave Meyer like that—when he heard noise in the main entry to the house.

Finn hurried back down the stairs.

Lena was there, along with Wella, the old apothecary.

"Finn," Lena said, running toward him and wrapping her arms around his neck. "I'm so glad that you're back."

"What happened?"

He nodded toward Meyer's office as he hugged his sister.

She stepped back from him. "I don't know. None of us do. He started getting sick. I think he tried to hide it from us, but while you were gone, he started getting weaker and weaker. Now he's like this. Barely defended the home when someone broke in. I don't think they took anything—"

"Someone broke in here?" Finn frowned.

"Like I said, I don't think they took anything, but I don't

know. And now he's like this. He had a small wound on his back, but that was easy to stitch. What's happening to him is like nothing I've seen before."

That was saying something, considering how Lena had worked with Meyer during the last few years, gaining as much or more experience than Finn did when it came to healing. She was the equal of almost any apothecary, and were Finn to be pressed, he would have figured her the rival of the physicians in the city.

"Wella?" he asked.

"I don't know. It is similar to what afflicted your friend."

Which meant magic.

"What happened to Oscar?" he asked.

Lena nodded toward the stairs. "When he was well enough to be moved, we brought him upstairs to recuperate. That was before we knew how badly Master Meyer was."

"Did you ask the hegen for help?" Finn whispered. He didn't want to announce that they had been using the hegen for healing lately.

"She was gone."

"I know she was gone, but there are others you could go to."

Finn only knew Esmerelda when it came to healing, but there would have to be other hegen healers. It would be a matter of finding them, something that Finn didn't know how to do, but there would need to be some within the hegen who would be able to guide her to them.

"I tried, but they told me... What do you mean, you know she was gone?"

"I met up with her outside of the city."

Lena frowned at him. "I thought you had left on a pilgrimage, not for you to fornicate with one of the hegen."

Finn snorted. "I *did* go out on a pilgrimage, and it wasn't until after I stopped in Torthen I encountered her. She was heading the same way as I was."

"Why?"

Finn shook his head. He wasn't going to tell Lena about the witchcraft. Not unless it made a difference to them. "You know how the hegen can be."

"I do. Which is why I'm asking why she would have been out on the road with you. What did she ask of you?"

He understood where his sister was coming from, but Esmerelda hadn't asked him for anything. All she had wanted was to travel with him. He had benefited as much as she had, he suspected.

"She didn't ask anything of me."

Lena eyed him for a long moment. "Finn... she would have asked something. That's how the hegen are."

"I think I know exactly how the hegen are."

He stormed off, heading up the stairs as he had intended. Once there, he could smell where he needed to go, even if Lena hadn't told him which bed it was to be. Meyer had three rooms on the second level: his, Lena's, and the one that had once been his mother's during the time that she had been with them.

Finn approached the door slowly, resting his hand on it

for a moment before pushing it open. Oscar lay on the bed, breathing steadily, only a thin sheet covering him.

The room hadn't changed much from the time that his mother had occupied it. She'd only been there for a little while—two years—but long enough to have made it her own. A mirror on a dresser reminded Finn of her, as did the brush resting next to it. A few books that Finn was surprised Lena hadn't taken, and nothing else. A lifetime lived, and that was all that she'd left behind.

He stopped next to the bed, looking down at Oscar. His eyes were darkened, sunken a little, and sweat slicked across his brow. At least he didn't look quite as ill as he had before Finn had left. A stool rested near the bed. Finn pulled it up and took a seat on it, leaning close to his friend.

Oscar stirred and rolled his head toward him, opening his eyes. "Finn," he said softly.

"It's me. How are you feeling?"

Oscar started to grunt, but it turned into a rough cough. "Probably about as good as I look."

"Like shit, then."

"Pretty much." Oscar took a deep breath. "Still feel weak. At least I'm awake." That meant the hegen magic had helped, but not enough. "Your sister told me you'd left the city."

"Meyer wanted me to take a pilgrimage."

"Which is?"

"A chance to go out of the city to prove myself."

He closed his eyes for a moment, rolling his head back around as if he were trying to stare up at the ceiling through his closed lids. "She said I had you to thank for getting me here."

"I wasn't going to let you die."

"I would have deserved it."

"Why is that? You wouldn't have let me die, either."

"That's different."

"Why?"

"I owe you," Oscar said.

"You don't owe me anything."

"Fine. Then I owe your father. It's the same thing, anyway." He coughed again and closed his eyes tighter. His breathing slowed for a moment, as if he were falling asleep. "He'd be proud of you." He rolled his head back toward Finn. "You probably haven't heard that before, but he would have been. I don't think that he ever wanted you to join a crew. Not the life for you, he would have said. It was the life for him. Not the one he wanted for his boy."

"I didn't know anything else."

"That's on him," Oscar said. "But you did the same as what he would have wanted you to do. Take care of the family. You took good care of your mother. Your sister. You've done well."

Finn glanced toward the door leading out into the hall and downstairs. "I don't always feel like I've done well by my sister."

"She's out of Brinder section. She's got a different kind of job—one where she uses her mind. That seems to me like you've done everything that you should have done for her."

He coughed again and took a deep breath to steady himself. "She tells me I'm not going to die from this."

"I guess not."

"You guess?" He cocked an eye open wider as he looked at Finn. "Aren't you the hangman who knows a thing or two about death? I would have expected this would be the very thing that you would be able to tell me."

Finn leaned back. Was that what he'd become? He didn't know how he felt about being considered an expert on death. It fit, though. As much as he might wish otherwise, it was an area where he now had some expertise. He had seen men suffer, broken, near death, and he knew what it took to bring them back—or push them over.

"I try not to get too involved with the magic in the world," Finn said.

"Don't we all," Oscar muttered.

"I'm glad you're going to survive."

"You and me both."

"Holden was responsible for the attack on you."

"That's what I gather," Oscar said.

Finn rested his elbows on his knees. "I'm going to have to deal with him."

Midnight. Full moon.

He didn't have much time.

"You don't deal with a bastard like that," Oscar said.

"I have to."

Oscar rolled his head off to the side. "No. You don't. I do."

"You aren't going to be able to do much of anything. You need to recover."

"I will. Lena tells me that it's not so bad. Just a matter of weakness. I've been getting older anyway, so that's not too surprising."

"You need time to come through this. It was a magical poisoning."

"Bastard," Oscar muttered. "Don't matter, though. Still going to handle my business."

He started to sit up but Finn held his hand out. "I don't think you should do that."

"Don't you go thinking you can tell me what to do as well. I've got enough of that with your sister. She comes here, trains with Master Meyer, and gets it all up in her head that she's going to keep me in bed." He grunted, coughing again. "The medicine that she's been giving me tastes awful."

"She probably told you the best medicines don't taste very good."

"She did tell me that," he said.

Finn only chuckled. He could see his sister doing that to Oscar. "What did you want to get up and do, anyway?"

"I'm not going to lie around while my business falls apart."

Finn smiled. "What business do you have to take care of?"

Oscar looked over at him. "The kind that I don't need you meddling in. If I tell you anything, you're going to have to go and investigate it, and the gods know I don't need that."

"What makes you think that I'm going to *have* to do anything?"

Oscar shifted where he was lying, managing to get up on his elbows and look over at him. "I've watched as you've progressed with Master Meyer, Finn. I know how you see your job. Can't blame you, either. This is what you always wanted. Something honorable."

Finn grunted. "I'm not sure *this* is what I always wanted, but it's what I've got. Anyway, you aren't going to leave and get yourself hurt again. I'm not willing to do that. You'll probably go back to Annie, and someone there will end up shooting a crossbow into you like they almost did to me."

Oscar waved his hand toward Finn. "Aw, I doubt Annie would shoot you."

"I didn't say Annie."

"You said *crossbow*. That's her weapon of choice. She's damn skilled with it. Learned to be once the King got pinched and she lost the protection she once had. That's how she's managed to stay in business for as long as she has."

Finn just stared at Oscar for a long moment.

"What? Did I say something that upset you?"

Finn shook his head and got to his feet. "Get some rest, Oscar. You can't get out of here until you're better rested."

"Now you're sounding like her too."

"Just because we're saying the same thing doesn't make the advice wrong."

"Just because you live in this nice house doesn't make it right, either." Oscar rolled his head away, staring at the wall.

Finn patted him on the hand before heading from the room. Once back down the stairs, he had reached the door leading out of the house when Lena caught him.

"What are you doing?"

"I've got something that I've got to check on," he said.

"You just got back! Master Meyer might need your help."

Finn took a deep breath. "Meyer needs help, but it's not my help. I've got to check on something." Whatever Holden planned was soon. Once Finn figured it out, then he would have to get word to Esmerelda. Only then could he deal with the Alainsith man. "Use the same hegen medicine Esmerelda gave me for Oscar on Meyer for now."

Wella stood in the door behind Lena, and her eyes widened slightly. The apothecary knew the hegen healer. That didn't surprise him. Finn suspected they all knew each other in some way. "That cannot be transferred in such a way."

He shot her a look. "I will pay the price. Whatever it is."

"Finn—"

"Just do it," he said softly.

With that, he turned, hesitating a moment to grab a cloak from the closet, decided to add the spike he'd taken from Holden, and headed out of the door and into the night.

CHAPTER TWENTY-SIX

Coming to the Wenderwolf tavern at night might have been a mistake. There weren't many people out now that they neared the curfew, though he hadn't passed any Archers along the way, either. He didn't know if that was a problem to be concerned about or not.

The streetlights seemed brighter than he remembered, though that might only be because he'd been wandering through the darkness of the forest for so long.

He approached the tavern slowly. The small plaza outside of the tavern was where he'd been attacked, so he made his way cautiously to see whether there was anyone moving out there, but didn't see anything. The tavern itself was quieter than he'd expected. Usually, there was the sound of music drifting out from inside, as if to tempt the Archers into coming to break up those who were out beyond the curfew. Often, Finn would find people making their way in or out of the tavern as well, though there was none of that.

He should have changed his clothes. He felt as if he still wore the dirt and grime from the road on him, the days of travel leaving him filthy, but he felt as if he needed to do this. Finn needed the answers he could only get there.

Pausing at the door leading into the tavern, Finn held his hand up from it, waiting for a moment. He heard nothing. The door was locked.

Had Annie closed the tavern early?

She normally stayed open as late as possible, keeping the tavern open until everyone left on their own. There was always ale to be sold, food to be eaten, so it surprised him she wouldn't have it open now.

Finn made his way around to the backside of the tavern through a narrow alley that ran this way. Even when he'd been a part of the crew, he hadn't come this direction that often. There wasn't a need. The tavern was the reputable front for the crew.

Finn reached the back door to the tavern and tested it. Unlike the other, it was unlocked. He wasn't beyond forcing his way in, were it necessary, but he didn't really want it to be necessary, either.

Once inside, he hesitated while his eyes adjusted to the dimmer light. The kitchen spread out before him. A lantern had been dimmed and rested on one of the counters, but there wasn't anything else. No smells, either. Nothing that would suggest to Finn that the tavern had been active recently. Only the stink of stale ale.

Where was Annie?

All of this felt off.

Finn headed through the kitchen, pausing at the door to listen to sounds on the other side. He heard nothing. Finn pushed open the door. It was dark, much like the kitchen. Finn found nothing.

No sign of Annie. No sign of any patrons in the tavern. No sign of anyone on any of the crews. The tavern was empty.

Finn made his way through the tavern and paused at the main entrance.

He tested the lock for a moment, tracing his fingers along the surface of the door.

"We're closed," someone said behind him.

Finn spun quickly.

A darkened figure stood in the doorway, a crossbow in hand.

"Annie?"

There was no response.

"We're closed," the voice said again. "Now, if I were you, I would consider moving as quickly as you can so you don't experience firsthand how badly one of these bolts can hurt."

Finn grunted. "I've seen it firsthand. It's Finn Jagger, Annie."

She didn't move.

The crossbow remained aimed at him.

Maybe Finn had it wrong, though he didn't think so. It sounded like Annie. Only, Annie would recognize him. Annie would have known.

He pulled his leather cloak around him. If nothing else, it might serve as a bit of protection, were she to fire at him. Maybe not as much as he would prefer. Finn would prefer that he not be fired upon at all.

"Annie," he said, this time more sharply than before. "Lower the crossbow. I'm just here to ask you a few questions."

"Like you did with the Hand?"

Finn frowned. "Like I did with what? Oscar is my friend. He's recuperating. He's getting as much help as I can provide him."

"I'm sure."

"What's that supposed to mean?" Finn asked.

Annie took a step toward him, though the crossbow never lowered. "You told me you were going to get him help. I thought the executioner was as skilled as any apothecary."

Finn nodded slowly. "He is. Probably more so."

"Where is he?"

"I told you. He's recuperating."

"The Hand wouldn't have stayed away so long."

There was something about the way she said it that struck a nerve for Finn.

She cared about Oscar. It wasn't just that she cared about him. She *cared* about him.

"I thought you and the King—"

"You won't mention him here," she said.

Finn raised his hands. "I'm sorry. That was uncalled for."

"Where is he?" she demanded.

"He's at Master Meyer's home. The poison used on him was"—Finn wasn't quite sure how to phrase it, not clear whether Annie would believe that Oscar had been poisoned with some sort of magical concoction, especially as he wasn't completely sure how to believe it—"different than anything that Master Meyer had seen before."

"He's going to get better, isn't he?"

The hand holding the crossbow seemed to quiver just a little bit. It was enough that Finn started to think she wasn't actually going to fire on him.

At least, he hoped she wouldn't.

The only chance he had was if she believed he was the only way she would get to see Oscar again.

Was that what he wanted, though? Did he want to use Oscar and whatever relationship he and Annie had in order for him to get the answers he wanted? Was that the person he'd become?

The answer came far too easily.

Finn knew what he had become. More than that, he knew *who* he had become.

An executioner.

It was his job to get answers. It was his job to question, regardless of what form that questioning took on. It was his responsibility to understand.

"Tell me what I need to know, and I'll make sure you can see him," Finn said.

"It's like that, is it?" she asked.

He shrugged. "I think it might need to be."

"I thought you said he was your friend."

"He *is* my friend." Finn almost made a comment about how Oscar was a friend who had said nothing about his relationship with Annie, whatever that relationship might be, before deciding against it. That seemed unnecessarily cruel, regardless of what he might need to know. "All I need is to have you tell me what happened here and what you know about the women Holden's crew are after."

"What happened is that I closed the tavern," she said. She took a step toward him, and lowered the crossbow. "There didn't seem to be much point in keeping it open, with the activity that's been going on here. Besides, too damn many girls going missing. I've got to make sure I protect *my* girls."

"You helped me."

She stared at him. "You didn't think I would?"

Finn remained standing near the doorway, one hand resting near the handle. He still didn't know what Annie might do and how she might react. It might be that he would need to move quickly. He was at a disadvantage in that she had a weapon and he did not.

"I thought you were angry about what happened with the King."

"Leon always knew what might happen to him. He could be a right bastard, especially when he got it in his head that he had been wronged."

"I never wronged him," Finn said.

"You didn't, but in his mind, the world had." She took a seat in one of the chairs, nodding to another chair across from her. Finn hesitated a moment, debating whether he would take a seat or remain standing. "That's why he always acted the way he did. Didn't you know that about him?"

Finn just shrugged. "I suppose I never really thought much about it."

"That's probably for the best. If you started to think too much about the reason why Leon did what he did, you might find yourself falling into a hole you never get out of."

"Why do you say that?"

"I thought I was special to him." She smiled ruefully. "Here, that's supposed to be my specialty, isn't it? Making someone feel as if they are more than what they are. I teach my girls that, too. It's how they get to be so successful. Build up a clientele and all. They get men to come back for them. Some men only come back for specific women."

"I know," Finn said.

Annie shrugged. "I figured you would. You always seemed a little sweet on a few of my girls."

"I always knew where I stood with them."

"I guess that's the difference between you and some of the others to come through here," Annie said. "You can see through to the truths within the world."

Finn settled into the chair, resting his hands on the table. His gaze darted down to the crossbow still clutched in Annie's hands.

"What happened with Leon?"

"He used me. That's all. Then he was going to use you. When I tried to caution him against it, he…" She looked up, meeting Finn's eyes, and shook her head. "It doesn't matter. Not anymore. I suppose in a way, Leon got what was coming for him. And, if you ask him, the world proved to him just how unfair it all was."

"He was trying to do something he shouldn't have," Finn said.

"You don't have to tell me. I know. Just as I know that he was never going to stop." She finally set the crossbow down next to her. "When you got pinched, taken to the gallows to hang, he'd already moved on." She shook her head. "I suppose that's hard for you to hear."

"I know," Finn said softly.

"Did you? You came back here enough times, I started to wonder. It's not my place to tell a man where he belongs in the world. I figure he's got to come to those terms on his own. Besides, at that point, even the Hand wasn't willing to go against Leon."

"I know." He took a deep breath, looking around the tavern. "Gina's the one who set me up."

"She's been dealt with."

"You got revenge for what she did to Oscar."

"Not me. *Them.*"

It was an admission of something. "I need to know. Whatever is taking place is happening tonight." And too soon.

"Gone," she said.

"Gone where?"

Annie cocked her head. "Do you intend to take me to prison, Finn?"

Finn let out a frustrated breath. "Come on, Annie. You know I'm just trying to get to the bottom of all of this."

"The bottom of all of what? Why does that even matter to you? She's been dealt with. If you really care about the Hand—Oscar—then you'll just leave things alone."

"It's not just about what happened to Oscar." At least, not entirely.

It had to be more than that. Gina had used magic. It was the kind of magic the hegen had struggled against, and a different kind of magic. Witchcraft.

Had he not gone out of the city, and had he not seen what was taking place there on his own, he wasn't sure he would have known. Which meant that whoever Gina had been in contact with also had access to witchcraft.

"I dealt with her," she said.

"What exactly did you do to deal with her?"

"I turned her against her own crew." Annie crossed her arms over her chest and looked at Finn with a smug expression.

"And which crew is that?" he asked softly.

"I'm not going to get into that, Finn."

"Because I'm with the executioner?"

"Because you *are* the executioner."

He stared, debating what to say. Finn was going to have to tell her something more. It was the only way he would get the information he needed.

"Oscar was poisoned with magic," he said.

She started to laugh, watching him. "You can't tell me you believe in that sort of thing, too? When Oscar would go on about it, I never knew quite what to say to him."

"It's true. I had to go to the hegen to get him help. The

apothecary couldn't help. Master Meyer wasn't able to help. The only one who helped him was one of the hegen." Finn stared at her, debating how to explain. "I need to know which crew Gina worked with so that I can better understand what exactly happened to Oscar."

Even as he said it, Finn had a sneaking suspicion he already knew. Holden's crew. They were new to the city. And Gina had allowed herself to get caught up in them.

"What will you do to them?"

"It depends upon what I need to do," he said. "But first, I need to know what happened. Where did you turn Gina in?"

Annie clutched the crossbow to her. "I can show you."

"That's not what I need," Finn said.

"I'm not going to give her up and send you in there by yourself. If I did, and if something happened to you, Oscar would never let me live it down."

"I can handle myself," Finn said.

"Oh, I saw that, Finn."

"I could just bring Archers with me."

"The moment that you do, they will know you're coming."

"Because they've paid for the Archers." Annie nodded and Finn sighed. "Let's go."

"Now?"

Finn nodded. "I need these answers. And Meyer learned that whatever they're planning with those girls is happening tonight. Which means we have to get moving." He *should* be getting help for Meyer—or reporting what he'd discovered outside the city—but Lena would get Meyer the help he needed and Holden couldn't wait.

He had started toward the main door when Annie cleared her throat. Finn turned toward her.

"Not that way," she said.

"You want to go out through the alley?"

"It's less likely to be watched by Archers," she said.

"I didn't see any Archers when I came."

"I doubt you would have." She turned away from him and headed through the kitchen.

It couldn't all be related, could it?

Everything he'd been doing, all tied to some strange emergence of magic within the city? Not just any kind of magic but witchcraft. Magic that preyed upon torment. Blood magic. It would explain so much. All of the strange occurrences within the city. The disappearance of the women. Attacks around the city.

He had to see what Holden and his crew were up to.

She guided him through the alleys, twisting and turning, reaching intersections that Finn once knew as well as any in the city but now had faded to the background within his mind; finding his way to whichever section Annie intended to bring him on the main streets would be impossible.

Which was probably her point. Annie wasn't naïve.

It had nothing to do with Archers. It had all to do with her controlling how much Finn knew and learned about the various crews operating within the city. They hadn't gone very long before she raised her hand, motioning for him to come closer.

When he did, she leaned in. Her breath stank of ale. How much had she been drinking while sitting alone in the tavern? The shakiness to her hands while holding on to the crossbow took on a different meaning. Maybe she wasn't the best companion for this journey.

"It's only a few doors from here," she said, keeping her voice pitched low.

"You don't want to go all the way to it?" Finn asked.

She glanced to the upper part of the buildings surrounding it. Finn tried to look there, peering against the darkness, but he didn't see anything. Annie must have noticed something, though. She swung the crossbow, pointing it up and toward the rooftops.

"You wanted somebody to keep an eye on you."

Finn frowned at her. "I believe you were the one who wanted somebody to keep an eye on me."

"Fine. You needed somebody to keep an eye on you. I will do that."

"By waiting outside?"

"I think you can manage well enough on your own."

There was a part of Finn that questioned her motives. Why was she so willing to be left behind?

It wasn't that he thought she might betray him. Not anymore. If she truly was with Oscar, then he doubted that she would betray him, though Annie had her own motivations. She would act on behalf of the tavern. She would act on behalf of those she wanted to protect. Some small part of him questioned whether all of this was a long con and she was using Oscar in order to get back at Finn for what had happened to the King.

"Which door?" He didn't want to think about it any more than he already had. Doing so would only lead him to question whether or not he should take action.

"There will be one with a symbol of a bird on it."

He nodded, looking back at her for a moment, and waited before heading onward. He needed to get this over with. He needed to know what was going on with witchcraft within the city. Maybe he needed to have gone for Esmeralda.

Finn reached the door, and as he grabbed for the handle, he froze.

He saw the symbol that she described as a little bird, but as he stared at it, a different purpose came to him. This was witchcraft.

He fumbled through his pockets and found the long, slender metal spike he had taken off of Holden before. Witchcraft could be disrupted. That was what Esmerelda had said.

Finn used the spike, scratching against the door, displacing the symbol the way that he'd seen Esmerelda do in Ferd. He tore through the wood, marring the marking. It might be his imagination, but he thought he felt a soft puff of air, as if the wind gusted around him suddenly.

Finn stuffed the spike back into his pocket.

He glanced behind him. Annie watched, staring at him as if to ask a question of him, but Finn just shook his head. He tested the handle.

It was unlocked.

That surprised him, considering this was supposed to be the safe house of a crew, but perhaps they didn't expect there to be any trouble there. Situated as it was off of an alley, it would be difficult for anyone to reach without knowing exactly which building it was. That Annie knew where it was...

He glanced back, but she had slipped into the shadows.

He pushed open the door. Once inside, he hesitated. A dim lantern cast a soft glow throughout the inside of the room. It was a small entryway. Strangely enough, it reminded him of Meyer's home. Wood paneled the walls. A plush carpet ran along the floor. There was even a portrait along one wall.

As he stepped into the room, a strange, cold energy washed over him, as if he were stepping into a frigid stream. He didn't know what that energy represented, and worried that it was magic, the same sort of magic he'd encountered outside of the city.

Finn pushed those thoughts away.

He stepped in, closing the door behind him, and searched for where to go next. This was the crew hideout. Holden's crew.

Finn *should* have gone for Archers.

He still could, he realized. There would have to be another entryway to the home, and he could call to the Archers, regardless of whether or not they had been bribed.

Finn found two doors leading off the entryway. Both matched the rich appearance of the inside of the entryway, and on both he noticed symbols much like had been on the one leading from the alley.

Finn pulled the metal spike from his pocket, and he scratched through both of them. As before, he felt a soft puff of air, like a breath escaping, and a strange, pungent odor followed it. Maybe that was only imagination too. Finn hadn't been paying that much attention to the smell in the air before.

He pulled the first door open.

It was an office. It reminded him of Meyer's office. There was a desk. A row of bookshelves. A trunk along one wall. A ceramic basin. A strangely shaped metal base with several flowers that had wilted. And a candelabra, the wax having shown no sign of dripping, as if it had never been lit.

Finn pulled the door closed.

He went to the other door. He tested it. It came open, and he saw another office.

Finn lingered there for a moment, studying the contents of that office. Another desk. Another bookshelf. Several other decorative items inside. Much like the other, there was a vase with flowers, and these had wilted as well.

Finn pulled the door closed. Had he come to the right place? There were no other doors inside. Nothing other than the two that he had already tested.

He turned in place, looking all around him. There would have to be something, though. No way to the street outside. Only alley access.

He looked down to the ground. On a whim, he lifted the

carpet. There was a trapdoor. He looked along the surface, but he saw no other markings of witchcraft.

Finn grabbed the handle, pulling it open. Stairs led down into the darkness.

Now was when he needed to go for Archers, but if he did that, there was no guarantee he could find his way back there. It was also possible they'd been paid off.

Annie had guided him through the alleys so quickly that he had gotten disoriented, something that was rare for him. Given that there was no obvious street access, Finn didn't like the idea of heading into the darkness, but he needed to know. He took a few steps down and noticed a pale light.

When he reached the bottom of the stairs, he followed that light. It was a narrow hallway. A buried tunnel. It reminded him of the cells within the Declan prison.

A thump sounded behind him, followed by a soft rush of air.

Finn spun.

The trapdoor had closed behind him.

CHAPTER TWENTY-SEVEN

F inn stood in the narrow tunnel for a moment, gathering himself. The walls were unmarked, and the light that glowed around him didn't have an obvious source. He couldn't see anything clearly.

He waited, worried that it might mean someone realized he was there, but nothing came. It likely meant the door had closed on its own.

Finn let out a sigh of relief.

Finn made his way along the hall. All of this had the feeling of age. The building above him might have been newer, but his tunnel he now found himself in was *old*.

There were parts of Verendal that were like this. Old parts. Ancient. Most were tied to the Alainsith. Finn suspected this once had been too.

When he came upon an iron door, he stopped.

Symbols were worked along the surface of the door. There would be no scratching those symbols off. He looked across the hall, and there was another matching door, with matching symbols.

In this part of the hall, there were many doors, and all of them had similar symbols. The light seemed to come from all around. It was pale, soft, and glowing.

He tested one of the doors. When it came open, it took his mind a moment to catch up with what his eyes saw.

A body lay twisted on the ground, arms and legs chained, blood pooled all around them, shackles having cut into what had once been their arms but with little left behind.

The stench within the room was incredible. It was much worse than anything he'd ever experienced within Declan Prison. Much worse than anything he had ever smelled anywhere.

He forced himself to look.

Long hair near the head suggested that the person who had died there was female. There wasn't anything else that Finn would be able to learn there. The room was otherwise empty.

He closed the door and opened the door across the hall.

Much like the last, a horrible scene greeted him. The smell was almost too much for him. Finn gagged, and it was only because he hadn't eaten anything for much of the day that he managed to keep the contents of his stomach from spilling outward.

Blood had cooled and congealed around a strangely contorted body. There wasn't anything about the body that was recognizable, though something about it felt off.

That wasn't quite right, Finn realized. Within that congealed blood were shapes.

Witchcraft shapes.

Much like the last body, this one had long hair.

The missing women. All of them had been there. Held there.

Tortured there.

Which meant that the chancellor's daughter might be there.

He stepped out into the hall, closing the door.

This was what the crew had done?

He went to the next room, pushing open that door. Another body.

He went one by one, hurrying along the cells, and with each one, he began to grow increasingly nauseated. Not so much at the awfulness there, although that was enough to overwhelm him. It was because of the purpose behind this.

Power.

There was little doubt in Finn's mind that all of this was designed to draw upon the power of witchcraft and magic. For what purpose, though?

Finn checked each of the doors. Body after body. A half dozen in all.

When he pushed open the seventh door, Finn expected much the same.

Surprisingly, the person on the other side of the door was still alive.

Chain-bound wrists and ankles. A soft moan emanated.

Finn hurried forward.

Blood trickled out of the wound in her neck. Long black hair hung down on either side of her head. He shifted around her, positioning himself so that he could examine her, looking to see if there was anything that he might be able to do or whether the injuries were too far gone.

Finn staggered back, landing on his buttocks.

"Gina?"

She moaned.

It had to be her, though she looked awful. Bruises marred her face, and chunks of skin were missing. The blood that had cooled and congealed had not been formed in the shapes. Whatever witchcraft was intended there had not been carried out yet.

He looked toward the door. He had to get her out of there.

If Gina still lived, there was a possibility others would as well.

Finn left her. It pained him to do so, but he needed to know how many people he was going to try to rescue from this terrible place.

He checked the next door.

A twisted and rotting body greeted him. Congealed blood covered the floor. The stench overwhelmed him. Finn closed the door. There were only two doors remaining.

He pushed open one, and it was much like the last. That left one more door. Would Rachel be there? Finn tested it, found it unlocked, and pushed it open.

It was empty.

His heart sank.

One of these women had to have been her.

He stopped back in the room with Gina and tested the shackles. There wasn't going to be an easy way to open them. The metal spike might help. Finn had never been much of a lockpicker. That was a separate skill, and one highly prized by most crews. In this case, he wasn't sure if he needed that ability.

He pulled the spike out of his pocket and jammed it into the lock.

He slammed it down, eliciting a sharp cry from Gina.

"Hold on," he said.

He jammed it again. She cried out once more. Finn slammed the spike down one more time. The lock snapped, and the cuffs came off her wrist.

He did the same on the other side. Slamming the spike against the lock over and over until it came open with a sharp *crack*. When he moved to her feet, he worried that he was hurting her much more than he intended.

There wasn't anything to do about it, though. He had to get these shackles off of her ankles if he was going to get her out of here. After he had gotten one loosened, he was working on the other when Gina moaned again.

"No," she muttered.

Finn paused.

"I'm trying to help you," he said.

"No. You're going to disrupt it. I won't be the reason it fails."

"The reason what fails?"

She blinked, and for a moment, there was clarity in her eyes, but then it faded.

"Gina?"

"No," she said again, this time softer than the last.

Finn could only shake his head. He pounded on the lock. As he did, he ignored Gina's soft moaning. Finally, the lock snapped open.

Finn pried it off of her leg and slipped his arm around her, lifting her. She moaned again, more agitated than she had been before. Finn continued dragging her, pulling her from the cell.

Finn headed toward the stairs.

Once he was out, would Annie help him?

There might not be anything he could do to save Gina. She might be too far gone.

He reached the top of the stairs and pushed on the trapdoor. It came open slowly. He poked his head up, looking around. The room was empty.

Dragging Gina up the stairs, Finn set her off to the side and rolled the carpet back into place. He didn't want anyone to know he'd been there. Not until he had an opportunity to gather Archers to investigate further.

For something like this, Archers might not even be enough. Strangely, Finn had to wonder if the hegen might be better suited for it. He flipped the carpet back into place. When it was settled, Finn grabbed for Gina, slipping his arm under her shoulder again, and guided her from the room toward the door.

He pulled it open just a little bit, glancing along the

street. He saw no sign of Annie. Either she had slipped into the shadows or she had left him altogether.

She wouldn't have left him. At least, that was what Finn told himself. Maybe he was giving Annie far too much credit.

He dragged Gina out into the street, pulling the door closed, and carried her back the direction that he had come. He wound through the alleys, focusing on how Annie had guided him, and when he reached a branch point, Finn had to close his eyes to try to remember which way they had come. He thought that he remembered, and if he made a mistake, he was going to end up stuck.

He turned to the left.

Finn hurried.

Gina grunted, making a small whining sound every time they staggered forward a few more steps. Her head bobbed forward, and she was little more than dead weight against him.

Finn had to carry her as quickly as he could. He dragged her through the alley, taking turn after turn, until he finally they emerged near the tavern.

He looked over to Gina. She wouldn't withstand him bringing her all the way back to Meyer's home. The tavern. That was where he would have to leave her.

Finn pushed open the door, carrying her into the kitchen, looking around for a moment before heading into the main part of the tavern. He found a booth, and he rested her there. Ironic that it was the same booth that Oscar had been in when she had poisoned him. Perhaps fitting.

Finn hurried out, reaching the street, and he sprinted toward Meyer's home.

He had to gather supplies.

And he was going to need his sister's help. He needed another set of hands.

It was more than just another set of hands. He was going to need access to magic and someone who understood the inner workings of it, so he could counter whatever was taking place within Holden's crew.

When he reached Meyer's home, a different idea came to him.

He hurried through the gate, pausing in the entrance, and grabbed the sword out of the closet, taking a slender dagger off a shelf as well. He shut the door to the closet just as Lena emerged from the back office.

She looked over to him. "What happened?"

"I need your help."

"I can't leave Master Meyer like this."

Finn glanced to the door leading to Meyer's office. "I might have a way to help him, and he's not going to get any worse without you here for a little while. Besides, this is something that needs someone more skilled than me."

She frowned at him. "What do I need to bring with me?"

Finn considered for a moment. "Something to help with blood loss. Possibly poisoning. Sutures. General supplies."

She took a deep breath, letting out slowly. "I will need a moment."

Lena returned to Meyer's office, and she was gone for a few moments before coming back with a leather satchel.

She glanced at him again, her gaze flickering to the sword strapped to his back. "What is that about?"

"I might need it."

"I thought it was only for sentencing."

"It might be needed for a sentencing," he said.

She said nothing more.

They stepped out into the night, through the garden, out of the gate, and into the street. "Where now?"

"I need you to go to the Wenderwolf." He slipped the dagger he'd taken out of the closet into her hands, and Lena's eyes widened. "Lock the doors when you get in. Use this if you need. There's a young woman there who was tortured." That was the only word that seemed fitting, though he doubted that it was even right. It wasn't torment so much as it was that he suspected she had been used for something dark. Nefarious.

"What about you?"

"I need to go to get a different kind of help."

"Oh, Finn..."

"I don't want to argue about this now, Lena. I need to do this."

"What will you end up paying in return for your request?"

"If I'm right, then nothing."

"And if you're wrong?"

"If I'm wrong, then there might be more danger than I can imagine."

The hegen section of the city was quiet at this time of night, which left Finn feeling unsettled. Each time he'd come through there, people had been out in the streets. Sometimes, it was nothing more than children roaming; other times, it was other hegen giving him side-eyed glances. Tonight, there was no one out.

He stopped at Esmeralda's home, the bright red door taking on something of a new meaning to him in light of all of the dead back at the crew's facility. He stared at it for a long moment, his gaze lingering. He doubted the hegen had witchcraft symbols upon the doors the same way as he had just seen.

The door came open and Esmeralda looked out at him.

"Finn Jagger. I thought the two of us had spent enough time together over the last few days."

He looked around. There was something she'd needed to be back for, though she hadn't clarified that for him. "Did you finish what you needed to do?" When she frowned, he looked around. "With the Alainsith. Is it done? Did you learn anything?"

"Not quite. Is that the reason for your visit?"

He took a deep breath. "I need your help."

"With what?"

"Witchcraft." Her brow furrowed. "There have been disappearances throughout the city over the last month. We thought they were all tied to Holden and his crew, and they certainly might be, but I discovered witchcraft symbols on the door to their hideout."

"You have seen this?"

He nodded. "Seen it. Entered it. Found a place of... Gods, I don't even know what it was."

"Show me." She turned back, gathering a few things from her home quickly, carrying out a leather pouch along with a heavy wool cloak that she swung over her shoulders.

"Where are the rest of your people?"

"You realize the hour, Finn Jagger."

"I'm sorry I woke you."

"You have not woken anyone," she said.

They passed the Raven Stone, and Finn glanced over. He always had a feeling of power from the Raven Stone, and tonight was no different. When they passed through the Teller Gate, Finn guided her toward the Wenderwolf. He hurried into the alley and hoped that his memory of navigating back out would be enough.

"I sense something..."

Finn glanced over. "There was a woman there. My sister is with her now."

Esmeralda turned back toward the tavern. "She is nearby?"

Finn nodded to the tavern. "There. At least, she should be."

"I see."

"You can help her, if you would like, but I think Lena can manage."

Esmeralda smiled slightly. "I am most certain she can."

There was something knowing about the way that she said it, and Finn wondered just what it was that Esmeralda might know about his sister. A question for another time.

They moved along the alleys, and when he reached the building, Esmeralda traced her finger around the shape on the door. The bird symbol that Annie had seen.

"There was power here," Esmeralda said.

"I figured," he said.

She glanced back at him. "This was you?"

"I disrupted it."

"How did you know to make this marking?"

"What marking is that?"

She frowned at him. "You didn't know?"

"I just tried to disrupt the pattern. I saw you do something similar when we were traveling." Finn just shook his head. "This isn't the thing I wanted to show you," he said.

"Then take me to what you need me to see."

Finn pushed open the door, prepared for whatever he might find inside.

The room was empty.

There was no carpet. No portrait. Nothing that would suggest this place had been used recently. The trapdoor was closed and a heavy lock had been slipped into place.

Finn hurried past and opened one of the two doors. As he had suspected, there was nothing remaining in the room, either. The desk and bookshelves, but that was it. He stepped out, made his way to the other door, and found the same.

"What is it?" Esmerelda asked.

"These had other items in them before," he said.

"And this room? You looked as if you were worried when you came in here," she said.

"This room had a carpet covering the floor."

"Over this door?"

Finn grabbed the lock. It felt warm. Almost hot...

He jerked his hand back from it.

Esmerelda took his hand and turned it over. "You must be careful here, Finn Jagger. We have already seen the use of witchcraft. Everything in this place has the potential to have been infested with it."

"Infested?" Finn looked down at his hand but didn't see any obvious injury. The burn remained, though, and started to work its way from his palm up to his wrist.

Esmerelda held tightly to his hand and squeezed, twisting his hand from side to side, forcing him to look up at her. "Infested." She pressed a small metal circle up against his palm, and the cool that came from it soothed the suddenly irritated skin. "That should be better. I would advise caution, especially on something so obviously burdened with witchcraft."

He reached into his pocket and pulled the metal rod out, using that to probe at the lock. "If you say so," he said.

"I do. Where did you acquire that?"

"Holden had one in his cell."

She grabbed his wrist, pulling it toward her. "It's a Staff of Welu. Unmarked."

"It doesn't look like a staff."

"That is what those who practice witchcraft would call this. Typically, they have their markings along the side. They offer a way of summoning greater power borrowed from those they have tormented. These are incredibly rare and exceedingly difficult to craft." She looked up at him, her eyes narrowing. "Did you have this on you when you traveled out of the city?"

"I had this one. There were others..."

With Meyer.

That would be why the house had been broken into. Why Meyer had been targeted.

"They would come for the staff?"

"It would be difficult to acquire others without the necessary power to create them." She shook her head, looking around before returning her attention to him. "I should have questioned more. I found it odd that we were pursued by such magic. Perhaps it was nothing more than you carrying a Staff of Welu, but I fear there is more. What we saw suggests something greater."

Finn used the staff to shove into the lock, probing at it. "I used it to pry the shackles from the injured woman," he said.

"Unmarked as it is, it wouldn't have power of its own. Which makes it even more valuable." She took a quick breath. "And perhaps is why the Alainsith sought you out."

Could that be the reason?

Maybe even why the berahn hadn't attacked.

Finn stared at the staff, then shoved it into the lock, twisting until he heard a *snap*.

The lock popped open. When he reached for it, Esmerelda shook her head.

"Use that to move it out of the way," she said, pointing to the Staff.

Finn did as she directed, sliding it off to the side, then

pried the door open and looked down into the darkness. "It's down here. I understand if you won't want to come down."

"I think I must," she whispered.

"You're not going to like what you see."

"When it comes to witchcraft, I never like what I see."

They headed down into the darkness, and Finn braced himself. Knowing what he would encounter didn't make it any better for him. It didn't make it any easier. All that it did was increase his anticipation. When he had been down there before, the floor and everything had glowed softly with a light of its own.

There was no sign of that.

"This was an Alainsith place of power," Esmeralda said softly, handing a small, glowing object to him.

"What is this?"

"Something that might allow you to see what is coming."

It was a small circular item, and it was slightly warm. Finn held it out, illuminating everything in front of him. He moved slowly and carefully forward. Something had changed there, along with whatever had changed in the upper level, so he knew that someone had been there.

It made him cautious.

When he reached the first of the doors, he pushed it open slowly. It was empty.

Finn frowned.

There was no smell. No sign of the body. No sign of the blood.

Nothing.

"I can tell you were expecting something different," Esmeralda said to him.

"There was a body chained to the ground here before."

She stepped past him into the room, and she looked around, sweeping her gaze everywhere. She inhaled deeply, and Finn wondered if there might be something she could smell from here. Maybe magic had a signature to it that she could pick up on.

She crouched down, holding an item out from her, and there was a faint glowing from that item, much like the one that he now held.

"Can that help you detect whether magic was here?" he asked.

"I am searching for something else," she said.

"What, exactly?"

"The purpose behind all of this."

She got down on her hands and knees, crawling along the floor, lowering her face as she examined for something.

Finn moved away, giving her space. He headed across to the cell on the other side of the small hallway. When he pushed it open, he didn't expect to find anyone. He figured that whoever was responsible for this had already moved the body, much like they had in the other room.

He was not disappointed.

There was no sign of anyone. The chains were gone. The floor had been cleaned of any evidence that there had been a body. No blood pooled and congealed.

Finn made a steady circuit inside the room.

The witchcraft symbols on the doors had been removed.

The power was gone.

How had they cleaned it up so quickly?

They must have known that he'd come. Either Annie had warned them—something Finn didn't want to be the case—or they would have detected what he'd done when he'd disrupted the magic that was around the doors. That seemed the more likely of the two. *He* had felt it when he had done something with the magic, so it seemed likely enough that whoever was responsible for the magic there would have felt it.

Back in the hall, he found Esmerelda now crouching in the cell. She hadn't moved out of it, though.

"What do you detect?"

"You said there was a body here?"

"A body. Chained to the ground." There wasn't even any sign of where they would have been chained. *How could they have moved that so quickly?* "The blood had pooled, and in some of the cells, there were symbols marked in the blood."

She looked up at him. "What kind of symbols?"

"I told you. Witchcraft."

"What do you know about the women who've been missing? Is there anything consistent about them?"

"Nothing that I knew. I'd been looking into the missing women." He hesitated. "Well, that's not quite true. Meyer had been looking into one missing person and had only shared with me what he'd been doing."

"Who was that?"

"The chancellor's daughter. She'd come through here

with the contingent meeting with the Alainsith to further the treaty."

"The chancellor?" She frowned. "Was she here when you found the others?"

"I don't know. Most were unrecognizable. The only one that I was able to help was Gina, and she was the one who had turned me in."

"You said she was still alive?"

"She was, but not in good shape. She's the one my sister is trying to help."

Esmerelda stood and came back into the hallway. "I need to see her."

"Why?"

"This," she said, sweeping her hand around her, "is meant to collect power. I do not know the reason why, nor do I know where it is channeled, but that is the purpose. If what you saw is correct, then there would have been considerable power available here. Dangerous power."

"I can tell you where she is, but I need to go to Declan. Whatever is going on is happening soon."

"Go. Intervene before they have an opportunity to complete the task."

Finn only had to wonder if he would be able to get answers out of Holden this time.

CHAPTER TWENTY-EIGHT

It felt as if it had been a long time since Finn had been to Declan Prison. Having been out of the city for the better part of a week had left him feeling as if he were separated from it. Returning to the prison, especially returning with the sword strapped to his back, might be a mistake, at least until he knew if Meyer had been able to dig out the people who had intended to betray them.

Were there not a need, Finn might have taken a bit more time, but he believed Esmeralda that they had an urgency with what they were doing.

When he reached Declan, no iron master stood guard. Finn bore his city cloak, and within it was the ring of keys that granted him access to every prison within the city.

He fished them out, finding the key for Declan Prison, and turned it in the lock.

A sense of movement behind him caused him to turn,

but when he did, he saw nothing. His imagination. That was all it was.

Stepping inside Declan, Finn closed the door behind him and locked it once again.

He paused on the stairs leading down into the darkness. There should have been iron masters there. Finn looked around for a moment, then headed down the stairs. Into darkness.

He still had the hegen magic coin, and he held it out, illuminating the hall.

He shouldn't have needed it, though. There should be no reason for him to need something to light his way into the darkness.

When he reached the lower level, he looked at the cells.

The nearest one was empty.

That wasn't altogether uncommon. There were many times when these cells were not occupied, so Finn wasn't troubled by it.

When he reached the second one and found it empty, he started to frown.

He hurried along them, finding one after another emptied.

Then he reached the cell that should hold Holden. It was empty as well. Finn raced along.

Meyer had been sick for most of the time that he'd been gone. Could the warden have decided to take action on his own?

Holden had warned they didn't have time.

And with Meyer injured, he wouldn't have been able to learn the truth.

Finn had been around James enough to know he could sometimes get it into his head he needed to be more aggressive with interrogations to uncover things on his own, but it would be unusual for there to be no prisoners there. Some there were serving a sentence. Life in Declan was difficult and the sentence hard, so those were usually the worst of the worst prisoners. Then there were men like Holden, who would wait until his sentencing, likely facing death.

Not likely.

He *would* be facing death.

Finn unlocked what had been Holden's cell and stepped inside.

Faint markings covered the walls. He had to get close to recognize the style, but when he did, his breath caught. Witchcraft. All of it.

Finn could feel it work over him as soon as he stepped in, and he moved back out of the cell to avoid the possibility of it influencing him.

When he'd been there before, he remembered there being marking around the cell. It wasn't uncommon for prisoners to mark the walls of their cells. Finn didn't remember anything like this. That would explain why Holden had the staff. He'd been using it to cover the walls with magic.

He had to find where the others were.

Finn hurried back up the stairs. If there were no prisoners, it made sense that there would be no iron masters. He headed toward the warden's office, pausing in front of the door. Would there be a marking there?

He found no sign.

Finn tested the lock and pushed open the door.

The desk looked as he remembered it from when he had last visited James. The chairs were situated as he remembered as well. A lantern resting on the table suggested that someone had been there recently.

Finn closed the door.

Where would everyone have gone?

He headed through the halls more slowly. It felt eerie, coming through with it empty like this. At least he hadn't imagined that it was darker than it should be.

As he neared the end of the hall to return to the entrance, a muffled cry caught his attention.

He froze. It came from the other end of the hall. Toward the chapel.

He hurried toward the sound. His heart pounded and his mouth was dry.

When he reached the chapel, he stopped and listened.

There *were* muffled voices from inside.

Who would be using the chapel at this time of night?

It was a place for him and Meyer, and that was it. They were the only ones in the city sanctioned by the king for the kind of questioning that would take place there, not that the warden and Archers didn't occasionally use it.

Finn tested the door, and he pushed it open slowly.

The sound of voices from the inside echoed, louder this time.

Finn pushed the door fully open and stepped inside. What he saw made him freeze.

There was a body chained to the ground.

Five other bodies were chained around the one in the center. Each was naked, bleeding heavily. They were twisted, making it difficult to tell if they were male or female. Some had long hair, though even with that, Finn wasn't able to determine gender. Someone knelt over each of them, holding a long spike up against them. Each person was dressed in a black robe, a hood pulled up over their head. Symbols were embroidered on the cloaks; markings of witchcraft.

The chapel wasn't a large room. It certainly wasn't large enough that Finn thought there would be enough space for some sort of witchcraft ceremony, but there it was.

He had to stop this.

"In the name of the king, I command that you stop!"

The person in the center of the ceremony looked up. The others didn't move. They continued holding their strange metal spikes, pressing them up against the bodies. Soft moans emanated from the people they pressed the spikes up against. They were killing them.

Through their death, power would escape, captured by those performing the witchcraft.

"You cannot stop this."

Finn looked down at the person lying in the center. Golden hair flowed down. They were nude, covered in blood, though as he looked, it seemed as if they were still breathing.

That suggested the blood wasn't their own.

The chancellor's daughter. Elizabeth Jarvis. That was what this was about.

"Stop this."

He took a step forward and slammed into something that prevented him from going any further. The person at the center of the ceremony laughed, a horrible and dark sound.

Finn grabbed for the spike, pulling it from his pocket, and pressed it up against the witchcraft barrier that surrounded the inside of the room, though there was no change.

The Staff couldn't pierce the barrier. Finn shouldn't have expected it to. Not without having any markings on it.

Moonlight streamed down through the stained glass overhead. Finn had always found the light filtering through soothing, but now he only found it frightening.

The full moon.

That reason Holden had been waiting. And why he didn't care that he was in prison. They *needed* to be there.

He could try his sword. That had worked outside of the city, though he suspected he'd already drained some of the magic out of the sword. Whatever remained couldn't be enough, though he hoped that it had enough strength that he would be able to penetrate the magical shielding that prevented him from getting any closer.

Finn unsheathed his sword.

And realized he had grabbed the wrong sword. He'd been in too much of a rush.

Not the one that Meyer had gifted him when he had sent him on his pilgrimage; this was a different blade. The one he had practiced with since coming to work with Meyer. A blade that had been a part of Verendal for centuries, one that had been used in sentencings for nearly that long.

Justice.

Perhaps he had grabbed the *right* sword.

Finn brought it back and slammed it into the shielding.

The sword carved through it as easily as if it had carved through everything that it had been faced with.

He stumbled, the momentum sending him crashing into one of the people holding a staff over one of the bodies. Finn kicked at them, and they fell back. The hood fell away, and he stared for a moment.

Loren Thilson.

"What are you doing?" Finn asked, getting to his feet and glancing over quickly, worried that he might still be outnumbered.

"You wouldn't understand," Thilson said, glaring at Finn but not moving.

Finn grunted, squeezing the sword as he looked around him, worried that the others might disengage from what they were doing with the spikes and come at him, but they didn't. They remained fixated on the body in front of them, holding their spikes and pressing down, as if they were going to stab through the heart of their victim.

Which they might.

He lunged toward Thilson and was thrown back.

Finn staggered back toward the door and slammed into something else.

Another magical shield.

He swung the sword.

It carried him through the shielding, where he came face to face with the other person. Finn held the sword out from him carefully.

"Put down the staff," Finn said.

The person laughed. "You won't be able to stop this."

"You have no idea what I'm able to do."

"It's too late! We've already begun—"

Finn kicked.

His boot struck the person's arm, and the spike went spinning out of their hand. He followed by darting forward and slamming a shoulder into them. When they fell, Finn landed atop them. He grabbed for the hood and pulled it back.

James.

His eyes had a haunted look in them, and a smear of what looked like blood formed a pattern on each cheek.

"What are you thinking?" Finn asked.

This was a friend. Someone Finn had come to know.

How could he be involved?

A moan from the far side of the chapel caught his attention.

Finn stayed on top of James, pinning him to the ground. Finn held onto Justice, prepared to sweep around were it necessary, but given the length of the blade, it wouldn't be easy for him to do.

"You couldn't begin to understand."

Finn looked around at the others. They were still crouched over bodies. "You were helping Holden," Finn said softly, beginning to understand.

"Helping him? No, Finn. You have it wrong. He revealed something to me."

"And what, exactly, is that?"

"A different truth."

The warden's eyes were wide.

Holden might still be there. He'd been injured when Finn had last been there. *Or would he be?* Magic could heal. Finn had seen it himself.

He grabbed for James's head and slammed it against the stone floor. James blinked before his eyes rolled back.

Finn got to his feet.

He looked down at the person chained to the floor. He jammed the spike into the shackles at the wrists, prying one free, then another, and then working at the ankles.

The woman was younger. The golden blonde hair and sharp jawline were like the portrait he'd seen of her. Elizabeth Jarvis. The chancellor's daughter.

She moaned softly.

"Let me help you get out of here," Finn said.

He dragged her toward the barrier.

As soon as he got there, the others holding their staffs overhead suddenly jammed them down, forcing them into the chests of the five bodies surrounding them.

"No!" Finn cried out.

It was too late.

Elizabeth sucked in a sharp breath.

Were they using magic against her?

Finn needed Esmeralda's help.

He tried to take a step forward, but the shielding made it difficult. He needed to get this woman out of there before whatever magic they were using would overwhelm her.

"Hold on," he said.

He brought the sword up, attempting to sweep it at the shielding, but wasn't fast enough. Elizabeth sank to the ground.

He couldn't hold her up. The strange ceremony had done something, forcing something through her, perhaps magic.

Finn brought the sword back. Justice was meant to carry out the king's justice, for him to enact the sentences the jurors deemed appropriate. It was not meant as a weapon, and it was certainly not meant to cut through magic.

Finn fought through those thoughts.

The sword might be the only thing that could stop what happened there.

The blade connected with the shielding. Finn could feel the power fading. Then it was through. There was a blast and he was thrown back.

Everything went dark for a moment, and he blinked, trying to clear his vision.

His head pounded. Throbbing. His body ached.

How long had I been unconscious?

He had landed near James, and Finn looked over to see the spike he'd been holding had ended up piercing the other man's chest. His hands were wrapped around it, leaving Finn wondering if he had chosen to use it upon himself.

Blood spilled from him. Finn couldn't help him quickly enough and wasn't sure that he wanted to. He had betrayed Verendal.

Getting to his feet, Finn licked his lips as he looked around.

Elizabeth Jarvis was gone. The others involved in the ceremony were gone as well.

Finn staggered forward.

The power that had pushed against him was gone. Whatever had been happening there was over. Relief crept into him.

He'd stopped it—for now.

Finn had a feeling this wasn't over.

He looked at the mess within the chapel. Blood filled it. More than he'd ever seen before, and this was a place where there was often bleeding. He checked the fallen, pulling back the hoods of cloaks and seeing faces he recognized. Shiner. Grady. Jalen. All iron masters.

Dead, and because of James.

Because of witchcraft.

Thilson was gone.

The others—including the chancellor's daughter—were gone.

Escaped.

"What happened?"

Finn looked over to the door and was only mildly surprised that Esmerelda would be there.

"I found this," he said softly. "I don't even know what it is. Or was. But I stopped it."

"You stopped it?"

He held out Justice. "Not alone."

She eyed the blade. "What did you see?" He described the ceremony to her, and Esmerelda's frown grew deeper. "Whatever they intended is not finished, Finn Jagger." She met his gaze. "Why this place?"

Finn shook his head. "This is a place of pain. Torment. This is where we question the criminals."

It was hard to admit, and worse, it made sense why they would have used it for the ceremony.

But it wasn't a place of death.

"I know where we have to go. The Stone."

Unlike the chapel, the Stone *was* a place of death.

CHAPTER TWENTY-NINE

They reached the Teller Gate. There were no Archers out watching. Finn kept thinking that they would encounter someone, but they never did. It troubled him.

He looked around him again, sweeping his gaze everywhere.

"What is it?" Esmeralda asked.

"I would've expected there to have been Archers."

"Why would there be none?"

"They might have been paid off," Finn said.

"Could they have paid off so many?"

He let out a sigh. "I would have once said no, but maybe I'm wrong. With the right crew and enough wealth, anything is possible."

"Even bribing all of the Archers?"

Finn nodded. "Even that."

Holden and his crew must have been much more successful than he had known.

They were a newer crew, at least from what Oscar had said, and they had built up their position within the city rapidly. That kind of activity suggested either they were more aggressive or they had some sort of wealthy backer. It was another thing for him to consider in the future.

Finn hurried past the gate, into the darkness, and they headed toward the Raven Stone. It loomed in the distance, reflecting some of the bright moonlight. There were figures by the Stone.

"Has Master Meyer ever shared with you why executions are completed in the daytime?" Esmeralda asked as they made their way toward the Stone.

"I assumed it had something to do with not wanting to upset the gods."

"There is some of that," she said, nodding. "Perhaps a great portion of it is that. But there is more to it as well. The reason that executions are traditionally performed in the daytime is to protect the dying; to ensure they can be returned to their gods."

"Isn't that what I said?"

"In a way," she said. "Only, the greater concern is that if the execution were carried out in the nighttime, a different kind of power could be summoned."

"Let me guess. Witchcraft."

"In its purest form," she said.

Finn sneaked toward the Stone, following Esmeralda. He held Justice unsheathed. None of this made sense to him. Even having seen magic, experiencing it firsthand, he still

THE EXECUTIONER'S BLADE | 501

didn't fully understand just what it was that was taking place there.

And it would be up to him to stop it.

They approached the Raven Stone carefully, using the wall surrounding the city to shield them. Finn saw three figures atop the Stone. He suspected one of them would be Holden—who likely led the procession. Five more surrounded the base of the Stone.

Holden's crew. They were holding watch, of a sort.

"Can you tell what's going on?" Finn whispered, staying in the shadows of the wall.

Esmeralda shook her head. "They intended to summon power, but I do not know what they will do with it."

One of the figures looked to be held captive, their arms bound behind them, their legs tied together. That had to be Elizabeth Jarvis. Finn had rescued her, only for her to end up captured again.

"Will you be ready?" Esmeralda asked.

Finn turned briefly, looking over to her. "What, exactly, am I to be getting ready for?"

"They were summoning significant magic. Powerful magic. It's highly likely they were able to harness it." Her voice was a soft whisper that drifted to his ears.

"Will it be more than what we encountered outside of the city?"

"I don't know," she said.

"Are there other hegen who can help?"

"There might have been, but..."

"But what?" Finn asked, turning to her and frowning. "We could alert them somehow."

"You might need to stop whatever is happening on the Stone," she said. "It's not about you having magic. It's about the blade having it."

Finn held out Justice. "Maybe it's good I grabbed the wrong sword."

"I should be able to draw the five off from the base of the Raven Stone. You will need to use that blade on the other two," she said, moving away from the wall and toward the Stone. Soon they'd be exposed. "A sword like that will have stored power over the years. More power, I think, than they would anticipate."

Finn didn't get the chance to argue with her.

She threw something.

It landed, coming to rest near the Stone, and a burst of energy exploded from it, sending a gust of wind sweeping over Finn.

"Go!" Esmeralda said.

Finn hesitated, but only for a moment, then he darted forward.

One of the crew turned toward him, but Esmeralda threw another of her magical items, and it forced the crew to pay attention to her.

Finn reached the stairs and bounded up.

"Holden!"

Holden turned toward him. He was dressed in the same black robe, hood pulled up like the others had been, the embroidery along the sleeves and down the front of the robe marked with symbols of witchcraft.

What Finn hadn't expected was that Elizabeth wasn't bound and captured. She stood free, next to Holden.

The one who was bound and captured was the Alainsith man.

They had one of the strange spikes held up to his chest.

"The Hunter," Holden said. "Interesting. I'd thought my troubles would have come from the hegen." He smirked at Finn.

He nodded, and Elizabeth pressed the spike closer to the Alainsith.

"Stop!" Finn said.

He darted forward, met resistance of the strange magical barrier, and swept Justice toward it, cleaving through it. He grabbed for the Alainsith man, positioning himself between Elizabeth and Holden.

Was this all because her family didn't care for the Alainsith?

Are they in on this, too?

He had to push those thoughts aside for now. Questions for later.

Holden eyed him strangely. "Where did you get that blade?"

Before Finn could answer, Holden raised his hands and then flicked them down.

A cold sensation washed through Finn, and he was suddenly too weak to stand.

Finn stumbled and landed atop the Alainsith. It took him

a moment to gather himself, and in that moment Elizabeth was there, a spike held atop the Alainsith, ready to stab down.

Finn had no idea what it would do, but there was power in death.

And an Alainsith death...

Finn tried to react, kicking his leg, but was unable to. He was trapped.

He rolled over the flat surface of the stone, and the blade snagged on the bindings around the Alainsith's wrists. Elizabeth came toward the Alainsith. Finn jerked at the bindings until they cut free.

He rolled again, trying to get to his feet.

Something pressed down upon him, as if it were going to squeeze him to the Stone.

He couldn't move. Elizabeth slammed the spike toward him.

Then a burning light flashed over the wind, striking Elizabeth. She, along with the spike, went flying away, landing several paces from him atop the Stone.

Finn looked behind him. The Alainsith man had gotten to his feet, crouching near Finn. He held his hands out from him, and he twisted his fingers, wiggling them slightly.

He had used magic. It was different from what the hegen used. Different from witchcraft. The Alainsith had pure magic.

The Alainsith tipped his head. *"Thea il oul portena!"*

Finn shook his head. "I don't know what you're saying."

"He's saying, *Look out behind you,*" Holden said.

Finn spun, and something struck him on the forehead. He flew backward, his head striking the Stone. His vision blurred for a moment, and Finn struggled to get up but could not.

Finn looked around, trying to process what had happened, but his head pounded. The only thought that lingered was that he needed to get to the sword. If he could reach Justice, then he might be able to keep himself safe regardless of what they did to him.

"An executioner would not be able to stop this," Holden said. "This has been in the works for far longer than you could understand."

Pressure continued building upon Finn, and he tried to move, but he still could not. He needed help.

Would the Alainsith be able to help me?

Finn rolled, trying to look over to the Alainsith, but he was held in the same way as Finn.

"The king made the mistake of believing he could bargain with the Alainsith, and they made the mistake of sending their emissary." Holden stalked over to the Alainsith. "Now his power will become ours." He glanced behind him, and Elizabeth strode forward. She was nude, covered in blood, and seemed to radiate power. The hairs on the back of Finn's arms stood on end. "We will have what we need to defeat them. To defeat all of them."

"Treason," Finn muttered.

Holden laughed bitterly. "Treason? This is about much more than treason. This is reclaiming what is ours."

Elizabeth stepped forward again, and she took the spike

from Holden and brought it up to the Alainsith.

He needed time. Maybe Esmerelda could help. Perhaps other hegen. Something.

"Why did you need to kill the others?" Finn asked.

"Because we wouldn't be able to claim their power otherwise."

Finn tried to move. He could not.

"Esmeralda!"

He had no idea if she could hear him. His arms didn't work. The sword Justice remained just out of reach. He wasn't able to do anything.

"Esmeralda!"

Elizabeth brought the spike up.

It was going to crash into the Alainsith's chest.

Finn would be witness.

The power of the Raven Stone would somehow permit them to do this. It was a place of death. A place of power. It was a place that they would misuse. Abuse.

No.

Only, he couldn't stop them.

Something landed on the Stone, rolling toward Elizabeth. The hegen device.

Holden raised a hand toward the device, and it let out a sad fizzle and a puff of smoke. He started to laugh. "Do you really think that would work?"

It might not have exploded, but it had caused Holden to redirect his power enough that Finn could move. He slipped his arm forward, and he grabbed the blade.

Then he ripped his arms up, carving through whatever

held him. Finn lunged to his feet. He tried to move through the magic, but he barely managed to stay upright.

Holden turned toward him, pointing one of the staffs at him.

Finn strained against it.

"I don't know how you—"

Holden didn't have the opportunity to finish. The Alainsith man grabbed him, wrapping his arms around Holden. Holden struggled, but only for a moment. Then he stiffened before collapsing.

Elizabeth spun, swinging her spike at the Alainsith.

Finn launched himself toward the Alainsith, swinging the sword at her.

The spike went spinning away.

He held out the blade to her neck, keeping her from moving. Elizabeth eyed the blade but didn't come any closer.

"You have made a grave mistake. My father will not permit this to stand. He is the king's chancellor."

"I am the king's executioner. And you have committed treason." He looked over to Holden, glancing to the Alainsith. "Thank you." Finn had no idea if the Alainsith man even understood him, but he nodded. "You may have safe passage."

The Alainsith regarded him, and Finn felt a strange surge wash through him. With a large jump, the man cleared the Stone, landing on the ground before loping off toward the trees. There were two others waiting for him, one of them much smaller—a child, Finn realized—before they disappeared altogether.

Esmeralda joined him on the Stone. "His family waited for him," she said, her voice soft.

"Family?"

She nodded. "Yes. My people suspected there were Alainsith in the forest, but we saw nothing but a sign of their passage. It looks as if he has a wife and child."

Finn frowned to himself. There had been a woman and a child near Declan around the time the Alainsith had been brought in. *Could* that *be who had been there?* If so, they'd been waiting a long time.

There were so many questions about the Alainsith he didn't have answers to. Maybe he would learn them in time. For now, he had to deal with what he had before him.

Esmerelda swept her gaze to the chancellor's daughter, then to Holden, where she crouched, checking him.

"Is he dead?" Finn asked, unwilling to take his gaze off the woman.

"Not dead. Just incapacitated."

"What about the crew?"

"They turned their staffs upon themselves," she said. "They were likely coerced so they could grant the others even more power."

Finn looked down, but he didn't even see the bodies of the crew. How could someone be coerced into killing themselves?

He didn't want to think about that kind of magic.

"I suppose the hegen will claim their prizes?" he asked.

"If you would permit it."

"It's up to me?"

"In this case, it is," she said.

"Have you always asked Meyer before?" Finn asked, and she tipped her head. "That's why he can go to you for his questions."

"Yes."

"He never owed you a debt," Finn realized.

She frowned at him. "That is between Henry Meyer and the hegen."

"I need to take her to prison. Him, too, I suppose."

"I will have him brought to you."

Finn started to smile. "You will?"

"You don't trust me?"

"I trust you." It surprised him, but he did.

"We will need to speak again, Finn Jagger."

"Yes. We will."

He lifted Elizabeth, taking her spike, and frowned to himself.

He set the staff, along with the one Holden had used, on a section of timber in the middle of the Stone, and he swept Justice through them.

Much like everything, Justice split them easily.

"No!" the woman cried out.

Power exploded from the staffs and then disappeared.

Esmeralda looked over to him. "That blade is more powerful than I knew."

Finn stared at Justice a moment before forcing the

woman down the steps of the Raven Stone. "You will make this climb again."

"I wouldn't be so sure of that," Elizabeth said.

Finn said nothing more as he marched her back to the city, through Teller Gate, and off to prison.

———

"Are you sure of this?" Magister Yolath asked, looking through the bars of the cell at Elizabeth. He was taller than the last magister, with deep brown eyes and a balding head. There was a hardness about him that hadn't been there with Fol. Fol had tried to give a warmth, though it had been false. Magister Yolath made no such attempt.

Elizabeth sat huddled in the back of the cell, her arms wrapped around her knees, and managed to put on an expression of innocence, frailty, and almost delicacy. Within the cell, she looked pitiful, though still beautiful. The blood had been cleaned off of her, leaving her with no sign of what she'd gone through.

"I saw it myself. I will vouch for what happened." He nodded at her. "Another of the citizens within the city would also make that claim."

"I doubt the king is going to care for that," the magister said, pushing up his thin glasses and shaking his head. "And the chancellor, of course, denies any involvement. All of this is quite unpleasant."

"The king will want justice carried out. And given the nature of her treason..."

Finn had experience with the king and treason. This time might be different.

They would have to question the chancellor. His wife. Others who'd traveled with them.

"So many involved in this," the magister said, shaking his head.

"I doubt it's over," Finn said.

The magister took a deep breath. "I will bring this to the jurors. We will submit our recommendation and await word from the king. I fear that it may not be what you want, Mr. Jagger. With the treaty now signed…"

"It's not a matter of what I want. Justice must be served."

"Of course," the magister said, waving his hand. "How is Master Meyer?"

Finn nodded slowly. "Recovering."

"I hope so. When I heard he wasn't well… Perhaps it isn't as much of a concern as it once would have been. We have a skilled replacement already in place." The magister clasped Finn on the shoulder.

When the magister left, Finn lingered a moment. It was just the two of them, with a couple of iron masters at the end of the hall. He looked at her through the bars.

"I suppose you still think you are going to get away with this," he said.

"Think?" Elizabeth said, looking up. All pretense of frailty was gone. She had a darkness about her. "I know I will get away with this."

"The king will want justice."

"Not when it has to do with me," she said. She leaned

forward, sneering at him. "There are some within the kingdom above justice, unlike the fool who served here before. But then, you know that, don't you?"

He held her gaze. She meant Fol. "Then the gods will sentence you," Finn said.

"The gods care little about us. They let us claim their power." She laughed, a harsh and bitter sound. "Didn't you know that? That is what we were doing. Claiming what is ours."

"No. You were stealing what is someone else's."

She chuckled. "Says the executioner who knows only of death but nothing of the power within the world."

"That power over death is the reason you were stopped."

"You won't stop me again."

Finn stared at her. "Maybe not," he acknowledged. "It's possible the king will request a stay of the sentencing proposed by the magister and the jurors. If he does, then I will honor it, the same as I honor every sentence. If he does not, then you will face your punishment. Much like Holden will face his." Finn tipped his head to the side. "You care about him. I saw that. I had wondered why the two of you would have worked together, but I recognize it now. And there will be nothing you or your father will be able to do to keep him from his sentence."

She leaned forward and spat.

Finn stepped off to the side, letting it fly past him. "You aren't the first person to try to spit on me. I doubt you'll be the last. If your father was involved—"

Her high-pitched laugh cut him off. "My father doesn't

believe in the powers of the world. Which is why he will convince the king to release me."

That answered his question about the chancellor, though Finn would have more questioning to do. Mistress Jarvis. The physician they stayed with. Others.

That was later.

"Holden will swing soon enough," Finn said. He sensed an opportunity with her. She had reacted to Holden already. What more might she reveal to him?

"If you carry out that sentence, I will come for you next."

"Do what you must do," Finn said.

"You have no idea the kind of power I have access to."

"I have some idea. Much as I have some idea the power you don't have access to. If you want to share more with me..."

She glowered at him as she fell silent.

That was unfortunate. It meant he'd have to push others in her family harder than he preferred if he wanted to find out the depths of their involvement. Perhaps it was only Elizabeth. That might be for the best, but Finn had a feeling this threat went deeper.

He stood for a moment, debating what else he might say, before turning away. When he reached the end of the hall, he paused at the two iron masters there. Both were new. "If she gets free, it is on your head."

He stepped out of the women's prison, out into the street, and looked up at the bright sunlight. It didn't fit his mood.

He had a darkness within him.

He made his way back to Meyer's home. There were other assignments that he needed to do today. Supplies that needed to be purchased. Checks upon the prisons he needed to make, especially on Declan, now that there was a new warden and an almost entirely new guard staff.

That would come later. For now, he wanted to check on those he cared about.

When he stepped into Meyer's home, he found Oscar sitting in the kitchen, eating slowly. He looked up, nodding to Finn.

"There he is. The Hunter."

"You need to use a nickname?"

"This one's better than the last."

"I suppose it is," Finn said. He took a seat across from Oscar. "You're looking better."

"It's a strange thing. I started feeling better quite rapidly. I suppose I have you to thank for that."

"It was a magical poisoning. I suspect that when I destroyed the magic used on you, it released some of that. There might still have been some residual effect, but..." Finn didn't fully understand it. Not that it mattered. So long as Oscar was well, nothing mattered. "Why didn't you tell me about you and Annie?"

He frowned. "How did you find out?"

"I spoke with her."

"She would never have said anything."

"She didn't have to."

Oscar shook his head slowly. "You really have become

like him, you know." Oscar regarded him for a moment. "It
suits you. You wear it well."

Finn grunted.

"And Holden's crew?"

"His crew is gone. Holden will be sentenced. And I doubt
we will have to deal with anything like that for a while."

"You doubt it?"

Finn said nothing.

"I see. Secrets now."

"There are some things I won't be able to share."

"I see," Oscar said again.

"I'm glad you're better."

"You and me both."

Finn got to his feet and nodded to Oscar. "Thank you.
And tell Annie she has my thanks. I'll thank her properly the
next time I see her." He still didn't know how much to trust
her, but she and Oscar were together, and she *had* saved his
life.

Oscar nodded slowly, taking another bite of meat before
setting his hands on the table. "Your father would be proud,
Finn."

Finn just grunted. He turned away, heading back to
Meyer's office.

Lena was there, and she looked over to him. "I did what I
could for the other woman," she whispered as he came in.

Finn would have to deal with Gina. She'd been the
reason he'd been attacked, and had willingly been a part of
the witchcraft in the city. He had no idea how she'd be

sentenced, but perhaps that was just as well. She would face justice for what she'd done.

Wella tipped her head in a nod at him.

Meyer sat on the edge of the bed, and he looked up at Finn. "I suppose I have you to thank for this," Meyer said.

"You have me to thank for you being able to recover."

"Hmm. Not for these two watching over me like a hawk?"

"I think they are here because they care for you."

"They don't need to be here."

Finn chuckled. "Do you even know who poisoned you?"

Meyer touched his side. "A blade in the shadows. That's the only thing I can recall. As I made clear to your sister and Wella all along."

Lena held his gaze, a hint of defiance in her eyes. Wella just cackled softly.

When Meyer turned back to him, Finn sighed. "I solved it."

"What do you mean, you solved it?"

"The missing women. Your assignment. I don't know if I would have been in time, were it not for your notes. And I found the chancellor's daughter."

Meyer's brow furrowed. "And?"

"She is awaiting sentencing. I'll need to visit with her father and mother, along with anyone else who travelled with them."

Meyer pressed his lips together in a tight frown. "That will be difficult."

"I know."

"It's possible her father will intervene."

"That's what she believes," Finn said. "With what happened in Verendal with Fol, I am prepared for whatever the king decides." It would be hard, much like it had been with Fol, though he *had* faced sentencing.

"You really do understand your duty."

"I don't think I needed that lesson," Finn said.

Meyer sighed, his expression softening. "I suppose not. It's never easy." He fell silent, his breathing heavy. "I suppose I should send a missive to the king."

"I already have," Finn said.

"I see," Meyer said. "And your pilgrimage?"

"It was enlightening," Finn said.

Meyer nodded slowly. "They often are."

CHAPTER THIRTY

"Are you sure you don't need me?"

Finn gathered the supplies from the closet, strapping on the executioner's cloak, glancing down at the leathers he wore, making certain he was dressed for the event. Finally, he looked up to Meyer. "I have done this before."

"Not alone."

"I did. On the pilgrimage."

"I suppose you did," Master Meyer said. "You are ready."

"I am ready."

Meyer took a step toward him, but then he wobbled and nearly collapsed.

"You need to rest."

"I shouldn't need to."

"You're recovering, but it will still be a few weeks before you're at full speed. Let me handle this."

"I'm not stopping you."

"No, but you are hesitating," Finn said.

"Only because I've done this for decades."

"I know. And I have no interest in you retiring anytime soon."

"You might not, but others…"

Finn clasped him on the shoulder. "It doesn't matter what the others might want."

Meyer nodded. "I suppose it does not."

"Rest, and offer words for the condemned the way you always do. I've seen you mouthing the words before," Finn said.

"Have you?"

"I understand."

Meyer regarded him for a long moment. "I suppose you do."

Finn turned.

"Do not let emotion get in the way of exacting the sentencing."

Finn paused with his hand on the door before nodding. "I will not."

He made his way through the city and reached the prison. He nodded to the two iron masters standing at the door to the prison, men he didn't know, and waited for the condemned to be brought out. The people in the city likely didn't even realize how much had changed over the last few days. Would the king realize what Finn and Meyer had done?

When the Blood Court convened outside of the prison, beginning its slow march through the city, Finn prepared himself for what must be done. The familiar chant of the priest to the Poor Bastard stayed with Finn. He kept his eyes locked straight ahead of him, focused on the assignment at hand.

The sentencing was complete. Now he had only to carry out the sentencing.

He supposed he shouldn't take satisfaction in it, and he didn't, not really. This time, though, he couldn't deny the sentencing felt justified. It was one of those rare times when he felt as if what he needed to do were right and true.

Finn marched at the head of the procession, ignoring the festival around him. He heard the hawkers calling out their foods and items for sale. He heard the parade of people nearby, all of them waiting for a glimpse of the Blood Court. He heard the occasional shouts, some of them coming from people who cursed or swore at the condemned.

If only they knew.

Would they move away, or would they be more violent in how they dealt with the condemned? Maybe they would throw more fruits and vegetables, or rocks, perhaps. The Archers did their best to keep people from getting too close, but there was a limit to what they could do.

When they passed through the Teller Gate, Finn glanced over to the Raven Stone. The gallows stretched above it, a familiar sight to him. It seemed as if it had only been a day since he had been to the Stone, but it had been several since the fight. It had taken time for them to make preparations.

Finn reached the stairs leading up.

At the top of the stairs, he turned, focusing on the jurors and the magister. All were dressed in their formal attire. All of them with a grim expression on their face. All of them looked at Finn, a question in their eyes.

"Elizabeth Jarvis stands before you convicted and sentenced for treason," Finn said. He looked behind him. She glared at him, the same way she had glared at him when he had first come to question her. She had said nothing, and he didn't expect her to. Nothing other than her ongoing belief her father would save her.

Finn's questioning had turned up nothing more within her family. The chancellor had been angry, but Finn could handle anger. When Mistress Jarvis had railed at the Alainsith, the chancellor had intervened, silencing her. That would be something for the king to deal with.

Finn didn't know why the king hadn't intervened. Perhaps it had something to do with the nature of the treason. Perhaps that she had attempted magic. Perhaps even something else—that she had thought to attack the Alainsith while her father had been sent to coordinate the treaty. Maybe this was the king's way of sending a different message.

Whatever the reason, Finn didn't care.

"Do you have anything further to say?"

"You will suffer."

She refused to make her peace with the gods. That was her choice.

Finn looked at the gathered jurors. "She has been tried and convicted. She committed treason against the kingdom.

She has committed murder against fellow citizens. I bring her here to face her sentencing."

The magister just nodded.

The priest continued chanting near Finn, and he ignored it.

He readied himself for the sentencing, focused on what he needed to do.

Finn unsheathed his sword.

He could have brought Justice, but it had enough power.

He would need to name his sword, but that could come later. He had several ideas but wanted to choose the right name for his blade, one that truly fit.

Moving to stand alongside the condemned, he looked down at her. "Kneel."

"No."

"Have some dignity. You were offered an honorable death. It is far more than you deserve. It's more than what you gave those you attacked."

When she looked up at him defiantly, he nodded to the two Archers standing at the base of the Stone. They climbed the stairs, wide-eyed. Finn understood. No one really wanted to climb the Stone. They viewed it as tainted, somehow dirty, despite there being nothing truly dirty with the Stone. A superstition, but it was one Finn understood.

They stood on either side of her and forced her to her knees.

"Do you have anything more to say?"

She tried to spit, but Finn stepped off to the side. He readied himself. This time, he had no doubt of what he needed to do. He brought his blade back before swinging around in a smooth arc, carrying out the sentence.

The area around the Raven Stone emptied quickly, as it always did after an execution. Few wanted to be reminded of death, and fewer still wanted to be there as the crows began their feast. The jurors and the magister departed quickly, perhaps even more quickly than usual this time, reaching the city and dispersing. Even the Archers who had assisted Finn in the sentencing had departed, returning to their posts.

Preparing the body from there would be Finn's responsibility. This was something he had often done alone.

"You did well, Finn Jagger."

Finn looked down to see Esmeralda climbing the stairs. "I did what was necessary."

She glanced to the blade strapped to his back. "Her death has strengthened it even more."

"I don't think of it like that."

"I suppose that you do not. I do, however."

"Think of it as you must," Finn said.

"I think this one should be handled differently." She set down several small items around the remains of the woman.

"The hegen don't want to claim prizes?"

"Not with her."

When she was done, she pressed her fingers together and began to chant softly. Flames built suddenly from her, burning hot but low so that they wouldn't create much of a pyre. It didn't take long before the body was consumed and burned away.

"Why did you do that?"

"I fear for what this means for the kingdom." Esmeralda looked up at him, meeting his gaze for a moment. "I doubt she was alone. And it is time for you to be more than the executioner."

"That's what I am."

She regarded him a long moment. "For now. That doesn't mean you cannot be more. I think you must accept that you are a part of something greater."

"I don't know magic."

"Must you?"

Finn didn't know. For what he'd encountered so far, he thought that it would be needed, but maybe that wasn't true. He had Justice.

"You think all of this is about someone more than Holden," Finn said.

Esmeralda nodded. "More than Holden. Someone powerful. Someone who taught her. That is who I fear. Someone who will likely attack again… and the next time, they will be ready for you."

Pick up the next book in The Executioner's Song series: The Executioner's Rebellion.

SERIES BY D.K. HOLMBERG

The Chain Breaker Series
The Chain Breaker

The Dark Sorcerer

The Dragonwalkers Series
The Dragonwalker

The Dragon Misfits

The Dragon Thief

Elemental Warrior Series:
The Endless War

The Cloud Warrior Saga

Elemental Academy

The Elemental Warrior

The Dark Ability Series
The Shadow Accords

The Collector Chronicles

The Dark Ability

The Sighted Assassin

The Elder Stones Saga

Made in the USA
Columbia, SC
27 August 2022